Praise for *Nicky Pellegrino*

'A lovely read … with a genuine heart and true observation' Elizabeth Buchan

'A touching story about one woman's search for love'
Sunday Express

'The descriptions of Italian food will make your mouth water' *Cosmopolitan*

'If you like your love stories on the sensuous side, this debut novel is for you' *Glamour*

'A tale of love, families, their foibles – and food'
Woman

'Full-bodied as a rich Italian red, it's a page-turner combining the missed chances of *Captain Corelli's Mandolin* with the foodie pleasures of *Chocolat*' *Eve*

'Three generations of Italian women talk romance and cooking in *Delicious*, by Nicky Pellegrino, an evocative food-fest of a novel' *Prima*

Nicky Pellegrino grew up on Merseyside but spent childhood summers in southern Italy. As well as writing her internationally bestselling debut, *Delicious*, she has worked as a woman's magazine editor. She now lives with her husband in Auckland, New Zealand.

By Nicky Pellegrino

Delicious
Summer at the Villa Rosa
The Italian Wedding

The
Italian Wedding

NICKY PELLEGRINO

An Orion paperback

First published in Great Britain in 2009
by Orion
This paperback published in 2009
by Orion Books Ltd,
Orion House, 5 Upper Saint Martin's Lane
London WC2H 9EA

An Hachette UK company

1 3 5 7 9 10 8 6 4 2

A CIP catalogue record for this book is
available from the British Library.

ISBN 978-0-7528-8391-5

Typeset by Deltatype Ltd, Birkenhead, Merseyside

Printed and bound in the UK by
CPI Mackays, Chatham ME5 8TD

www.orionbooks.co.uk

For my parents with thanks for the love,
the food and the stories

Beppi's Recipe for Melanzane alla Parmigiana

This is so easy. Why do you even need a recipe? My daughters were helping me with this when they were children. You just make the Napolitana sauce. What do you mean you don't know how? *Cose da pazzi!* OK, I'll explain it to you. This is what you will need:

2 aubergines
1 onion
1 jar of tomato passata
2 eggs
plain flour
salt
pepper
fresh basil
lots of grated Parmesan
a little grated mozzarella
olive oil
vegetable oil

This is my way of doing it. The best way, of course. First you cut the aubergines into rounds – not too thick but not too thin. Salt them and leave in a colander for an hour to drain. Then wash off the salt with cold water and pat dry with a clean cloth.

Now make the Napolitana sauce. Chop an onion finely, fry it in olive oil and then pour on the jar of tomato passata. Add basil, a little salt and pepper and then simmer the sauce for twenty minutes. Now your kitchen is smelling wonderful, eh?

Next beat two eggs with a little salt and pepper. Dip both sides of each aubergine round in plain flour, then in the beaten egg and shallow fry in vegetable oil until golden brown. Oh, and don't be mean with the oil. *Mannaggia chi te muort*, you people, always so worried about the oil. Pour it from the bottle properly – don't just dribble it in.

Layer the fried aubergine in a shallow oven dish – four layers maximum – and cover each layer with some Napolitano sauce and plenty of grated Parmesan. Sprinkle mozzarella on the top and bake for twenty minutes at about 150ºC.

(Yes, yes, I know two aubergines will be too much, but who can resist tasting a few pieces as they come out of the frying pan?)

Addolorata's note: Papa, I don't believe this. No wonder you have high cholesterol.

I

The mannequin was propped up in the corner of Pieta's attic room. The dress she'd put on it was nothing more than a roughly stitched calico toile but Pieta could see what it would become. The fine beading, the fall of the train, the sash tied at the waist. It was going to be magnificent.

This was the time Pieta loved most. When both the gown and the bride's future held so much promise. Later there might be disappointments, or even heartbreak. But right now, with the dress no more than a plain shape and all its beauty still locked away in Pieta's imagination, was the best time of all.

Usually Pieta knew the dress before she got to know the bride. Her vision of what she would create with her rolls of lace, tulle and silk was nearly always complete in her head by the end of the first consultation. It was later, at the endless fittings, that she would bend the bride to her will, but so gently and persuasively they always seemed to think it was their idea. Forget the fabric flower on the hip; get rid of the handkerchief hemline. Yes, yes, that's what you want.

At the final fitting, when the bride stood in the Mirror Room and they slipped shoes on her feet and put a veil in her hair, Pieta always felt sad. She was sending her creation out into the world, and who knew how it – and the woman who wore it – would fare? For there were worse things than torn lace and grubby hems, Pieta knew that.

And this dress, the one clothing the mannequin in her bedroom, was different. More important than any that had gone before, more difficult to let go of. Pieta sat in bed, propped up on pillows, and stared at the calico toile. This plain-looking thing was to be her little sister's bridal gown and everything about it had to be perfect.

Pieta heard a door open and close and footsteps on the wooden floors below. She wondered who it was. Her sister Addolorata, too excited about all her plans for the future to sleep? Or their mother, who had gone to bed hours ago but might have woken and realized she'd forgotten to take whatever pill or potion she was relying on these days?

The footsteps sounded heavier now and there was another noise – a banging and crashing of pans and crockery in kitchen cupboards. It must be her father Beppi then. He was too restless, too busy in mind and body, ever to sleep a whole night through. And of course he'd be in the kitchen, nowhere else. In the morning, when Pieta went down to make her first cup of strong black coffee, there would be freshly made pasta drying on the kitchen table, or a stock pan filled with a sauce of tomatoes and slow-cooked beef.

As if there wasn't enough food already. There were bundles of his carefully dried pasta wrapped in linen tea towels in the kitchen cupboard, and containers of his sauces and soups neatly labelled by her mother and packed away in the deep chest freezer. And still Beppi kept on cooking.

Pieta loved the food her father made but there was always so much of it. Sometimes she dreamed of leaving the big four-storey house they all shared, living alone and making her own meals. And then dinner would be a simple soup of Swiss chard, flavoured with a little bacon and eaten in peace instead of the extravagant portions her father served up amidst the noise and fuss that accompanied whatever he did.

Yawning, Pieta took a last look at the calico toile. Mentally she adjusted the neckline slightly and made the shoulder straps wider. Then she turned out her light, wriggled down under the covers, closed her eyes and was asleep in minutes.

Early the next morning Pieta came downstairs to find the kitchen exactly as she'd expected. Yellow ribbons of fettucine covered one end of the long pine table, dusted with flour and spread out erratically. The other end was crowded with thin shards of lasagne, and in the middle there was the tiniest space, where Pieta's mother Catherine had put her cereal bowl and a mug of tea.

Pale and tired, her greying hair pulled back harshly from her face, her flower-sprigged robe wrapped round her, Catherine spooned cereal into her mouth disinterestedly.

'Good morning, Mamma. How do you feel today?' Pieta pushed open the kitchen door and headed straight for the coffee pot.

'Not so good, not so bad.'

'Do you want some coffee?'

'No, no, I can only drink tea in the mornings, you know that.' Catherine jabbed an angry finger at the confetti of pasta covering the table. 'And anyway, I don't know where you're going to sit to have your breakfast. Look at this!'

'It's fine.' Pieta shrugged. 'I only want a coffee and a cigarette. I'll sit on the back doorstep and have it.'

'Smoking, always smoking,' Catherine lamented. 'When are you going to give up, eh? Your sister doesn't smoke. I don't know what made you start.'

It was the same every morning. Her mother was always the first to wake and would sit with the newspaper, clucking over the bad news stories, as the milk soaked into her cornflakes. Pieta would find her at the kitchen table, her mouth pursed as though she were eating something slightly bitter, and often she would read aloud a story that particularly displeased her.

If Addolorata had been working late at the restaurant she would usually come down and join Pieta on the doorstep for a quick coffee and an illicit puff of her cigarette before going back to bed to snatch a little more sleep.

But it was when their father Beppi got up that the whole house seemed to wake for the day. If he was in a good mood he would burst through the kitchen door, sweep away his wife's half-eaten bowl of cereal and rattle it in the sink, noisily pour himself coffee, all the while calling, 'Good morning, my bella Caterina, and good morning, Pieta. Are you out there smoking? Come inside and eat some breakfast like a good girl before you go to work.'

It was different if he had woken in a bad mood. Then he would shuffle round the kitchen, pinching the bridge of his nose between a forefinger and thumb, and groaning noisily.

But this morning it was just Pieta, sitting on the step, drinking her coffee as she looked out over the small patch of garden where her father grew his vegetables, and listened to her mother turn the pages of her newspaper.

In the background, as always, was the rumble of London traffic, but Pieta barely noticed it. She had been born in this tall house in the backstreets of Clerkenwell and had lived in it all her life. When she sat here in her favourite place, eyes half-closed and the morning sun on her face, she heard only the sounds she wanted to hear – birds singing in the trees of the churchyard opposite, children shrieking in the little playground. This high-walled garden, with every inch of its earth cultivated and useful, was the safest place she knew. But she couldn't stay here all morning. One more cup of coffee, one last cigarette, and then it would be time to go. She felt the usual sense of dread at the thought of the day ahead.

'What's wrong? You look a bit pale this morning, Pieta.'

Her eyes flew open. It was Addolorata, of course, bending down to take the cigarette from her hand and sucking on it greedily.

'Nothing's wrong.' Pieta shifted sideways and her sister jammed herself in beside her. 'I was just thinking about something, that's all.'

'Worrying about something, you mean.'

Addolorata topped up Pieta's coffee cup from her own and took a regretful last pull of the cigarette before handing it back to her.

The two girls didn't look like sisters. Addolorata was her father's child, all curves and untamed curly hair, with round cheeks and small brown eyes. Pieta had lighter eyes and darker hair that she wore in a neat bob, the heavy fringe grazing her eyebrows. In temperament they were just as different, and yet, while they had fought with each other all their lives, they had always stayed the best of friends.

'Are you working today?' Pieta tossed the spent cigarette onto the concrete path and stubbed it out with the toe of her slipper.

'Mmm, yes, and I need to get in reasonably early. I want to try something new. I've been thinking about orechiette pasta with broccoli and leeks braised in a little chicken stock, some lean bacon, maybe even some chilli and a tiny squeeze of lemon.' Addolorata's voice sounded almost dreamy as she described the dish. 'Why don't you come by the restaurant for lunch and I'll make it for you.'

'Maybe. I'll see if I've got time.'

'Just come in for half an hour. He can't expect you to work all the time. Even he must see that you've got to eat.'

'We've got brides coming in all day for consultations and fittings. I have to be there.'

Addolorata rolled her eyes. 'Honestly, I don't know why you do it. He steals your ideas, expects you there all hours, makes you do all the work.'

'I know, I know. But he's Nikolas Rose so he can do whatever he likes.'

'Leave him, Pieta. Go out on your own. You know you can do it.'

'Not yet.' Pieta shook her head. 'The time's not right. I'm not ready.'

'If it's money you're worried about, Papa will help you.'

'I know. He reminds me at least once a week. Just leave it, will you?' Pieta tossed another cigarette at her sister, who put it in her pocket.

Almost on cue, Pieta heard a rattling of pans in the kitchen and smelt an onion frying. And then, scissors in hand, her father appeared in search of fresh herbs, almost tripping over his daughters as he erupted out of the back door.

'Girls, why do you have to sit out here like peasants, eh? Why do you think I bought those kitchen chairs? Go and sit on them like normal civilized people. And Pieta …' He raised his voice. 'Have some breakfast. You need to eat more.'

'No time, Papa, sorry. I have to get to work.'

'Well, in that case come home at a reasonable hour tonight. I'm going to make a beautiful lasagne and I want all my family around the table to share it with me.' He beamed at her happily and waved his little bunch of freshly cut herbs in the air.

Pieta kissed him quickly on the cheek. As she hurried back through the kitchen and headed upstairs to be the first in the shower she heard her mother complaining: 'Always the smell of cooking in this house, Beppi, even first thing in the morning.'

Not for the first time, Pieta wondered why her father had left Italy all those years ago. Why would such a brightly coloured man fall in love with a washed-out woman like her mother? But then, what made any man fall for any woman? Pieta was nearly thirty and still she didn't know.

2

'Tell me about your wedding style.'

It was the first question Pieta asked new brides. And the reply was what gave her the first glimmer of an idea for the dress she would design.

Today's bride was blonde with perfect skin, although she had too mean a chin to be truly beautiful and barely a teaspoon of hair. She was perching on the very edge of the white sofa in the Chandelier Room, looking around at the ivory-clad mannequins and shelves full of accessories that lined the walls. Pieta sat opposite her in a high-backed chair, a block of white paper on her knee and a pencil in her hand.

'Oh, I expected . . .' The young bride looked confused. 'Are we starting now? Only I thought we'd be waiting until Nikolas Rose arrives. I don't mind waiting.'

Pieta gave a half-smile. 'I'm sorry. I thought it had been explained to you. I take care of the first consultation and the initial sketches. Then Nikolas takes the design and refines it. That's the way it works with every Nikolas Rose gown. So, tell me . . . your wedding style?'

The bride took a sip from the glass of chilled champagne Pieta had poured for her. 'Well, my fiancé's family are Catholic and so the wedding will be a big one in a very grand church and afterwards there'll be a feast with music and dancing. It will be very traditional. But the thing is …' She gulped down a little more champagne. 'I want to feel glamorous on my wedding day. Like I'm on the red carpet at the Oscars. That's why I'm here, at Nikolas Rose, because everyone told me he does the most exquisite gowns.'

Pieta's pencil was already moving across the white paper. 'So we want something classic but still quite sexy,' she mused. 'Not too much décolletage or shoulder on display but fitted to your figure, do you think? You have such a lovely shape it would be a shame not to show that off.'

The bride looked nervous. 'I brought some pictures I've cut out of magazines but I wasn't sure if Mr Rose …' She dipped into a big handbag and produced a folder full of glossy pages.

Pieta tucked the folder beneath her block of paper. 'That's fine,' she said, her pencil still scratching down ideas. 'Nikolas will be happy to take a look at it. Now what about colour themes? Had you thought about what you might like your bridesmaids to wear? And flowers. What are you thinking of having in your bouquet?'

'I … I'm not sure. There's so much to think of, isn't there?'

'That's all right. We can help you with ideas for all of those things if you need us to. So the next step is for me to take some measurements and a few quick photographs of you. And then, as soon as I've consulted with Nikolas, we'll make another appointment for you.'

She'd just placed the measuring tape round the

bride's waist when she heard him coming. He must have thought she was alone. 'Pieta, Pieta, Pieta,' Nikolas was calling petulantly. 'Pieta, have you seen my—?'

When he realized she was with a client he stopped and rearranged his expression. He was wearing narrow-legged pin-striped trousers, a black shirt and a long black jacket with a red gerbera in the buttonhole. In one fluid movement he crossed the room, turned the bride to face the mirror, gathered her fine hair in his hands and piled it on her head and then gazed at both their reflections. 'Lovely,' he said. 'Just lovely.'

'This is Helene Sealy,' Pieta informed him. 'She is getting married next summer and she is going to be dressed by Nikolas Rose.'

'Of course she is.' Nikolas allowed the bride's hair to trickle out of his fingers and glanced down at the sketches Pieta had made. 'I see her in something fluid, fabric that moves when she moves, nothing too stiff and formal. I see white orchids in a bouquet hand-tied with a simple mint-green ribbon. And maybe the hair up and some white flowers and pale green leaves right here by her ear. Yes, yes, lovely. I'll leave you to it, Pieta.' He turned on his heel and was gone just as quickly as he'd appeared.

'That was Nikolas Rose?' The bride seemed dazzled.

'Yes, that was him.'

Pieta continued with the things that needed to be done – the measurements and the photographs for her files, the filling-in of forms and, last of all, presenting the bride with her business card, which read 'Pieta Martinelli, Assistant Designer'.

'Oh, you've got an Italian name.' Helene sounded pleased.

'Yes, my father is Italian,' Pieta told her.

'That's a coincidence. My fiancé is Italian, too. His name is Michele DeMatteo. Isn't that lovely? Soon I'll be Helene DeMatteo ...'

Pieta stood very still and let the young bride talk on until she was sure she had complete control of herself. It took a few moments and she wondered if it was obvious there was something wrong.

'And your fiancé,' she said at last, 'does he know you've come to Nikolas Rose for your wedding gown?'

'Oh no, of course not. It's meant to be a surprise, isn't it? A big surprise.'

Pieta nodded. 'Oh yes, it will be a surprise,' she said softly. 'I can promise you that.'

She slipped out without even telling Nikolas. If he'd known she was going he'd have found countless ways to hold her up and most likely made a list of things for her to bring back for him. And Pieta couldn't wait. She had to go to Little Italy and see Addolorata at once. She couldn't keep this news to herself for very much longer.

Little Italy had once been the narrowest of restaurants with barely enough room for a waiter to slip between the tables. There had been no menu and no choice. Instead the customers ate whatever Beppi had decided to cook for them. Perhaps a pasta soup, followed by a plate of slowly braised meat and peperonata with a glass of rough red wine and a communal basket of hard, chewy bread on each table. At first only

Italians had eaten there but slowly word had spread and now, all these years later, Little Italy had expanded into three of the adjacent shops. There was a big white canopy over the pavement at the front with silver aluminium tables and chairs beneath it, and planters filled with trimmed green bushes to separate the diners from the bustle of the street market that was always there on weekdays. This was where Beppi, who had supposedly retired years ago, could be found on warm days, playing cards with his friends and keeping an eye on Addolorata as she chalked up the menu on the blackboard each morning and fed their customers all day long.

The decor hadn't changed. The white stucco walls were covered in large black-and-white prints of the old days: Beppi as a child eating spaghetti at the dinner table; the whole family dressed for church on a Sunday morning; Beppi and his sister, Isabella, laughing as they rode a borrowed Vespa together. The tables were covered in red-checked cloths and the food served in big white bowls. This was how it had been at Little Italy since the very beginning.

Now, slowly, Addolorata was making small changes, adding new flavours and textures to dishes: a handful of walnuts thrown into a creamy risotto, a pinch of cumin seeds in a lamb ragu. Between his games of cards, Beppi would come inside and taste a spoonful of sauce or a ladleful of soup, and often that was when voices would be raised most loudly in the kitchen.

But today Pieta found her father at his favourite sunny outdoor table, stripped down to his white vest and deep in a card game with Ernesto Bosetti.

'Are you winning, Papa?' she called out.

He looked up, frowning. 'Well, I might have a chance if this *stronzo* would stop cheating.'

Ernesto threw his cards on the table and his hands in the air. '*Porca la miseria*, thirty years I've been playing cards with you and you can't forget that one mistake all those years ago.' He looked up at Pieta and shook his head. 'I don't know why I still play with him, *cara*, really I don't. Anyway it's good to see you. Find a chair and join us for lunch.'

She patted him on the shoulder. 'I'd love to have lunch with you but I'm going to eat with Addolorata. She has some new dish she wants to try out on me.'

'New dish?' her father muttered. 'Don't eat too much now, Pieta.'

Exasperated, she laughed. 'But only this morning you told me I need to eat more.'

'*Si, si*, but remember the beautiful lasagne I have made for dinner tonight. I want you to have some appetite left.'

'Don't worry, Papa,' Pieta called over her shoulder as she headed inside. 'Your beautiful lasagne will get eaten, I'm sure.'

The restaurant was busy today. All the tables outside were occupied and there was barely an empty one indoors. Noise levels were high and white-clad Italian waiters darted about delivering steaming plates of food and clearing them away again once they were almost wiped clean. The older waiters all had moustaches and the younger ones wore long hair in ponytails, gold studs glinting in their ears.

Frederico was the head waiter and had been there

almost since the beginning. He was serving bowls of black squid ink risotto when he noticed Pieta. With a nod of his head, he motioned towards an empty table. '*Ciao, bella*. Sit down and I'll tell your sister you're here.'

As she waited she watched people enjoying their food. The risotto table were regulars. They ate with gusto, dabbing at their squid-ink-stained mouths with red napkins and swigging at glasses of Chianti. Beside them was a man in a suit, eating alone while he read the newspaper. He was making his way through the one dish Addolorata always left on the menu – venison shanks slow-cooked in lots of onion and tomato with a silky sauce that seeped into a big mound of potatoes mashed with roasted garlic. Pieta could tell from the expression on his face that every mouthful was heaven.

When she appeared, Addolorata was flushed from the heat of the kitchen and in her hands were two white bowls filled with the pasta dish she'd been perfecting all morning.

'Here, try this. Tell me what you think. I've made so many different versions of it but I think I've finally got it right.'

Pieta tasted a spoonful. It was more of a light soup really. The broccoli was cooked the old-fashioned way, until it was soft and breaking apart, the leeks fried in olive oil and then braised gently in a little of the broccoli water until they were almost melting. There was a hint of chilli and lemon, and some roughly chopped black olives, a few pine nuts and thick shavings of pecorino cheese mixed in with the little ears of pasta to add flavour and bite.

'You left out the bacon,' Pieta observed.

Addolorata spooned a little into her own mouth, tilted her head and shrugged. 'It didn't feel as though it needed bacon in the end. You like it?'

Pieta tasted a second spoonful and then a third. 'Mmm, I do. I like it a lot. You should definitely put it on the menu. Serve it with a big slice of crusty bread so people can mop up all the juices.'

'Is it too liquid? Does it need a little potato to thicken it up maybe?'

'No, no, it's better like this, light and healthy. Don't put potato in.'

'Still …' Addolorata stirred her soup. 'Maybe it does need bacon …'

This was one of the things that divided her family. Her sister and father lived for food. They could eat it greedily and talk about it passionately all day and half the night without ever getting bored. But Pieta, although she was enjoying the soup of vegetables and pasta, would have been just as happy with a poached egg on toast.

'So what do you think?' Addolorata prompted her. 'Bacon or no bacon?'

'Never mind that.' Pieta leaned across the table. 'I have news.'

'Oh?' Addolorata tore herself away from contemplating the contents of her bowl. 'What?'

'We had a new bride come in this morning for a consultation and guess who she is marrying.'

'Tell me.'

'Michele DeMatteo.'

Addolorata dropped her spoon into her bowl. 'No! Really?'

'Yes, really.'

'Does she know who you are?'

'I don't think so.'

'My God, are you going to say something to her? Old man DeMatteo will have a fit when he finds out.'

Pieta nodded. 'I know but I don't see how I can say anything. Apart from anything else he's seen her already.'

'Nikolas?'

'Yes, he came in while I was measuring her. So I can hardly put her off now, can I? He never forgets a customer. He's already decided what colour ribbon she should have in her bouquet.'

'So, what will you do?' Addolorata pushed her bowl aside and rested her elbows on the table.

'I don't know. Just carry on, I suppose, and design a gown for her. It's going be rather beautiful, I think. She wants to go discreetly sexy and glamorous.'

'And what about her? Is she sexy and glamorous, too?'

'She's pretty, blonde and younger than Michele by a good few years, I think. But not glamorous exactly.'

Addolorata looked thoughtful. 'You know, I always thought Michele DeMatteo was sweet on you when we were at school.'

'No!'

'Really I did. He always seemed to be trying to attract your attention.'

Pieta laughed and shook her head. 'He used to tease

me, you mean. And sometimes he would steal my lunch.'

Frederico came over and raised an eyebrow, and Addolorata nodded a yes for him to clear away the plates. Minutes later he brought them tiny cups of espresso with a square of dense chocolate cake balanced on the side of the saucer. Pieta bit into hers before touching the coffee. She loved sweet things.

She sipped her coffee and shook her head again. 'Michele was never interested in me that way, and even if he had been, what could have happened? Papa and old man DeMatteo would have had fits if we'd gone anywhere near each other. Don't tell him, Addolorata. Don't say anything about Michele's bride coming to me. It'll only cause more trouble.'

'Well, there's going to be trouble eventually, isn't there?' Addolorata looked glum. 'I thought weddings were supposed to be happy things but it seems to me there's always some sort of drama.'

'Not with yours, though,' Pieta promised. 'Your wedding will be perfect. I'm going to make sure of it.'

She was late back from lunch. Nikolas would be furious. Hoping her next appointment hadn't yet arrived, Pieta hurried along the crowded pavements back towards the bridal salon. Nikolas Rose Couturier occupied a series of interlinking rooms on the top floor of an old mansion block in Holborn. Right now, if Pieta were very unlucky, the great man himself would be in the Chandelier Room making conversation with a bride who had come in for her final fitting. Her gown was hanging ready for her in the Mirror Room but Nikolas wouldn't think to take her through. That was Pieta's job. He liked to appear at the very end, brush the bride's hair, fluff the train of the gown and then disappear into the Design Room next door until another bride appeared and he needed to switch on his charm again.

The most important room at Nikolas Rose Couturier was the Make Room, and the five older women who worked there, in cramped conditions around a long sewing table, were the main reason Pieta found it so difficult to walk away from the salon and set up on her own. They were the finest seamstresses in London, producing gowns with the exquisite cut, fine stitching and hand-beading for which Nikolas Rose was renowned. Often they could just glance at a design and see a detail she had missed. On quiet days, if Nikolas was not around, they'd play around with fabrics on the mannequin and help her dream up ideas for the ready-to-wear collection she planned to launch some day. Pieta thought she knew what she wanted. Just a capsule collection at first, no more than eight simple styles that each bride could customise a little to make her own, and inside each one would be a label that read 'Pieta Martinelli, Bridal Designer'.

But it wasn't easy to break away from Nikolas Rose. She would miss those five experts in the Make Room and she would miss other things, too: Nikolas Rose's reputation; the wealthy brides who came to him ready to spend money on beautiful fabrics and intricate work; and, surprisingly, Nikolas himself. For, although he was capricious, infuriating and demanding, he often had flashes of brilliance. He could take a perfectly lovely design Pieta had created and make it truly special. Every day she worked there she learned something new. And that was why she couldn't leave and set up on her own. Some day, yes, but she wasn't ready yet.

Pieta was in such a hurry she ran up the six flights of steep stairs in her high heels. The old lift with its double doors and creaking wooden panels took forever to arrive and she didn't have the patience to wait. More importantly, neither did Nikolas.

She was breathless as she pushed open the door of the Chandelier Room. As she feared, both the bride and Nikolas were waiting for her there. They looked a little flushed and there was a half-finished bottle of champagne on the low table between them.

'I'm so sorry I'm late.' Pieta tried to steady her voice. 'I had to go out to take care of a few errands and I was held up.'

Nikolas gave the tightest of smiles. He wouldn't let his anger show in front of a client. 'Miss Laney is anxious to see her finished gown, Pieta. Please take her through to the Mirror Room.'

This bride had been difficult. She had changed her mind about fabric and style countless times; cried about the shape of her arms and the thickness of her thighs; lost weight, then regained it and lost it again. The gown had been through endless alterations but Pieta had guided the bride through the whole fraught process with a steady hand and now she wondered if the finished gown wasn't one of the most beautiful they had ever created.

The wedding dress was hanging where she'd left it

in the Mirror Room. It was full-skirted, made from the finest silk satin, with long buttoned sleeves, matching covered buttons down the back and finished with a floor-length black satin bow. The bride's eyes filled with tears when she saw it. 'Oh, Pieta, you and Mr Rose have made all my dreams come true.'

Pieta smiled gently. 'Let's try it on you one last time to make sure it fits perfectly. A Nikolas Rose gown shouldn't pinch, slip or ride up when you move. It should be the most comfortable thing you've ever worn as well as the most exquisite.'

There were more tears as the bride stood before the mirror in her gown and Pieta handed her the large box of soft tissues she kept in the Mirror Room for emotional moments like these.

'It's perfect, isn't it?' she said.

'Oh yes.' The bride seemed overwhelmed. 'Am I really going to be allowed to take it home with me?'

'Not until Mr Rose has seen you in it and we've made sure he is entirely happy.' Pieta rang the decorative brass bell that hung in the corner of the Mirror Room.

Nikolas waited a few moments before making his entrance. Today he was wearing fitted trousers, with black suede ankle boots and a tight black shirt. He was an impish man with a slender figure, a thick head of spiky, prematurely silver hair and a sulky pout to his mouth.

He stopped in the doorway, his bad mood forgotten. 'Pieta darling,' he breathed as he surveyed the gown. 'I really do think this may be the most divine thing we have ever created.'

'I think so, too.'

He moved forward and touched the sleeves that had been cleverly draped to disguise the bride's upper arms. 'It's so modern, so now and so original. I am happy, very happy indeed.'

The bride's tears were flowing steadily. 'This is the most beautiful gown I've ever seen in my whole life. I never want to take it off.'

He smiled at her. 'Every Nikolas Rose bride is beautiful. We wouldn't have it any other way.'

And then he was gone, leaving Pieta to take the final payment, slip the gown into a protective bag and put it, and the bride who would wear it, into a taxi and send them home. In a few weeks' time they would receive an envelope of photographs of the bride on the steps of a church, clutching her bouquet and looking even more beautiful and joyful than she had today. Pieta could almost feel tears forming in her own eyes as she imagined it.

'Good luck, be happy … and don't forget to have the gown dry-cleaned and wrapped in acid-free paper after you've worn it.' Those were always the last words Pieta said to her brides as they and their gowns disappeared towards their new lives.

3

This was what made her father happiest – his family gathered around the kitchen table, laughing and arguing while they shared something delicious he had created. He liked to sit at the head of the table with his wife at his right and his daughters on the other side. But now there was a new chair at the table and another man in the family and, while Beppi was doing his very best, the strain of it was starting to show. For although he liked Eden Donald well enough, he was not the man he wanted for his daughter Addolorata.

Eden's father was Scottish and his mother came from Ghana. He was a builder and had skin the colour of milk chocolate, a sprinkling of freckles over his nose, full lips and dark hair with a slight auburn tinge that he'd twisted into long dreadlocks. When he sat down in the chair at the far end of Beppi's table the atmosphere was slightly tense. Tonight was no different.

'So, Eden.' Beppi's tone was domineering. 'You and my daughter have spoken to the priest at St Peter's and booked a date for the wedding?'

'No, not yet.' Eden seemed uncomfortable.

'Well, you need to hurry. St Peter's is a busy church and you won't get the date you want if you leave it very much longer.'

Eden nodded. He had been told at the very beginning that he and Addolorata would be marrying at St
Peter's, the Italian church in Clerkenwell, and holding
their wedding feast at Little Italy.

'And Ernesto tells me they have this other thing
you must do.' Beppi was so busy talking he had barely
touched his lasagne. 'Special classes for couples who
are getting married. It is obligatory, he says.'

Addolorata looked up from her food. 'Papa ...' she
began and then hesitated.

'*Si, cara*. I know you are busy at the restaurant. I will
speak to the priest if you don't have time.'

'No, don't do that yet.' She dug her fork into the
thin layers of pasta oozing with béchamel sauce, meat
and tomatoes. 'Eden and I were thinking we might
look at some other venues first.'

Beppi looked confused. 'Other churches. Why?'

'No ... not other churches. Some place quite different ... like a hall or a hotel. Even a private members'
club. There are some beautiful venues.'

'And you could get married by a priest there?'

'Well, it would be a civil ceremony, Papa. But the
great thing would be—'

'*Mannaggia chi te muort!*' Beppi slammed his wine
glass down so violently that it shattered and a lake of
Barolo spread across the tablecloth.

'It's only an idea, Papa. We just want to think about
it.' Addolorata's tone was pleading.

'Are you trying to insult me and my family?' Beppi
was addressing Eden directly now. 'Have you got no
respect for me?'

Eden just looked at him, holding his gaze but saying nothing.

'*Va bene, va bene.*' Beppi threw his hands in the air. 'If my daughter says she must marry you then so be it but she will do so in St Peter's, nowhere else. Do you understand?'

No one said a word. Beppi lowered his head and finished every last scrap of pasta on his plate. Then, tossing down his fork, he pushed back his chair and stormed out of the room.

There was silence for a few moments and then Catherine spoke in her soft, exhausted voice.

'Are you trying to break your father's heart, Addolorata?'

'No, Mamma.' She sounded close to tears.

'Then why are you and Eden thinking of marrying anywhere but St Peter's?'

'It's just because … it's my wedding and … .why does everything have to be the way Papa says it will be?'

'Because he's the head of the family,' Catherine said simply.

'Oh, for God's sake.'

'You live here under his roof, you make your living in the restaurant he worked so hard to build up into what it is today. Everything your father does, he does for you and your sister. And now you would refuse him this one thing that he wants.' Pushing away her plate of uneaten lasagne, Catherine quietly left the table and the room.

Addolorata's head fell into her hands. 'Oh my God.'

'Well, I told you,' said Eden mildly.

'I just want to look at some other venues, that's all. Is it such a big deal?'

'Apparently.' Eden was the only one still eating.

'Pieta?' Addolorata appealed to her sister. 'Am I being so unreasonable?'

'Honestly?' Pieta considered it. 'No, you're not. But still I think you should get married in St Peter's.'

'Oh, is that a fact? Well, I'm sick of being told what I should do, and I'm tired of this family and the way that everyone has to interfere in each other's lives.' Addolorata stood up. 'I won't put up with it any longer.' She slammed the door behind her as she stormed out of the house.

Eden wiped a piece of bread round his plate to soak up the last of the sauce. 'I'll talk to her,' he said to Pieta.

'Just get her to book a date at St Peter's. You can have everything else your way,' Pieta promised. 'Well, pretty much.'

'Yeah, yeah, OK.' Still chewing his bread, Eden got up from the table. 'I'd better go after her anyway. See you later.'

Pieta was left alone, the table still covered with dirty plates, broken glass and wine stains, the cooker crowded with used pans and dishes. Sighing, she began to clear up. Addolorata was right – sometimes it wasn't easy being part of this family.

Pieta slept badly and woke late. She drank her coffee standing up, looking out of the kitchen window at her father, who was stripped to the waist and digging

28

in his vegetable garden. His movements were quick, almost frantic, as he turned the soil beneath his spade. Beside him was his old cassette player, blasting out Neapolitan love songs. From time to time, he sang along in his reedy voice. He seemed happy enough but then her father's anger was like a flame in dry tinder – quick to flare but just as fast to die down if it wasn't fuelled again. Her mother was different. As she pottered around the garden, pulling out a weed or tying up a tomato plant, she would be mulling over last night's argument and, most likely, dreaming up fresh problems to worry about.

Finishing her coffee, Pieta climbed the steep stairs to her room in the attic. The house was shared out, floor by floor, between the family. Downstairs was the large kitchen and a small, hardly used living room. On the first floor lay her parents' bedroom and her mother's sewing room. Addolorata occupied the floor above, although she wasn't there now so she must have stayed the night with Eden. And at the very top was Pieta's domain, the room she slept in and another that, over the years, had become a giant walk-in wardrobe.

Pieta never threw clothes out. They could always be altered and worn again. She hunted at markets, sales and second-hand shops, greedily adding to her store. At one end of the room was a rail of beautiful silk dresses from the 1920s and 1930s. They were beginning to rot and fall apart but Pieta still put them on from time to time. There were flowered gypsy skirts and smock tops, dresses Pieta had run up quickly on her mother's sewing machine hours before a big night out, expensive designer clothes she had spent far too much

29

money on. Every rail was so overcrowded it sagged in the middle, but Pieta could always find room for something new and special.

Each morning she liked to stand for a few moments gazing at her clothes like they were old friends, before choosing something to wear. Today she picked out a simple black cotton dress, tied an orange silk scarf round her waist like a sash and slipped two chunky resin bangles on her wrist. A pair of wedge-heeled espadrilles on her feet and she was ready.

Unless it was raining, Pieta liked to walk to work. She never varied the route she took. First she cut through St James's churchyard with its stretch of lawn and mature trees, then across Clerkenwell Green and along the busy main road towards Little Italy where they were washing down the pavements and setting up for the day.

Just a few steps further down the road, Pieta smelt the pungency of roasting coffee. DeMatteo's Italian Grocer created its own fine blends. Pieta never allowed herself a takeaway coffee, however, for members of the Martinelli family were not supposed to speak to Gianfranco DeMatteo and his son Michele. The feud between them was longstanding and bitter.

Even as a child Pieta could remember her father turning his back on the DeMatteo family outside St Peter's church. It was the same whenever they had to meet. Each January, when the local Italian families gathered to celebrate La Befana and give their children gifts, the DeMatteos would be at one side of the room and the Martinellis at the other. In July, at the procession of Our Lady of Mount Carmel and at the *festa* afterwards, they gave each other the cold shoulder.

Pieta had never been told what the feud was about. Her father refused to talk about it and her mother was vague on the subject. Sometimes, when they were younger, Addolorata would try to guess, but her ideas were always so crazy they only made Pieta laugh. And the feud was just one of the many mysteries of her father's life. For all the noise he made, he very seldom talked about himself.

This morning the door to DeMatteo's lay open and the smell of coffee was strong and tempting. Pieta was sure that on the counter they would have the deliciously sweet *sfogliatelle* she loved so much. The fine layers of pastry crisp beneath her teeth, the soft ricotta oozing inside, the hint of candied peel, vanilla and cinnamon – it was impossible to resist. She glanced around quickly. There was no sign of anyone she knew. Through the shop window she could see Michele DeMatteo stacking boxes of pasta on a shelf, but his father didn't seem to be around. Pieta decided to risk it.

'Good morning. I'll have a caffe latte and a *sfogliatella*, please.' She glanced at her watch. 'And I'm running late so …'

Pieta turned and browsed in a rack of Italian magazines while Michele made her coffee. She picked up a copy of the latest Italian *Vogue* and started flicking through the pages.

'Eh, lady, don't touch the magazines unless you're going to buy them.' Gianfranco DeMatteo had appeared out of nowhere and his expression was sour.

'OK, OK.' Flushing, Pieta flung the magazine down on the counter. 'I'm going to buy it, all right?'

The old man had been spoiling for a fight and he wasn't going to give in yet. 'This is not a library, you know. I have to make a living. You people think you can just come in here and ...'

He was still ranting as Pieta put her money on the counter, grabbed her purchases and headed out of the door. She glanced quickly at Michele, still lurking behind the coffee machine. He smiled slightly and shrugged apologetically. But he wasn't going to bother sticking up for her. He knew there was no point.

As she nibbled on her pastry and hurried towards Holborn, Pieta wondered what the old man would say if he knew her first task this morning was to design the gown his only son's fiancée would wear on her wedding day. If he didn't want her in his shop touching his magazines, then she was certain he wouldn't want her anywhere near the future Mrs DeMatteo.

Nikolas never arrived early and Pieta relished the first few hours of each day when she could be alone in the Design Room. This morning she sat beside the pinboard she'd covered with fabric swatches and references from international magazines, and thought about how much work she had ahead of her. There were more brides than ever on their books, and each dress they designed seemed to take longer than the last. Plus she had Addolorata's gown to think about now. Pieta didn't know where she would find the time to manage it all.

Sighing, she opened her sketch pad and looked at the notes she'd made for the DeMatteo dress. Nikolas Rose gowns were all about simplicity – strong shapes, beautiful fabric and fine workmanship. But when Pieta flicked through the folder of tear sheets Helene had given her she realized Michele's fiancée preferred something more embellished. She found page after page of full-skirted gowns with lace overlays, appliqué detailing, feathers and ruffles. She sighed again. It was going to be an effort to guide her towards the soft understated style that Nikolas Rose demanded. Pieta wondered if she should save everyone a lot of trouble by persuading her to go to another salon for her bridal gown.

She was still flicking through the folder when Nikolas appeared. Today he was in slouchy tweeds with a red paisley scarf knotted round his throat.

'Oh dear,' he said, peering over her shoulder at one of the more extravagantly ruffled gowns. 'What's going on there?'

'Everything,' said Pieta glumly.

'Yes, so I see. And why are you staring at it like that? Is this some sort of self-torture you've dreamt up? Staring at a hideous gown for five minutes a day? Is it character-building?' His tone was sarky and she could tell he was vastly amused by his own wit.

'No, this is the style of gown one of our new brides, Helene Sealy, likes. She came in yesterday morning, remember? You saw her in fabric that moves and mint-green ribbon.'

'Ah yes.'

Pieta held up a picture of a feathered lace creation

from the folder. 'The thing is, I'm not sure she's really a Nikolas Rose bride. Maybe we should turn her down.'

'Turn her down?' Nikolas repeated. She could see the idea appealed to his vanity. He'd never turned down a client before. It might give him a kind of cachet and exclusivity.

'Yes, exactly.' Pieta's voice was hopeful.

'No, no.' Greed had won out. 'Pretty little thing, wasn't she? We can't refuse to design for her. Perhaps you will need to revise your original ideas, though. And look at something with a little more detail and … erm … volume.'

'You want me to design a meringue?' Pieta regretted her words as soon as she spoke them.

In reply Nikolas merely hissed at her from between his teeth and stalked out of the room, walking, as he always did, almost on tiptoe and with his head back, as if he were heading into a high wind.

Miserably, Pieta abandoned her desk and sought refuge in the Make Room where there was noise, laughter and endless cups of tea. Maybe they could help her come up with a design for the DeMatteo gown that would keep both the bride and Nikolas Rose happy.

Pieta worked late and London was in a party mood by the time she left the salon. The pub crowds were spilling out onto the pavement and the restaurants were filling up. Pieta wondered if Addolorata would be finishing her shift at Little Italy. It would be good to have a chance to talk to her before she got home.

She walked slowly, hugging her unread copy of

Italian *Vogue* to her chest, her mind still caught up with designs and ideas. She couldn't have been looking where she was going because suddenly she collided with someone walking fast in the opposite direction.

'Pieta, I'm sorry. Are you all right?' It was Michele DeMatteo. Blushing a little, he bent down to retrieve the magazine she had dropped.

'Yes, yes, I'm fine.'

'I'm sorry about this morning.' He noticed Pieta's blank look. 'I mean, Papa shouting at you like that.'

'Oh, that's OK.' She reached out for her magazine but he was clutching it tightly.

'It is their feud not ours, you know.' His voice was slightly hesitant. 'There's no reason why we can't be friends.'

Pieta wasn't sure what to say.

'And no reason why you shouldn't come into DeMatteo's for a coffee and a pastry if you want to.' He sounded more confident now. 'Come by tomorrow and I'll give you one on the house to make up for this morning.'

'Michele?' She had never thought to ask him this before. 'Do you know what it's about, the feud between our fathers?'

'No. Do you?'

'Papa won't talk about it. I think it's something that happened at home, though, back in Italy.'

'Strange that they should both end up here in the same neighbourhood, isn't it?'

'I know. It doesn't make sense. I'd love to get to the bottom of it.'

'Well, if you ever do then let me know. Meanwhile,

I'll see you in the morning.' He gave her back her magazine. 'A caffe latte and a *sfogliatella*, right?'

'Right,' Pieta replied. 'And your father won't shout at me?'

'No.' Michele looked thoughtful. 'At least, I hope not.'

Pieta found Addolorata sitting alone at one of Little Italy's outdoor tables, a bowl of olives and a glass of red wine at her elbow.

'Waiting for someone?' she asked as she dropped down into the seat opposite.

'Actually I was hoping you'd stop by.' She poured Pieta a glass of wine and pushed the olives closer to her.

'How are you?' Pieta took a big sip of the wine.

'Tired. It's been a long day. What about you?'

'I'm tired, too. My day has been eventful. Want to hear?' She filled Addolorata in on everything that had happened to her, from Gianfranco DeMatteo's outburst to Michele's sudden friendliness.

'But he says he doesn't know the cause of the whole feud, either,' she finished.

'Frustrating, isn't it?' Addolorata sipped her wine thoughtfully. 'It's ancient history and it shouldn't matter, but I wish I knew.'

'I always wondered if it had something to do with Papa's sister.'

'Poor Isabella?' They'd never heard her referred to any other way.

'Yes, he hardly ever talks about her.'

'But there are lots of things he hardly talks about,'

Addolorata pointed out. 'How he met Mamma, why he ended up here …'

Pieta laughed. 'I found a beautiful English girl and I promised to follow her to the ends of the earth,' she said, mimicking her father.

'Exactly. So Papa won't tell us a thing and poor Isabella is dead and gone, so it's hopeless. We'll never know.'

'No, I suppose we won't. Ah well, at least I'm getting a free coffee and a pastry out of Michele in the morning.'

Addolorata raised her eyebrows. 'Didn't I tell you he's always been sweet on you?'

'Not that sweet. I'm in the middle of designing his fiancée a wedding dress after all. And that is a whole other story.' Pieta smiled. 'Come on, let's walk home and I'll tell you about it on the way.'

Pieta made her sister laugh so much as she regaled her with descriptions of the DeMatteo wedding gown that they were still giggling as they came through the front door and smelt the sweetness of frying onions.

Their mother was sitting at the kitchen table podding peas from the garden, and their father was at the stove.

'What's for dinner?' Addolorata lifted the lid of a pan.

'Oh, just a *pasta e piselli* and then some fish cooked in a Napolitana sauce with a little salad,' said Beppi. 'That lasagne last night was too heavy. I had the indigestion all night long. So this evening we're having something light for a change.'

'Papa, it's two courses,' Pieta pointed out. 'That's hardly light.'

'Pieta *cara*, the day you cook a meal in this house you will earn the right to comment but until then …'

'Wait, Papa,' Addolorata interrupted before Beppi's temper could catch and flare. 'I have something to tell you. I talked to the priest at St Peter's today. I've booked a date for the wedding.'

Beppi dropped his wooden spoon and, taking his daughter's face in his hands, he kissed her quickly on both cheeks. 'Ah, my good girl,' he said. 'And the marriage preparation course Ernesto told me about? You have booked that, too?'

'No, Papa.'

He gave her a disappointed look.

'But I'll talk to them about it and sign up,' Addolorata finished.

'Good, good. Dinner won't be long. Pieta, could you grate some parmigiano? And Addolorata, go and pick some salad from the garden. Your mother will set the table.'

Catherine looked up from her colander of freshly podded peas. 'Will Eden be joining us?'

'Not tonight.'

'What a pity,' Beppi said a little too enthusiastically. 'Never mind, maybe tomorrow night.'

Pieta had always liked *pasta e piselli*. The nuttiness of the peas and the freshness of spring onions made up for the bits of fatty bacon she always picked out and pushed to the side of the plate. And tonight she was hungry.

'Look at my daughter – she has some appetite at last,' said Beppi happily as he watched her tuck in. 'But Pieta, you look tired. Are you working too hard?'

'We're pretty busy,' she replied but didn't mention the DeMatteo gown. He would be no happier about that than Gianfranco was likely to be.

'And you have your sister's dress to make, too. How will you manage?'

'I'm not sure,' Pieta admitted.

Catherine sprinkled some more grated Parmesan on her pasta and mixed in a little butter. 'What will it be like, then, this wedding dress? You haven't told us.'

'Well.' Pieta glanced at her sister. Addolorata had promised her free rein with the design but still she felt jittery about describing the gown in case her sister couldn't imagine how beautiful it was going to be. 'It will be made of taffeta and have a full skirt that flows into a train at the back, a fitted bodice with wide shoulder straps and a sash that falls to the floor. And the whole thing will be encrusted with tiny Swarovski crystal beads so that even from a distance it shimmers.'

'It sounds fantastic,' said Addolorata.

'Yes, it does,' their mother agreed. 'But it also sounds like a lot of very fine work. Like your father says, how will you manage?'

Pieta cast her eyes down to the table. 'I'm not sure but I'll fit it all in somehow. I have to.'

There was silence for a moment and then their mother said hesitantly. 'If you want me to … I could help you.'

'Really?'

39

Catherine nodded. Years ago she had been a seamstress but she never went near her sewing room now. She hadn't used it for a long time. 'Yes, I can help. I'd like to. All that hand-beading, though … it will take us hours and hours.' She looked almost as though she relished the idea.

'So, Addolorata, what date did you book at St Peter's?' There was a wobble of anxiety in Pieta's voice.

'Um, two months tomorrow. They had a cancellation so I thought I should take it.'

'Well, that doesn't leave us an awful lot of time.' Oddly Catherine was sounding more cheerful by the minute. 'Pieta, you had better order the fabric and the beads, and we'll get started as soon as we can.'

Pieta nodded. Mentally she cancelled plans for movies and nights out with friends. It would be worth it, though, to see Addolorata in her perfect gown. And if the thought of spending so many hours alone with her mother bothered her slightly she pushed the thought away, right into the back of her mind.

4

It was hot again. Pieta couldn't remember the last time it had rained. Beppi kept declaring it was almost like an Italian summer. He had taken to waking early to water his garden, for he lived in fear of his rocket bolting or his cherry tomatoes splitting in a sudden rainstorm. Often, by the time Pieta was awake, he'd removed his shirt and was soaking in the morning sunshine as he moved about the small garden tending to his vegetables.

This morning Pieta found her mother sitting on the back doorstep chatting to him as she drank her tea. She was full of talk of the wedding and more animated than she'd been in a long time. The business of bonbonnières and bouquets would have absorbed her completely if Addolorata had allowed it to. 'Mamma, don't worry. We have it all under control. You don't have to do a thing,' she kept saying.

And so all that was left for Catherine to obsess over was the wedding gown. She had been into Pieta's room to examine the calico toile that still hung on the mannequin and had made some suggestions. She had even tidied her sewing room and taken a bus up to Oxford Street to buy bits and pieces at John Lewis. Pieta tried not to be resentful. She knew she should be glad to see her mother with some purpose and, anyway, she would need her help when the hard work of hand-beading started. But it wasn't easy. The gown had been all hers and now she had to share it.

'Mamma,' she called, 'can I get you another cup of tea?'

'No, no, I think I might share some of your coffee,' her mother replied. 'But not too strong, plenty of milk.'

'Coffee, are you sure?'

Her mother didn't answer. She was too busy worrying about flower girls and bridesmaids. 'How many will there be and who will make their dresses?' she was asking Beppi plaintively. 'Addolorata hasn't told us.'

Pieta sat down on the step beside her and passed over a cup of milky coffee. 'I don't think she's decided yet, Mamma. But that's fine because we can buy ready-made dresses for them.'

'But the cost … it seems a shame. Could we … ?'

'No, don't even think about it. We have enough work ahead of us.'

Catherine took a sip of her coffee. 'So when do we begin?' she asked eagerly. 'When will the fabric arrive?'

'It's here. It arrived yesterday and it's all ready to go.'

'So we should start tonight when you get home from work. I'll set up the sewing room so we can begin cutting.'

Pieta was hesitant. It was such a big task and she would have been happier to continue planning and dreaming for a little while longer.

'*Si, si*, start tonight,' her father urged. 'There is no time to waste.'

'All right, I'll try not to be too late home. I have a bride coming in for an after-work appointment but I'll come back straight after that.'

'Beppi, wash your hands.' Catherine stood up. 'You need to help me move the mannequin down the stairs and into my sewing room. And maybe we should shift the sewing table over slightly. No, not later … come and do it now …'

Pieta had been touched by Michele's offer of coffee and a pastry but she hadn't taken him up on it. His father always seemed to be skulking round the shop and she wasn't interested in another confrontation. But she did allow herself to think about sweet ricotta and shards of crisp pastry for a few moments as she walked past DeMatteo's each morning.

Today she was hungrier than usual. Perhaps it was the thought of the working day ahead. It would be a long one thanks to the late appointment, which happened to be with Michele's young fiancée, Helene. Pieta was curious about her. She wondered when she and Michele had met.

Caught up in her thoughts, she found herself walking through the doorway of DeMatteo's and smelling the sharpness of wheels of Parmesan and pecorino, and the smokiness of the thick salamis that hung from metal hooks, all overlaid with the rich aroma of coffee beans.

'Good morning.' Michele was standing behind the counter. He had cut off all his dark curls and his hair

43

was now just dense fuzz that lay close to his head. The shortness of it distorted his face somehow, making his nose look longer and his chin more angular. Luckily his father was nowhere to be seen.

'I thought you must have given up eating *sfogliatelle*,' he said to her.

'No, never.' She smiled at him. 'I always seem to be in such a rush to get to work, though. I don't have time to stop to get coffee.'

'The bridal world is busy, then? Lots of dresses to make?' Michele asked as he began frothing the milk for her caffe latte.

'Yes.' Pieta paused for a moment. 'And I heard that you are getting married soon. Congratulations.'

He hit the button on the coffee bean grinder and for a moment they were half deafened by the noise. 'Me? Oh yes, thanks.' She thought he looked uncomfortable.

'Will you have the ceremony at St Peter's like my sister Addolorata?'

Michele seemed to be struggling to decide how best to answer. 'Well, yes, we were going to but ...'

'But what?' Pieta couldn't help herself.

He looked up, his expression unreadable now. 'We both decided things were happening too fast, so we decided to postpone it for a bit.'

'Oh, I see.' Pieta wondered what that meant exactly. 'Well, at least your fiancée will have longer to think about her wedding gown.'

'Yes, there's plenty of time for that. No need for her to rush into anything.'

'That's good. Rushing is a bad idea when it come to

weddings,' she murmured, adding hurriedly, 'There's so much to plan.'

Putting her coffee and pastry on the counter, Michele gave her a half-smile. 'Enjoy it. See you next time,' he said before turning away.

As she walked towards Holborn, sipping coffee from the cardboard cup and nibbling on her pastry, Pieta wondered if Michele had got cold feet. Perhaps she would arrive at work to find Helene's name had been crossed out of the appointment diary and she wouldn't be working late on the DeMatteo gown this evening after all.

There was almost a holiday feel about the salon today. Nikolas was at home with a bad summer cold, and since he hardly ever took a day off, his absence encouraged everyone to behave a little badly. The Make Room girls took their tea break in the Chandelier Room. There was loud laughter and a lot of time wasted. And all day Pieta found herself returning to her designs for the DeMatteo gown and making modifications. She had convinced herself Michele had called off the wedding and the idea that the dress would never be made somehow gave her a sense of freedom she hadn't felt for years. She added fanciful details she knew Nikolas would never approve: an asymmetric shoulder strap of fabric peonies edged in palest pink; a hemline that was caught up at the front in an extravagant ruffle to show a little leg. Michele's fiancée would most likely never see the sketches she had made. They were just a flight of her imagination. But although she checked several times throughout the day, Helene's name remained in the diary.

When Nikolas's secretary started tidying her desk at the end of the day, Pieta asked, 'Are you sure my last bride didn't call to cancel?'

'No, sorry, Pieta. You can't get out of working late.'

'But did you check for any messages?'

'Yes, of course I did. There have been no cancellations. Your bride is on her way.'

Pieta closed her sketch pad and put it with Helene's folder of tear sheets on the shelves behind her desk. The poor girl was probably too upset to call and cancel. All the same, she waited until fifteen minutes or so after the appointment time before turning out the lights and switching on the alarm. She was just double-locking the front doors of the salon behind her when she heard the lift clang open.

'Pieta, Pieta, I'm so sorry I'm late.'

'Oh, I didn't think you were coming.'

'I got stuck at work.' The girl was pink-cheeked and breathless. 'And then I couldn't get on a bus and had to run most of the way. Please say you can still see me. I can't wait to have a look at the design you've come up with.'

'Really?' Pieta was confused. Perhaps she had misread the signs and the wedding was still going ahead. 'Well, everything is locked up but, since you're here, just let me deal with the alarm and turn all the lights back on, and then I'll show you through.'

Normally Pieta would seat the bride in the Chandelier Room and pour her a glass of champagne but, thrown off balance, she showed Helene through to the Design Room and sat her down there instead.

Helene was excited. 'Oh, is this where you work? And what's through there? Is that where the gowns are made? Can I see?'

'No, no.' Pieta knew Nikolas would be furious she had made it this far. He believed in glamour and mystique and, above all, only spending money where it needed to be spent. So the carpet in the Design Room had holes in it and the walls needed painting, while the Make Room was cramped and untidy.

'Clients really aren't meant to be in here, but since it's so late and I don't have much time I'll quickly show you my ideas for your gown and then we'll make another proper appointment for you for later in the week. You do want another appointment?'

'Yes, of course, if you think it's necessary. Can I see the design now?'

Pieta thought about the peony creation she had doodled and shuddered inwardly. Pulling out the sketch pad, she placed it in Helene's hands. 'Look, this is a little bit different,' she admitted. 'If it's not what you want then I'll go back and start again. I might have got carried away, to be honest.'

Helene gasped. 'Oh no, I love it. Honestly I do.' She stared at the sketch pad and traced the peony shoulder strap with her finger. 'You've just so totally, totally got me, it's unbelievable.'

Pieta's heart sank. 'Really?'

'I can't wait to try it on.'

'Well, that's a while away, I'm afraid. Now just let

me double-check the date of your wedding and then we'll book in another appointment, shall we?'

'Actually there has been a bit of a hitch with that.' Helene's smooth young forehead creased into a frown. 'There was a double-booking at the church so we've had to postpone for a while. But never mind. There's so much for me to plan that I'm sure I'll be glad of the extra time.'

Pieta realized she felt disappointed. She must have been hoping that Michele wouldn't marry the girl. And then the second realization hit. The DeMatteo gown, which already had the potential to cause so much trouble, was now a bigger problem than it had been before. A big, ruffled, peony-covered problem.

All the way home she mulled over the situation she had found herself in, but by the time she slid her key into the lock of her parents' front door she was no nearer to a solution than before.

Pieta sensed something was wrong the moment she walked into the house. There was no smell of cooking, no one in the kitchen at all. She found her mother in the garden sitting in an old deckchair, while her father busied himself pinching the laterals from the tomato plants so they would grow straight and tall.

Beppi looked pale. His lips had formed a thin line and his dark eyes were hard. Beside him, her mother sat cradling a half-drunk cup of tea. Everything about her look worried.

'We've been waiting for you, Pieta,' she said, her voice soft. 'You are later than we thought you'd be.'

'I got held up. I'm sorry. I know we'd said we were going to start Addolorata's dress but—'

'This isn't about the dress, Pieta,' her father interrupted.

'It isn't?'

'No.'

Pieta stood in front of her parents, shifting her weight from foot to foot, just as she had on the rare occasions she'd been in trouble as a child.

'So what have I done?' she asked.

Beppi held out his hands, green with the sap of tomato vines. 'You know we don't have anything to do with them,' he said in a disappointed voice. 'Our family has not spoken to their family since before we left Italy. You know all that, Pieta.'

So that was it. Someone had seen her going in or out of DeMatteo's this morning and reported it back to her father.

'It was only a coffee and a pastry, Papa. There's no need for you to be so angry.'

'No need?' He sounded furious. 'Who are you to tell me there is no need? You know nothing.'

'That's right, I know nothing.' She was cross, too. 'I have no idea why you and Gianfranco DeMatteo have been feuding for all these years because you refuse to tell me.'

'He dishonoured my family. I've told you that plenty of times.'

'Yes but how, Papa? What happened?'

He only shook his head. 'If you need to drink coffee while you walk to work then go into Little Italy. They will make you one for free, which is much better than

49

putting money into that man's pocket. Now, Caterina,' he glanced down at his wife, 'let me go and find something for you to eat. You must be starving.'

As he shuffled towards his kitchen, Pieta noticed how the skin on her father's arms looked dry and his legs were beginning to knot with veins. He was getting older.

'It was just a coffee, Mamma,' she said once they were alone. 'There was no need for Papa to overreact like that.'

'Well, like he says, get your coffee somewhere else. That's not so difficult, is it?'

'No.' It was so pathetic, all this feuding, but Pieta knew there was no point trying to discuss it any further.

'So, will we start working on the dress tonight?' Her mother looked hopeful.

'No, I'm too tired. We'll start it at the weekend, OK? And then we can have a decent run at it.'

She saw the disappointment on her mother's face and felt guilty. It was a strange sort of guilt that left her feeling half sad and half resentful, and Pieta felt it often.

'We'll start first thing Saturday morning, I promise,' she repeated. 'But right now I need an early night.'

It was a relief to climb the stairs to her room, shut the door and curl up on her bed. It had been a bad day and tomorrow promised to be worse. When Nikolas Rose saw the design for the DeMatteo gown, Pieta suspected she was going to find herself being shouted at all over again.

5

It was worse than Pieta expected. When he set eyes on the designs for the fantasy gown of peonies and ruffles, Nikolas threw an epic tantrum. He tore up her drawings into tiny pieces, lectured her about style, taste, restraint and, most of all, his reputation, then suggested she take two weeks' holiday, starting immediately.

Pieta hadn't argued. Let him run the place for a fortnight. She was tired and needed a rest. And she could use the time to start work on her sister's gown.

She walked home slowly, feeling a sense of freedom at being out on the streets in the middle of the afternoon. As she passed DeMatteo's she looked purposefully in the other direction so she didn't see Michele raise his hand to wave at her.

Her father was sitting outside Little Italy playing cards with Ernesto, but last night's argument was still fresh in her mind and she didn't stop to chat to them. She walked all the way to the churchyard and sat on a bench for a while beside a couple of office workers enjoying a late lunch from the sandwich bar round the corner. Pieta remembered when that café had been run by Italians who used to give her dolcelatte cheese spread on ciabatta bread as a treat. Now they had gone and everything cost twice as much and was half the size.

Round here there used to be lots of those old coffee bars and smoky little cafés where you could get a lunch of spaghetti and veal escalope. One by one they had closed, as the Italians who ran them grew old and tired of living in the city. Some went home to Italy at long last; others moved out to the suburbs. There were just a few clinging on to the old life in the old place. You could see them flocking to St Peter's for morning mass on Sundays: shrunken old women dressed in dark clothes and expensive gold jewellery; old men with tired brown eyes and noble faces. Pieta knew them all by name and they knew her. Sometimes it felt like living in a village that had somehow found itself transplanted into the middle of a big city.

Every Italian family in the area knew about the longstanding feud between Beppi Martinelli and Gianfranco DeMatteo. It was impossible to ignore it. If one man walked into a coffee bar, the other would leave. If one went to mass in the morning, the other went in the evening. They would even cross the street to avoid walking past each other. The hatred they felt was so strong and implacable that neither man ever spoke the other's name.

Pieta had grown up not questioning it. At school they had fights and feuds all the time. They would gang up on each other and send someone to Coventry. It was only as she grew older that she realized it wasn't the normal way for adults to behave. But she couldn't question her father or suggest he 'forgive and forget'. The priest had tried it once and her father had become so enraged he hadn't gone to mass for six months. And so the feud had been carried on through the decades and now it looked as if she and Addolorata were supposed to continue it. It seemed so pointless.

Pieta stood up, scattering a flock of pigeons that were pecking at someone's discarded filled roll. She would go home, make herself a coffee and plan what she was going to do with her two weeks of freedom.

She found Addolorata sitting on the back doorstep, smoking a cigarette she must have pinched from her room.

'Shit, what are you doing here?' said her sister. 'You gave me a fright.'

'Where's Mamma?'

'Upstairs, having a lie-down. She's got a headache.' Addolorata took a drag of the cigarette then passed it to her. 'I'm doing a double shift so I came home to have a quick shower. It's bloody hot in that kitchen.'

'I bet.' Pieta sat down beside her.

'But you didn't answer my question. What are you doing home so early?'

'I'm taking a couple of weeks' leave so I can work on your wedding dress.'

Addolorata seemed worried. 'Look, I don't want you taking this on if it's going to be too much work. Honestly, I can just buy something from a shop.'

'No, I want to do it. It's not too much trouble. And Mamma is really excited about it.'

'Yeah, I know.' Addolorata took back the cigarette and flicked some ash on the ground. 'Everyone seems more excited about this wedding than me. I keep telling Eden that it's not too late to elope but he says he's not prepared to face Papa afterwards, even if I am.'

Pieta smiled. 'He has a point.'

'I'm almost wondering if we should postpone the whole thing. I feel like we're rushing.'

'How weird that you should say that.'

'Why is it weird?'

'Because that's exactly what Michele DeMatteo has done.'

'Really?'

'Yes, but that's not the strangest thing. When I spoke to his fiancée she claimed they'd had to postpone because of a double-booking at St Peter's, but that's not what he said to me at all.'

'Those guys at St Peter's are so organized. I can't imagine them double-booking someone's wedding,' said Addolorata. 'I reckon Michele has got cold feet but he just hasn't got the guts to tell her.'

'That's what I thought.'

So that means Michele is free again?'

'What do you mean?'

Addolorata gave her a teasing sidelong look.

Pieta laughed. 'Are you mad? I'm in trouble for going into DeMatteo's to get coffee, so don't think you can start cooking up any romance between me and Michele.'

Addolorata looked thoughtful. 'But it's not our feud.'

'Papa doesn't see it that way.'

Addolorata stubbed out the cigarette. 'Don't I know it. I'd better get back to work. I've put a beetroot risotto on the menu and he's bound to have discovered it by now. All hell will have broken loose.'

Pieta stayed on the doorstep for a while thinking about Michele DeMatteo. Why had he chopped off all his beautiful curls and why had he postponed his wedding? And, more importantly, was he telling the truth when he claimed his father had never told him what this ridiculous feud was all about? Surely someone must know what lay behind it?

6

The next day Pieta slept in late and then sat in the garden with her coffee relishing her freedom. Life was always such a rush; there never seemed to be any empty time. And although the work on Addolorata's gown lay ahead of her, she was tired and needed a few hours of doing nothing at all. It was her gift to herself, she reasoned.

And then the phone rang and stupidly she answered it.

'Oh, Pieta, thank God you're at home.' It was Addolorata and her voice was frayed with worry.

'What's happened?'

'Two of the waiters have rung in sick and we've got this huge group booking at lunchtime. I can't find anyone else to work. I hate to ask you because I know it's your first day off but ...'

'I'll come in and help. Just let me shower and get dressed.'

'You're a star. I owe you.' Addolorata sounded distracted. 'See you in a bit, then.'

Pieta had waitressed at Little Italy on weekends and during summer holidays throughout her teenage years. It had been a while since she had taken an order or carried steaming plates to a table but she had always liked the controlled chaos of the place, her father yelling in the kitchen, the chefs scrambling to work at the speed he demanded and the buzz of the dining room filled with contented people sharing wine and food. As she put on a pair of narrow black trousers and a fitted black shirt, she realized she was almost looking forward to spending the day working there.

It was obvious from the moment she arrived that Addolorata was tense. The kitchen was in the middle of prepping for the day and the place was filled with the heady smells of onions sizzling in olive oil and beef braising slowly in tomatoes. Everyone was doing something – chopping, stirring and peeling as quickly as they could – and yet the atmosphere was strangely subdued.

Unlike their father, Addolorata didn't shout when she got stressed. She had a reputation for never losing her cool. But Pieta could see the mood she was in from the set of her shoulders and the way her skin seemed paler than usual.

'Hey, I'm here,' Pieta called out. 'Put me to work.'

Addolorata gave a half-smile. 'Thank God. I just need you till the lunch rush dies down and we've got rid of that big table.'

'That's fine. I'll go out and help set up but if there's anything you need me to do in here just yell.'

There wasn't another chance to exchange a word with her sister for the next four hours. Pieta had forgotten how busy Little Italy could get. Soon every table was full with people who wanted to order and eat within a lunch hour. Some were peremptory, treating her like an inferior because she was taking their order;

others were regulars Pieta remembered from years ago. As she raced from the kitchen to their tables and back again, her arms overloaded with plates, there was barely time to think, never mind pause for a moment. Pieta wondered how anyone had the stamina to do this day after day.

The rush seemed to die down as quickly as it had begun. Suddenly Pieta realized the tables they had wiped down and set again weren't filling up and there were just a few people lingering over coffee and dessert.

She headed back to the kitchen to see if there was anything she could do. Addolorata met her at the door with a bowl of spaghetti tossed with chilli, garlic and olive oil and covered in torn rocket leaves.

Confused, Pieta glanced up at the wall where the orders were pinned. 'What table is this for?'

Addolorata laughed for the first time all day. 'Idiot, it's for you. Go and find somewhere quiet to enjoy it. And thanks, I don't know how we'd have got through today without you.'

Pieta took her lunch out to her father's favourite table and ate in the sunshine as she watched the theatre of the street market – the stallholders competing noisily to attract customers for their cut-price clothes and cheap jewellery, the shoppers searching for a bargain. She was wiping up the last of the chilli-infused oil with a crust of ciabatta when Ernesto appeared.

'No sign of your papa, eh?' The old man sat down opposite her. 'He must know that I'm feeling lucky today.'

Pieta smiled. 'Papa hates to be beaten at cards.'

'He hates to be beaten at anything, *cara*, always has.'

Ernesto had known her father since they were both young men, struggling to establish themselves in a strange city. They were the same age and both from mountain villages in the south, but it was their love of a glass of red wine and a game of cards that had sealed their friendship. Pieta could remember them sitting at this table when she was a child. Sometimes they laughed, often they shouted, and from time to time they fell out, but they always picked up their friendship before too long and the card games would continue.

Then she had a thought: if her father had confided in anyone, it would be Ernesto. Pushing aside her plate, she leaned towards him. 'I don't know if he's told you, but Papa and I haven't been getting on so well lately,' she told him.

'No? Ah well, he can be a difficult man sometimes, your papa. And you have a temper, too, I think.' Ernesto laughed. 'All Italian families argue. I wouldn't worry too much about it.'

Pieta wondered how best to phrase her next question. 'He talks to you, doesn't he? He tells you things?' she asked at last.

Ernesto nodded. 'Yes, I suppose he does. Why?'

'If you knew the reason for the feud with Gianfranco DeMatteo, would you tell me?'

'Ah, the feud.' Ernesto shook his head. 'If you had any idea of the number of times I've tried to get him to explain exactly what lies behind it. But he says the same things to me that I expect he says to you. It's about honour, respect and a wrong that was done many years ago.'

'He must have told you more than that.' Pieta was exasperated.

'No, and to be honest I can understand why. It's Beppi's business not mine.'

'So that's all you know?'

Ernesto looked thoughtful. 'Your mother may have let something slip years ago in the days when she was still your father's waitress.'

'What did she say?'

'Oh, I don't remember exactly, but my impression was that it had something to do with Beppi's sister.'

'Isabella?'

'Yes, that's right.'

Pieta had learned nothing new. She was sure the old man must know something more. 'But what?' she pressed him. 'What could possibly be so awful that they'd still refuse to have anything to do with one another all these years later?'

Ernesto sighed and gestured to a waiter to bring him a glass of red wine. 'You know, you're looking at this the wrong way,' he said gently.

'I am?'

'You're looking through your own eyes when you should be trying to look through your father's. You grew up with all this prosperity.' He gestured towards Little Italy. 'You always had food on your plate and shoes on your feet. It was different back then when we were growing up.'

'I know.'

'Try to imagine it, Pieta. Some days there was so

little food in our house that my mother would just put one plate of spaghetti in the middle of the table and the person who talked the least ate the most.'

Pieta smiled. She had heard reminiscences like these from her father.

'I had more brothers and sisters than Beppi so we were perhaps a little poorer but it wouldn't have been that different for him. There was never enough to eat. And we had no toys. When I was little I used to play with pebbles in the dust. For fun my brothers would catch eels or songbirds, and my mother used to cook them so at least there was some food on the table.' He sipped at his wine. 'I still remember how it felt to be so hungry. You never forget it, you know.'

Pieta looked at Ernesto, at his wrinkled skin, thinning hair and large belly. It was difficult to imagine him as a hungry young man.

'And then we left our villages and came here.' Ernesto was deep in his memories now. 'And we were determined to work hard and make a big success. Your father borrowed money, risked everything. He worked day and night. When you were born, your poor mother hardly ever saw him. She was upstairs in their tiny flat, all on her own with a little baby.'

'And then she got pregnant with Addolorata so quickly, didn't she?' Pieta had often wondered about that.

'That was a mistake for your mother, a big mistake. No wonder ...' Ernesto broke off and shook his head. 'So you see, Pieta, don't try to judge your father by your standards. We come from a different time and place.'

'I'd still like to know, though,' Pieta told him. 'What the feud was all about and what happened to poor Isabella.'

'Maybe he'll tell you some day.'

'I doubt it.' Pieta stood up. 'I'm going to see if Addolorata needs any more help. Sorry you didn't get your card game, Ernesto. I'll tell Papa you were here, though.'

Instead of walking straight home Pieta took a detour through the market, browsing at the stalls filled with things she didn't want: cheap perfume, nylon clothes, dodgy electronic goods. She bought a bunch of sunflowers for her mother and then turned to head for home.

'Pieta! Wait for me.'

It was Michele, hurrying up behind her. He was carrying two plastic shopping bags filled with leafy green vegetables. He smiled. 'You're not working today?'

Uncomfortably, Pieta glanced around her. 'No, no, I'm not.'

'Do you have time to stop for a coffee?'

'I can't, Michele, I'm sorry.'

He looked at her quizzically. 'Is everything all right?'

'Yes ... no ... oh, look, the problem is my father will be furious if he hears I've been talking to you. This whole stupid feud business, you know. I'm so sorry, but I can't have coffee with you.'

'They're such stubborn old men, aren't they?' Michele looked rueful. 'After all these years you'd think they could get over it.'

'You know I agree with you ...' She shrugged. 'But what can I do? It's easier if we just stay away from each other ...'

She glanced back once as she strode off through the market. Michele was still standing there, clutching his plastic carrier bags and staring at her. He didn't seem to have noticed that it was beginning to rain.

By the time Pieta made it home the soft summer rain had turned into a storm. The wind was crashing through the trees and the water running in rivers down the gutters. Wet and cold, she hurried through to the kitchen, always the warmest room in the house. But there was no sign of her father.

She peered through the window to check if he was out in the garden, tying his precious tomatoes more securely to their stakes. Although sheltered by its high brick walls, the garden was still being stirred by the winds and the rain was pelting down. But her father was nowhere to be seen.

Pieta headed upstairs to change into dry clothes, calling out, 'Mamma, are you here? Is anybody home?'

'I'm in here.' Her mother's voice came from her parents' bedroom. 'I'm having a lie-down.'

Pieta put her head round the door. 'Are you all right? Can I get you anything?'

'It's just a bit of a headache, that's all. I've taken some of my pills. I'll be OK.'

'Where is Papa?'

'He had to go out. He shouldn't be too long.'

'Ernesto was looking for him at Little Italy.'

Her mother pulled herself up in bed and rested her

63

back against the pillow. 'Was he?' she asked disinterestedly. 'Actually, Pieta, could I get you to make me a cup of tea?'

'Yes, of course, Mamma. I'll dry myself and then I'll put the kettle on.' Pieta paused. 'And then I thought I'd make a start on Addolorata's dress, but if you don't feel up to helping me that's fine.'

The sewing room had a musty, unused smell, even though her mother had been in and out of it for the past few days, checking and re-checking that everything was ready.

Pieta had already put hours of work into this gown. She had planned and sketched it, chosen the perfect silk taffeta in a subtle, soft shade of white, and had it backed so that it was heavy enough to work with. Then there had been a taxing hour or so while she measured Addolorata, who had fussed and squirmed with impatience.

'Don't tell me what my hip measurement is because I don't want to know,' she had groaned, as Pieta worked out the precise angle of her shoulders, the distance between her waist and the nape of her neck, the length of her legs.

Next had come the technical part, drafting a body block and developing it into a pattern. She had made four calico toiles to get the fit and shape exactly right, and now at last it was time to start working with the fabric.

As she unfolded the pieces she'd already cut into large blocks her mother came in carrying her second cup of tea and settled in the old armchair in the corner. Quietly, she watched Pieta work.

'I'm so proud of you, Pieta, you know,' she said at last. 'I'd never have had the confidence to achieve what you have. Look how far you've come in so short a time.'

'Oh, Mamma ...' Pieta found conversations like this embarrassing. Her mother had a way of pouring out her love unbidden and Pieta couldn't help pulling away from it.

'But it's true. Your father and I are both so proud of you and your sister. We couldn't have asked for two better daughters.' Tears began to form in Catherine's eyes.

'I know, Mamma, I know.'

Pieta tried to focus on laying out her fabric but her mother was still talking. She was saying the things she always said, remembering how hard it had been when they were babies, the struggle to keep a roof over their heads, the way they had worked and worried all day and half of the night. Pieta had heard it all many times but now, with Ernesto's words still fresh in her mind, she was more curious than she had been before.

Looking up from her work, she asked, 'Why did Papa come here if it was such a struggle? Why didn't he stay in Italy?'

'I suppose he came partly for me,' her mother replied. 'He knew I missed my family. And there was nothing there for him either, no future. He was determined to make a better life for himself, and he wanted his children to have all the things he never had.'

'Was he very poor when he was young, Mamma?'

'Everyone was poor in Ravenno. It was so isolated up there in the mountains. Your grandparents had a little plot of land and kept chickens and goats, so they weren't as hungry as many families. And there weren't too many children, only your papa and his younger sister, because all the other babies died. She had a hard life, your grandmother Adriana. By the time I met her she was old before her time and almost toothless. We hardly understood a word the other said, but she was always kind to me.'

'But Papa lived in Rome when you met him, didn't he?'

'That's right, because there was no work in Ravenno. He was a waiter in a big hotel and sent most of the money he earned home to Adriana and Isabella. By then your grandfather had died and life was even more of a struggle for them.'

Pieta had seen the old black-and-white photographs of her parents looking glamorous beside a big baroque fountain. Her father was handsome and black-haired, her mother pretty in a headscarf and sunglasses.

'Why did you go to Italy, Mamma?' Pieta had always wondered why her mother had left her home in London and travelled to Rome. How had she ended up standing with her father beside that fountain? Looking at her now, sitting in the old armchair, an empty teacup in her lap, it seemed extraordinary that such a timid woman had embarked on such a big adventure.

'Why did I go?' Catherine mused. 'Oh, I was young and that's the kind of thing you do when you're young, isn't it?'

'But why choose Italy?'

'Actually, that wasn't my choice. It was my friend's idea. She started taking Italian classes and made me go along with her, too. We learned about the art and the food and the beautiful buildings, and wanted to see them for ourselves.'

'But how did you afford it? The fare must have been expensive.'

'We didn't have any money and we hardly paid any fares.' Catherine smiled at the memory of it all.

'So how did you get there?'

'Oh, we ...' Catherine paused and, standing up, came over to take a closer look at the taffeta. 'If you cut the fabric shell today then I'll help you start on the beading tomorrow,' she offered.

'You didn't answer my question, Mamma,' Pieta insisted. 'How did you get to Italy? And what happened once you were there?'

Catherine laughed. 'What do you want to know all that for? I don't remember most of it anyway. I haven't thought about it for so many years.'

'I just do. I'm interested.'

'All those old stories ... I don't know ... we'll see,' her mother murmured, and Pieta was certain she had no intention of telling her any more than she already had.

Beppi's Beautiful Lasagne

Lasagne, I don't see what all the fuss is about. It's too heavy for me, too rich. I prefer the spaghetti. But people seem to love my lasagne and so I make it, of course. My way is to make a *ragù* sauce and then ... but I'll tell you about the sauce first because it is superb.

You must use the Italian tomatoes in tins. The fresh ones you buy here, they are like pulp, tasteless. Even the ones I grow in my garden aren't as good as the tomatoes back home.

This is what you need:

olive oil
2 cloves of garlic (not like Caterina's friend
    Margaret who understood two bulbs – so every-
    body was avoiding her in work the next day)
2 medium finely diced onions
2 sticks of celery and some celery leaves
4 oz of button mushrooms
fresh basil
1 medium carrot
6 tins of tomatoes
1 tin of tomato purée
1.5 kg of beef mincemeat
1 large glass of red wine
salt
pepper

OK, so in a large saucepan add some oil (not too much because the meat is going to release fat). Cut up the onions as finely as you can and fry on a low heat. When the onions are nearly done chop garlic finely and fry for a few minutes with the onion (add a drop of water if necessary to stop the onions burning.) Add the mincemeat a little at a time and stir fry till the meat is browned. Add the diced mushrooms and stir with the mince until beginning to cook. Now add the chopped celery, chopped carrot and the tins of tomato and puree. Finally add salt and pepper to taste. Bring to the boil and simmer for one and a half hours minimum. Add the wine or water during the cooking to stop the sauce becoming too dry, and stir occasionally to stop it sticking to the bottom of pan.

OK, that's enough for now. You go away and practise the sauce. When you get it right then I'll give you the rest of the recipe.

Addolorata's note: You forgot to put in the basil, Papa. I like to stir lots of it through at the very end and maybe use some Italian parsley too for a really fresh, herby flavour.

Beppi: My God, Addolorata, always you put in too many ingredients. Try to restrain yourself.

7

The beading was the part of her job Pieta loved most. It took time and patience, and that was why so many other designers preferred to farm it out, but to Pieta, beading was what gave a design its signature look. She believed it could make or break a gown.

The beads she'd chosen for this dress were delicate because, rather than a fussy, embellished look, she wanted to create the impression that Addolorata was shimmering as she stood beside the altar. Now, as Pieta sat and looked at the virgin fabric and her boxes of crystal beads, she was grateful to have her mother's help. To do this properly was going to be a lot of work.

She stretched out the fabric over the frames and put cushions down on the hard wooden chairs she'd set beside them. If they were going to be sitting here all day, they might as well be comfortable.

Below her a phone was ringing. She heard it stop and then start again. This time someone must have answered it because it rang only two or three times. Pieta thought she heard a voice cry out and the sound of china clattering on a hard floor.

She opened the door of the sewing room. 'Mamma, are you OK?' she called down the stairs but there was no reply.

The front door slammed and afterwards everything went quiet.

'Mamma?'

The house was empty. In the kitchen a broken cup lay on the floor in a pool of milky tea. Pieta noticed the phone was lying off the hook. Before she replaced it, she held it to her ear. 'Hello?' she said uncertainly.

'Oh, Pieta, it's you.' It was Addolorata. She sounded panicky. 'Is Mamma there? Put her back on quickly. I need to tell her exactly where we are.'

'She's not here. What's going on?'

There was a moment's silence and then the words rushed out of Addolorata, shocking and raw. 'Oh God, Pieta. I think I've killed Papa.'

Pieta did exactly what her mother had just done – slammed the front door behind her and ran to find a taxi. Because she'd managed to stay on the phone long enough to listen to Addolorata's instructions, she arrived at the hospital first.

She found her sister pacing back and forth in a small waiting room, looking dishevelled and fraught.

'How is he?'

'I don't know. I'm still waiting to hear.' Her face looked ashen. 'It was my fault, Pieta. All my fault.'

'What do you mean? How could it be your fault?'

'We were arguing over something I'd put on the menu. He was complaining that everything I cook is unnecessarily complicated, like he does about three times a week, but this time I just lost it. I started shouting at him, told him I was sick of him trying to control me and that I was going to leave Little Italy

71

and start up my own place where I could do things my way.'

'What did he say?'

'I thought he was going to yell back at me but instead he went quiet and pale, and then he fell down onto a chair and sort of slumped and groaned. Frederico was there and he called an ambulance. When we got here they whisked him away and told me to wait in here.'

'Do they think he's had a heart attack or a stroke?'

'I think so but they haven't said yet.'

'Oh God.' Pieta sat down heavily. 'Poor Mamma.'

'I hope she hasn't gone to the wrong hospital. I don't know how much she listened to after I told her Papa had collapsed.'

Together they waited in the cramped room beneath the harsh strip lighting. After a while Pieta fetched some undrinkable coffee from a vending machine and they watched it go cold.

'What if he dies? What if he's dead already and they've forgotten to send someone to tell us?' Addolorata was panicking.

Pieta said nothing. She had been thinking the same thing.

They both shot to their feet when the door opened and the doctor came in.

'He's OK,' he assured them quickly. 'And you can go in and see him in a minute.'

'Was it a heart attack?' Addolorata asked.

He nodded. 'We've done some blood tests and an ECG, and yes, it was.'

'Oh God, it's my fault. I stressed him out so much I nearly killed him.'

The doctor was softly-spoken and kind. He made Addolorata sit down and explained that, although heart attacks can be caused by extreme stress, it was more likely in this case to be a blockage in one of their father's arteries. There would be more tests and possibly surgery.

'In the meantime we've got him on drugs to improve the blood flow and prevent another attack. He'll have to stay in hospital a few days and look at changing his lifestyle when he does get home.' He smiled at them both. 'And yes, less stress would probably be a good thing.'

'You go in to see him, Pieta.' Addolorata sounded close to tears. 'I'll only get him all stressed out again. It's better if I wait here for Mamma.'

As she walked down the corridor, Pieta tried to prepare herself for the sight of her father in a hospital bed, robbed of his usual febrile energy, diminished into a frail old man.

His eyes were closed when she entered the room. She sat down beside him quietly in case he was sleeping.

'Caterina?' His voice sounded hoarse.

'No, Papa, it's me, Pieta. Mamma is on her way.'

He opened his eyes and tried to smile. 'You are so like your mamma. So like her when she was about your age.'

Reaching out, Pieta took one of his hands. It was roughened by knife cuts and kitchen burns. 'Are you OK?'

'Tired. Very tired.'

'Go to sleep, then. Get some rest.'

'Addolorata, where is she?'

'She's worried she caused this, Papa. She's blaming herself.'

'We had a fight?' He frowned as he struggled to remember.

'I think so but it's not important now.' Pieta didn't want to upset him again.

'She told me I am overbearing and impossible.' His voice was hoarse and slow.

'Papa—'

'She said she is going to leave Little Italy and start her own restaurant.'

'I'm sure she didn't mean it.'

He squeezed her hand hard. 'I don't want my daughter to think such bad things of her father.'

'Sshh, don't worry about this now. Go to sleep.'

'Little Italy is all I have to give Addolorata and now she says she doesn't want it.' He sounded lost and confused.

'It was just a silly fight and it doesn't matter any more. What's important is that you get well.'

He managed to smile at her. 'You are so like your mamma.'

What surprised Pieta most was the way her mother took control. As soon as she knew the immediate danger had passed and she'd seen Beppi with her own eyes, her fear and panic gave way to a determined efficiency.

She told Pieta she should go home. 'I'll stay with your father and make sure he's comfortable.' Her voice was calm. 'You start work on the beading, if you like. Don't sit around doing nothing. Keep busy.'

'What about me?' Addolorata asked.

'You should go to the restaurant and take care of things there. It's the least you can do.'

Chastened, Addolorata didn't argue. But Pieta was reluctant to leave so quickly. Only when she saw her parents didn't need her, and how holding her mother's hand seemed to give her father some strength, did she slip quietly out of the room.

She asked the taxi driver to drop her off at Little Italy so she could make sure Addolorata was all right. It was late afternoon and, apart from a few lunchtime stragglers, the dining room was empty. In the kitchen they were busy, prepping for the night ahead, but Pieta noticed the atmosphere was subdued. There was none of the normal joking and teasing, none of the usual kitchen bustle. Instead everyone was focused on their tasks and trying not to stare at Addolorata, who was sitting at the counter pretending to read through the order book, quietly letting tears slide down her face.

She looked worried when she saw Pieta. 'What's wrong?' she asked.

'Nothing, they're both fine. I just came to see how you are.'

'Oh, you know ...' She stood up and led Pieta out of the kitchen in search of somewhere more private to talk. 'I still feel pretty awful but I'm OK.'

They sat down at a corner table and Frederico, who'd been tidying away bread baskets and pepper grinders, went to fetch them some coffee.

'You're not really going to leave Little Italy?' Pieta asked.

Addolorata looked awkward. 'I've been thinking about it. Eden thinks I should.'

'But why?'

'This place is all about Papa. It's always going to be his restaurant no matter what I do. I'd like to go out on my own, prove myself.'

Pieta remembered her father's words. 'But he built this place from nothing and made it into what it is for you. He wants you to have it. You'll break his heart, Addolorata. You can't leave.'

'That's easy for you to say but you don't have to work here with him interfering all the time.' Addolorata's head sank into her hands. 'Oh, obviously I'm not going to go now. Not with him sick and everything. I'll put the whole idea of leaving on hold until he's better. I should probably postpone the wedding as well.'

'No, no, don't do that. Papa wouldn't want that.'

Addolorata shook her head. 'It's always about what Papa wants, isn't it?' she said. And then she got up and went back to her kitchen.

Pieta didn't follow her. When Addolorata was in this mood she was better left alone. Instead she wandered between the market stalls in search of something to occupy her.

Usually Pieta lived life at such a run there were no leftover hours to fill. Feeling lost and edgy, she walked past the rows of cheap handbags and knock-off perfumes, past the greasy spoon cafés stinking of fried potatoes and fatty sausages, and the hawkers yelling about miracle cleaning products, and then back up through Hatton Garden past the diamond merchants' shops and towards home.

Everything was as she had left it: the fabric stretched over the frames waiting to be beaded; the comfortable cushions on the chairs where she and her mother were meant to be sitting and working by now. To Pieta's eyes it all looked sad.

She wasted time, fiddling with the crystal beads, rearranging things that were fine as they were, making cups of tea she didn't really want. So often Pieta longed for the house to be peaceful. And now that it was, now there were no pans being clanged and no smells of frying onions or searing meat drifting up the stairs, she couldn't bear to be there.

Pieta went out and sat in the churchyard for a while. At least here she was surrounded by the bustle of office workers seizing ten minutes for a cigarette. But after watching people come and go for a short time, she'd had enough. She was worried about her parents; concerned her mother would be feeling lost in the cold efficiency of the hospital or that her father's condition might be worsening. So, walking quickly down through Clerkenwell Green, she headed towards the main road in search of a taxi.

The moment she arrived at the hospital it was clear her father was feeling much better. He was groaning as her mother arranged his pillows, and had one hand cupped over his chest. 'No, not like that, Caterina. A little higher. One behind my head, too. And then I need some water. Oh, it is so terrible to be an invalid.'

'You're not going to be an invalid, Beppi. Stop being so melodramatic,' her mother said crisply.

'I have to change my lifestyle, you heard the doctor. No more stress. And I am going to join the gym like Eden. Do the weightlifting and go on the exercycle. I am going to get fit and strong again, Caterina, you'll see. There is a young man inside of me just bursting to get out.'

Pieta met her mother's eyes and they both tried not to smile.

'Beppi, you must rest,' her mother reminded him. 'Don't think about that now. Just take it easy while you're in hospital and we'll worry about you getting fit again once you're home.'

'But what about you?' He sounded anxious now. 'How will you manage with me here in the hospital? What will you eat?'

'I'll be fine. Food is the last thing on my mind.'

'No, no, you need a proper meal,' he insisted. 'Go to Little Italy on your way home. Get them to give you some of the sauce with the braised venison. Very lean, you'll like it. Not the sauce with the pancetta, though, as Addolorata puts too much chilli in it for you.'

'I'm happy with eggs on toast,' she insisted.

'Bah, always you say that. But just have the venison and some salad if the pasta is too heavy. Or some soup? Maybe Addolorata could make you a pan of *minestre* ...'

Pieta listened to them bicker for a while until her father's eyes closed and he began to doze.

'It's been such a shock,' her mother said softly, watching his chest rise and fall with the deep breaths of sleep. 'Your father has always been so fit and healthy, always on the go. To see him lying here like this ...'

'The doctors say he'll be fine, Mamma. They started treatment quickly and that's the important thing. We have to trust them.'

'I know, but still … I don't think I can bear to leave him alone. I'm going to spend the night here. I can snatch a few winks in the chair if need be.'

Pieta looked at her mother. Her skin looked dull and grey, and the web of lines on her face more deeply strained and furrowed.

'Papa's right. You need to come home and eat a decent meal,' she told her. 'And then get a good night's sleep. You can come back first thing in the morning.'

'But what if something happens and I'm not here? I won't be able to sleep for worrying.'

'Then you can help me with the beading. We'll keep busy and tire ourselves out. Come home with me, Mamma.'

'Not yet … just let me stay a few hours longer until I'm sure he doesn't need me. Then I'll come home and help you with Addolorata's dress. If it isn't ready in time for the wedding that will upset your father more than anything.'

By the time she heard her mother open the front door, Pieta had made a start on the beading. She felt better now she had begun. There was a soothing rhythm to the work and once she'd settled into it her mind was free to wander.

Her mother came in and picked up her needle without saying a word.

'Is everything all right?' Pieta asked.

'I hope so.' Her voice sounded small.

79

'You look tired, Mamma. Why don't you go and rest? I'm sure I can manage alone.'

'I don't want to rest, Pieta. Or eat. Just leave me be and let me get on with some beading.'

They worked together in silence for a while, stitching each small crystal bead carefully in place. Progress was slow and Pieta was glad to have help, although she worried about her mother. Her expression seemed dazed, and her silence suggested she was brooding.

'So, Mamma,' she said trying to distract her, 'weren't you going to tell me about when you and Papa were young, back in Italy?'

Catherine looked up from her work. 'Was I?' She sounded confused. 'You know, I was thinking about those days in the hospital while your father was sleeping. So many things came back to me that I'd thought I'd forgotten. Like the trick Beppi played on me on our very first date ...'

'What did he do?'

'Oh, he was always full of jokes, always laughing.'

'But what happened on the date?' Pieta persisted. 'And how did you even meet Papa in the first place?'

Catherine looked uncertain. She'd never told her story before but Pieta could see she was tempted to now. The shock of the day she'd been through and the knowledge her husband was lying sick in hospital made her long to talk about him.

'If I'm going to tell you about your papa then I ought to start at the beginning,' she said slowly.

Pieta nodded her encouragement.

'And actually the beginning wasn't about Beppi

at all, it was about Audrey. I've told you about her, haven't I?'

Pieta shook her head. 'No, I don't think so. I don't remember you mentioning anyone called Audrey.'

Her mother didn't seem to be listening. 'I haven't heard from her in years.'

'Who was she?'

'Audrey was … Audrey is …' she faltered, and then her needle stilled and she began to tell her story.

* * *

8

There were three of us and we did everything together. Audrey was the glamorous one. She had white-blonde hair and knew how to make the most of herself. Margaret was a redhead, fiery but always ready to have a laugh. And then there was me. Well, you've seen the photos, I wasn't anything special to look at. Dark hair, slim like you, always the quiet one. I used to think the other two only bothered with me because I could sew. We never had any money for clothes but I was clever at altering things and making an old outfit look like it might be a new one.

The Italian lessons were all Audrey's idea. 'Come on, we can do evening classes at the college,' she said. 'It'll be fun, something different.'

I wasn't keen. I was working in a grocer's shop and on my feet all day. Going to evening classes afterwards sounded like more hard work.

'Oh, I don't know, won't it be just like going back to school again?' I asked.

None of us had liked school. We'd all left at sixteen, the minute we were allowed to. Audrey was a waitress at a Lyons Corner House, and Margaret had trained as a nanny and was looking after some rich family's children.

'Yes, do I really want to waste a precious night off?' Margaret worked long hours. 'I'd rather go dancing.'

Audrey gave a little toss of her head, which meant there was no point arguing with her. Once she'd got an idea she just wouldn't shut up about it.

'We could go dancing after the class,' she reasoned. 'It won't take all night, you know, just a couple of hours. And it would be a great way for us to meet new people.'

We knew what that meant. Audrey was hoping to meet a man. It wasn't as if she had any shortage of them. But Audrey got bored quickly and no one was ever quite right for her. They'd be too romantic or not romantic enough, too mean or too extravagant. She started looking for faults from the moment she met them.

'But what about that dark-haired one, the bus driver?' Margaret asked. She was better at keeping up than me.

Audrey shook her head. 'He didn't have anything to say. Could only talk about football.'

'So do you think you might meet someone more interesting at an Italian class?' Margaret asked.

'Well, it's worth a try, isn't it?' Audrey asked. 'I'm twenty-two next birthday, you know. I don't want to end up being an old maid. And my mum reckons evening classes are a great way to meet people. So are you going to come with me or do I have to go alone?'

'I'll come.' She had me interested. I wondered what sort of people we'd find at this Italian class and whether Audrey would click with any of them.

'Margaret?'

'Yes, but only if you promise me we'll be going dancing afterwards.'

Audrey allowed herself a tiny smile of triumph. 'Right, so that's agreed. Italian lessons on Thursday evenings after work. I think there's a book we're meant to buy but I'll get one and we all can share it.'

'I don't know what good it's going to do any of us being able to speak Italian,' Margaret complained.

Audrey ignored her. She had won and that was all that mattered.

What I don't know is why Audrey picked Italian classes. Because when we got to the college that first Thursday evening I discovered there were all sorts of other things we could have chosen to learn. There were courses in everything from woodwork to creative writing. I suppose Italian seemed romantic to Audrey.

Anyway, we got a shock when we walked into the classroom. There were only two men there. One was the teacher, who must have been over forty, and the other was there with his wife. But we couldn't exactly turn round and walk out again, particularly as Audrey was holding the beginners' Italian book she'd bought. So we took our seats and got ready for a long couple of hours.

Straight away there was something about the sound of the language that I liked, the way the teacher rolled his tongue round the words. It was richer and more alive than staid, clipped English. Sexier, too, according to Audrey.

'I know he's old but don't you think there's something attractive about our teacher?' she said as soon as the class was over. Then she giggled. 'And his name, too … Romeo. I didn't think anyone was actually called that.'

'So we're coming next week, then?' I asked.

'Yes, of course.' Audrey looked surprised I'd even asked. 'We're coming every week. We're going to learn Italian.'

It turned out to be a little more difficult than that. All of us struggled with the grammar and at the end of the first term I think only Margaret could string a sentence together. Audrey had moved us to desks at the front of the class and developed a crush on Romeo, which meant she had trouble concentrating on nouns, verbs and adjectives. And for me the best part of the classes was when the lights were dimmed and Romeo showed us slides of beautiful old paintings and ancient buildings, talking all the while in the melodious language I still barely understood.

'I'd love to go there and see all those places in Rome,' I said one night to Audrey. 'You know, the Colosseum and the Pantheon and those frescoes in the churches. Wouldn't it be amazing?'

'I suppose.' Audrey sounded unexcited.

'And we could drink espresso on the Via Veneto and say *buon giorno* to all the handsome Italians,' Margaret said, giggling.

Of course, that interested Audrey. 'Well, why don't we go, then? Let's do it,' she said as if it were the easiest thing in the world.

'We can't afford the train fare and we'd never get the time off work. Still, it's a nice dream.' Margaret smiled at me. 'Maybe one day, eh?'

Audrey gave that familiar toss of her head. 'No, I'm serious. I think if we want to go then we should. Let's make a plan.'

'My only plan is to get a few days off in the summer and take a day trip to Brighton to sit on the beach,' said Margaret. 'And I'm not sure how great my chances are of managing that.'

I didn't say anything. I was wondering if somehow Audrey could make it happen. She had a way of getting what she wanted.

She shared her plan two weeks later when we were sitting up in her bedroom in her mum's house. She still had on the little black waitress uniform they made them wear in the Lyons Corner House. I'd taken the hem up for her so it showed more of her legs.

'So,' she said, lighting a cigarette, 'I've got it all worked out.'

Audrey's plan involved us all finding extra work to earn as much money as possible over the next six months. She was going to do extra shifts at the coffee house, I could take in sewing, and Margaret could do some babysitting on her nights off.

'We still won't have enough money,' Margaret complained. 'Have you any idea how much it costs even to get to Italy?'

'We won't be paying for our travel, though, will we?'

'Why not?' I asked.

'Because we're going to hitchhike!'

It wasn't as crazy as it sounded. Hitchhiking wasn't so dangerous back then and, with three of us, Audrey thought we'd be pretty safe.

'I'll never get the time off,' Margaret said. 'But you two should go without me.'

'We're not going to take time off.' Audrey sounded triumphant. 'We're going to chuck in our jobs. And when we get to Italy we'll see if we can find some work. Maybe we'll teach English or look after people's children.'

Margaret and I must have both looked dubious because Audrey tossed her head again. 'There's no point going all the way there and then only staying for a week,' she pointed out. 'Come on, we're going to have an adventure. We'll find new jobs when we come back, won't we?'

On my own I'd have never come up with a plan like that. But the more I thought about it, the more I liked it. This could be our only chance to see a bit of the world. And I had images floating in my head of grand fountains, pretty piazzas and churches filled with candles to light their frescoed walls. A feeling of freedom sort of rushed at me and suddenly I felt like I could do anything and I didn't have to stay working in the grocer's shop until eventually someone married me and we had children.

'Yes, I'll come. I'll do it,' I said.

Margaret looked surprised. She must have expected me to say no. 'Will you really? What will your mum and dad say?' she asked.

My parents had a reputation for being strict. But I knew they'd never stand in the way of something I really wanted to do.

'So long as it's the three of us and we stick together and stay safe, they'll be fine,' I told her.

'That's right,' added Audrey. 'We have to stick together. So, Margaret, it's all up to you now. Are you coming with us to Rome?'

Margaret said nothing for a moment and we both sat there looking at her, willing her to say yes. Then she burst out laughing. 'Honestly, you two are awful. But yes, I'll come. Since I'm the only one who can speak any Italian you'll be in trouble if I don't.'

None of us were very good at working hard and saving. There was no fun in it at all. Audrey and Margaret both smoked and even though they cut right down to one cigarette a day, they refused to give up. I spent all my spare time doing clothes alterations and repairs, and was probably the one with the most money at the end but it didn't matter anyway as we'd decided to pool our resources.

We sat up in Audrey's room and agreed on some rules. We had to travel light with small bags, we wouldn't accept a lift from anyone we didn't like the look of, and we'd never let anyone buy us anything. Also Audrey had a thing about not smoking anyone else's cigarettes, so we put that on the list, too.

Romeo had agreed to give us extra Italian conversation classes at the weekends, and we'd all improved a lot by the time the six months were up.

'Shall we work a bit longer? Save a bit more?' Margaret asked. Of all of us, she seemed the most nervous at the prospect of throwing in her job and taking off. I wasn't really worried about any of that because I was so focused on what would happen once we got to Italy. I'd been reading a book Romeo had lent me and I couldn't wait to be there.

'No, it's now or never, Margaret,' Audrey told her. 'Tomorrow all of us will go into work and the first thing we'll do is resign.'

They were really nice to me in the shop. Told me that when I got back I should come to see them first for a job and they'd find me something if they could. The Lyons Corner House was used to staff coming and going so Audrey was fine. But Margaret had a terrible time. The mother actually cried and begged her not to leave, and the children were distraught. But she stuck to her guns and on her last day they gave her an envelope stuffed with cash to take with her.

The morning we set off is one I'll never forget. We'd packed our belongings into tiny duffel bags. All I could fit in were plain trousers and shirts, a warm sweater and a few changes of underwear. At the last minute I wedged in a lipstick and some face powder. I wasn't going to look very glamorous in Rome but at least I'd be able to make a bit of an effort.

Audrey's uncle had a car and he'd offered to drive us to the ferry at Dover so we wouldn't have to start hitching rides until we'd crossed the Channel. We sang all the way there, all the silly songs we'd learnt when we were kids.

We went to a café in Dover and Audrey's uncle bought us soup with bread rolls, and then apple pie and cream for afters.

'This will be your last taste of English food for a

while,' he said. 'No telling what sort of foreign rubbish they'll be serving up over there.'

I hadn't even thought about the Italian food but it turned out to be one of the things Margaret was most looking forward to.

'We'll be eating spaghetti with *ragù*,' she told Audrey's uncle.

'Best fill up on that apple pie, then,' he replied.

The ferry ride wasn't as much fun as we'd imagined. The grey English Channel was sloshing about, and the boat heaved and rolled. Margaret and I felt sick in no time.

Audrey had gone to explore and when she came back to find us sitting there groaning she made us go right to the top of the boat and walk about in the fresh air. 'Honestly, it'll make you feel better,' she promised.

There were seagulls wheeling and shrieking over-head, and all I could see was water stretching away on every side of us. It didn't make me feel much better at all. Only when Margaret shouted, 'Look, there's Calais', and I saw the dark mass of land did I begin to perk up.

There was so much to take in – the bustling little port and the strangeness of everything from the build-ings to the cars. It was all so foreign and somehow I hadn't expected that. I don't know why. We heard our first French voices, a soft and guttural sound, not like Italian at all. And as we passed through customs I realized it even smelt different – of mothballs, coffee and something else I couldn't identify.

We must have looked strange, three young English

girls dressed in sensible trousers and shirts, carrying matching duffel bags.

'So what now?' Margaret asked once we had shown our passports and were officially on French soil.

'We need to find somewhere cheap to stay the night and then we'll start hitching first thing in the morning,' said Audrey.

I felt a little anxious. Never in my life had I not known where I was going to sleep that night. 'Do you think we'll find something close by?' I asked.

'Ought to. It's a port, after all, and there are lots of people coming and going. But why don't I ask someone?' said Margaret.

She went back and talked to one of the customs officers. That's when we realized that, not only was Margaret's Italian much better than ours, she also spoke a smattering of French. 'I learnt it at school, remember?' she said later. Audrey and I hadn't taken that class. I'd done sewing and she'd learnt shorthand (which she'd hated).

The customs officer suggested a couple of places within walking distance, and so we set off to investigate. The first one looked really run-down and the woman who opened the door had an unclean look about her.

Margaret shook her head when she told us the price of one night's stay. 'It's too expensive. We're not paying that to stay here.'

So we kept walking and knocking on doors whenever we saw a sign that said hotel. But everyone wanted to charge us far more than we could afford.

Even Audrey was beginning to worry. 'We're just

going to have to pay what they're asking. We can't sleep in the street,' she said.

'Let's try walking a bit further,' Margaret suggested. 'I'm wondering if it's better to be away from the port. Things looked so scruffy there, and they probably think they can charge what they like because that's where all the travellers land.'

We walked through some narrow streets that opened out into a little square. It was really quite pretty. There was a statue in the middle and some pots with colourful flowers in them. And there was a café with tables and chairs set on the cobbles outside and a little bakery beside it.

It was me that noticed the sign on the doorway between the café and the bakery. 'Hotel Richelieu,' it said, in old-fashioned script.

'Funny-looking hotel but it's worth a try,' said Margaret.

The man who answered the door was probably about the same age as Audrey's uncle. He had a big moustache and slightly greasy long hair that he wore brushed across his head to hide a bald spot.

He nodded enthusiastically when Margaret explained that we were looking for somewhere cheap for the night. 'I do very good price for pretty English girls,' he told us. 'You want?'

'Yes, yes, we do want,' Margaret told him.

He took us up some stairs that had the same odd foreign smell of mothballs and coffee. Audrey said we should bunk in together to save money, so he gave us a key and showed us to our room. It was tiny, with one double bed and a chest of drawers, but we told him it looked fine.

'I will come back later and check you are all happy,' he said and then, before he turned away, he winked at us.

Margaret shut the door and leaned back against it. 'Why do you think he's happy to do a cheap price for English girls?' she asked. 'And what was that winking about?'

Audrey stared at her for a moment and then squeaked, 'Ew, no! An old man like him? That's disgusting.'

I still hadn't cottoned on. 'What do you mean? What's disgusting?'

'Never mind, Catherine, just help us move this bed against the door, and if you hear anyone knocking in the night, don't make a sound,' Margaret said.

We pushed the bed right up to the door so no one could open it, and then we all squashed in beneath the covers, which smelt musty and old. None of us had eaten anything since the soup and apple pie at lunchtime and we could smell the most delicious things being made in the café below. But although our stomachs were growling, we didn't dare to leave the room again till morning.

When I woke up and found myself wedged in between Audrey and Margaret I was confused for a moment until I realized we were in France. Then I felt a quick stab of excitement followed very quickly by hunger pangs.

'Girls, wake up,' I said, nudging them. 'Let's go and see if that bakery downstairs is open. I'm starving.'

Audrey couldn't be hurried. She dug about in her bag and produced bits and pieces of make-up that she applied to her face. Then she shook the creases out of a pretty summer skirt and slipped some sandals onto her feet.

'What else have you got in there?' I asked, peering into her duffel bag. 'And how did you fit it all in?'

'It's just a matter of careful packing,' she said in a slightly superior tone. 'We have to look presentable if we're going to have any chance of hitching a lift later.'

There was no sign of the creepy desk clerk so we left some cash and let ourselves out. The most delicious buttery smells were coming from the bakery. The woman there sold us croissants fresh from the oven, and told us the café next door would make us coffee to go with them. I couldn't wait. I tore into one of my buttery sweet croissants standing right there in the street. I'd never tasted anything quite like it.

The waiter at the café was nice to us. When he could see I didn't like my coffee much he brought me a cup of tea for free. It wasn't very nice – too weak and milky – but I drank it anyway.

Margaret asked him where he thought the best place for us to start hitching might be.

'You need to get onto one of the roads that head out of town,' he told us in passably good English. 'But it's a long walk from here. If you wait a little while, my cousin will come by for his coffee and then maybe he'll give you a lift.'

The waiter advised us to stay away from big towns and cities. 'Lots of cars will be going to Paris but it's expensive there. You'll find cheaper accommodation in the smaller places and people will be kinder to you.'

Suddenly the enormity of what we were doing hit me. We had no idea how long it would take us to get to Rome, where we would stay or what sort of people we might meet. Hugging my duffel bag to my chest, all I wanted was to get back on that ferry and head across the English Channel towards home.

Margaret must have been feeling the same because she said in a small voice, 'What if no one stops to give us a lift?'

Audrey frowned. Even she didn't seem so certain any more.

But the waiter only laughed. 'Three pretty English girls like you won't have any trouble, I'm sure,' he said, then he brought us more hot drinks and a free pastry filled with chocolate that we shared.

His cousin was an older man and very gruff, but he agreed to take us to the outskirts of Calais in his little car and leave us in a good hitching spot. Audrey sat in the front seat and shared her cigarettes with him, and, in the back, Margaret and I stared out of the window and tried not to think about how fast he was driving.

He left us beside an old stone church and, as I stood and watched him speed off, I felt abandoned, even though he hadn't seemed like a terribly nice man and his driving had been appalling.

Audrey fluffed up her hair and applied more lipstick, then stood at the side of the road and stuck out her thumb. We stayed with her, smiling hopefully every time a car approached. A few drove past quickly, their drivers ignoring us, but Audrey didn't seem perturbed.

She kept on standing there in her pretty skirt, waggling her thumb and smiling at each approaching vehicle.

Finally a lorry slowed down and pulled in a little way ahead of us. Grabbing our duffel bags, we ran towards it. The driver said his name was Jean-Luc and he was heading to Amiens. Audrey turned to us, nodded briskly and then climbed into the cab beside him.

Jean-Luc drove at a leisurely pace. Sitting high in the cab of his lorry, we had the perfect view of the farmland and the little villages of Nord-Pas-de-Calais and Picardie with their steep-roofed old houses and tumbledown barns. Margaret practised her French, telling him we were travelling all the way to Rome, but I was content just to stare out of the window and try to imagine the lives of the people in the houses we rumbled past.

We stopped in one of the villages and Jean-Luc took us to a little café where they seemed to know him. He insisted on buying us each a glass of rough red wine and on paying for a wooden platter covered in crusty bread and thick slices of ham.

'We agreed we wouldn't accept food from anyone,' I reminded Audrey.

'Never mind,' she said. 'It would seem rude to refuse. Once we get to Amiens I'll give him a packet of my cigarettes.'

The ham was succulent and tasty, and we sat in the sun while we ate it and watched some old men playing boules. There was a lot of laughter and plenty of red wine was being drunk. Jean-Luc waved at them but stayed sitting with us. He seemed almost proud to be sharing his table with three young English girls.

Once we were on the road again, Margaret told us Jean-Luc had recommended a place to stay in Amiens that was cheap and clean. He would take us there if we wanted.

'Should we try to go a bit further?' asked Audrey. 'See if he'll drop us off on the outskirts and hitch another lift?'

Margaret looked uncertain. 'He says Amiens is really pretty. We'd have some time to explore. I don't suppose we're in any hurry really, are we?'

So it was agreed and we ended our day's journey in Amiens. It turned out to be just as pretty as Jean-Luc had promised. There was an old Gothic cathedral and lots of houses with brightly coloured awnings squashed beside the wide river and along a network of narrow canals.

We ate a meal in a smoky bistro beside a canal where they offered a fixed-price menu. The food was too rich for me, flavoured with garlic and onions and sauced with cream, but Margaret finished everything I couldn't eat. Afterwards the waiter brought out some really smelly cheese and even Margaret could only manage a mouthful of that.

Walking back along the canal towards our hotel, which was just as clean as Jean-Luc had promised, we decided it had been a good first day.

'Let's hope we get a lift as quickly tomorrow,' said Margaret.

I hoped we did, too. The thought of standing at the side of the road all day with our thumbs stuck out and no one stopping had become my greatest fear.

* * *

Pieta looked at the clock and realized how much time had passed. Her mother's story had filled half the evening. Something about her had changed as she revisited the memories she'd left alone for so long. Her voice had grown lighter and less husky, the lines on her face seemed almost to soften. At times she put down her needle and her hands moved to join her voice in the telling of her story. Lost in the past, she seemed closer to her younger self than the mother Pieta knew.

'Will I go and make us a cup of tea and a sandwich, Mamma?' Pieta stood up and stretched out her cramped legs.

For a moment, Catherine looked dazed, then she glanced over at the section of fabric Pieta had filled with glittering crystals and at the little part she herself had managed.

'Oh, I'm sorry.' Her voice had deepened and she sounded like herself again. 'You've been doing all the work and I've just been sitting here talking.'

'That's OK.' Pieta had been fascinated by the story. She didn't want to say anything that would discourage her mother from continuing it.

As she sliced cheese, chopped up tomatoes and buttered slices of bread, Pieta's mind played with the image of the three pretty English girls setting off on their adventure. It was difficult to believe that one of them had turned into her mother.

9

They ate their food and drank their tea quickly. Then they tidied everything away and cleaned their hands scrupulously before they touched the dress again. Pieta was surprised at how much beading she had managed to get through. The work was neat and the crystals caught the light, bringing the fabric alive, just as she had known they would.

'It's going to be beautiful, isn't it?' her mother said. 'It will be so wonderful for Addolorata to wear it on her wedding day knowing it was made with love.'

Pieta looked at the many boxes still full of beads. 'There's a long way to go.'

'I know. I'll try not to get distracted and work a little faster.'

'That's not what I meant, Mamma. It's getting late. You've had a long day and you look so tired. Go to bed.'

'I can't lie in that big bed all alone thinking about your father in hospital. I'd rather stay here and talk to you.'

Pieta picked up her needle. She wanted to hear more of the story so wasn't going to argue. 'Tell me about hitching through France,' she prompted. 'Did you manage to get another lift that next morning? Or did you have to wait for hours?'

'Oh, you don't really want me to go on with that, do you?'

Her mother bent her head over her beading. For a while she said nothing. And then Pieta saw her expression change, her face soften and her mouth lift in a half-smile. Slowly she began talking again.

* * *

We were so pleased with that first day's hitching and Audrey kept saying that if we could just meet a few more people like Jean-Luc we'd be in Italy in no time. The next morning we ate coffee and croissants again, just as we had the morning before. I remember being astonished by the flavour of the coffee. The stuff we'd drunk at home had come out of a bottle and tasted of chicory. I think it was called Camp coffee and it was nothing like this strong, bitter brew. But the other two seemed to like it so I tried to force some down. Afterwards we walked for a while, carrying our duffel bags, until we found a busy road.

This time Margaret held out her thumb and a car stopped pretty quickly. It was only going to the next village but we jumped in anyway.

By lunchtime Audrey was getting frustrated. Although we'd had lifts in three different cars, no one was travelling very far and she didn't think we'd made enough progress. Gradually, though, the countryside was beginning to change and we saw vineyards instead of farmland. We checked the map Margaret had brought and realized we were in the Champagne district.

At last we hitched a lift with an old couple who were travelling a decent distance. In the back of their ancient car were cages full of chickens that kept squawking and pecking at each other. Margaret didn't want to get in but Audrey gave her a push.

The three of us were crushed together on the back seat. Its springs had gone and the road was full of potholes, so we bounced around a lot. The old lady seemed quite worried about us and kept turning round and babbling in French. All Margaret could understand was that they were farmers and they were driving beyond a town called Troyes where they had a small farm.

The three of us kept nodding and smiling until our cheeks ached, as the old lady chattered on and the chickens behind us shrieked in reply. At last we saw a sign marked Troyes and the farmer drove slowly through narrow lanes filled with tall timbered buildings, past a street market and a café with gaily-striped umbrellas over its tables.

'We should get them to stop here,' suggested Audrey.

Margaret tried but the old lady only shook her head and babbled even faster while the old man kept driving.

'Why won't they stop? You don't suppose they're kidnapping us?' I asked nervously.

When the car began bouncing over a narrow rutted farm track we were almost jolted out of our seats. The old lady kept letting out little screams but her husband just hunched over the wheel and said nothing.

Finally he pulled up beside a low, ivy-covered farm

building with a sagging tiled roof. There were chickens and ducks running all over the yard and some old cats lying in the sun. The old lady turned and gave us a toothless grin.

'*Nous sommes ici*,' she declared.

'We're here,' Margaret translated. 'Wherever here is.'

A younger woman came out of the house, drying her hands on a linen tea towel, and there was a rapid exchange of French as we all climbed out of the car. It was a relief to stretch my legs and escape the musty smell of caged birds, even though I was worried and confused about why we'd been brought here.

The old couple herded us inside and made us sit around a pine table in a dim room. They brought us a cool lemon-flavoured drink and some dry biscuits.

'My parents would like to offer you a meal,' said the younger woman in halting English. 'And a place to sleep for the night, even though it is only in our barn and not very comfortable, I'm afraid.'

None of us felt right accepting such kindness from strangers. We tried to refuse politely but the old lady started pulling out pans and a large casserole pot.

'It is useless arguing,' the young lady smiled. 'My mother's mind is made up.'

So that night we ate a casserole made from a rabbit they must have killed themselves. It had been slow-cooked so its meat fell softly from the bone, and the gravy tasted of earth and mushrooms. Afterwards we slept wrapped in blankets on hay bales in the barn. It was so prickly and dusty it made us sneeze, but we were tired and slept the whole night through.

The next morning we were woken by the sound of cockerels crowing. The old lady gave us bread, jam and strong coffee for breakfast, and then, just before we left, she pressed a brown paper parcel into my hands. It was tied with string and filled with boiled eggs, ham and cheese. She smiled and bobbed her head. I think she'd finally realized we didn't understand a word she said.

Her husband drove us back to Troyes in his old wreck of a car, only this time there were no chickens in the back.

'*Au revoir. Bonne chance*,' he said as he dropped us off. They were the only words I'd heard him speak.

We found other kind people as we travelled through France: waiters who would give us extra bread rolls with our soup; bakers who slipped a free croissant or two in a bag for us; drivers who swapped chocolate for cigarettes. The waiter in Calais had been right – it was better in the rural areas. I think perhaps the war was still fresh in a lot of the older people's minds. Or perhaps it was simply that we were three young girls and they were charmed by us.

What I remember most about France is the hills. Some of the older cars we travelled in struggled up them. One French man made us sing to his battered Citroën van as it laboured up a steep slope. 'She's an old, old woman,' he told Margaret. 'She needs the encouragement.'

I began to like France, the tall churches topped with bell towers, the fields full of lavender. I even grew to like the food. Not all of it, but the toasted sandwiches melting with cheese and tender ham, or the pastries sticky with butter and almonds. The only thing I couldn't stand was going to the toilet. Often we had to go in corner bars where there would be a squalid room out the back with a hole in the ground and two spaces either side where you were meant to put your feet. They weren't clean and some of my worst moments were spent crouching over a stinking hole and wishing I were somewhere else.

A lot of the places we slept in weren't much better. We spent one night in a bed that was jumping with fleas.

'Let's put our bags on the top of the wardrobe. The fleas won't be able to jump that high surely,' said Margaret.

We knew there was no sense in that but we tried it anyway.

As we neared the Swiss border, the hitching became more difficult and we waited longer between lifts. One morning we stood at the side of the road for almost an hour and were relieved when at last a shiny new car pulled over in front of us.

'Damn, there are two men in it,' said Margaret, peering through the back window. 'I don't think it's safe. Shall we pretend we're going somewhere else?'

But Audrey was ahead of us and was already climbing into the car. 'They're servicemen,' she hissed at us, 'Americans. Get in, quickly.'

They were clean-cut boys, wearing their uniforms and with a map spread out between them.

'Maybe you can help us, girls,' said one in his loud, drawly voice. 'We're trying to locate some place we've been told we need to head to. It's called Douane but we can't find it on the map.'

'Douane?' asked Margaret. 'But that means customs. Are you looking for the Swiss border?'

'Yes, that's right.' They sounded relieved as they pushed the map over to her. 'Thank God. Maybe you can make sense of this.'

It wasn't so difficult really. Margaret and I read the map and gave directions and Audrey sat between us, leaning forward slightly and chatting to the American soldiers. The further we travelled, the more animated she grew, sharing out her cigarettes and throwing her head back to laugh at their jokes.

We reached the border and showed our passports to the official. Finally we were in a new country, Switzerland. We could see snow-capped Alps and isolated villages reached by tracks that zig-zagged up the mountains. The soldiers were going all the way to Italy so we travelled over the Grand St Bernard Pass together. The views of mountains and lakes were breathtaking but Audrey didn't seem to notice. She was too busy talking, smoking and laughing.

When they dropped us off in Aosta, Audrey swapped addresses with them and stood in the road waving until their car had disappeared. She hid her face from us and I think she may have been crying a little.

'They were nice boys,' I remarked.

Audrey's hand lay against the pocket of her cardigan where she had stowed the precious piece of paper they'd scrawled their addresses on. 'I suppose so,' she said, and her voice sounded flat.

But I was elated. At long last we were in Italy and I could hear the language Romeo had taught us being spoken all around us. The accent was different, clipped at times and almost whining the next, but it was unmistakably Italian.

'What now?' I was almost hopping on the spot in my excitement. 'Shall we try to hitch further south or find a place to stay the night?'

Audrey shrugged. She looked as if she didn't care much either way.

'Let's stay here,' decided Margaret. 'This is a place people come to for skiing so in summer there must be lots of empty hotel rooms. I'm sure we'll find somewhere cheap.'

We found a room in a place that looked like a mountain chalet. Audrey went straight to bed but Margaret and I stayed up, drinking mulled wine and celebrating our arrival in Italy.

'Poor Audrey, she really liked those soldiers,' I said, leaning against Margaret and feeling warmed right through by the wine.

'She'll meet a handsome Italian boy and they'll be forgotten in a moment. You'll see.' Margaret sounded certain.

But as we travelled onwards Audrey seemed to retreat further into herself. She pulled her hair back harshly into a ponytail and let Margaret and me take care of all the hitching. We made our way to Genoa and then followed the coast south, stopping at Pisa where we had to drag an unenthusiastic Audrey to see the famous leaning tower. Margaret grew addicted to drinking tiny cups of strong black coffee every morning, and in Grossetto she finally got to eat her spaghetti with *ragù*. Audrey bought an unfamiliar brand of foreign cigarettes in a soft shiny packet and said they tasted strong.

Tuscany was beautiful but I wanted to push on and reach Rome. I'd grown tired of life on the move and longed to stop in one place for a while, for the sights and faces to become familiar and to have the comfort of some sort of routine. Tuscany's wooded hills, ruined towers and glimpses of the sea weren't enough to keep me on the road any longer than I needed to be.

Also I was sick of being frightened half to death by people's driving. Some drove too fast, some too slow, and the further south we travelled, the more erratic they became. Everyone seemed to have their own style. Some hunched over the steering wheel; others held it casually with one hand and slouched back into the seat.

The morning we drove down the long, straight road that led to Rome we were surrounded by flowers. We'd been picked up by a van driver who was delivering a load of long-stemmed fragrant blossoms to the market in Campo dei Fiori.

'I think that's a piazza right in the centre of Rome,' said Margaret, struggling to open her map in the confined space. 'Couldn't be better really. We're bound to be able to find a cheap *pensione* somewhere nearby.'

The driver dropped us off near the Piazza Navona and, with our duffel bags slung over our shoulders, we walked slowly past the fountains and the street cafés filled with well-dressed tourists enjoying milky coffee and freshly squeezed orange juice. The three of us felt scruffy and not terribly clean. It hadn't been easy doing laundry while we were on the move – only the most basic rinsing of underwear had been possible. So by now my trousers looked tea-stained and tired, and even Audrey's summer skirt had lost some of its jauntiness.

'What I'd like is to be wearing pretty clothes and sitting at one of those tables watching other people walk by,' I sighed.

'You will, but not perhaps today.' Audrey seemed to have regained some of her spark at long last. 'Let's follow one of these side streets off the piazza and see if we can find somewhere to stay. Then we can have baths, wash all our clothes and be ready to start exploring Rome first thing tomorrow.'

We plunged into the tangle of narrow cobbled streets between Piazza Navona and the River Tiber, and began knocking on the doors of every *pensione* we passed. Prices were steeper than we'd expected, so we decided to keep walking and knocking, just as we had in Calais. 'If the desk clerk is a man who offers us a good deal perhaps we should be careful,' I said. 'We don't want to sleep with the bed pushed against the door every night.'

Margaret said she was feeling thirsty and tired, so we stopped for a while at a little corner bar. It was a lively place with a jukebox in the corner, little red booths down one wall and lots of shiny chrome and mirrors. The owner spoke Italian with a strong accent and was difficult to understand.

'I'm Greek,' he told us, extending his hand across the counter so we could shake it. 'My name is Anastasio. How do you do?'

Sometimes you just know people are kind and with Anastasio it was like that. He had a big, round, smiling face and tight black curls of hair that looked as if they'd slid down from the steep dome of his head and arranged themselves round his ears. We stood at the counter drinking coffee and told him how we'd arrived in Rome and had nowhere to stay.

'There is a place near here that is very cheap. Lots of young girls live there,' he told us.

'Is it like a boarding house?' asked Margaret.

'Yes, something like that. If you come with me I'll show you where it is. You'll never find it on your own.'

We stood on the corner and he pointed out an archway about four doors down. 'Go through there and then into a narrow alley,' he instructed us. 'At the end you'll find some back stairs and, at the top, there is a door. Knock on it and ask for Signora Lucy.'

'Doesn't this *pensione* have a name?' wondered Margaret.

'No, I don't think so. It's not a place that tourists usually find. The girls who stay there are all Italian.'

The alley was dark and the back stairs even darker. I wasn't certain about the place at all but Audrey pointed out that if we all went up together we should be safe enough.

As Anastasio had promised we found a door at the top of the stairs. It was old and made of heavy dark wood with a brass knocker that hadn't seen polish for a while. Audrey knocked once or twice and at last we heard the sliding of bolts. The door opened a little way. 'Yes? Who is it?' The women's voice was slow and sounded distrustful.

Margaret spoke up. 'Signora Lucy? We wondered if you had a room vacant?'

'How many of you?'

'There are three of us. Three English girls.'

The door opened and the woman standing behind it looked us up and down carefully. We stared back at her. She was wearing a faded floral housecoat but her face was carefully made up with blusher, powder and lipstick, her dark hair had a copper rinse and was set in soft waves, and she wore chunky gold earrings. She looked glamorous and formidable.

'I don't rent rooms by the night, only by the week,' she said sternly.

'That's fine,' Margaret told her.

'I'd want a week's money upfront.'

We nodded our agreement.

And then she fixed each of us with a fierce stare. 'No men, do you understand? No men on the premises at any time, day or night. That is the rule and if you break it your bags are packed, you're on the street and you don't get any of your rent refunded.'

She was so vehement that we must have looked slightly taken aback and she started to shut the door in our faces.

'No, no, that's fine,' Margaret said quickly. 'We understand, no men. That's not a problem.'

She opened the door again and let us in. It was as dark inside as it had been in the stairwell. Signora Lucy led us up more stairs, four or five flights of them, until we were at the very top of the building.

The room she showed us into was spacious with one double bed and two singles. There was a tiny window with a view over the rooftops of Rome and a shared bathroom down the hallway. It was perfect, and Anastasio had been right – it was also the cheapest place we'd come across.

The first thing each of us did was soak in the bath. Then we started scrubbing our clothes, wringing them out and hanging them up from some string Audrey had found in a nearby shop and hung from one end of the room to the other.

Exhausted, we all crawled into bed. 'Let's go back to Anastasio's bar and say thank you to him later,' said Audrey, leaning back on her pillow and closing her eyes. 'Maybe we could have something to eat there, too. But right now I just want to lie here feeling clean for a while.'

I must have slept for a couple of hours and when I woke I was disoriented. I could hear Italian women chatting and laughing with each other somewhere down the hallway.

'Audrey, are you awake?' I whispered.

'Um … yes.' Her voice was hoarse.

'Let's get up. I want to go to the Trevi Fountain.'

She groaned. 'Just give me ten minutes.'

I let her sleep a little longer and then spoke again. 'Audrey, Margaret, come on, wake up. Let's go to the Trevi Fountain.'

'Why are you in such a hurry?' Audrey complained.

'I want to put a coin in it to make sure I'll come back to Rome one day.'

Margaret laughed sleepily. 'You've only just got here and already you're worried about coming back.'

And for some reason I was. It had been a long hard

journey to get here and arriving in the city had seemed unreal. Now I felt like Rome could be snatched away from me in an instant if I wasn't careful. Putting a coin in the famous fountain might be some sort of insurance.

'Fine, I'll go on my own,' I said.

I put on the driest of my clothes, let myself out of the room and went back down Signora Lucy's steep, crooked stairs. Margaret and Audrey probably didn't believe I was really going. I was always the timid one.

It was bright on the street and I stood there blinking for a while. Then I consulted Margaret's map and decided it didn't seem too far a walk so I set off in what I hoped was the right direction. There were so many ancient buildings and beautiful fountains everywhere. It was like walking through history.

Somehow I had imagined the Trevi Fountain would be in the middle of a vast piazza so when I found it, squashed into a cobbled clearing between tall buildings, I was taken by surprise. I sat for a while just looking at it. I think I knew it was always going to be a special place for me. Then I found a coin in my pocket and carefully dropped it in.

It would have been nice to stay there a little longer but I thought Audrey and Margaret might be worried about me. So I walked back faster than I'd come and found them in Anastasio's bar putting their spare coins into the jukebox and jiving with each other. A small crowd of young men had gathered to watch the beautiful girl with the white-blonde hair and her pretty red-headed friend. Anastasio was busy selling them all drinks and ice-cream.

*

We spent the next week exploring Rome, half starving ourselves to help our savings stretch a little further. When we paid Signora Lucy her second week's rent upfront we didn't have an awful lot left.

'What about that idea Audrey had of giving English lessons?' suggested Margaret. 'There must be lots of Italians who'd like to learn. Maybe some of the girls who live here would be keen.'

We didn't see much of the other girls who lived at Signora Lucy's. They seemed to come and go a lot. Sometimes we'd catch sight of one of them chatting on the phone in the downstairs hallway. They were always very glamorous, with lots of make-up, bright clothes and high-heeled shoes. Like Signora Lucy, many of them had rinsed their hair a coppery colour. Sometimes they would smile and say '*Ciao*' to us, but we were a bit intimidated by them, even Audrey.

'Why don't we put an advertisement for our English lessons in *Il Messagero*,' I said. Lots of people seemed to read the newspaper and I was sure we'd get some response.

So we arranged it the next day. The advertisement said we were three girls from London prepared to give English lessons, and we gave the phone number of the *pensione* as we didn't think Signora Lucy would mind. The only thing she seemed to care about was that no men were smuggled into her building. She became quite hysterical if anyone tried.

The phone started ringing a lot but because it was several floors down one of the Italian girls would always get there first. A couple of times we heard them say the words *'fare una passeggiata'* and then they'd make a date to meet the caller. None of us could work out what was going on.

Then Margaret heard one of them say to a caller, 'No, no, they're good girls. I will come and meet you instead.'

Anastasio laughed when we asked him what he thought was going on. It turned out that the glamorous girls at Signora Lucy's were all prostitutes and this was where they stayed when they couldn't afford anywhere better. Our advertisement for English lessons had been completely misinterpreted. All of us were horrified, Audrey especially so. Right away she went and bought a huge bottle of disinfectant and spent ages scrubbing the room with it.

'No men have been here,' Margaret pointed out. 'Signora Lucy would never allow it.'

'I know but I'm not taking any chances,' said Audrey as she drizzled disinfectant round the room.

We didn't end up teaching anyone English but neither did we move out of Signora Lucy's. Our room was nice and we felt safe there. Besides we got to know some of the girls quite well and they were pleasant enough. One evening Signora Lucy asked if we could fit one in our room for the night. She was a pretty girl from the country and I don't think she'd been working as a prostitute for very long. Nevertheless, Audrey pulled out her bottle of disinfectant again the moment she had gone.

To make sure everyone knew we were truly good girls Audrey rigged up a washing line right across the well between the buildings. Then she made me hang all my knickers out on it like bunting. I had six pairs and they were huge, made from white Aertex and waist-high. Later we heard the Italian girls giggling about them. They wore skimpy bits of coloured lace and I don't think they'd ever seen anything like my underwear before.

10

Anastasio truly was a kind man. Sometimes we'd see him giving old customers warm milk and bread in the mornings if he thought they were looking ill or hungry. He must have realized we were running out of money when we stopped going into the bar to drink coffee and jive to the jukebox music. One day he called out to Audrey on the street. 'You worked in a café in England, yes?' he said. 'So why don't you come and work for me?'

Audrey looked crestfallen. 'I'd really love to but my Italian is still so awful. What about Margaret? She speaks it so much better than me.'

But Anastasio wanted Audrey. I suppose he knew that with her blonde hair and pretty face she'd be a draw for all the young men in the area. And he was right. When Audrey was working the little bar was always busier. No one seemed to mind if she misunderstood them or mixed up their orders. On warm evenings, if it got really crowded, Anastasio would turn up the jukebox and people ended up jiving on the narrow street outside.

It was a relief that Audrey was earning some money but it wasn't really enough to keep things going. All of us were looking shabby and desperately needed new clothes, so I bought some cheap floral fabric in the market and asked Signora Lucy if I could borrow her sewing machine. I made three skirts, each of them a little different. Margaret's flared softly over her hips, Audrey's was more fitted and shorter, and mine had a circular skirt that swished around satisfyingly when I was jiving. The girls at Signora Lucy's were intrigued when they saw us wearing them. Margaret explained that I'd made them and they started bringing me yards of fabric and asking me to make skirts and dresses for them, too. I even sewed cushion covers and curtains for Signora Lucy. Word got out to the neighbours and soon I was kept busy sewing most days. I didn't charge much but I was earning my share.

Margaret told me she felt bad because she was the only one not contributing. She started borrowing Anastasio's newspaper every day and searching through the 'help wanted' ads.

'Here's one,' she said one morning as we were drinking coffee and sharing a pastry. 'Contessa Cecilia De Bortoli is looking for a nanny to help her with her two delightful children and do a few light household duties. Sounds perfect. I should call her quickly before she hires someone else.'

It turned out not to be all that perfect. The children weren't always delightful and the Contessa was very grand. She made Margaret wear a long-skirted white uniform, and the light household duties included serving coffee and little cakes to visitors as though she were a maid. But Margaret said the apartment was very beautiful, with high ceilings and marble floors, so it felt cool even on the hottest days. And some mornings she took the children to the gardens at the Villa Borghese and sat by a fountain while they played on their bicycles.

The weeks went by quickly and we were so busy we hardly saw each other. For me, sewing in our little room for hours each day, it could get a little lonely at times.

'You know the thing we've never done,' Audrey remarked one rare Sunday afternoon when we were all together. 'We've never been to one of those pavement cafés in the Piazza Navona like Catherine said she wanted to on the very first day.'

'But it's so expensive,' said Margaret. 'A coffee costs about six times what we pay at Anastasio's. God knows what they charge for food.'

'It's about the experience, though, isn't it?' Audrey argued. 'Let's dress up in nice clothes, put on lipstick and go and sit with the rich people. We can afford to do it once.'

Margaret had most likely had enough of rich people but she knew how much I wanted to go. 'I suppose a few coffees aren't going to bankrupt us,' she agreed.

We had a giggle getting all dressed up. Audrey did my make-up, choosing bolder colours than I would ever use. I felt a bit like one of Signora Lucy's girls but she wouldn't let me rub it off.

Then we chose our clothes. By now I'd made us lots of bits and pieces so we didn't have to wear our floral skirts or the tired old clothes we'd arrived in. Once we'd finished we all looked very sophisticated and even one of Signora Lucy's girls whistled at us appreciatively as she saw us leave.

Everything they say about Italian men is true – the bottom-pinching, the whistling, even the hissing between their teeth, which isn't very pleasant at all. We'd attracted plenty of it since we arrived in Rome and, although flattering at first, it quickly grew tiresome. The three of us together, dressed up to the nines, drew an unprecedented amount of attention. It was only a short walk from Signora Lucy's *pensione* to the piazza but by the time we got there all of us were heartedly sick of having our bottoms pinched.

'Honestly, do they think we like it?' Margaret asked, disgusted. 'As if I'd ever go out with any man who behaved like that.'

'Some of them are very handsome, though,' mused Audrey.

'I don't care,' Margaret declared. 'It doesn't matter how good-looking they are if they can't keep their hands to themselves.'

We chose a café next to one of the fountains and a waiter showed us to an empty table and took our order. It was lovely sitting there watching people stroll by.

'Sip that coffee as slowly as you can,' Audrey told us. 'Let's make this last.'

Every woman around us was beautifully dressed with sleek hair and manicured nails. Their musky perfumes were mingling in the warm air and the three of us sat mostly silent, listening to their laughter and to the clinking of glasses and crockery as they shared expensive food.

Suddenly Audrey smiled.

'What?' asked Margaret.

'You see those two boys over there? The skinny dark

one and the one who looks like he could lose a little weight? Well, that's the third time they've walked past us and they're both staring at Catherine.'

'Rubbish,' I said. Audrey was the one who attracted all the attention and after her it was Margaret. Sometimes I wondered if the boys only pinched my bottom because they felt they had to.

But the fourth time they walked past I looked up and it really did seem like they were staring at me.

I started to giggle. 'They probably think we're rich tourists because we're sitting here drinking coffee instead of standing up at the bar.'

Margaret laughed as well but then she noticed the pair of them lingering by the fountain, smoking cigarettes. Every now and then they glanced over at us.

'Oh no, they're waiting for us. I bet there'll be a frenzy of bottom-pinching when we leave the café.'

'Well, there's only one thing for it, we'll have to have another coffee,' said Audrey. 'Maybe they'll get tired of waiting around.'

But they were still there when we left. The skinny one broke away from his friend. 'Excuse me, madam,' he called over to me. 'Please may I speak to you?'

Perhaps it was the polite way he asked, trying so hard to pronounce the English words properly. Or maybe it was because he was the first man who'd approached me without trying to pinch my bottom. But I surprised myself by turning round and saying, 'Yes, all right.'

His friend joined us and we all walked round the piazza together chatting as we went. They told us their names were Gianfranco and Beppi and they were waiters at a big hotel nearby. 'Very smart, expensive,' Beppi, the skinny one, said solemnly. 'I am only a commis but my friend Gianfranco is a *chef de rang*. He is the important one.'

I liked him straight away. The other one, Gianfranco, seemed solemn, almost sulky, but Beppi had a ready smile and a kind face. He told me he hadn't been in Rome for very long and didn't know many people.

'Gianfranco is my only friend. He and I have known each other since we were very small. We come from the same village, Ravenno. It is in the mountains of Basilicata. Very beautiful. One day I will take you there.'

I smiled politely and wondered why Italian men felt they had to be so ridiculously effusive around women. Still, at least he and Gianfranco were keeping their hands to themselves.

We'd walked round the piazza four or five times when Beppi turned to me and said, 'Tomorrow is my day off but Gianfranco he must work. I will be so lonely by myself. Maybe you will come with me and we will explore Rome?' He managed to sound at once heartbroken and hopeful. 'Don't make me spend the whole day alone,' he added theatrically.

'Where would we go?' I was struggling to resist him.

He grinned. 'I will take you to an exhibition and show you the world,' he declared grandly.

Audrey looked interested. 'That sounds good. I wish I could come as well but I'm working.'

'Me, too.' Margaret sounded glum.

'It is settled, then. Just you and me, Catherine,'

Beppi chirped happily. 'I will meet you at ten o'clock by the fountain near the café. We will have a wonderful day together.'

As they walked away I noticed Gianfranco turning and staring back at me. There was something about him that made me think he was angry.

* * *

Pieta was pleased her father had entered the story at last. Although it was very late, she wanted to hear more.

'So tell me what happened on the date,' she urged. 'What was the trick he played on you?'

'No, no, I'm tired enough to sleep now,' her mother murmured. 'And you must be, too. Let's leave this and go to bed. In the morning I want to buy some food and take it to your father. Can you imagine what he'll think of what they serve up in hospital?'

Pieta felt guilty. 'I've kept you up talking far too late.'

'It's been good remembering. But now I have to sleep. I'll help you again tomorrow so long as your father doesn't need me.'

'And you'll tell me some more? You'll pick up where we've left off.'

'Maybe. We'll see.'

II

Pieta woke much too early. It would be more than an hour before she could expect her mother to be up and about. She went downstairs to make a cup of coffee and drank it scalding hot, sitting out on the back doorstep.

Already the sky was hazy and she could tell it was going to be warm. She filled in time pottering about the kitchen and setting out her mother's breakfast things: her favourite cereal, a jug of milk, a bowl and a spoon with the newspaper folded beside them. Then she brewed a pot of tea.

But her mother, when she came downstairs, was dressed to go out. 'I'm not bothering with breakfast,' she said briskly. 'I want to get to the hospital as quickly as I can.'

'At least have a cup of tea.'

'No, no.' She was determined. 'I want to see if I can talk to a doctor and find out what happens next for Beppi. But so long as he's OK I'll be back some time later this afternoon. You should stay here and get on with the dress.'

Pieta drank the tea by herself. The house was quiet and there was no sign of Addolorata, who must have run away to Eden's place last night. Most likely she couldn't face any of them right now.

There was a part of Pieta that resented locking herself away in the stuffy sewing room with her sister's wedding dress, but once she'd started working on it, the resentful feeling seeped away. As she sewed, she thought about the story she had listened to the night before. It seemed like something that had happened to strangers not people she knew. Pieta was impatient to hear more. She wanted to learn how her parents had fallen in love and, most of all, how they'd turned into the people they were now.

But when her mother returned late that afternoon the corners of her eyes were reddened and Pieta suspected she'd been crying.

'What did the doctors say? Is it bad news?' she asked quickly.

'No, not really,' her mother reassured her. 'It's just your father seemed so much better this morning I thought the worst was over.'

'But it isn't?'

'They want to do things to him – X-ray his heart and his blood vessels. Maybe put this little tube into his artery to keep it open so the blood can flow properly. They say they do it all the time but ...'

'But what?'

'There are risks. The doctor told me that less than two per cent of people die during the procedure, but that's still some people, isn't it? What if Beppi is one of them?'

'You can't think like that, Mamma.' Pieta was just as worried but trying not to show it.

'I can't help it.' Her mother's face crumpled and for

a moment she looked like a lost child. 'What would I do without him, Pieta? How would I live?'

Pieta wrapped her arms around her and they stood there together, physically closer than they'd been in a long time, feeling the same things.

'What do you want me to do?' Pieta broke the silence. 'Shall I come back to the hospital with you? Talk to the doctor and make sure this is the right thing for Papa?'

'No, no, we mustn't take up any more of his time. He's a busy person. And anyway, your father has decided it's what he wants. He has to feel strong again. His mind is set on it.'

For a while they stayed in the kitchen. Pieta made a pot of tea and reheated some soup she'd found in the freezer, but her mother didn't seem terribly interested in either.

'What about the wedding?' Pieta asked as she watched her stir her spoon through the soup. 'Maybe Addolorata should postpone it.'

'I don't know. If things go well Beppi will only be in hospital for a few days. He'll be fine in time for the wedding. But if ...'

'Things will go well,' Pieta insisted. 'They have to. So let's just keep all the plans as they are, shall we?'

'OK.' Her mother was still playing with her food. 'If you think that's best.'

'Leave that.' Pieta took the still full bowl from her, put it in the sink and swiped at the messy table with a tea towel. 'Come upstairs for a minute and see how far I've got with the dress. It's looking really good.'

Once they were in the sewing room, her mother

couldn't help but pick up a needle and take her place at the table. Pieta sat beside her and they began to bead together in silence, both lost in the same worries, both struggling to imagine the world without Beppi.

'Thirty years we've been together.' Catherine paused for a moment. 'It's difficult to believe time could have gone by so quickly.'

'Tell me about the first time you went out with him,' Pieta asked as she fastened a bead into place. 'You must have been so nervous.'

'Nervous? Yes, of course I was.' This time her mother didn't seem so reluctant to share her story. It seemed almost a relief to escape to the past again. Her voice lightened as she began to speak.

* * *

I was terribly anxious about that first date. It wasn't that I'd never been out on one before. I'd courted a couple of nice English boys. But they'd always done things properly, coming to meet my parents first and bringing me home again nice and early. And with them I'd never felt the way I did with Beppi. I liked him a lot and was desperate for him to like me just as much.

Audrey and Margaret were excited about my date but I was panicking. 'I can't go off with him for a whole day by myself. What will I talk to him about for all that time?' I kept asking.

'He's taking you to an exhibition so there'll be lots of things to look at and talk about,' pointed out Audrey, adding with a sly grin, 'And anyway, you might not want to spend the whole time talking.'

To decide what I was going to wear we laid out all

our clothes on the beds. I chose my floral skirt, a pretty blue top and some sandals I'd bought in the market that we'd been taking turns to wear.

'I'll do your make-up again,' offered Audrey.

'No.' I shook my head. 'I want to look like me.'

That night I kept waking and remembering Beppi, his lean body, the dense brown of his eyes and his smile, of course, with the neat row of white teeth, which, as I later learned, were strong enough to crack a walnut.

I woke early and filled with nerves. Getting ready didn't take me long enough, even though I spent ages running one of Audrey's pencils over the arch of my eyebrows, blackening my lashes, pinking my lips and then wiping my face clean again. There was still more time to waste so I stopped at Anastasio's for a coffee.

Audrey was already there and she gave me a knowing look.

'You look nice.'

'Thanks.'

She could tell I was anxious so she fed me pastries and milky coffee until it was nearly time for me to go. Then she slipped her sunglasses across the counter and said, 'Wear these today; they suit you. Oh, and have fun.'

Beppi was waiting for me in the piazza, pacing and looking impatient. I hung back, hidden in the crowd, and watched him for a moment. He'd gone to some effort with his appearance, taming his unruly black hair with Brylcreem and carefully ironing his short-sleeved white shirt. But still I couldn't quite bring myself to walk the few steps to his side.

Then he looked up and saw me, and a smile changed

his face. '*Bella* Caterina, you are here.' He kissed me lightly on both cheeks. 'I am so happy to see you. A little part of me was worried you might not come.'

'So where is this exhibition?' I asked.

'We must take the underground train. Don't worry, it is easy.'

He insisted on paying for my ticket and, as the train swayed and clattered through the tunnels, he reached down and held my hand, but softly so it felt like I could easily pull away from him if I wanted to.

We got off at a station called Esposizione. 'Isn't that the Italian word for exhibition?' I asked him.

'That's right.' He nodded and I caught another quick flash of those strong white teeth.

I'd thought he was going to take me to a museum or gallery, so when we came out of the station I was confused. This was a modern part of the city, with wide avenues lined with new apartment buildings. There were no museums here.

He led me to a little park and stopped at a bench near a fountain. With a flourish he produced something from his pocket and, unfolding it, laid it out on the seat. I was taken aback to see it was a map of the world.

'There you are. Please, sit down,' he said. His tone was polite but he was grinning widely.

'I don't understand? Where is the exhibition?'

'We are at Esposizione and here I am, showing you the world. See?' He gestured at the map and began to laugh, but when he saw my face he stopped. 'I'm sorry, Caterina, it was a joke. But you don't find it funny, do you?'

'Not really.' I wanted to storm off but I wasn't sure I could find my way back. 'You've made me feel silly.'

'I'm sorry,' he repeated. He wasn't grinning any longer. 'I wanted so much to spend a day with you. Gianfranco told me it was a mistake. He said you would be angry. But I was so sure it'd make you laugh.'

'I still don't understand. Why didn't you just take me to the Colosseum or the Spanish Steps?'

He crinkled up his face. 'Everyone goes to those places, all the tourists. I thought I needed to come up with something special to tempt you to spend time with me and make you like me.'

I couldn't think what else to do so I sat down on his map of the world. Beppi sat beside me looking as though he was desperate to take hold of my hand again. He edged his fingers a little way towards me, across the map. I watched as they marooned themselves in the middle of a wide patch of blue ocean and, despite myself, I began to laugh. Once I'd started, it was impossible to stop. Beppi looked uncertain for a moment and then he joined in. We laughed until tears ran down our faces, and passers-by hurried past us looking the other way.

'Next time I will take you to the Colosseum,' he promised when at last our laughter had subsided. 'Or to the Spanish Steps.'

'But no exhibitions.'

'No,' he agreed.

I let him take my hand again and we talked until we were hungry. Then we found a little bar that sold us sandwiches and went back to the park to talk some more. He told me how his father had died when he was young and his mother had struggled to bring him up. He'd left home to do his military service and stayed in Rome after that, working in the hotel with Gianfranco and sending most of the money he earned to his mother and sister back home.

In turn I told him about my life. It seemed awfully dull until I got to the bit about us hitchhiking to Italy.

And then I let him kiss me as softly as he had held my hand. It was lovely, but when his arms fastened round me I knew I had to be a nice girl and pull away, saying, 'No, no.'

When the light began to fade he took me back on the train and then we walked round Piazza Navona one more time, staring at the rich people sitting at the pavement cafés.

'I'm not like them, you know,' I told him.

He smiled and kissed me quickly on the cheek. 'Not yet, maybe,' he said.

Audrey told me I was pathetic but I couldn't stop going on about Beppi. He occupied my mind all day long while I was sewing alone in our room, and as soon as I had company I started to talk about him. It wasn't really the way he looked, more that I'd never felt so comfortable with a boy before. Perhaps his ridiculous joke about showing me the world had broken the ice but I felt like I could talk to Beppi as easily as I could to Margaret or Audrey. On his next free day he was going to show me the Roman Forum and I couldn't help wondering if he'd take my hand as we wandered around the ruins.

'Why does he speak such good English?' Margaret was suspicious. 'Didn't he say he comes from some little mountain village down south? It doesn't make sense to me.'

I defended him. 'Well he's been in Rome a while, hasn't he? Perhaps he's spent time with other English people.'

Margaret rolled her eyes. 'I'll bet.'

'What's that supposed to mean?'

'Honestly, Catherine, you're such an innocent. Isn't it obvious? You're not the first English girl your Beppi has shown the world to.'

'I won't see him again then, if that's what you think.' I was near to tears.

Audrey sighed. 'We're not saying that. Just don't fall madly in love with him after one date, that's all.'

I agreed that I wouldn't but of course it was too late. Beppi had charmed me and I spent half my time remembering our first date and the rest imagining the next one.

So when I turned up to meet him at our fountain in the Piazza Navona and found his friend Gianfranco there too I was disappointed. At first I hoped Gianfranco might join us for a coffee and then go his own way. But he stuck with us, dawdling around the ruins of the Forum and then following us to the Colosseum.

'I hope you don't mind,' Beppi said when Gianfranco went to buy ice-cream and left us alone for a moment or two. 'It was his day off too and I didn't want him to spend it all alone.'

'No, of course not, I'm pleased he's come,' I lied.

The more I saw of Gianfranco, the more I disliked

him. There was something about his attitude towards Beppi. He sort of patronized him. And he always seemed to be showing off, reminding us he had the more important job and earned more money. It was very clear he thought of himself as the leader. But Beppi didn't seem to mind, or perhaps he just hadn't noticed.

I never knew when Gianfranco would be there waiting by the fountain with Beppi, his expression sulky and stubborn. He trailed round the gardens of the Villa Borghese with us and walked through the narrow streets of Trastevere. He was there when I first saw the Sistine Chapel and he even sat beside us at the Trevi Fountain. Always I pretended to be happy to have his company. But whenever I left Signora Lucy's and walked towards our fountain I used to pray I'd find Beppi alone. I invented rituals and omens. If I drank one coffee not two then he wouldn't be there. If I saw three nuns in the street I'd find Beppi alone. Silly things but I started to believe in them.

We saw a lot more of Rome when Gianfranco was there. We visited museums and galleries and walked for miles. Once he insisted on us stopping to drink tea and eat little cakes at the grand hotel where he worked. He seemed so proud to be there, pulling out his wallet and insisting on paying for us all. But I felt out of place, sitting on an uncomfortable, ornate chair surrounded by soaring marble pillars and vast, dark oil paintings of people who had died long ago.

When Beppi and I were alone we often didn't go very far at all. We might walk as far as the Trevi Fountain and sit there talking for half an afternoon. As dusk fell and the street lights came on, he would take my hand and say tender things, and I would let him kiss me. Once we stayed there so late we were asked to move on by the street cleaners.

Audrey and Margaret had given up lecturing me, but sometimes the three of us would lie in bed chatting about Gianfranco. None of us could understand why he insisted on tagging along. It was so frustrating when all I wanted was to be alone with Beppi.

'We're going out on Sunday. They're taking me up some hill where we'll get an amazing view of Rome. Will you come, too, Margaret?' I begged her.

It was too dark for me to see her expression but I knew she was pulling a face.

'Please,' I begged again.

'Oh, Catherine.'

'It'll be fun. We'll have ice-cream and we can take photographs.'

'But I don't even like Gianfranco. He's podgy and always looks so miserable. If I come then he's going to think I'm interested in him.'

'No, he won't,' I promised. 'I'll just say what Beppi always says, that it was your day off, too, and I didn't want you to spend it alone.'

Audrey made a muffled snorting sound. Her head must have been under the covers but still she had been listening.

'Why don't you ask Audrey to tag along instead of me?' Margaret groaned.

'Because I know she'll refuse,' I admitted. 'Oh, please, Margaret, please.'

She was too nice to say no. So on Sunday morning

we met Beppi and Gianfranco by the fountain. They had borrowed two Vespas from some other waiters at the hotel and we jumped on behind them. I put my arms around Beppi's waist and saw Margaret glancing over at me and reluctantly doing the same with Gianfranco.

We dodged through the traffic, Gianfranco in front, leaning on his horn. I worried he was showing off. 'Tell him to slow down, Beppi. We're not in any hurry, are we?' I shouted but he took no notice.

It was a warm morning with enough of a breeze to whip through my hair as the Vespas climbed the steep hill. Once we got to the top I was glad I'd come. There was an old stone balustrade and beyond it a view of Rome like no other I'd seen. It was all laid out – the domes, the fountains, the crumbling rooftops, and the river snaking through. Then the church bells started ringing, echoing up towards us.

'*Bella*, eh?' Beppi said.

I leaned my head against his shoulder and reached for his hand. 'Yes, *bella*.'

Gianfranco bought us all strong, sweet coffee in paper cups from a little roadside café and we walked beside the balustrade together. I noticed he seemed to be avoiding Margaret. He hardly looked at her, and when she asked him a question in her nearly perfect Italian, he shrugged and mumbled in reply.

Beppi tossed his empty paper cup into a rubbish bin and then squeezed my hand. 'Caterina, I have something I have to tell you.' His voice was grave.

'What?' Was he going to say he didn't want to see me any more? Had one of those other English girls returned? I knew I sounded alarmed. 'What's happened?'

'Some news that is not so good,' he told me. 'I received a letter from my sister Isabella. She says our mother has been ill for weeks. She has a bad chest and always it causes her problems. But this time Isabella sounds very worried. She wants me to go home to Ravenno.'

'For how long?'

He shrugged. 'I don't know.'

'But what about your job?'

He grimaced. 'They won't hold it for me. But there are other hotels. I'll find work when I come back.'

'So you will come back, then?' I couldn't keep the hope out of my voice.

His fingertips brushed my face. 'Yes, of course I'll come back, Caterina. And don't worry, I've made sure you won't be too lonely while I'm away. I have asked Gianfranco to look after you.'

It may sound like a cliché but I really did feel my heart sinking. 'I don't want to be a bother,' I said.

I was only being polite but Beppi can't have understood that. 'The weather will be hot enough to go to the beach soon,' he said. 'Gianfranco will take you there.'

'But I don't want to go to the beach with Gianfranco,' I whispered plaintively. 'I want to go with you.' I saw Gianfranco shoot a dark glance towards me, but I didn't care if he'd overheard me.

'The beaches here are nothing,' Beppi said. 'Wait until you see what we have further south. I will take you there one day, I promise.'

'But not this time?'

'No.' He sounded regretful. 'My mother is sick. She wants to see her son.'

'When will you leave?'

'Tomorrow morning, quite early. So today it will be goodbye. But Gianfranco will look after you and keep you safe till I come back again.'

I stopped trying not to cry. Beppi didn't seem to mind my tears. He wiped them away with a handkerchief Margaret lent him and then kissed my damp cheeks. 'Gianfranco will take care of you,' he repeated.

12

I'd have avoided Gianfranco if I'd been able to. But my world in Rome was small and he knew where to find me. Early most mornings I went to Anastasio's bar to drink coffee and chat to Audrey while the place was still quiet. She was working double shifts to earn extra money and was squirrelling away as much cash as she could. She'd even stopped spending so much on her precious cigarettes and now only smoked one or two a day. She hadn't explained why but I'd noticed she'd been writing to one of the American servicemen we'd met while we were hitchhiking. He'd left the army and was back home in New York. I wondered if Audrey was trying to save the money for the fare over there but didn't dare ask her. I hated the idea of our little trio being broken up.

I suppose in a way it already had. A couple of days after Beppi left, Margaret had gone away with the Contessa and her family. They spent every summer in their house down in Battipaglia and went for at least two months, missing the hottest time in the city. We'd had a letter from her already and she sounded lonely. She said her only consolation was that the place was famous for its buffalo mozzarella.

I was lonely, too. After I'd spent an hour or so

with Audrey in the morning all I had was my sewing. Already I was missing Beppi desperately. Somehow everything seemed different when he was around. I could have wandered around Rome by myself and sat beside the Trevi Fountain or on the Spanish Steps, but I'd have felt too sad and even more alone than ever.

So when Gianfranco came to find me at Anastasio's café one sunny Sunday morning I was almost grateful. He was still the same doughy boy who wore too much cologne and looked like he spent too long combing his hair, yet there was something different about him. After a while I realized it was his smile. It sort of opened up his face and made him instantly more likeable. For some reason the sulkiness that usually dogged him seemed to have gone.

'I am taking you to the beach,' he told me. 'It is so hot today it will be good to be near the sea.'

Audrey leaned her elbows on the counter and her shoulders sagged. 'Oh, the beach. Wouldn't that be lovely? Catherine, I'm jealous. It's going to be boiling in here today.'

'There's room for you in the back of the car I've borrowed. You're very welcome to come, too,' said Gianfranco politely.

'Oh yes, do come, Audrey. See if Anastasio will give you the day off,' I begged her.

She looked tempted but shook her head. 'No, I've told him I'll work today so I've got to. And anyway, I need the money.'

Gianfranco smiled again. 'It's just you and me then, Caterina.'

It gave me a jolt to hear him use Beppi's special name

for me. Suddenly I felt disloyal going off to spend the day with another man, even if it was his best friend and he'd suggested it in the first place.

'Maybe we should wait and go on a day when Audrey can come, too?' I suggested.

But Gianfranco wouldn't hear of it. 'We can take her with us another time,' he promised. 'Hurry up and fetch your things. It's a long drive so we need to get going.'

He waited for me in the bar while I went back to Signora Lucy's to find my swimming costume and sun hat. I couldn't help wondering what I was going to talk to Gianfranco about on the long drive and felt a bit uncomfortable at the thought of being alone in the car with him. But there was no getting out of it. So with my beach bag packed, I returned to the bar.

As it turned out Gianfranco did most of the talking. He made me laugh with stories of the trouble he and Beppi had got into as boys. They'd known each other for as long as he could remember. Too poor to afford toys, often with barely enough to eat, he said they'd rampaged around the mountain village of Ravenno, building forts, climbing trees and hunting small birds. I could imagine Beppi as a young boy, his skinny little body in scruffy shorts, knees scabbed from some adventure and skin darkened by the sun. It made me feel happy to hear Gianfranco talk about him.

The road to the coast was straight and long, and when we drew near to the beach we found a queue of traffic. Even with all the windows rolled down we were sweltering in the car and I was envious of the girls buzzing past on their scooters with the wind in their hair.

Gianfranco honked his horn and fanned himself with his hand. There was a line of sweat on his upper lip and it was trickling down his brow. 'Ouf, everyone wants to go to the sea today. This is ridiculous. At home we never have to queue like this and the beaches are a million times better.' He honked his horn again and swore beneath his breath.

The sand, once we got there, was crowded, too. Families had staked out their space with sun umbrellas and deckchairs, and some had unfolded tables and covered them with dishes of baked pasta, foil-wrapped meat, crusty bread and cheese. Beautiful girls stretched out to bronze their bodies, old men played cards while the younger ones were playing bat and ball games, and children built sandcastles in the wet sand. There was noise, laughter and loud arguments.

We found a space and put down towels to sit on. Gianfranco had borrowed a small striped beach umbrella and planted it in the sand.

'I brought no food with me,' he said apologetically. 'But there is a café where we can maybe get some pizza later.'

He stripped off his clothes and I saw the way the elastic of his swimming trunks dug into the mound of his stomach. His belly was as soft and milky as a ball of mozzarella, but he didn't seem self-conscious about it. No one did, I realized. Old women with vast, dimpled thighs and young mothers still thick round the middle lounged in their swimming costumes, seemingly un-concerned about appearances.

But I felt uncomfortable as I stepped out of my skirt and pulled my shirt over my head. I was aware that

Gianfranco's eyes were on me as I stood exposed in my swimming costume.

'I'm going for a quick swim first,' I told him. 'I'll be back in a minute.'

It was a relief to cover myself in the cool water. Gianfranco didn't follow me, but he sat up and watched as I swam away from the crowds into the deeper water. I was a good swimmer. My dad had taken me to the pool every week and in the summer we'd always spent a few days in Brighton and swum in the sea there. Here it was different. The water was warmer and saltier, and everything seemed more brilliant and blue. I turned onto my back and let the sun warm my face. This was heaven.

Gianfranco insisted on covering my back with sun oil when I got back to the beach. 'It will help you get a nice tan,' he told me. I felt awkward. His hands were soft and the feel of them massaging the scented oil into my back was too strange to be pleasant.

I drifted off to sleep for a while. When I woke up I discovered Gianfranco had brought us slices of pizza on plastic plates and bottles of cold Coca-Cola with straws.

'I thought you might be hungry,' he said.

'Yes, I am. It must be the sea air.'

I felt awkward again. The memory of his hands on my back and being here beside him on my towel, both of us half-naked, seemed wrong. I wished we weren't alone together.

'I wonder what Beppi is doing now?' I said as I swallowed a mouthful of oily, garlicky pizza.

Gianfranco shrugged. 'Running round after his

sister and mother, I expect. They will be thrilled to have him home.'

'What is his sister like?' I asked, desperate to keep the conversation on safe ground.

'Isabella? She is a nice girl.'

'Is she beautiful?'

'Not really ... no, I don't think so. But she is a good girl. She looks after her mother.' Gianfranco shaded his eyes with his hands so he could see me better. 'But she is not beautiful like you are, Caterina,' he added softly.

I said nothing. As soon as I'd finished my pizza I lay back and shut my eyes, pretending to be asleep again. I heard Gianfranco go off for a swim, hopping across the scorching hot sand as fast as he could. And I lay there wondering what to do. I was certain this wasn't what Beppi had in mind when he'd asked his friend to look after me.

We stayed there for most of the afternoon, swimming and sunbathing, until I noticed both of us were turning pink. I was relieved to have an excuse to cover myself up.

'Come on, let's go up to the café and have a cold beer and some olives before we drive home,' said Gianfranco. 'I want to miss the traffic heading back into the city.'

There was a breeze out on the balcony of the café. We sat in the shade and looked out over the beach.

'I have another day off on Wednesday,' Gianfranco told me. 'Would you like to come back here or should we go somewhere else?'

The last thing I wanted was to spend another day

at the beach with him. 'Let's go somewhere else,' I suggested.

'OK. I'll see if I can borrow the car again and try to think of a good place.'

On the way back he talked about the hotel where he worked. I'd heard most of the stories already from Beppi. I knew all about the chef who drank his way through a bottle of wine before lunchtime and the head waiter they'd had an argument with about tips, but I listened all the same. It was better to be bored with second-hand stories than have Gianfranco pay me excruciating compliments.

'Wednesday then,' he said as he dropped me off outside Anastasio's bar. 'Be ready nice and early so we can have a whole day together.'

All I wanted to do was to talk to Audrey. My skin was salty and crusty with sand but I didn't bother going back to Signora Lucy's to get cleaned up. Instead I headed straight in to the bar and found Audrey fanning herself with a glossy magazine.

'Oh, lucky you,' she said as soon as she saw me. 'You've been swimming in the sea, haven't you? I should have come. This place has been dead anyway. Ah well, maybe next time.'

'Oh yes, please come with us next time,' I said fervently.

Audrey raised her eyebrows. 'Why, what happened?'

I felt silly because Gianfranco hadn't actually done anything. In fact, he'd been nicer than ever. But there was something oppressive about being with him, something that didn't seem right.

'Well, don't go out with him again,' Audrey said when I told her. 'Just say no.'

'But I've already said I will and Beppi wanted me to … and well, it would be rude,' I wailed. 'Please try to come on Wednesday. It'll be better with you there.'

She looked dubious. 'Maybe … I don't know.'

'You can't work all the time.'

She pulled a face. 'The thing is, I won't be working here for much longer. I've nearly saved up enough to pay my fare to America. I'm going to New York to see Louis. He was the darker of those two soldiers we hitched a ride with, remember? The better-looking one. You knew I'd been writing to him?'

'Yes.'

'I feel bad about leaving you, Catherine. It's been great being here but …'

I was angry with her. 'You think you're in love with this American?'

'Maybe … well … I don't know.' She looked away from me and stared out of the window.

'You were stuck in a car with him for less than a day. You hardly know him. And you're going to travel halfway round the world to be with him?'

'Don't be like that, Catherine.' Audrey sounded sad.

'It sounds pretty stupid, that's all.'

'I know, I know. But there's something about him. Remember how you were when you first met Beppi? How you couldn't stop thinking about him? Well, I've been the same about Louis only I didn't say anything to you and Margaret because it all seemed so hopeless. Then we started exchanging letters and got to know each other that way. He could be the one I've been looking for, Catherine, and if I don't go to America I'll never know.'

I stared at her. Audrey had always been the adventurous one. She made life exciting. I hated to think I was going to lose her.

'I don't want you to go ...' I realized I was crying.

'Oh, Catherine.' She came round to my side of the counter and hugged me. 'I know, I know.'

She cried a little bit, too, and stroked my hair. 'You know, it probably won't work out and then I'll come crawling back here, begging Anastasio for my job back.'

'But if it does work out, will you stay in New York?'

She sat down on the stool beside me. 'Honestly, I haven't planned that far ahead. I've been so busy working to save the money to get there, and all I've been thinking about is seeing Louis again.'

'I can understand that.'

'And what about you?' she asked me. 'What will you do? Will you go home to London or down to Battipaglia to see Margaret?'

'No, I've got to stay here in Rome to wait for Beppi. He promised he'd come back.'

'But will you be OK all on your own?'

I scrunched my face into a frown. 'I won't be on my own, will I? I've got Gianfranco to look after me.'

Both of us laughed then and hugged each other again. Audrey poured us each a glass of Campari and lemonade, and we toasted her future in America.

'How long before you go?' I asked.

'Two weeks. I've already booked my ticket and told Anastasio. But I'm a coward so I've been putting off breaking the news to you. I knew it would be awful.'

I couldn't imagine how I was going to cope in Rome without her. As soon as I'd finished my drink I left the bar and hurried back to Signora Lucy's where I knew I could bury my head in my pillow and have a good cry.

Audrey's last two weeks in Rome went by in a flash. On her final day she came to the beach but we were too sad to really enjoy ourselves.

'I'm scared, you know, Catherine,' she told me as we sat side by side on the sand. 'What if I see him again and don't like him?'

Privately I'd been wondering the same thing but I hadn't expected Audrey to worry about it. She seemed so different these days, less confident, more vulnerable. I hadn't seen that trademark little toss of her head for a long time.

'If it doesn't work out you can come back,' I re-assured her.

She stared out towards the sea. 'I don't know if I'll ever come back here,' she mused and I saw she was frowning. 'And what will happen to us – you, me and Margaret? Do you think we'll ever all be together again?'

The future was something I'd been worrying about since the day I met Beppi. I couldn't imagine being without him, but neither could I see how we might stay together. Our lives were too different, our worlds so far apart.

'I've no idea,' I said at last. 'I'm like you. All I'm

thinking about is seeing Beppi again. I can't plan any further ahead than that.'

Then Gianfranco came back with some cold Coca-Cola and we drank it and lay in the sun, listening to the happy noise made by the other beachgoers and trying not to think too hard about what lay ahead for us.

* * *

Pieta noticed her mother had once again abandoned all pretence of beading as she lost herself in her story. At times it was almost as though she had forgotten there was anyone listening to her. Mostly, as she talked, she stared out of the window, but she wasn't looking at the sky or down at the patterns made by the bamboo canes in the vegetable garden below. All she could see was the past.

As she steadily worked on alone, covering more of the taffeta with crystal beads, Pieta thought about love and how hard it was to come by. Her mother had found it by a fountain in Rome, her friend Audrey in a car travelling through Switzerland. For a long time Pieta had thought it might happen like that for her, too. One day in some unexpected place she'd come across the one she'd want to marry. But so far the men she'd met in bars and clubs had only been interested in knowing her for a night or, if she were lucky, a month or two. Then they'd start to murmur that they needed more space or just stop calling her.

Addolorata always said it was because she was too intense, but Pieta didn't think so. As her twenties had gone by she had become convinced there simply wasn't a man out there for her. She was meant to be alone. So she concentrated on making wedding gowns for other girls, heard their love stories and their marriage plans, and tried not to think too much about it. But now, listening to her mother, Pieta couldn't help wondering if she had given up on herself too soon.

13

Pieta had known she wouldn't be able to sleep. She'd sipped a milky drink, made her room warm, taken a bath – done all the right things to get a good night's rest. When she lay down and closed her eyes, her body felt tired but her mind refused to shut down. It spooled through her parents' love story and reminded her that, if things went badly, then soon it might be over. It made her think about her father going about his normal life, playing cards outside Little Italy, digging in his garden, and all the time his arteries clogging up without him knowing. It forced her to imagine how they would cope without him.

In the middle of the night she got up and went down to the sewing room, tempted to put the sleepless time to good use. But in the end she worried that tiredness might make her work sloppy so she left the dress alone and returned to bed.

It was a relief when she realized it was starting to grow light and there was no point trying to fall asleep any longer. She switched on her bedside lamp and found a notebook and pen, so she could write a list of things she wanted to ask the doctor if she got a chance.

Pieta was making a strong brew of coffee when she heard her mother moving around upstairs.

'Did you sleep?' she asked when she appeared, although she could see for herself what the answer would be.

'I dozed a little on and off.'

'Why don't you go back to bed for a bit? I'll visit Papa this morning.'

Her mother shook her head. 'I'm not staying here alone, Pieta. And anyway, I want to see him.'

'But you look exhausted.'

'And so do you. So why don't you be the one who goes back to bed?'

In the end they went to the hospital together, travelling in silence in the taxi, both impatient to get there yet dreading the metallic smell of the place and the endless rooms full of sick people with their sad families.

Beppi seemed relieved to see them. 'I can't sleep here,' he grumbled once he'd kissed them hello. 'Always noise, light and people moving about … but never anybody there when you need them.'

Pieta noticed a booklet that had been left by his bed. 'Your Angioplasty: What to Expect' it said in plain type on the cover. She picked it up and started to read while her mother fussed about with the bedclothes and poured coffee from a flask into a plastic cup.

'It doesn't sound so bad,' she volunteered. 'It says here you only have a local anaesthetic and you shouldn't need to stay in hospital too long afterwards. And then you just have to take the drugs they give you and be careful about what you eat. No more butter, cheese and prosciutto, Papa.'

'So they say.' He sounded mournful. 'Yesterday they

brought me cottage cheese and lettuce for my dinner. It tastes of nothing. What is the point of it, eh?'

'At least you're OK, Beppi.' There was a scolding tone to Catherine's voice. 'At least you're alive to eat cottage cheese. Thank God Frederico was so fast to call an ambulance and you got here so quickly.'

'Yes, thank God,' Beppi agreed. 'I love my restaurant but I don't want to die in it.'

They spent the morning there, trying to keep him from becoming bored and fractious. Pieta slipped out to buy newspapers, more coffee and some flowers to cheer up the room, and when she got back she found her mother crying and Beppi trying to comfort her.

'Take her home now,' he told Pieta. 'It's not good for her to spend too much time here.'

'No, no, I want to stay.' Her mother sounded querulous. 'Why are people always telling me what to do? Go to bed, go home … I can make up my own mind. I'm not a child.'

'But there's still so much work left to do on the dress, Mamma,' Pieta reminded her. 'It would be good if you'd come back and help me with it.'

'Don't be silly. You don't really need my help. And anyway, I've talked more than I've sewn.'

'I'd like it if you were there, though.'

'Oh, all right then.' She sounded resigned. 'Give me five more minutes … ten minutes maybe. Wait outside. I want to say goodbye to your father properly.'

The pattern of beads on the fabric was starting to take shape and the work was good. But Pieta hadn't been exaggerating when she'd said there was still a long way to go. Already she had stiff fingers and tired eyes from the long hours of fine work. Only the thought of hearing the next part of her mother's story made the prospect of more beading bearable.

'Tell me what happened when Audrey left you in Rome?' Pieta prompted as soon as they began sewing. 'Did you really stay there alone?'

'I had no other choice.'

'Were you OK?'

'Not really. No, I wasn't OK at all.'

* * *

Anastasio saved me in those first couple of weeks in Rome without Audrey. He asked me to work some shifts in his bar, and even though I was worried I'd be hopeless, I said yes. It was quiet in Rome because so many families had gone away to their summer houses, so I expect he could have managed without me, but he was such a kind man and I'm sure he could tell how lonely I was.

Sometimes Gianfranco would come and sit at the bar, order a drink and watch me as I worked. Often it felt like he was laying claim to me, letting all the regulars know I was taken. Anastasio never said anything, but I got the feeling he didn't like him much.

It turned out I wasn't as useless behind a bar as I'd feared. I quite enjoyed memorizing what people drank and how strong they liked their coffee. We didn't serve much in the way of food, just pastries in the morning and little plates of bread, mozzarella and salami later in the day. It was a meeting place really, somewhere for people to refuel and relax for a few moments before they got on with their day. Often the regulars would stop and chat to me for a while, and I got to know little things about them – the names of their children, the people they'd fallen out with, their hopes and plans. I didn't talk much about myself because I didn't want anyone to know I was alone in Rome. Or for them to guess that with every day that passed my worry that Beppi was never coming back grew stronger.

I'd had a few short notes from him but his writing was strange, the words scribbled erratically on the page, and I struggled to understand them. So I bought a great big block of writing paper and, when I wasn't working in the bar or busy sewing, I'd sit and write long letters to him and Margaret. I told them very different things. Margaret heard all about Gianfranco and how uncomfortable I felt around him sometimes, and to Beppi I wrote funny anecdotes about people I knew from the bar. Once a week I wrote to my parents and that was always difficult. I couldn't let them know Audrey and Margaret weren't with me because I'd promised we'd stay together. Even though I felt guilty lying to them, I never considered going home. If Beppi came back to Rome and didn't find me there then he might think I didn't care about him any more.

Gianfranco had been promising me an extra-special outing and was nagging me to take a break from the bar. I ought to have refused but there were times when I enjoyed his company. Not when he showed off and talked about how much money he had made that week, or how smart a car he was going to buy once he'd saved a little more, but when he forgot to be self-important and instead clowned around and made me laugh.

'Exactly where are you taking me on this special outing?' I asked him the next time he mentioned it.

'Like I said, it's a mystery,' he told me. 'But I'll be here on Sunday morning very early, so tell Anastasio you won't be working.'

'Can't you at least give me a clue?' I didn't completely trust him and it seemed unwise to head off without letting someone know where we were going, even if it was only Anastasio.

Gianfranco's expression seemed arrogant. 'You won't guess so there's no point in me giving you a clue. Just be here nice and early on Sunday morning.'

I ought to have been stronger and told him no, but somehow Gianfranco always managed to make me feel powerless. It seemed easier to let him have his way. I was fairly sure he'd only take me to a different beach or the top of another hill to admire the view and eat an ice-cream.

So I was there on Sunday morning. Anastasio had only just opened the bar and we were drinking our first coffee of the day together when Gianfranco came in, a swagger in his walk, and tossed some car keys down on the counter in a showy sort of way.

'Are you ready?'

'Well, I think so, although since I don't know where we're going I'm not sure what I should bring.' My voice probably sounded sulky but I didn't care.

'I have everything we need.' He took my arm. 'Come on, it's a long drive so there's no time to waste.'

Gianfranco had a different car today. It was

polished to a high shine and something about the way he unlocked the door made me guess he wanted me to notice it.

'Who did you borrow this one from?' I asked.

'I didn't borrow it.'

As soon as I was in the passenger seat he started the engine and roared off far too quickly down the narrow street, the radio blaring and all the windows down.

'Did you buy it?'

He nodded, pleased with himself. 'Nice, eh? I got a really good deal.'

We took the main road south and Gianfranco pointed out the abbey of Monte Cassino up on the hill. I'd have preferred him to put both hands on the steering wheel and concentrate on the road. The speed he drove at was terrifying and he liked to stay close to the car in front so he could hoot his horn repeatedly and overtake the minute it was possible.

'She goes fast,' he said patting the dashboard. 'We'll be there in no time.'

When I began seeing road signs marked for Naples, I started to wonder how far Gianfranco was taking me, but I knew there was no point asking. Only when I realized we were heading into the city did I speak up.

'Gianfranco, you've brought me to Naples. Isn't it meant to be dangerous here?'

He shrugged. 'For tourists maybe but not for me.'

I kept expecting him to stop but he carried on driving through the cobbled squares and rattling over tramlines. I wound down the window further and leaned out. The city smelt quite different to Rome and it seemed less well cared for but somehow more alive.

'Are we going to pull over soon?' I asked.

Gianfranco shook his head. 'Not yet.'

We drove past Vesuvius and I was excited because I'd never seen a volcano before. Finally we took a road that began to wind around the coast. Soon it became little more than a narrow track carved into the cliff with a mountain on one side and a steep drop on the other. Even Gianfranco had to slow for the hairpin bends and pulled over perilously close to the edge to let a bus through.

He cursed beneath his breath. 'Just my luck if I smash her up on my first proper drive,' he muttered.

At long last we arrived in the prettiest town I'd ever seen. Pink and white houses were stacked up on the cliffs, and just above a little stretch of beach was a church with a domed roof covered in a pattern of coloured tiles. Beyond us stretched a brilliant turquoise sea bobbing with little boats. I was captivated by the place. I couldn't imagine living here and not feeling happy to wake each day.

Gianfranco found a place to park, and my legs felt stiff and a little shaky as I climbed out of the car.

'This is Positano,' he announced. 'You stay here. I'll go and get us some coffee and a snack.'

He came back with balls of rice wrapped in paper serviettes, and when I bit into mine, warm mozzarella oozed into my mouth.

'Can we go and explore now?' I said as soon as we'd finished eating.

He looked dubious. 'It might not be safe to leave the car.'

I couldn't help laughing. 'Gianfranco, you can't

bring me all the way here and make me stay by the car. Come on, I want to have a look around.'

Nearby were three boys kicking a football about. Gianfranco gave them a few coins from his pocket and pointed at his car.

'Keep an eye on it, OK?' he said and, after one or two concerned glances over his shoulder, followed me up the narrow, steep streets.

Together we climbed hundreds of steps and walked past tightly packed buildings, stopping every now and then so I could glance into the window of an expensive boutique or look inside a dark cool church. Gianfranco seemed bored but I didn't care. I might never visit Positano again, and I wanted to see everything if I could.

After an hour or two Gianfranco started to complain. 'My legs are tired with all this climbing, Caterina. This is my day off so I need to rest. Let's go back and stay on the beach for a bit.'

Down on the sand it was all glamour. Women wore wide-brimmed hats, lots of gold jewellery and bright red lipstick as they lounged in their canvas chairs. I felt out of place in the cotton skirt I'd stitched myself.

We hadn't been there long when Gianfranco decided he was hungry again and wanted to have lunch on the terrace of a grand-looking hotel above the beach.

'Won't it be terribly expensive?' I asked.

He made a dismissive gesture with his hand. 'I can afford it. I don't send all my money back home like Beppi does.'

Nevertheless, I hung back when we got to the entrance. I felt sure the waiters would be able to tell we didn't belong. Gianfranco didn't share my concerns. In fact, he embarrassed me by refusing the first table we were shown to and insisting we were given something with a better view.

He ordered spaghetti with clams and a carafe of chilled white wine. I'd never eaten shellfish before and had to watch him carefully to see what I was supposed to do. Twirling the pasta round my fork I was careful not to splash myself with the oily liquid it was swimming in. When I did manage to eat some it was delicious. It tasted of the sea mixed with garlic and fresh parsley. I couldn't help thinking how much Margaret would have enjoyed it.

Then an old man with a guitar took a seat at the end of the terrace and started singing Neapolitan love songs in a soft, deep voice.

'I wish Beppi were here,' I said. 'Wouldn't he love it?'

Gianfranco looked sullen. 'He's never been anywhere like this in his life,' he said shortly. Waving the waiter over, he ordered ice-cream and coffee.

'What shall we do after this? Go down to the beach again?' I asked.

'No, we'll go back to the car. I want to drive further so you can see all of the Amalfi coast.'

'We don't need to …' I began but his mind was made up and he didn't want to hear me.

Taken more slowly, it would have been a beautiful drive, but Gianfranco raced like a madman around a road that seemed barely to cling to the steep grey cliffs. The last place we stopped was called Vietri sul Mare where the roadsides were cluttered with brightly-painted vases that spilled out of shops full of plates, bowls and tiles decorated in a similarly colourful style. Gianfranco insisted on buying me a hand-painted tile as a keepsake, although I was worried that he'd already spent more than enough on me.

Then we drove back along the terrifying road and stopped at Amalfi for a while so Gianfranco could refresh himself with a beer and a dish of olives before the long drive back to Rome.

Finally he agreed it was time to go home. We got back into the car and that was when things began to go wrong. Gianfranco turned the ignition and his foot sank down onto the accelerator, but the car only coughed in reply.

'Damn,' he muttered.

'What's wrong?'

'That doesn't sound good.'

Gianfranco turned the key once or twice more and pumped his foot up and down on the pedal. He seemed angry. 'Come on, come on,' he muttered.

The car made a moaning, dying sound and then there was silence.

I felt helpless. I'd never driven a car and had no idea why it might suddenly stop working, so I stayed in the passenger seat while Gianfranco took a look under the bonnet. He rummaged around for ten minutes or so, then slammed the bonnet back down and got back into the car. By now his mood was as black as the oil that covered his hands.

'Heap of shit.' His fist crashed down on the dashboard.

It had been a long day and Gianfranco's driving had

put me on edge. I lost my patience. 'It's no use swearing and hitting things. What are we going to do?'

Gianfranco threw his hands in the air dramatically. 'I don't know.'

I was angry but not just with Gianfranco. If my friends hadn't abandoned me, if Audrey, Margaret and Beppi were still in Rome, this would never have happened.

'Well, why don't you go and see if you can find a garage or a mechanic to help us?'

With a petulant twist of his lips, Gianfranco got out of the car again. He marched off down the road without looking back.

He was gone for ages. I didn't have a book or magazine to occupy me so I stared out the window and watched the life of the town. A fat waiter was serving tables at the corner café where we'd drunk our beer, a young mother and two little girls strolled along together, and a hunched old lady rushed past carrying a basket heavy with food for her supper. It struck me that they all had homes to go to and people waiting for them, and I wished I was where I ought to have been – working in the grocer's shop and about to head home for a meal of stew and boiled potatoes at the kitchen table with my parents.

I must have closed my eyes and dozed off because when I looked out of the window again the street lights had come on and the warmth had gone out of the day. There was no sign of Gianfranco. My mouth was dry and I thought about getting a glass of Coca-Cola at the café, but I'd have felt awkward sitting there alone so I stayed in the car, my head resting against the window, hoping Gianfranco would be back before it got dark.

When he did get back he slammed the car door so hard that I didn't dare speak to him for a moment. The news was obviously bad and he was angry so I knew I had to be careful. I waited for him to tell me what had happened.

'Stupid town, idiot people,' he said eventually.

'No mechanic?'

'Oh yes, I found one. But he was shutting up shop for the day and said he couldn't look at the car until first thing tomorrow morning. Unbelievable. No mechanic in Rome would be so lazy.'

'So what will we do? Find a place to stay for the night?'

'I tried that but you have no idea how expensive this town is. It's for rich foreign tourists not Italians.' His tone was scathing. 'And I've spent all of the money I brought with me on lunch and that present for you.'

'I have some money.' I pulled the purse from my handbag and took out a sheaf of notes. 'It has to be enough, surely.'

'For one room maybe …'

My throat was dry and my head hurt. I wanted to go home, even if that only meant my empty room at Signora Lucy's.

'Isn't there a bus?'

He shook his head

'So we're stranded here.'

'Yes, yes … I'm sorry.' His voice was more glum than angry now. 'I think we'll have to sleep in the car.'

The thought of sleeping so close to him, listening

to his snores and snuffles, feeling his sour breath on me, horrified me. I'd never spent the whole night with a man before and I didn't want Gianfranco to be the first.

'We can't.'

'What choice do we have? The seats recline and I think I may even have a couple of rugs in the boot. Once the café is closed there'll be no one around. It may not be so bad.' He grinned at me. 'We'll be quite comfortable in here together, I think.'

I thought back to how we'd always managed to find a decent place to sleep while we were hitching no matter how late it was. And I looked across at Gianfranco and wondered about the odd little smile I saw on his face. My mind ran fast with suspicion. Was he telling me the truth? Or was this some sort of ploy to keep me with him for a whole night? I was certain I knew what Audrey and Margaret would say if they were here.

He reached across and put his hand over mine. 'I'll look after you,' he said. 'Don't worry.'

I glanced out the window and saw the round waiter leaning over to put a fresh ashtray on one of the outdoor tables. 'I'm going to go and ask at the café,' I said. 'They might know of somewhere cheap I could stay.'

The waiter's Italian was heavily accented and I struggled to understand him. I looked over at the car, hoping Gianfranco might come and help me, but he was staring determinedly in the opposite direction.

'I need a room for the night,' I said, stumbling over the words. 'Something cheap because I don't have much money. Please help me. I don't have anywhere to go.'

He must have been confused. I saw him glance at Gianfranco sulking in the car, then he shrugged and told me to follow him. Breathing heavily, he took me up a steep flight of stairs and showed me into a little room. There was a single bed pushed against a peeling wall and a bare bulb hanging above it that cast a yellow light. It was a dump and yet I was relieved to be there.

'How much?'

The price he named wasn't cheap. I'd be using up most of the cash I had on me with just a bit left over to buy some bread and soup for dinner. Again I thought about Audrey and Margaret and wondered what they would do.

I shook my head. 'Too expensive,' I said and offered a smaller amount.

He knew I was desperate so could have insisted but instead he nodded, his jowls wobbling, and held out his hand for the money.

He didn't seem to care that I had no bags. Tucking the money into a little pocket sewn into his apron, he nodded again and backed out of the room.

I sat down on the bed for a moment and leaned on the lumpy, peeling wall. Gianfranco would be down there still, sitting in the car, and I knew I ought to go and tell him what was happening.

He was sulky, of course, but there was nothing much he could say or do.

'I'll be fine up there,' I told him. 'And I've got enough money left over to buy us some dinner so it's all worked out. We just have to hope the mechanic can help us sort out your car in the morning.'

Gianfranco only grunted in reply. His expression was still sour as he followed me into the café. Thankfully the food we ordered came quickly and I only had to sit beside him in silence for half an hour or so. Then I went back up to my room and he returned to sleep in his car. The waiter looked amused but said nothing.

The first thing I did was to push the bed against the door just as we had that first night in France. Then I crawled beneath the covers, turned out the light and shut my eyes. I was tired but I couldn't sleep. I was lonely, angry with Gianfranco and utterly confused about my future. I kept thinking how much I envied Audrey her courage. She hadn't thought twice about sailing all the way to America to be with her service-man. Beppi was only a few hours further south from here and yet I hadn't dared to go to him.

I slept badly and woke with a headache. The clothes I'd worn the day before were lying where I'd left them, in a pile on the floor, and I put them back on. Pulling the bed away from the door, I went downstairs.

Gianfranco was sitting at one of the outdoor tables with a coffee and a basket of pastries in front of him.

'Have you been to find the mechanic?' I asked.

He looked up but didn't quite meet my eyes. 'I had another look at it myself,' he said. 'I think I may have sorted the problem. Have some coffee, then we'll go.'

I didn't believe him but what was the point in getting angry? All I wanted was to get safely back to Signora Lucy's. Once I was there I'd decide what to do.

Anastasio had been waiting for me. He'd expected me to turn up for work first thing and when I arrived closer to lunchtime and still in the clothes I'd been wearing the day before, he looked concerned.

'It's fine. I'll tell you later,' I said, tying on an apron and slipping behind the counter.

I worked for three or four hours and then Anastasio spotted me yawning and sent me back to my room at Signora Lucy's. When I closed the door behind me I cried for a little bit and then I opened the shutters and lay on my bed listening to someone practising the piano in an apartment nearby.

Once I'd rested for a while I got my towel and went down the corridor to take a bath. Then I combed my hair, put on fresh clothes and walked back to Anastasio's bar.

He seemed surprised to see me. 'Are you OK?'

'Yes, yes,' I assured him.

'If that Gianfranco comes sniffing round here for you, I'll send him away,' he promised.

'I don't think he'll come,' I said. 'I hope we've seen the last of him.'

He poured me a Coca-Cola and I took a seat at the counter.

'Anastasio, how would I get to a place in Basilicata called Ravenno?'

He looked surprised. 'Why do you want to go there?'

'I'm going to visit a friend.'

'Ah, I see. Well I suppose you'd take a train to Naples, then change onto another train that would take you further south. And then I don't know. A bus or a taxi maybe? It's in the mountains, I think, very remote. How long are you going for?'

'I don't really know. But I don't want to pay for the room at Signora Lucy's while I'm away so could I leave a bag of my things here?'

'Of course you can.' He was such a kind man. 'When are you leaving?'

'As soon as possible … tomorrow maybe.'

He wasn't angry with me for abandoning my job. 'Well, you want to be careful down there. It can be dangerous,' was all he said.

That night I couldn't sleep for worrying. Just the thought of the journey was daunting and, even if I did manage to get there, I wasn't certain Beppi would be happy to see me. I only dared to go because by then it felt as if I had no other choice. I couldn't stay in Rome and I didn't want to go home, so that only left Ravenno. Bunching up the pillow beneath my head, I shut my eyes and tried to get some sleep. Tomorrow I had to pack up my room and go to Stazione Termini to find a train that would take me south to Beppi.

* * *

Pieta wondered why her mother had never told her any of this before. How could such a faded woman have had so vibrant a story inside her and never thought to share it with her children? To her shame Pieta realized she had never really thought of her as a person before. She was just someone who had always been there, fussing over things like warm clothes and early bedtimes when they were children, worrying if they stayed out late as teenagers. She saw her mother every day but never once had Pieta asked herself who she really was. She'd never wondered what her secrets were, what she

166

was thinking or who she'd been before children came along.

When she had first asked for this story to be told Pieta had been thinking only of how she might learn the reason for her father's feud with Gianfranco DeMatteo. Now she realized she was discovering something much more valuable – the mystery of her mother.

14

It was the day of Beppi's procedure. No matter how much the doctors reassured them, the thought of him being wheeled away from them and the chance, tiny as it was, of him never coming back was preying on all their minds.

Addolorata came with them to the hospital but she didn't stay for long. She seemed relieved to make her excuses and leave for Little Italy.

'It's going to be a big day,' she muttered. 'Lots of tables booked and a large party coming tonight. And we're short-staffed ... some flu bug ... I want to stay but ...'

'You go, *cara*,' Beppi said lightly. They still hadn't talked about their argument or Addolorata's threat to leave, and the unspoken words formed a barrier between them. 'It's good the place is so busy. But don't work yourself too hard.'

There was some crying and clinging from Catherine as they took Beppi away, but once he had gone and Pieta settled her down in the waiting area, she seemed a little calmer.

'All we can do now is wait,' she said quietly. 'It's in the doctors' hands.'

'It's a routine procedure, Mamma. They've probably done it a thousand times. It's going to be fine.'

They sat in the small room on uncomfortable chairs beneath strip lighting, drinking bad coffee and wondering what to say to each other.

'So you went to Ravenno to see Papa,' Pieta said, as much to distract herself as her mother. 'Was he pleased to see you? Were you glad you'd gone?'

'Well, yes,' her mother said, casting her mind back over the years. 'In the end I was glad. But things weren't easy to begin with. There were problems.'

'What problems? Tell me while we wait to hear about Papa.'

* * *

I booked my seats on the train and packed my bags. I only realized how low I'd been feeling once they were piled up on the bed. It was a big room and I'd hated being the only person in it. Maybe one day Margaret and I would come back and stay here again, but somehow I doubted it. That time seemed to be over.

Anastasio and I drank a last coffee together and he gave me a salami sandwich wrapped in greaseproof paper. 'Take care, Caterina,' he said, kissing me lightly on both cheeks. 'Send me a postcard so I know you have arrived safely.'

In the months I'd spent in Rome I'd accumulated more than I really needed – clothes I'd stitched myself, second-hand books and a box of sewing things. I left most of it with Anastasio and only took what I could carry in the tiny duffel bag I'd brought from England.

I felt so alone walking up the crowded streets

towards Stazione Termini. I kept asking myself if I was doing the right thing, and dwelling on what might go wrong. As soon as I chased one worry out of my head another would replace it. By the time I found the railway station I was a bag of nerves. The place was seething with people, some of them travellers, others begging for small change. More than one suspicious-looking man cast a sidelong glance at me as I walked by. I held on tightly to my duffel bag and was glad I'd put most of my money in a belt I wore beneath my clothes.

Somehow I managed to buy a ticket and find the right platform. Once I was on the train I felt a little bit better. I'd taken the first step of my journey and for the next few hours all I had to do was sit there while the train rushed towards Naples.

The journey turned out to be nowhere near as difficult as I had imagined. At Naples I changed onto another train that was much older and very rattly, but it followed the coast and the views were enough to distract me from the occasional alarming swaying when we hit an uneven section of track. When I got off at a little station right by the sea I discovered I only had to wait an hour for the bus that would take me to Ravenno. I would be there before nightfall. That's when I wished it hadn't been so easy. I'd have liked a little more time to build up my courage before seeing Beppi and to decide what I was going to say.

I rehearsed in my head as the bus wound its way through the mountains towards Ravenno. I wouldn't mention Gianfranco and his strange behaviour, I promised myself, as we thundered through a long, dark tunnel. I wouldn't cling to Beppi or tell him that I loved him, I decided, as the bus slowed so the driver could shout a greeting at an old peasant tending a crop of onions on the rough ground beside his tumbledown stone house.

Once we had to stop because the road was full of goats. Even when the driver hooted his horn they refused to move, so some of the passengers at the front had to get out and shoo them away. The toothless old lady beside me wheezed with laughter and said something I couldn't understand in her fast, misshapen Italian. This seemed like another Italy, a different country. I wondered what Ravenno would be like.

We were still some distance away when I saw it. Perched on the top of a mountain, the houses were the same dusty grey as the rock they sprang out of. I couldn't see a hint of green anywhere. Just like Amalfi, the buildings seemed stacked one on top of the other, but their shutters were closed against the light. Surrounded by a high rock wall, the place looked cold and unfriendly.

'Next stop, Ravenno,' sang out the driver, and the engine screamed as the bus began to climb towards the town looming above us.

We stopped in a small piazza beneath Ravenno's walls. I was jostled and poked by people trying to get on the bus before I'd managed to jump off. An old man swore at me beneath his breath and his wife butted me with her basket.

I watched the bus leave, raising dust with its wheels, and then took a steep flight of crumbling steps towards the lowest street of the town. Although

I had Beppi's address, I had no idea how to find his mother's house. It didn't help that Ravenno was so confusing. The streets seemed to curve in circles and the houses weren't numbered properly. I might have asked for directions but there was hardly anyone around, just a few black-clad old women, who stared at me and then hurried away when I looked back at them.

I wandered around, hoping I'd stumble across Beppi's street or find an open shop or bar where someone might help me. But everything was closed, shuttered or dark. There were no smells of frying onions or roasting peppers like there were on every side street in Rome. I began to wonder what this place was and if I'd really find Beppi here.

At last I rounded a corner and found a lone market stall. It wasn't selling much, just a few lank bunches of spinach, some flaky red onions and a box of bruised tomatoes. There was an old, depressed-looking man sitting beneath a torn canopy beside it.

'*Buona sera*,' I said, and he looked up and grunted in reply.

I showed him Beppi's address and he grunted again. When he spoke it was as if he begrudged every word and I struggled to understand him. Finally he lost patience. Heaving himself up from his stool, he gripped my shoulder and pulled me over to the high wall that enclosed Ravenno. With a yellow finger he gestured towards a house halfway down a steep paddock beneath us. There were goats grazing on its low mossy roof and I could see one shuttered window set deep in the blackened old walls.

'Are you trying to tell me Beppi Martinelli lives there?' I asked, pointing towards the house.

He nodded, grunted again and went back to his lonely market stall.

For a moment I stood there, staring at what amounted to little more than a hut with a sagging roof that sloped down into the steep hill. I had known Beppi's family didn't have much money but still I had expected his mother to live somewhere better than this. Half of me wanted to run back to the piazza and see if there was another bus coming. But I was here now and if Beppi really was in that lonely little house then I wanted to see him.

Only as I grew closer did I realize just how rundown the place was. There was a couple of dusty olive trees growing out of a crumbling rock wall and I could hear chickens squawking. Beside the house was a small patch of earth that had been recently turned over and planted with some leafy vegetables that were still drooping from the day's heat.

'Beppi,' I called out, but there was no reply.

The shutters were ajar and I could smell the sharpness of tomatoes cooking down into a sauce.

'Hello, Beppi ... is there anybody here?'

I heard the front door creak open and a familiar voice said, 'Caterina?' but when I looked up it wasn't my Beppi standing there. His glossy curls looked unwashed and dull, his face was skimmed with stubble and he was wearing an old white vest splattered with yellowing tomato stains. 'Caterina?' he repeated, sounding amazed.

'Yes, it's me.' Despite all my rehearsing I didn't know what else to say.

'But …' Beppi opened the door a little wider and I caught a glimpse of the dingy room behind him. 'What are you doing here?'

'I don't know. I shouldn't have come.'

He took a step towards me and the door swung shut behind him. 'Are you all right?' he asked.

I shook my head. 'Not really.' And before I knew it my face was buried in his neck and his arms were reaching round my waist.

He smelled as always, musky and earthy like liquorice. I closed my eyes and breathed him in.

'Caterina, what has happened?' he murmured into my hair. 'Why have you come here?'

He walked me over to the low rock wall and sat me down. 'Tell me,' he urged.

And so I lay my cheek against his bare shoulder and told him how sad I'd been once everyone left me alone in Rome.

When I'd finished, he pulled his shoulder away from my face. 'I'm so happy to see you of course but …' he began awkwardly.

All my usual worries crowded into my head at once: he had another girl; he'd fallen out of love with me; he'd never really cared for me in the first place.

'But what?' I asked.

'I don't know where you're going to stay.'

'Can't I stay here?'

He clicked his tongue against his teeth in reply.

'Why not?'

'It's not the sort of place a girl like you stays in. And anyway, there is no space here.'

'I don't mind what it's like. I just want to be with you.'

He stood and held out his hand. 'Come and see, then.'

The house only had two rooms. In the first there was a small Formica table and four plastic-covered red chairs, a long narrow couch with hard cushions, a yellowed enamel sink and a gas stove with a pan of spaghetti sauce bubbling on it. The door to the second room was closed but Beppi pointed to it. 'That's where my mother and Isabella sleep. They share a bed. I sleep in here on the couch.'

He was right; there was no space for me.

'What will I do? … I hadn't thought …'

Beppi held his forefinger and thumb up to his nose while he considered the situation. Then he grinned, paused for a moment to stir the sauce and said, 'I have an idea – you can stay with Gianfranco's family.'

'No, I don't want to do that,' I said hurriedly. 'Isn't there an inn or a cheap hotel I could stay in for a couple of nights?'

'In Ravenno?' Beppi look wry. 'I don't think so. People don't come here for their holidays. You could go back to the coast and stay in a hotel there but you've missed the last bus back. No, Gianfranco's place is your only option.'

I looked down at the cracked tiled floor and the chicken roosting beneath the table. 'All right, I'll stay with Gianfranco's family if that's OK.'

Beppi smiled. 'Of course it will be OK. I've known

his parents since I was a boy. They're like my second family. Why don't I run up there now and let them know? You stay here and watch the sauce. Stir it now and then to stop it catching. I won't be too long.'

Left alone I took the opportunity to look around a little more. My own family weren't well off and there were times when my parents worried about paying the bills, but these people had nothing. On one wall there was a simple wooden cross and some colourful cards of saints. Against another was a very old dresser that contained a little chipped crockery, and hanging above it were a few black-and-white family photographs. I looked closely at a picture of a little boy smiling as he brought a forkful of spaghetti to his mouth. I was sure he must be a young Beppi. Beside it was a wedding portrait of a couple looking stiff and uncomfortable in their formal clothes. And next to that was a shot of Beppi and a girl I hoped was his sister. They were sitting on a Vespa together and laughing. Beyond those few things there was nothing to decorate the bare little room, not even any pretty curtains at the window.

I stirred the sauce and licked the edge of the wooden spoon. It tasted of basil and green olive oil, and I wondered if Beppi had made it.

From behind the closed door I heard the sound of someone coughing. I guessed it was his mother but didn't like to go in and check she was all right. I felt like an intruder and was beginning to wish I could just quietly slip away when the front door flew open and a young woman came in.

She wasn't pretty. Her nose was too broad and her teeth were crooked, but she had a vivacity about her that gave her face so much life you quickly forgot she was no beauty.

'Ah, it's true!' she said, smiling. 'I saw Beppi and he said you had come. The English girl I have heard so much about. I am Isabella and I'm so pleased to meet you.'

She untied the headscarf she wore over her glossy black curls and then came over and kissed me on both cheeks. 'I've never known my brother fall for a girl like this before. What have you done to him, eh, English?'

I didn't know what to say. 'My name is Catherine,' I managed at last. 'I met Beppi in Rome.'

'Yes, yes, English, I know all that. Now, come and meet Mamma. She will want to say hello to you.'

Isabella threw open the door to the second room and I saw a woman lying beneath a white sheet in a high double bed. She looked very old and I could easily have believed she was Beppi's grandmother rather than his mother.

'Mamma, look who is here. She couldn't stay away from our Beppi so she has come to find him,' Isabella called.

The old woman pulled herself up and lay back against a big pillow shaped like a sausage. She put a thin hand over her mouth and smiled at me. 'Welcome to my home,' she said, and her accent was so strong I struggled to understand her.

I never once saw Beppi's mother smile without first putting her hand over her mouth. She was ashamed of her missing teeth, I expect. But she always spoke and acted with tremendous dignity, even on the days when she was so sick she couldn't get out of bed.

'I'm sorry to appear without letting you know I was coming,' I told her in my stumbling Italian.

'Well, we are pleased to see you.'

'She's going to stay with the DeMatteo family, Mamma,' Isabella told her as she closed the window against the cool evening air. 'But she will eat dinner with us first. Beppi is cooking so I hope she likes our Italian food.'

We ate around the small kitchen table. First spaghetti with the sauce Beppi had made and then some spicy sausages he fried quickly with red onions, chilli and peppers. Before he'd started cooking he had shaved his stubble and slicked down his hair so he looked like my Beppi again.

As we ate and drank the rough red wine Isabella poured from a dusty, unlabelled bottle, I tried not to think about the night I was about to spend with Gianfranco's parents. I was dreading meeting them.

I found as many reasons as I could not to leave too early. First I helped Isabella wash up the dishes and then I went with her to feed the chickens. I would have stayed for longer but when he saw the moon hanging above Ravenno, Beppi insisted it was time for us to go.

'It's just for the night, Caterina,' he promised. 'I will come and get you first thing in the morning.'

We walked back up towards Ravenno and stopped to kiss when we reached the steep stairs that led into the town. We stayed there for a long time.

'I've missed you,' Beppi told me. 'I'm glad you came.'

*

Gianfranco's parents were as grey as the Ravenno stone their house was built from. Their narrow rooms were filled with solid pieces of dark wooden furniture, and the only one that felt truly lived in was the kitchen.

They had been waiting up for me. The moment I arrived they took me upstairs to the room I was to sleep in and left me there with a jug of cold water and a square of pressed white linen that I assumed was a towel. I was happy to be alone. All I wanted was to curl up in bed and think about Beppi's kisses as I slipped off to sleep.

Just as he'd promised, Beppi came to find me first thing in the morning. He was riding a Vespa he'd borrowed from his cousin and was grinning broadly.

'Come on, Caterina, I'm taking you to the beach.'

'But isn't that miles away?' I asked dubiously. 'Do we have to go back the way the bus came, along that winding road and through the tunnels?'

'Don't worry so much. It'll be fine. I've done it a hundred times.'

'All right,' I conceded. 'But don't go too fast.'

The beach he took me to was almost surrounded by a wall of rock and covered in fine pebbles instead of sand. We spent the day there, swimming in the sheltered waters and lying side by side in the sun. It felt so natural to let him rub oil on my shoulders or drop a kiss on my bare back. Not like those awkward times lying on beaches beside Gianfranco.

We ate lunch in a clifftop café shaded by pines. Wrapped in our towels, we munched on pizza covered in fresh tomatoes and basil, and sipped a drink that tasted of sweet lemons. It was there Beppi first told me that he loved me and I felt a little bubble of happiness pop inside me as I said I loved him in return.

'I don't have anything to offer you, though, Caterina,' he said sadly. 'No money, no house. You've seen how we live.'

'None of that matters.'

'Yes, it does,' he insisted. 'Eventually it does.'

'All I want is to be with you, Beppi.'

'In Ravenno?'

I thought of the low, two-roomed house in the shadow of the mountain town. He was right; I couldn't live there.

'But you said you'd be coming back to Rome?'

He looked troubled. 'I don't know what to do. My mother is still not well, as you saw, and it's hard on Isabella being the one who has to take care of her all the time. But there is no work for me in Ravenno.'

'What about here on the coast?'

'For summer maybe, but all this is closed in winter.'

'Come back to Rome,' I said selfishly. 'Your mother will be fine. Please come back.'

'We'll see,' he said, and then he smiled. 'Let's not think about it now. I want to go back down to the beach and enjoy the rest of our afternoon.'

I tried to relax as we lay on our towels and the sun warmed our bodies, but my mind was busy with thoughts and plans. There had to be a way that we could be together.

The next day we stayed in Ravenno and Beppi took me for a walk around the town. It was a desolate place filled with decaying buildings and old people who were suspicious of strangers.

'Where are all the young people?' I asked Beppi.

'They've left to find work. Some have gone to America or England. Others just to Naples or Rome like me. There's nothing for them here.'

'Would you come to England?' I was hopeful.

'I'd like to see it some day, but who would look after Mamma and Isabella? Anyway, people say it's cold there and the food is bad.'

I'd been in Ravenno four days and was helping Isabella in the vegetable garden when we heard a car pull up outside.

'I wonder who that is?' Isabella said, putting down her trowel. And then a smile spread across her face and she squealed, 'Gianfranco, is it you? At last you've come home to us.'

She ran to him and put her arms around his wide body. Seeing his shiny car, she squealed again and jumped into the passenger seat. Putting her feet up on the dashboard, she demanded, 'Take me for a ride.'

But Gianfranco didn't seem interested. He was looking at me.

'So this is where you've been hiding, Caterina.'

I tried not to make it obvious how unhappy I was to see him. 'That's right. I came down to see Beppi.'

'And you're staying at my parents' house, I hear.'

'There was no room for me here.'

'Gianfranco!' Isabella demanded his attention. 'You can talk to English later. It's me you haven't seen for months. Take me for a ride!'

'OK, OK, give me a minute. Why do you always have to be so noisy, Isabella?'

She looked hurt for a moment but then she bounced back. 'I have to be noisy to get your attention. Will you give me the keys? Will you let me drive? Go on, Gianfranco, I've never driven a car before.'

As I watched them drive away I realized I hated Gianfranco. It took me by surprise because I wasn't used to feeling like that about anyone.

I thought about saying something to Beppi. But they'd known each other since childhood and he wouldn't want to hear anything bad about his friend.

Beppi had gone to buy some meat for dinner because he liked to choose the food himself. When he got back he would be happy to see Gianfranco. I didn't want to spoil that happiness.

In retrospect I wished I had. If I'd had any idea then of what was about to happen I'd have told Beppi how I felt about his friend.

Of course, the next day Gianfranco wanted all four of us to go to the beach together in his car. Isabella was excited and Beppi pleased because it meant we could travel further down the coast to where there were sandier, prettier beaches than the one he'd taken me to.

'It's so beautiful, Caterina. Just wait,' he said happily.

I sat in the back with Isabella, who bounced up and down and sang most of the way. She hadn't had much fun in life. Her days were filled with housework and looking after her mother. So I was glad to see her enjoying herself, and tried to smile and join in with the singing.

Isabella clung to Gianfranco, although I could tell he wasn't interested in her. She insisted on linking arms with him as we took the steep path down the cliff to the beach and she put her towel next to his on the sand. But I was certain Gianfranco's eyes were on me. He talked to Beppi, gossiping about people they knew from the hotel and boasting about his car. But it was me he watched.

Beppi hadn't noticed. He was happy to be here on a hot summer's day with the people he loved most. He ran into the sea, yelling at the top of his voice, and dived beneath the waves. I saw the water running off his slim, hard body as he resurfaced.

'My brother, he's a madman,' Isabella murmured fondly.

Gianfranco rolled his eyes. 'Do you think he will ever grow up?'

We spent all day there, sunning ourselves and swimming. In the afternoon Isabella went for a long walk along the tide-line, splashing through the shallow water. She wanted Gianfranco to go with her but he only went a little way before turning back.

'Your sister likes Gianfranco a lot,' I said as I watched him walking down the beach towards us.

'She's always had a crush on him,' Beppi agreed, 'even when we were small. Poor Isabella. What are the chances of her finding a husband in a town like Ravenno?'

'Maybe she will marry Gianfranco?'

'I don't think so. He is fond of her but I can't imagine him settling for a girl from Ravenno.'

In the car on the way home I watched Isabella. She was one of those people who chose to be happy unless she had a good reason not to be. Always laughing, always telling jokes. She was like Beppi in many ways but not blessed with his good looks. I hoped she did find someone who would love her but privately agreed it was unlikely to be Gianfranco.

The next night Isabella wanted to go out in the car again. 'Let's go for a moonlight drive,' she urged us. 'Mamma will be fine on her own for a few hours.'

The thought of careering round those hairpin bends after dark horrified me and I glanced over at Beppi. 'But we left your mother alone all day yesterday,' I said. 'I don't mind staying here with her if you all want to go.'

Beppi was torn. He knew he ought to chaperone his sister but I suppose he thought Gianfranco was more like a second brother to her. And anyway, he preferred to be with me. So we stayed at the house and, once his mother was asleep, spent our time talking and kissing.

It grew late and both of us started listening for the sound of Gianfranco's car returning. 'I hope they're OK. He drives like a madman sometimes,' I said.

Beppi looked worried. 'He'll take care with my sister in the car,' he said without much conviction.

An hour later there was still no sign of them and Beppi was no longer trying to hide how anxious he was. Every few minutes he jumped up and went to look outside, thinking he'd heard a car pull up.

'Maybe the car has broken down,' I said. 'Once, when Gianfranco took me out, it wouldn't start.'

'Maybe,' said Beppi, but he didn't sound as if he believed it.

When it was time for me to leave he walked me through the dark back to Gianfranco's parents' house. There was no stopping on the steps to kiss and, as he said goodnight to me, his voice sounded tense.

No one was waiting up for me so I let myself in and went straight to bed. I lay awake, hoping to hear Gianfranco come in, but there was no sign of him.

It was late when I drifted off to sleep in the narrow single bed and early when I woke. I could hear someone moving around downstairs and knew it was Gianfranco's mother mopping floors or scrubbing down walls. All she ever seemed to do was clean.

'Where's Gianfranco?' I asked her when I got downstairs.

She shrugged. 'In bed, I suppose.'

I didn't like the idea of going into his bedroom but I wanted to make sure he and Isabella had made it home safely so I went back upstairs and hesitantly pushed open his door.

There was a musky stale smell and I could see his bag on the floor with clothes spilling out of it. But although his bedclothes were rumpled, there was no sign of Gianfranco.

Usually in the mornings I hung about until Beppi came to get me but today I couldn't wait. I ran down the Ravenno steps and kept on running until I reached his cottage.

His mother was sitting outside in an old cane chair

with a rug over her knees. It was the first time I'd known her to leave the house, and her skin, always pale, was now chalky white.

'Beppi isn't here,' she explained, speaking slowly in her heavily accented Italian so I could understand her. 'He's borrowed his cousin's Vespa and gone to see if he can find Isabella. She and Gianfranco didn't come home last night.'

I made her a cup of coffee she didn't drink and tried to comfort her with stories of how unreliable Gianfranco's car was. But after a while we stopped trying to talk and waited together in silence.

After several hours we heard Beppi return.

'I've ridden all the roads around Ravenno but they must have gone further,' he said, looking grim.

'What shall we do?' I asked.

'I don't know. They could be anywhere.'

His mother and I sat there looking at him, waiting for him to come up with a plan. We were talking about whether he should aim for the coast or head further into the mountains when we heard the squeal of tyres followed by the slamming of a car door.

All of us, even his mother, ran out to the road. We got there in time to see Gianfranco's car disappearing and found Isabella sitting in the dust, tears running down her cheeks. 'He doesn't want me, he doesn't want me,' she kept repeating.

Somehow we got her inside and lay her down on the hard couch. I gave her a glass of water while her mother bathed the tears from her cheeks and stroked her hair. 'It's all right, it's all right,' she kept repeating.

Only Beppi hung back. Without either of us notic-ing he slipped out of the cottage.

It took a while for Isabella's hysteria to subside. Her mother didn't ask any questions, just stroked her hair until eventually she fell asleep. I wasn't sure what to do. Everyone but me seemed to understand what had happened.

When Beppi returned he was holding my little duf-fel bag. 'You'll stay here tonight,' he told me.

'But where will she sleep?' asked his mother. She had collapsed onto one of the kitchen chairs and put her head in her hands. I saw now that she'd been cry-ing, too.

'None of us will get much sleep so it doesn't matter,' he replied.

That day it felt as if someone had died. All of us moved around the house softly, hardly speaking. I spent the afternoon weeding a patch of garden so Beppi could plant out vegetables there. It seemed bet-ter to stay out of the family's way. We ate very little, just a bowl of spaghetti at dinnertime that hardly any of us touched.

When it grew dark Beppi threw a blanket over Isabella, who was still lying on the couch, and made up a bed for himself on the floor. I'd never seen him like this before. His expression was fierce and even the way he moved had a fury about it. When he told me it would be best if I slept with his mother, I was horrified but didn't dare argue.

So I crept in beside her in the spot Isabella usually occupied and lay, stiff and uncomfortable, listening to her laboured breathing. She slept with her arms thrown above her head and made little whimpering sounds every now and then.

Daybreak wasn't far away when I heard her whisper, 'Caterina, are you awake?'

'Yes,' I whispered back.

'You must leave on the first bus. Go back to Rome.'

'But I don't understand. What has happened?'

I couldn't see her face but her voice was harsh and bitter. 'Gianfranco has disgraced my daughter,' she said. Turning her back on me, she pushed her face into the pillow.

* * *

Even Pieta knew that things had been different back then, especially in Italy. A girl didn't spend a night with a boy unless she was married to him. As she thought about the Gianfranco DeMatteo she knew, a middle-aged man behind a glass counter filled with sides of ham and rounds of cheese, she wondered how Isabella could have been so in love she risked everything for him.

15

The nurse came into the waiting area wearing a smile so practised it was almost part of her uniform. It was impossible to tell anything from it.

'Mrs Martinelli?'

'Yes, that's me.' Catherine jumped up from her seat.

'I just came to tell you that everything went well. Mr Martinelli is in recovery now. He has to lie completely still for a few hours and we'll be checking his heart rate and blood pressure regularly.'

'When can he come home?' Pieta asked.

'Not for a couple of days. We'll keep him under observation and make sure his drug therapy is established.'

'Can we see him? We don't mind waiting.'

The nurse gave her mother an appraising look. 'You'd be better off taking Mrs Martinelli home, I think,' she told Pieta. 'Her colour doesn't look so good to me. Have a rest and then come back in the morning when he'll be up and about and feeling chipper.'

'I don't feel right not seeing him ...' Catherine insisted. 'I'd rather wait if you don't mind.'

'Well, it's up to you, of course.' The nurse shrugged. 'But this was a very routine procedure and Mr

Martinelli didn't have any bad reactions to it so there's really nothing to worry about.'

'Come on, Mamma.' Pieta took her arm. 'Let's go home. The nurse is right, you do look awful. Now we know that Papa is out of danger maybe you can have a decent sleep and then you'll feel so much better.'

Her mother must have been exhausted. She fell asleep in the taxi and Pieta felt terrible having to wake her when they pulled up outside the house. She put her to bed and then made some tea, but when she took it upstairs she found Catherine had already fallen asleep again.

Pieta left the tea and went to the sewing room. The thought of beading without the distraction of her mother's story was unappealing and, for the first time, Pieta regretted attempting something so ambitious. Addolorata had no idea how much time and work was going into this gown. She thought she was the busy one, running Little Italy. She would never appreciate what Pieta was doing so that she looked beautiful on her wedding day.

An hour or so after she'd started work, Pieta heard the creak of floorboards and realized her mother was already awake again.

'What are you doing up so soon?' she asked when Catherine came in carrying a fresh cup of tea.

'I rang the hospital to check your father was OK and they said he is sleeping but that everything's fine. I don't want to go back to bed yet. I thought I'd sit here and talk to you for a bit. I wanted to tell you what happened after Gianfranco disgraced Isabella. I've been lying there thinking about it.'

Pieta smiled. She was pleased her mother wanted to continue with the story. She'd been wondering what had happened next. 'Did you leave Ravenno like you were told to?' she asked. 'Or did you stay with Papa?'

Catherine settled in the armchair in the corner of the room and cradled the mug of tea in her hands. 'How could I stay after what had taken place? I had no choice but to go. I wasn't welcome there any longer.'

* * *

As soon as I heard the first birds singing I slipped out of bed and found my duffel bag. Beppi and Isabella were just two huddled shapes and neither moved as I tiptoed past them and out of the door. I was scared by what had happened and didn't want to witness any more of this family's heartbreak, so I left without saying goodbye.

All the way to Rome I tried only to think of practical things. I totted up how much money I had, planned for how I might earn more and worried about finding myself a place to live. If I thought about Beppi waking to find me gone or allowed myself to wonder when I might see him again, warm tears would start to seep from my eyes and I had to hide my face from the other passengers.

It seemed such a defeat to be sitting on that train heading back to the city. I couldn't help suspecting Gianfranco had known it would happen. Why else would he have spent the night with Isabella if he didn't love her and had no intention of marrying her?

Anastasio's bar was the first place I went when I arrived in Rome. It was reassuring to be back there, surrounded by all the mirrors, chrome and little red booths. Things had changed so much for me in those few days that somehow I felt the rest of the world might have changed, too. But Anastasio's place was just the same, of course.

He seemed pleased to see me and kissed me quickly on both cheeks.

'Margaret has been looking for you,' he told me. 'She is back from Battipaglia and staying at Signora Lucy's.'

I was so pleased I almost kissed him again. If Margaret was back in Rome then maybe things weren't so bleak after all. Grabbing my duffel bag, I ran down the alleyway and up the dark stairs. One of Signora Lucy's girls answered my knock on the big wooden door.

'*Ciao, bella*,' she said casually.

I found Margaret in a room that was smaller than our old one. She seemed relieved to see me. We sat side by side on one of the narrow single beds, leaning back against the wall, and talked ourselves nearly hoarse.

It turned out she'd had a terrible time in Battipaglia. The rich family's holiday house was rundown and full of mice. The children ran wild and she was expected to chase after them from dawn till dusk. Worst of all, they'd made her wear her starched white uniform every day and when she went for the bicycle rides that were her only way of escaping the house for an hour or two, the long skirt had caught in the wheels

'That's it. I've had it with being a nanny,' she told me. 'I'm going to resign first thing tomorrow morning.'

'What will you do instead?'

'Go home, of course. What's the point of staying here? Audrey has gone and it was all her idea in the first place. We should both go home.'

'But I can't, not yet.'

Margaret rolled her eyes. 'You're not still waiting around for Beppi? Isn't it about time you gave up on him?'

She was astonished when I told her about my trip to Ravenno. I don't think she'd expected me to have the nerve to travel so far alone.

'I still think you should come home with me,' she said when I'd finished. 'Write to Beppi and give him your address in London. If he really loves you then he'll come to find you.'

'It's not that simple for him. He has his mother to think of ... and his sister.'

'The thing is, Catherine, you can't stay in Rome waiting for him for ever. How do you even know he's going to come back?'

She was right, of course. But as well as being braver than she'd imagined, I was also much more stubborn. 'I don't care, I'm not leaving,' I insisted. 'And I don't think you should go yet, either. You've been so busy working that you've hardly seen anything of Rome. Why don't we stay a few more weeks? We could have such a good time together.'

'Oh, Catherine, I don't know ...' Margaret sounded weary and fed up.

'Please,' I begged. 'We might never come back to Rome again. This may be our last chance to really enjoy it.'

For some reason I had always been able to persuade Margaret round to my way of thinking. Most likely she was too nice to say no.

'All right, then.' She sounded reluctant. 'Just for a few more weeks, though, and then I'm going home with you or without you.'

I hoped this would give me the time I needed. In the morning I would mail a letter to Beppi telling him if he didn't come soon then I would be gone. It was a gamble. I knew he had other things to worry about – his sister's disgrace, his mother's illness, his friend's betrayal. Most probably I was the last thing on his mind. But as Margaret said, I couldn't wait for him for ever.

In some ways those next few weeks were the best yet. It was as if we were saying goodbye to Rome. Each morning Margaret and I woke early, drank a coffee with Anastasio and then set off on foot to explore a different part of the city. One day we might walk the narrow backstreets of Trastevere, the next stare at the riches of the Vatican or sit at a street café on the Via Veneto and pretend we were movie stars. Always there were Italian boys offering admiring whistles and promising to show us parts of the city we'd never find alone. But we only smiled, shook our heads and walked on – Margaret because her mind was set on going home and finding a nice English boy to settle down with, and me thinking only of Beppi and wondering if he'd received my letter.

I had heard nothing from him and, as each day passed, began to lose hope that he would ever come. I never said anything to Margaret and she didn't mention it, but both of us were thinking the same thing: he had forgotten me.

So when a furious Signora Lucy hammered on our door late one evening we both got such a fright we thought a fire had broken out or someone had been murdered.

'I told you no men,' she shrieked at me when I opened the door.

'There are no men here. Look.' I opened the door wider so she could see inside. 'Just me and Margaret.'

'He is outside the front door asking for you.'

'Who is? Beppi?'

I didn't even bother to check that I looked presentable. Pushing past Signora Lucy, I ran down the stairs. 'No men,' she yelled after me. 'He mustn't come inside.'

When I saw it really was him I almost cried. There were violet shadows beneath his eyes and he looked sad and worn down.

'Caterina, I'm so sorry,' he said. 'I got your letter weeks ago and it's taken me so long to come. Thank you for waiting for me.'

He stepped forward, almost over the threshold. Behind me I heard a shriek from Signora Lucy. Pushing him back with the flat of my hand, I closed the door behind me. 'Not here,' I told him. 'Let's go to Anastasio's bar. You can have a drink and tell me what's been happening.'

The bar was noisy, with the jukebox blaring out songs. But we found an empty booth and huddled close together. I felt Beppi's lips brush my hair and he slipped his arm around me and squeezed my shoulder.

'It has been a disaster, Caterina,' he told me. 'I feel like I have lost my sister and my best friend. Now I only have you.'

Slowly he gave me the whole story. The night of their moonlight drive Isabella and Gianfranco had gone all the way to the coast and walked on the beach together. When they'd got back in the car Gianfranco hadn't been able to start it. He'd declared they'd have to spend the night there and find a mechanic in the morning. I think I may have gasped when I heard that, but I said nothing about my own experience in Amalfi.

Beppi wasn't sure exactly what had happened in the car that night. Neither Gianfranco nor Isabella would speak of it. But in some ways it didn't really matter. She had spent the night alone with a man and that meant she was ruined in the eyes of everyone that mattered. No other man would touch her now.

'Fifteen, twenty years ago the solution would have been simple,' said Beppi bitterly. 'The Carabinieri would have fetched Gianfranco and he'd have been forced to marry my sister. Maybe I could have made him do it. But my mother said no. She preferred Isabella to be alone rather than have anything more to do with him.'

Still Beppi hadn't been satisfied. He had to have some sort of revenge. So late one night he had stolen Gianfranco's car, parked it in the piazza just below Ravenno and set it on fire. Half the town had come out to look. But Gianfranco and his family had slept through the whole thing and woke in the morning to find the car nothing but twisted black metal and ash. Apparently Gianfranco cried when he saw it.

'I don't care,' declared Beppi. 'He ruined something of mine, so I destroyed something of his.'

'So now you are even?'

'Of course not.' Beppi sounded scathing. 'He ruined my sister. We will never be even. The worse thing is she really thought he loved her. It was only as he drove her back the next morning that he told her he is in love with someone else.'

'Who?' I asked, dreading the answer.

Beppi shrugged. 'I have no idea. When we were in Rome together I never saw him with a girl. He was always hanging around with us on his days off, remember?'

If there was a moment when I might have told Beppi the truth about his friend then this was it. But I didn't dare. He had already burned a car. What sort of revenge would he exact if he knew Gianfranco had also tried to spend a night with me? So I stayed quiet.

'What will you do now?' I asked instead.

'Find work as quickly as I can.'

'Here in Rome?'

'Yes, of course,' he replied, squeezing my shoulder again. 'So we can be together again, Caterina.'

'But Margaret and me, we're leaving Rome. I've only stayed all this time to wait for you. It will be winter soon. It's time for us to go back home.'

He looked confused. 'I thought you wanted to be with me.'

'I do. But you could come back to London, too. You'd earn more money there and you'd be far away

197

from Ravenno and Gianfranco. Won't you at least think about it?'

He agreed that he would, although I was certain he was just humouring me. Beppi had never left Italy before. Rome was the furthest he'd been from home.

He kissed me goodbye at the foot of Signora Lucy's stairs. I wouldn't let him come any further in case she started having hysterics again.

'Where will you stay tonight?' I asked.

'With a waiter from the hotel I used to work in. Tomorrow I'll go and see if I can get my old job back.'

'What if they say no?'

'Then I'll keep looking. Don't worry, I'll find something. Meet me at Anastasio's bar tomorrow evening and I'll let you know how I've got on.'

Margaret was in bed when I got in. 'Catherine, is that you?' she asked sleepily. 'What happened?'

I sat on her mattress and she curled her legs around me while I told her about my night.

She was silent for a while after I'd finished. 'What will your parents say?'

'What do you mean?'

'If you arrive home with an Italian boy you say you love, how will they react?'

I'd spent so much time worrying about other things but for some reason I'd never considered my parents. Now suddenly, thanks to Margaret, I could see so many more problems standing in our way. Not only was Beppi Italian but he was Catholic. That might not go down well with my father, a staunch Protestant.

My parents had always been plain-living, honest people. Dad's idea of excitement was doing the football pools or playing darts in the corner pub. Mum liked a cup of tea and a quiet time in their narrow little house on Balls Pond Road. Beppi wouldn't fit into their world.

'I don't care,' I told Margaret. 'They can't stop me being with him.'

'No, but are you sure this isn't just a holiday romance? What if you do persuade Beppi to go to England and then decide you don't love him after all? Wouldn't it be better if you left him here and just had happy memories of him?'

'No.' I couldn't believe she was saying all this.

'Come back with me and we'll both go on the hunt for a couple of nice English boys,' said Margaret. 'Who'd want to settle down with an Italian anyway? They all have terrible tempers and they're always on the edge of hysteria. I wouldn't want an Italian boy, however nice he might be. I think tomorrow we should find out how much it would cost us to get to Calais by train. And we should leave as soon as we can.'

I went back to my own bed and lay listening to Margaret's even breathing as she drifted off to sleep. If she wanted to leave Rome so badly that was fine. Everything she had said had been true but I didn't care. I'd made up my mind.

Beppi was full of excitement when I met up with him the next night at Anastasio's bar. His old manager at the hotel had been glad to see him. Not only was there a job for him but, even better, he'd been promoted.

Now he had Gianfranco's old position as a *chef de rang* and he would be responsible for six tables, serving the vegetables, meat and fish from a silver salver, or cooking crêpe Suzette at the *gueridon* beside the table.

The whole thing was a performance really and everything had to be done very precisely. For example they might bring in a whole salmon that had been steamed with celery and onion and decorated with slices of lemon. All around it were little jugs full of different sauces – lemon and butter, horseradish, or mayonnaise with mustard. Beppi's job was to carve off a boneless piece of fillet and then serve the chosen sauce. It had to be arranged on the plate beautifully and the whole time Vittorio, the head waiter, would be watching to make sure he did nothing wrong.

'It's a big promotion,' he told me proudly. 'Normally a commis like me would be promoted to demi-chef first and then you only get to serve the tourists. But all the high-class people will be at my tables. It's more money, too, Caterina, so if I'm careful I should be able to save as well as send some home to Ravenno. But it means I won't be able to come to England, at least not yet.'

'One day, though?'

He smiled and kissed me, but he didn't say yes.

It was a cool evening. Autumn was coming to Rome and already the smart women had changed into their woollen suits and elegant knits. I only had the cotton skirts and dresses I'd made for myself and had been feeling chilly all day, so when Beppi suggested we leave Anastasio's bar and take a walk around Piazza Navona I wasn't keen.

'But it's warm in here,' I said. 'Why don't we get another drink and stay where we are?'

'No, no.' Beppi seemed jumpy and excited. 'Let's go for a walk. Piazza Navona looks so pretty after dark with all the fountains lit up.'

'But I'll freeze in this thin dress.'

'We'll warm up quickly, you'll see.'

As always I couldn't resist him. Within ten minutes I was walking through Piazza Navona with my arm through his. There were still people at the street cafés, eating late suppers or enjoying a *digestivo*. And there were other couples walking hand in hand or sitting by the fountains.

Beppi was silent and seemed distracted as we circled the piazza. I wondered what was wrong and whether he was brooding about his sister's problems.

'Do you remember the first time you saw me when I was drinking expensive coffee outside the café with Audrey and Margaret?' I asked, trying to take his mind off things.

'Yes, of course I remember.' He smiled. 'It seems like a long time ago, doesn't it?'

'Not so long really, just a few months,' I reminded him.

'Long enough, though.' We stopped beside the fountain that had always been our meeting point and Beppi tilted his face towards me.

'Long enough for what?' I asked.

'For me to know how much I love you.' His voice was quiet and I almost had to strain to hear it.

'I love you, too, Beppi.' I was happy to tell him that again and again.

He stared at me for a moment as if he was trying to decide what to say next. 'I don't have much, Caterina, you saw that,' he began. 'But with this new promotion I may have some prospects. So what I want to know is ...'

'Yes?'

'I don't even have a ring to give you but ... will you marry me, Caterina?'

For a moment I was too stunned to speak.

'Caterina?' he prompted in a strained, anxious voice.

'Yes, yes, I will. Of course, I will.'

'Really?' He seemed incredulous.

'Yes, really.'

He let out a big whoop. 'She's going to marry me,' he shouted to the people sitting at the pavement café. 'Aren't I the luckiest man on earth?'

And they cheered and called, '*Auguri!*'

I was a little embarrassed, especially when someone sent a waiter out with two celebratory glasses of prosecco for us. But as we sat by the fountain, sipping the bubbles, I felt as happy as any girl who has just got engaged. I didn't care that I had no ring on my finger or think about the problems that might lie ahead for us. I was only interested in the feeling of being a girl that someone loved. A girl with a fiancé.

We didn't even talk about wedding dates. Both of us were content just to be together, enjoying the little piece of happiness we'd made for each other.

It was late when he left me with a kiss outside Signora Lucy's. As I'd known she would be, Margaret was fast asleep, her packed suitcases piled at the foot of her bed. She had discovered she had enough money for the train and boat fare home and was leaving in the morning. I'd been feeling sad at the thought of saying goodbye to another friend, but now all that had been pushed out of my mind because Beppi had chosen me. He would be my family now as well as my friend. I lay awake half the night thinking about him.

16

The next morning I needed plenty of Anastasio's strong coffee to startle me out of sleepiness. Margaret and I had decided to have a last breakfast together before she caught her taxi to Stazione Termini. We splashed out on some little *cornetti* dusted with icing sugar and oozing with custard. And Anastasio brought us some pastries filled with chocolate and nuts and said they were his treat.

'I'll miss these,' Margaret sighed. 'And I'll miss the fresh mozzarella and the little squares of pizza from the shop down the road.'

She had put on a little weight in Italy but it suited her.

'It'll be mashed potatoes with sausages in onion gravy for you in a couple of days,' I reminded her.

She frowned. 'I know, and I'm not looking forward to it. I wish we had Italian food back home. I'd never eat anything else.'

I didn't care about food the way she did but I could see how even the poorest Italian families ate better than the English. They might be simple dishes but they were always bursting with the flavours of garlic or basil, and each mouthful was relished not forked down dutifully.

'Maybe you could make Italian food at home?' I suggested.

'Where would I even buy the ingredients? No, it'll be sausages in onion gravy just as you said.'

I didn't say anything to her about Beppi's proposal. I was afraid she wouldn't be excited for me and that she'd have something sensible to say that I preferred not to hear. So far the only people who knew were the strangers outside the café and I thought it best to keep it that way until I'd written to tell my parents the news.

We loaded Margaret's suitcases into the boot of a taxi and I said goodbye to her on the pavement.

'I'll see you soon,' she said, hugging me.

'Yes, I expect so,' I replied.

As the taxi pulled away I felt completely alone once more. But then I reminded myself that I had Beppi now and he was going to look after me.

It helped that there was a letter waiting for me when I got back to Signora Lucy's. It was covered in American stamps and had Audrey's neat, cursive writing on the envelope. I couldn't wait the few minutes it would take to run up to my room so I tore it open and read it right there in the hallway with Signora Lucy's girls coming and going.

Dear Catherine and Margaret,

Sorry it's taken me so long to write but I'm so busy there never seems to be a good time to sit down with a pen and paper. First of all I expect you'll want to know about me and Louis. Well, we're married … and I'm pregnant! I'm having a honeymoon baby, which wasn't really what I intended, but Louis is happy enough for both of us.

I'll admit at first I thought coming here had been a mistake. When he came to meet me off the boat, Louis' hair was much longer and out of uniform he looked a bit scruffy. And then we went back to his mother's apartment in Brooklyn and she didn't exactly make me feel welcome. I was just about ready to pack it all in but then Louis took me to Coney Island for the day and we had such a good time. That's when I remembered why I'd fallen for him.

Anyway, his mother has warmed up a bit since we got married. We're still living with her and I hope to God we can afford a place of our own before too long. Louis is working extra shifts down at the docks to save money and I've been waitressing in a diner. It's a bit like Anastasio's bar with mirrors and little booths, but the customers all ask for thing like 'eggs over easy' and the coffee tastes awful.

I think about you girls all the time and remember our adventures. Wasn't it the best fun? Even though things are a bit tougher now, I'm glad I came to New York. Louis and me are madly in love and I know as soon as we escape the old harridan things will be perfect.

Write to me soon and let me know how you're getting on. I miss you both so much.

Love Audrey

Reading Audrey's letter strengthened my resolve. If she can do it then I can, too, I told myself. That afternoon I sat down and wrote a letter to her in reply. It went on for pages and pages and I told her everything, even the news that Beppi and I were engaged. It felt good to share it with someone and I was sure she wouldn't have any difficulty understanding how I felt. After all, she had done more or less the same thing.

The letter to my parents was more difficult. Part of me was frightened to write it in case they somehow tried to stop me marrying Beppi. I didn't know if I could make them understand how wonderful he was or just how much I loved him. Nothing I wrote seemed right, so I crumpled my first attempts into little balls and gave up. As the days went by I made excuses for myself. I had started working for Anastasio again and was tired and busy. Signora Lucy had asked me to make her some more cushion covers. One of the girls wanted a red dress. There was always something else I could find to do.

It was about a fortnight after Beppi's proposal that I first thought I'd seen Gianfranco. He was standing at the end of the alleyway that led to Signora Lucy's. When he realized he'd been spotted he disappeared. He must have run fast because there was no sign of him when I got out onto the street.

I thought I saw him again two days later in the middle of a swirl of tourists as I walked through Piazza Navona. Then, when I was buying myself some flowers at the market in Campo dei Fiori, I turned to find him a few feet behind me. Again he darted away as soon as he realized he'd been seen.

I started to worry that he was following me but I was too scared to say anything to Beppi. I was certain he had no idea Gianfranco was back in Rome. So I stayed quiet but whenever I was out alone I found my eyes sweeping through the crowds, looking for his face.

There were times I imagined I'd seen him and it turned out to be someone else. I started to feel nervy and uncomfortable whenever I went out. It seemed easier to stay in my room or at Anastasio's bar unless Beppi was with me.

With his first wage packet he had bought me a thick winter coat. 'I'm sorry it's not an engagement ring but I thought you needed this more right now,' he said, smiling.

It was blue with a fur-trimmed collar and I loved it. All the same, when I unwrapped it my stomach turned over. If Beppi had bought me a coat it was because he expected me to spend the whole winter in Rome.

All my problems began to pile up on top of me. While I was sewing in my room or pouring drinks for Anastasio's customers my mind was free to worry. I began waking in the middle of the night and I'd torment myself with worries until the light crept through the cracks in Signora Lucy's shutters and I heard the birds start singing.

Still I said nothing to Beppi. Even though we were engaged I felt I might lose him if I wasn't careful.

I loved spending time with him. Some nights when he wasn't working we would walk up to the streets around Stazione Termini where there were dozens of inexpensive little restaurants. Beppi always knew where to find the best food. Often I would only manage a little pasta with tomatoes and basil while he ate his way through plates of tripe or liver, slow-roasted piglet and hard crusty bread, or bowls of plump little baby squid.

Beppi ate fast with his head held low over the plate like a person who had known what it was like to be hungry. He always wanted to talk about the dishes he'd tried. The whole way back to Piazza Navona he'd tell me about the flavours he'd picked out and imagine what the chef had used to flavour a sauce, or rhapsodize over pork that had been roasted so slowly and so long that the meat was shredded and sticky. It amazed me that he could bear to think about food after serving it to other people all day but he never grew tired of it.

Even though I was always looking out for him, I never once saw Gianfranco when Beppi was with me. Perhaps he was there somewhere in the shadows of an alleyway, slyly watching us, but he kept himself hidden.

I started to feel safe again, protected by Beppi, Anastasio and Signora Lucy, even though none of them knew it. But then one day I was alone behind the counter at the bar. Anastasio had slipped out to buy a newspaper and, when I looked up from what I was doing, there was Gianfranco standing in the doorway, staring at me.

He looked different. All his puppy fat had gone and there were new lines around his eyes. For a moment neither of us spoke.

'Caterina,' he said at last. His voice was low and he said my name slowly.

'What do you want, Gianfranco?' I sounded braver than I felt.

'He took my job, you know.' He came a little closer. 'He took you and then he took my job.'

Through the window I saw Anastasio crossing the street, a newspaper tucked under his arm.

'Go away.' I raised my voice. 'Just go away.'

Who knows what he had been planning? Fortunately, when Anastasio came in and gave him a sidelong look, Gianfranco backed away.

'I'll see you later, Caterina, OK?' he called over his shoulder as he left.

Anastasio threw his newspaper down on the bar. 'What is he doing back here?'

'I don't know.'

'So why were you shouting at him when I came in?'

I wanted to tell him. My worries had been stored up for so long that I needed to share them with someone but Anastasio, no matter how kind he had been, was still almost a stranger.

'Oh … nothing important,' I muttered, and went back to polishing glasses.

Anastasio shook his head. 'I don't like that boy. There's something not right about him,' he said. And then he picked up his copy of *Il Messagero* and went off to read it in the far booth where he knew he'd find some peace and quiet.

It was about a week later that Beppi came into the bar, distraught. He sat down at the counter and his hands began shaking when he tried to lift the drink I'd poured him.

'I've lost my job, Caterina,' he told me. 'They've sacked me.'

'What? How could they sack you?'

'They accused me of stealing but I didn't do it.' He put his head in his hands. 'I didn't do it, Caterina, honestly.'

Slowly I coaxed the story from him. Vittorio, the head waiter, hadn't taken his eyes off him all day, and Beppi had made certain to do an especially good job. At the end of his shift Vittorio followed him to the small cloakroom where all the waiters kept their street clothes.

'He told me there had been reports that someone in the restaurant was stealing. The very next moment I put on my coat and a fork fell out of my pocket. There were other things stuffed in there – knives, a spoon, a small jug – all the best silverware. But I didn't put it there and I don't know who would. Who could hate me that much, Caterina?'

I knew the answer but I was still afraid to say. It was Anastasio who came to my rescue. He poured a big glass of whisky for Beppi and then said quietly, 'Your friend Gianfranco, that's who.'

Beppi's head snapped up fast and his eyes widened. 'Gianfranco? But he isn't even in Rome.'

Anastasio only raised his eyebrows. Then he turned to me and said, 'Catherine, I think you two have things you need to talk about. Why don't you let Beppi drink his whisky and then take him for a walk round the piazza? I'll manage here alone.'

So I wrapped my blue coat around me and brushed my cheek against its soft fur collar. I was nervous but I knew Anastasio was right. It was time I told Beppi everything.

We sat beside the fountain, our moods so very much bleaker than they had been the last time we were there. As I told him about his friend's fumbling attempts to spend a night with me in his car, Beppi became angrier than I'd ever seen him.

'Why didn't you tell me sooner?'

'I was afraid.'

He swore beneath his breath. '*Cose da pazzi*. Don't you see what you've done? If you'd told me all this, it might have saved my sister.'

'I'm sorry.'

'Sorry? Yes, I'm sure you are.' His voice sounded bitter. It was almost as though he blamed me for what had happened, as though I'd courted Gianfranco's attention. The unfairness of it swamped me but I could see that this was no time to argue with him.

'Maybe if you explain it to them, they'll give you your job back,' I said instead.

He shook his head. 'You only get one chance in this business. I'm finished in the big hotels. They'll all know by now. Maybe I can get some work in a trattoria somewhere.' His head fell into his hands again. 'What a mess, what a mess.'

He walked me back to Signora Lucy's and turned to go without kissing me goodbye. The next morning Anastasio told me that he'd gone back to the bar and drunk the bottle of whisky dry. I didn't see him that day or the next and I wasn't sure where to find him.

He'd been sharing a room with another waiter from the hotel, but I'd never been there and only knew it wasn't far from the Spanish Steps.

I felt miserable and guilty, but angry, too. This wasn't my fault. Surely when Beppi calmed down he would see that he was the one who had asked his friend to take care of me. He'd set the ball rolling himself.

I filled my time with cleaning. The mirrors and chrome in Anastasio's bar had never been polished to such a high shine and no broom had ever reached so far to sweep tendrils of fluff and hair from the furthest corners. I tried to take my mind off Beppi by pulling down all the bottles of liqueur and wiping a film of dust from them, and I made Anastasio help me heave the big refrigerator away from the wall so I could scrub away the dirt behind it.

A week went by without Beppi appearing. I was in despair. One night I sat in my room and counted my money to see if I had enough for the fare home. Leaving seemed the best thing to do.

I was walking up to Stazione Termini to see about buying a ticket when I heard Beppi calling my name. 'Caterina, stop. Wait for me.'

I turned to see him running towards me. I felt a bit like the way you do when you think someone is about to touch a badly bruised part of your body and hurt it again. Protective, nervous. Even though I'd been longing to see Beppi, the moment I set eyes on him I panicked. Instead of waiting, I began to run, weaving in and out of the clusters of people blocking my way, all the time hearing Beppi shouting my name behind me.

'Caterina, don't run away. I only want to talk to you.'

I turned into a side street that led to the Trevi Fountain and ran into a wall of tourists. An American woman clutched her handbag closer to her chest as if I were going to snatch it from her, and her husband scolded me, 'Hey watch where you're going.'

They stared when Beppi ran up behind me and grabbed my shoulders.

'Caterina, why did you run from me?' He was breathing harder than I was.

I tried to wriggle free from him. 'Let me go.'

'Not until you tell me why you ran away.'

'You can't just ignore me all week and then expect me to be pleased when you decide to turn up.' I was the angry one now. 'And you can't blame me for everything that's gone wrong. That's just not fair.'

'I know, I know. Let's go and sit beside the fountain and get away from these people, who seem to think we're some sort of sideshow.' He grimaced at the group of curious tourists. 'I have something to tell you.'

I let myself be led to a wooden bench and sat beside him, staring dead ahead at the fountain and waiting for him to speak.

'I'm sorry I disappeared but I needed some time to think.' He paused and waited for my reaction. I nodded slightly and he went on. 'I know none of it was your fault and it was stupid of me to blame you. It's Gianfranco I should have been angry with.'

'How could you not have seen what he was like?' That's what I had never been able to understand. 'Even Anastasio doesn't trust him and he hardly knows him.'

'He was my friend.'

'Yes, but why?' I turned to look at Beppi and saw how sad and confused he was.

'He's been my friend for as long as I can remember,' he said quietly. 'We're the same age and we've done everything together since we were little boys. He used to help me walk the goats to the fountain in the piazza in the days before we had water at home. We went spear fishing for eels in the summer and trapped the songbirds that were flying south at the start of winter. Gianfranco was a brother to me. I loved him, Caterina. I still can't believe what he's done.'

'But he was always so jealous of you. That's why he had to be the one with the better job, the car, more money.'

Beppi shook his head. 'That's crazy.'

'I know.'

We watched the tourists for a while. There seemed to be an endless parade of them but they all did much the same thing: stare in awe at the spectacle of the fountain, throw a coin into the water and then stand with their backs to it grinning while someone took their photograph. I was no longer one of them. By now I felt part of Rome.

'Gianfranco isn't really in love with me, you know,' I said. 'He only wants me because I belong to you.'

'And you think because he can't have you he's trying to destroy me?' Beppi asked.

'Yes, I suppose that's it.'

'Well, it's worked. He's destroyed my family, my prospects …' Suddenly he grabbed my hand and squeezed it hard. 'Marry me, Caterina.'

'I already said yes.'

'I mean now, this week. Once we're married we'll be safe from him. He won't be able to destroy you and me, like he has everything else.'

'But I can't. What about my parents? I haven't even told them and …' I stopped and thought for a moment. Perhaps Beppi was right. If we were married then Gianfranco couldn't touch us. He would have to leave us alone.

'All right then, let's get married as soon as possible,' I agreed. 'This week, if we can.'

I didn't wear a gown on my wedding day. Instead I went to a smart shop on the Via Condotti and bought a cream woollen trouser suit that I knew I'd get some wear from later on.

Beppi picked me up from Signora Lucy's on a borrowed Vespa and took me to the register office. The ceremony was short and spoken in rushed Italian. Before we knew it, we were signing the register, with Anastasio as our witness along with the waiter whose room Beppi was still sharing.

Afterwards we went to the Piazza Navona and Anastasio took our photograph as we posed in front of our favourite fountain. Back at the bar he had some prosecco chilling in the fridge and we toasted our future together. It was a happy day even though it wasn't the wedding I'd dreamt of having.

We spent our first night as newlyweds apart. Signora Lucy would never have allowed a man in one of her rooms even if he were now my husband. But still I felt different with the thin gold band warming on my finger and the memory of promising to love and honour Beppi so fresh in my mind.

The next morning we met in the bar for coffee and to discuss our future. Beppi still hadn't found work and he was running out of money. Meanwhile I was worried about my parents and how I was going to explain what I'd done. It seemed as if we had hurried through our share of happiness already and now all we had left were problems.

'You go back and see your family,' Beppi suggested. 'And I'll stay here and see if I can find any sort of a job.'

'I won't go without you,' I said stubbornly.

'But we don't have enough money for two tickets.'

'Let's hitchhike. That's how I got here, remember?'

He clicked his tongue. 'Easy for three pretty girls to get lifts maybe. Not so simple for you and me.'

I was exasperated. 'Well then, what are we going to do?'

'I don't know, Caterina.' He threw his hands in the air. 'I wish I had some answers but I don't. Even if I had the train fare, how could I go to England and leave my family behind? I can't abandon my mother.'

'I'm your family, too, now, Beppi,' I reminded him. 'I belong to you as much as they do.'

'Yes, yes, I know that.'

I pressed him harder. 'And your mother and Isabella rely on the money you send home, don't they? How will they manage if you can't support them? In England we could live rent-free with my parents, get good jobs, save money and still be able to send something to them.'

He looked defeated. 'I don't know, Caterina, I just don't know.'

'Rome will always be here. Just come to England with me for a little while,' I begged him. 'Please.'

'OK,' he relented. 'If we can find a way for me to get there then I will come ... for a little while.'

Anastasio had been busy serving customers but he must have been listening to our conversation because when he came over to bring us more coffee he lingered for a moment and then said, 'Do you mind if I offer a suggestion?'

Beppi shrugged. 'Of course not.'

'I have a friend who runs a Greek restaurant in Soho. If I write to him then maybe he'll be able to help you out with a job.'

'Thank you, but I can't even afford the fare right now,' Beppi told him.

'Then I'll lend it to you.'

'Why would you do that?' Beppi, who had once been so trusting, now seemed to trust no one.

'Because I know you'll pay me back.'

Beppi frowned. 'That's kind of you but I can't accept.'

Anastasio sat down on the spare chair at our table. 'Look, Beppi, someone helped me once – that's how I came to have this place. Now I want to help you. Maybe some day you'll be able to help the next person. That's how life ought to work, even though it doesn't always.'

I spoke before Beppi had a chance to reply. 'Thank you, we accept your kind offer. And I promise we'll pay you back as quickly as we can. Won't we, Beppi?'

Reluctantly, he nodded. I could tell he wasn't happy about leaving or accepting money from someone he barely knew. 'Thank you,' he said almost begrudgingly.

'*Prego*,' Anastasio replied, and then he got up and went back to serving his customers.

17

I wrote to my parents and told them I was coming home. Imagining them reading my letter in the dark basement kitchen that smelt of cabbage and roasted meat, I added one last line. 'I won't be alone,' I wrote. 'I'm bringing my new husband home with me.'

That would have to do. The rest we would take care of once we were in the same room. I was dreading it but Beppi and I were married now and no one could do anything to change it. We were safe.

A week later we caught a train from Stazione Termini. Someone had told Beppi how much colder it would be in England and he'd bought a second-hand greatcoat he'd found on a market stall. It was grey, a bit moth-eaten and about three sizes too big. 'I'm leaving Italy, Caterina,' he said mournfully. 'Who knows when I'll come back?'

We'd booked couchettes and he cheered up a little when he realized we had a carriage to ourselves. That night the attendant came and folded out six bunks from the wall. Somehow both of us managed to wedge ourselves onto one of them. It was our first night together as husband and wife.

When I woke in the morning Beppi was on the floor. He'd been shaken out of bed in the night by the movement of the train and was so exhausted he'd curled up and slept where he landed.

We were both tired. The strain of the past weeks, worrying about Gianfranco and how we were going to find a way to be together had been harder on us than we'd realized. So the train journey was like a holiday, the honeymoon we'd never had. There was nothing to do except talk, stare out of the window and walk to the dining car every now and then, clinging to each other as the train rocked over the tracks.

'What will it be like in England?' Beppi kept asking. 'Do they have pasta? Red wine? Will I like it there?'

'You'll see soon enough,' was all I'd say. Sometimes, while we were watching the scenery fly past, I'd worry that he'd hate the rain and cold, and that the greyness of London would leach into him and he'd be miserable.

It was raining hard the day we arrived. Beppi took our bags and we ran to the bus shelter. It seemed so strange to be back, surrounded by voices speaking my own language. The smells and sounds of home felt foreign to me, and I could see how much I was going to miss Italy. It made me worry even more about Beppi's chances of adjusting to this new life.

But if anything he seemed excited. He bombarded me with questions as the bus trundled through the traffic.

'Which way is this place Soho where Anastasio's friend has his restaurant?' he asked.

'That way.' I pointed. 'Not far from here really.'

He jumped to his feet. 'Well, come on, let's go and see him now.'

'But we've only just arrived. We should go home first so you can meet my family.'

'Won't it be better if I meet them as a man with a job? Come on,' he urged, 'let's get off the bus and go to see if they have anything for me.'

The Greek restaurant was in a basement, and the short flight of steps that led to it smelt strongly of disinfectant. Beppi wrinkled his nose in disgust. To him restaurants were meant to smell of onions frying slowly down to gluey sweetness, or meat juices and roasting garlic. But still he knocked on the open door and called out to the owner.

It turned out they didn't need a waiter but were looking for a chef who could cook Greek staples like moussaka, pork souvlaki and beef stifado served with crispy fried potatoes and green salad.

'No problem,' said Beppi. 'At the hotel in Rome I cooked things all the time.'

He was exaggerating, of course. For a *chef de rang* in a big hotel it was more about performance and presentation. He'd light the Grand Marnier on top of the crêpe Suzette or prepare pasta at the table, tossing it with the chosen sauce and sprinkling cheese on top. None of it was real cooking and Beppi hadn't even held that job for long.

'It doesn't matter,' he told me once we were back on the bus, his mood quite jubilant. 'No one goes to a restaurant like that for the quality of the food. They eat there because it's cheap and the portions are large. I'll manage, you'll see.'

He stayed in his good mood as the bus edged up the Essex Road. It was only at the very top, when I told him we didn't have much further to go, that he showed signs of being nervous.

'Will your father be very angry? What sort of a man is he? You've told me nothing about him.'

I was anxious, too. Not of my father's anger, because he was a gentle man who hardly ever raised his voice. But I knew he'd be disappointed in me and in many ways that was harder to bear.

My dad held back as we came through the front door, letting my mother hug me in her thin arms. I looked over her shoulder and saw how he seemed to have aged. His hair was greyer and his eyes were tired behind the large, thick-lensed glasses he always wore.

They were so nice to Beppi and for that I was grateful. In the dining room there was a special tea laid out for him with ham on the bone, buttered white bread and cucumber salad. My mother had even put a paper doily on the plate and she gave me a sharp look in case I was thinking of commenting on its presence.

It was Beppi who commanded all their attention. As he ate, they asked him questions about his life and family, trying to weigh up what kind of man he was.

'And now you're in London, what will you do?' my father asked.

Beppi told him about the chef's job he would start the next day and I saw my father give an approving nod. For him life was about hard work, and showing he was not a shirker was the best thing Beppi could have done.

For a year we lived on the top floor of my parents' house and Beppi took the bus into Soho each day to work in the Greek restaurant. Sometimes he'd work so late he'd miss the last bus back and then he'd walk for over an hour rather than waste any money on a taxi.

Paying Anastasio back was his first goal and once he'd managed that Beppi seemed to relax. He went to the pub with my dad a couple of times and learned to play darts and drink warm beer.

He was still sending money home to Ravenno and saving what he could, so I was surprised when he began taking me to Italian restaurants. We would go on his nights off and every time Beppi would choose a different one. Some were cheap little basement places tucked away on Charlotte Street, while others were grander and more expensive.

Beppi found fault with every single place. Either the food wasn't right or the service not attentive enough. It was funny to watch him eat. He'd lift the first fork-ful with a sour expression on his face and then smile the minute he'd tasted it. 'There's too much sugar in this sauce because they're trying to make up for the bitterness of the tomatoes they've used,' he'd declare happily. 'It's terrible, terrible.'

The more he found to complain about, the happier he'd look. 'They used cream in that dish because they think it's what the English people want,' he'd say. 'They cut the fish against the grain, the barbarians. They put the meat and the spaghetti on the same plate. Don't they know anything about food?'

Then, abruptly, the restaurant visits stopped and after that, when he wasn't working, Beppi would shop for the cheapest vegetables he could find at Berwick Street market and bring them home with strange cuts of meat or revolting parcels of fish heads and take over my mother's kitchen. As soon as spring came he planted herbs in her garden, flat-leafed parsley and basil, rosemary and sage. He was always on his feet doing something, putting a pan of beans on to boil or making notes about the food he'd cooked the day before. Whenever he did sit down, within minutes his eyes would be shut and he'd be snoring.

One night he and my dad stayed in the pub until closing time and then sat up late in the kitchen talking. When I got up I found an ashtray with two cigars stubbed out in it. I wondered what they'd been celebrating.

It was my father who told me later that morning while he was eating poached eggs for breakfast. He'd slept in late and his hair was sticking up in tufts. I thought his eyes looked a bit bloodshot.

'This restaurant that Beppi wants to open, do you reckon it will work as well as he thinks?' he asked.

I knew nothing about any restaurant but I tried not to show my surprise. 'He's a good cook,' was all I said.

'That's what I think, too. A lot of the stuff he makes looks like foreign muck but it tastes OK. That rice thing he made the other night with the cabbage and the bacon was good, even if he did put too much garlic in it.'

I smiled as I remembered my father eating a second helping, carefully pushing the soft chunks of cooked garlic and the fatty bits of bacon to the side of his plate.

'But a restaurant, well, I don't know,' he continued,

polishing off his eggs. 'I've told him I'll think about it.'

'Think about what?'

'Lending him some money to help him get started, of course.'

I cleaned away my dad's plate and wiped down the kitchen surfaces, all the while wondering what Beppi was playing at.

That night he explained, as we lay side by side in the lumpy double bed in our room at the top of the house. All this eating and cooking he'd been doing was research. He was determined to open his own restaurant and he'd planned every last detail.

'I've found an empty place near a busy market. It's close to Clerkenwell so there are lots of Italians in the neighbourhood. The rent is low, it's perfect,' he told me excitedly. 'All I need is the money to get started.'

Beppi had surprised me. All this time I'd been waiting for him to suggest it was time for us to return to Italy. I knew he missed his mother and felt guilty about neglecting her. And although he was still so angry with Isabella, I was certain he must miss her, too.

'A restaurant will keep you here in London,' I said hesitantly. 'Are you sure that's what you want?'

'This is my opportunity to make something of myself. I might not get another one.' Beppi sounded proud and animated.

I was worried. 'But you miss Italy, don't you ... and your mother?'

He nodded. 'Once the restaurant is up and running I may go back for a visit. But for now I have to focus on making a success of myself. In Rome there

226

are hundreds of restaurants like the one I'm planning. Here it seems there are none. This is my big chance, Caterina.'

He took me to see the place the next day. It was so narrow and gloomy that it was more like a tunnel. There had been a leak and one of the walls was bulging and covered in mould. But in Beppi's mind it was already a restaurant.

'We'll plaster the walls roughly and paint them white. The kitchen will be there in the back with a small hatch I can look through to see the whole restaurant. We'll put tables and long benches along that wall and on every table there will be a basket of bread, a jug of water and a carafe of wine. So it will feel as though people are coming to my home to share my food.'

I looked around. 'But it's awful, Beppi. How are you going to make it into a place where people will want to come and eat?'

'I'll decorate it myself when I'm not at work.'

'And where will my father find this money you're asking for?'

'He'll borrow it from the bank against his house.'

'But what if you can't pay it back?'

'I paid back Anastasio, didn't I?' He sounded offended.

'That wasn't nearly so much as this will cost.'

It wasn't that I wanted to destroy his dream but I was scared of the risk he was taking. He had a job and we had each other. Weren't we happy enough with the way things were?

'Why do you always have to look for the problems,

227

Caterina?' He sounded grumpy. 'Stop worrying for once. It will be fine. I will make it work.'

For the next few weeks Beppi didn't get much sleep. As soon as my father's funds came through and the lease was signed, he made himself a funny little hat out of newspaper and started clearing up the interior of the shop. When he wasn't cooking at the Greek restaurant, he was there decorating.

He saved money wherever he could, doing little deals with people and offering to pay them in meals rather than cash. On the walls he put the few family photographs his mother had sent from Italy. I recognized the one of a young Beppi eating pasta that had once hung above the dresser in her house in Ravenno, and the shot of him and Isabella laughing as they rode a Vespa. He even put our wedding portrait up on the wall much to my embarrassment. There I was in my cream woollen suit, standing beside the fountain in the Piazza Navona and squinting in the bright sunlight.

'You can't hang that there,' I told him.

'Yes, yes. I want people to feel like they are eating with family when they are here. And I want them to see my beautiful wife, Caterina.'

The day when the signwriter painted the words 'Little Italy' in big bright red letters above the door, I felt so proud of Beppi. He had done it and now we had our own restaurant.

But really the hard work had only just begun. To make enough money to pay off the loan we had to open for lunch and dinner seven days a week. During the day I was working in a shop on Oxford Street but at five p.m. I'd race to Little Italy as fast as I could and

228

waitress for the night. We didn't even have printed menus. People ate whatever Beppi chose to cook, usually a soup, a pasta dish or a risotto, followed by meat or fish with vegetables and salad. At first I just told the customers what was on offer that night, but later we bought a little blackboard and wrote it up in chalk.

It was a cheap place to eat, particularly because the wine and bread were included in the set price. But Beppi made sure the food was good. He got so excited about it that sometimes he'd dart out of the kitchen to show a customer a bowl of fresh clams he was going to cook with spaghetti he'd made himself the day before.

It wasn't always easy to find the ingredients he needed, which was why we kept the menu short. Also, we couldn't afford to have any waste. Beppi had discovered that the owner of the Greek restaurant had kept prices low by using everything. Vegetable trimmings went into a stockpot, and the fat pared from a piece of meat was used to flavour a sauce. So he did the same.

He bought the most inexpensive pieces of meat, often deboning chicken thighs, flattening them, rolling them and stuffing them with cheese and ham to make *involtini*. His soups would be full of beans and celery leaves and flavoured with a little bacon fat, and his *ragù* was simmered for hours to make the cheap meat tender. Beppi recorded his weekly earnings meticulously in a little notebook, and all the money he made went back into the business.

At first only Italians came to us but then slowly English people discovered Little Italy and soon there was a queue outside the door most nights, with people often waiting half an hour for a table. In the kitchen Beppi worked like a maniac, mopping his brow with an old tea towel, and I was run ragged delivering the food he cooked to the tables and collecting the empty plates.

At least once a week Margaret came in for dinner but I never had time to stop and chat to her.

At long last the loan was paid off and my father's house was safe again. We didn't celebrate because there wasn't time. But when the apartment above Little Italy came up for rent, Beppi decided we could afford to take it. At last we had our own place.

If I thought that was enough to keep Beppi happy, I was wrong. He was ambitious for more. He took out another loan, this time directly with the bank, and leased the shop next door. The kitchen was expanded and we knocked arched doorways through to link the two dining rooms. Beppi hired Frederico as a waiter and a Neapolitan man called Aldo to help him in the kitchen. He said having a trained chef to work with had made everything easier. I tried not to look for problems but I was scared things were happening too fast.

It was summer and Little Italy was noisy and hot. Once or twice as I was hurrying to the kitchen to give Beppi an order, the room would start to swim around me and I'd have to find an empty seat and sit down. Everything in front of my eyes would go black and I was afraid I was going to throw up.

'Don't worry, love, I was the same when I was pregnant,' said one of the regular customers cheerfully. 'It usually passes after the first few months.'

We'd been so busy I hadn't noticed the changes that were happening to my body. As soon as I realized I was pregnant, it became obvious that my waist had thickened and my stomach was curved like one of Beppi's pasta bowls.

He started fussing over me straight away. 'We'll have to hire another waitress because we can't have you on your feet all night,' he insisted. 'You must give up work altogether and rest.'

But once the nausea had passed, I felt well enough and went back to helping Beppi again. I'd have hardly seen him otherwise, as he worked from early in the morning when he shopped at the markets to the moment the last customer left.

I was seven months pregnant when Beppi expanded Little Italy again, this time putting a canopy outside with tables and chairs beneath it. That caused a big fight between us.

'It means in the summer months we won't have to turn customers away,' he told me. 'We'll have all this extra space for them.'

'But what about me, Beppi?'

He looked confused. 'You won't be working. Aldo's sister is going to help us out, remember?'

'That's not what I mean. We've got a baby coming and here you are making more work for yourself. I hardly ever see you as it is.'

'I'm working to make a future for our baby, Caterina. You know that.'

I sat down heavily on one of the chairs and looked away from him, towards the daytime bustle of the market.

'What about me?' I repeated quietly.

'Stop worrying … it will be fine … you'll see.' He seemed to say those words to me more and more these days.

I disappeared upstairs to our little apartment and lay alone in bed. We still hadn't decorated the place and it was rundown and depressing. I hated the wallpaper with its faded pattern of pink roses, the nicotine-stained ceiling and the yellowing paintwork. Now I was going to be stuck up here alone for hours on end with a small baby while Beppi worked downstairs. Part of me was scared, as any new mother has a right to be, but another part of me resented this child that was coming too soon. I felt I'd never had enough of Beppi, and now I was going to have to share him.

It was then I started writing to Audrey again because, even though she was an ocean away, her situation was much the same. If anything she had it worse, she wrote, as she was still living with her mother-in-law while Louis kept on working extra shifts so they could one day have a place of their own. When the blue-edged airmail letters arrived I always felt my spirits lift. It made me feel better reading about how tired, irritated or sad Audrey was and how she missed our carefree days.

But once the baby came, even Audrey's letters failed to stir much interest in me. I felt as if I was fading away like the roses on the wallpaper. Every day was the same routine: feed time, nappy time, nap time. I did everything as efficiently as I could, and waited to love this baby.

I could see how other people responded to her,

holding her close, smelling the top of her head and exclaiming how beautiful she was. Beppi ran up from the restaurant every chance he got and stood beside her crib, staring at his child. But when I looked at her, all I saw were the same chores to be done, time and again, when what I wanted was to curl up in my bed, close my eyes and forget everything.

'We have to gave this baby a name,' said Beppi one night. He'd come to bed late as always and was sitting on the edge of the mattress peering into the crib. 'People keep asking what she's called and it's embarrassing me that I can't give an answer.'

'Call her what you like,' I said flatly.

Beppi gave me a disappointed look but said nothing. He didn't know how to deal with this new mood that I was always in.

'I want to call her Pieta,' he decided.

I found out later it meant 'pity', which seemed a good name for a child whose mother had forgotten how to feel.

When my parents decided I should move in with them for a week or two while my father decorated the apartment, I let them bundle me into a taxi and arrange my things in my old bedroom like I was the baby.

I chose the colours I wanted for the apartment walls from a paint chart my father brought me: red for the kitchen, yellow for the living room and blue for the bedroom. The brightest shades I could find.

'Are you sure?' My father looked confused.

'Yes, the place needs cheering up,' I said definitely.

'Well, OK, if that's what you want.'

My mother would have taken the baby and done

everything for her if I'd let her. But it seemed to me that the least I could do was change nappies and bathe and feed her. So I carried on grimly with my routine.

Both of my parents were worried about me. Late at night I'd hear them murmuring to each other and, if I strained, I could make out their words.

'She'll be fine. She just needs some time,' my father often said.

My mother wasn't convinced. She tried to fuss over me but I pulled away from her, and as soon as my father declared the apartment habitable again, I put the baby in a taxi and moved back there.

Beppi was overjoyed to have us home. He seemed to have forgotten I had turned into a stranger. But as the weeks went by he began avoiding me. If he did have free time he'd put the baby in her pram and park her beside one of the outdoor tables while he played cards with his Italian friend Ernesto.

Upstairs, alone and shut into my world, I didn't much care what he did. Most days I didn't even bother to get dressed properly. If it got cold I'd pile on more layers over my nightgown so I could be ready for bed again in an instant.

Finally he lost patience with me. 'Caterina, enough of this,' he said one morning. 'It's a beautiful day so get up, get dressed and take Pieta out for a walk in her pram.'

I knew he was right. I needed to get out. So I nodded. 'OK.'

'Really? You will do it?'

'Yes.'

'I'll be watching out for you and if I don't see you

leave the apartment in the next half an hour I'll come back up and get you.' He was anxious, but he sounded angry.

It felt strange to wear proper clothes and shoes on my feet instead of slippers; to be tightly buttoned in instead of swathed in soft layers. I felt unsteady on my feet, as if I had suffered from a long illness, and everything in the world seemed bigger, brighter and noisier than before.

I pushed the pram between the market stalls, pretending to browse for bargains, although really I was wondering how long Beppi expected me to be out. Perhaps an hour and then I could creep back up to the apartment?

I walked around the block and back up through Hatton Garden, past the diamond merchants. I was nearly at the top when I realized something in the familiar scene was out of place. I was looking at a face that didn't belong. There, standing beside the window of a jewellery shop, with a woman who was as heavily pregnant as I had been just a few months before, was Gianfranco.

I let out a scream and then clapped my hand over my mouth. A couple of passers-by turned to look at me and, just as quickly, looked away. Only Gianfranco's eyes stayed on me. He didn't come any closer or try to speak to me. He just stood next to the pregnant woman and watched me.

Grasping the pram handle a little tighter, I put my head down and hurried on. My mind was jumping with questions. What was he doing here? Had he followed us? Was his presence just a coincidence?

I half ran back to Little Italy to tell Beppi what I'd seen.

But when I pushed the pram through the door he looked up and said, 'Back so soon?' in such a disappointed way that I swallowed my words and went back up to the apartment without mentioning Gianfranco's name.

Each morning, unless it was raining hard, Beppi made me take the baby for a walk. And every morning I thought about telling him the new reason I didn't want to go but the words wouldn't come.

I didn't always see Gianfranco because I made sure to alternate my routes. But sometimes I'd catch a glimpse of him on the pavement opposite. Then a bus would trundle past and by the time it had gone he'd have disappeared. Once or twice I saw him standing in a shop quietly watching me go by. At first the pregnant woman was with him but after a week or so he was always alone. I was certain this was the same game he'd played with me in Rome.

In the end it was Margaret I told. She still came to eat at Little Italy once a week and would always stop by the apartment to see me first.

'I think he's following me,' I admitted. Although I hadn't told her about the night in Amalfi when he'd tried to trick me into spending a night with him, or about what he'd done to Isabella, I knew Margaret had never liked Gianfranco.

Her advice was predictable. 'Catherine, you have to let Beppi know straight away. How could you have kept this from him?'

'But he'll be so angry and …' I wasn't sure how to put my fears into words. 'Maybe he won't believe me. We haven't been getting on so well since the baby came.'

'Of course he'll believe you. This is Beppi you're talking about.'

I'd always put on a brave face when Margaret came. She had no idea how difficult life had become for me.

'I can't tell him,' I insisted. 'He's so happy with his restaurant and this will make him furious. It will ruin everything.'

Margaret shook her head. 'I still can't believe the little creep has turned up here. And he doesn't say anything, just stares? Oh, that's awful.'

I promised I'd speak to Beppi before her next visit. But what Gianfranco did next made my promise irrelevant. He announced his presence in London in a way that neither Beppi nor anyone else could ignore.

* * *

18

Pieta's days had settled into a rhythm of visits to the hospital, where her father was feeling better but growing restless and impatient, and afternoons in the sewing room, working on the dress and listening to her mother unfold her story. Pieta could sense it was all coming to an end; the dress was nearly finished and the story almost over. Soon Beppi would be home and the house would be filled with noise and the smell of food cooking once more. Pieta was looking forward to it and yet she would miss being closeted in this small room, her hands busy with work and the only sound her mother's voice recalling the past.

'How was it that Gianfranco announced his presence in London and took you all by surprise?' she asked the next time they sat together in the sewing room.

Her mother frowned. 'I think you know what he did,' she said. 'You've been there often enough.'

* * *

There was a great deal of excitement in the kitchen of Little Italy when they first heard about the shop that was opening up around the corner.

'A *salumeria*,' Beppi told me later. 'A proper Italian delicatessen selling salami and cheeses imported from

Italy as well as good pasta and olive oil. Maybe I'll be able to do a deal with them to buy some of the things we need in bulk.'

'Who is opening this *salumeria*?' I asked.

'No one seems to know.' Beppi sounded upbeat. 'There is newspaper up over all the windows but there are workmen in there so it can't be too long before they open.'

Three days later the sign was painted above the shop door. 'DeMatteo's Italian Grocer' it said in scarlet letters.

'It can't be.' Beppi sounded so certain.

'Yes it can,' I replied, and told him why.

Now it was Beppi's turn to retreat. For the next week he barely seemed to remember he had a wife and baby. I left him to his black mood but when he took a whole day off work and stayed in bed, leaving Aldo to manage alone in the kitchen, I started to worry.

'What are you complaining about? You spend half your life in here,' Beppi pointed out. 'I work hard so why shouldn't I have a day in bed if I want one?'

I sat down on the mattress but made no move to touch him. 'Because it's not like you,' I said. 'It's not what you do.'

I heard him mutter an Italian swear word. '*Mannaggia* ...' And he sank deeper beneath the covers.

'But Beppi, what are we going to do?'

'About what?' His voice was muffled but the tone was impatient.

'Gianfranco, of course.'

'Just ignore him. Don't speak to him. If you see him turn your back on him.'

'But I don't want to be here if he's just around the corner.'

Beppi pushed back the covers. 'We were here first,' he said angrily. 'If he thinks by opening his *salumeria* he's going to scare me away or destroy Little Italy then he's wrong. We're not going anywhere, Caterina.'

'OK, so I'll just ignore him … turn my back on him,' I murmured, not wanting to see Beppi become any angrier. 'Maybe his business won't do well and he'll be the one who leaves.'

He reached out and touched my arm. 'Every time I see him I'll remember what he did to my sister and what he tried to do to you. It will kill me.' He spoke each word as if it hurt.

I leaned in closer so he could wrap his arms around me, and we lay there together in the semi-darkness listening to one another's breathing. For some reason, even though such a bad thing had happened, I felt a little better.

DeMatteo's had a big, showy opening and Gianfranco hired musicians, hung up bunting in the colours of the Italian flag, and gave out free tastes of prosciutto and cheese to passers-by. Beppi and I stayed away but we heard all about it from almost everyone who came into Little Italy that day. I sat in the sunshine, folding napkins and listening to the chatter.

'Wonderful cheese: parmigiano, pecorino, dolce-latte,' Ernesto told me. 'Salami hanging from metal hooks just like at home, shelves full of pasta, anchovies and oils. It even smells like Italy.'

Beppi and I both wondered where Gianfranco had found the money for such a venture.

'Borrowed it, I expect,' said Ernesto. 'Taken a risk just as you did when you opened this place. If you don't take risks nothing happens, eh, Beppi?'

I walked past DeMatteo's every so often and took to glancing inside to see how many customers he had. There was always someone in there waiting for a piece of cheese to be wrapped in glossy white paper or stocking up on bottles of balsamic vinegar and jars of olives. If Gianfranco looked up and saw me, I turned my head away quickly and walked on. I felt better knowing he was busy behind his counter and couldn't be somewhere ahead, lying in wait for me.

Gradually I started helping out in Little Italy again, taking the baby with me. I stayed away when customers were there but I could help with setting tables, peeling vegetables or chalking up the day's menu. It meant I got to see a little more of Beppi even if we were both busy.

Every day things felt a little lighter, and I realized that, instead of driving a wedge between us, Gianfranco seemed to have brought us together. Beppi and I spent ages trying to piece together how he might have found us. It was obvious, of course. Beppi still wrote to his mother regularly. Once he'd made me take a photograph of him standing outside Little Italy cradling a big ham in his arms and had sent that to her. He wanted everyone to see how well he was doing.

It was only natural that his mother had spoken to friends and neighbours, proudly showing them the photo of her Beppi who was making such a big success in England. Ravenno was a small place and soon everybody had heard, even Gianfranco's parents.

'But why would he follow me here?' asked Beppi. 'It doesn't make sense.'

'For the same reason he did everything else; he wants whatever you have.'

'And maybe he is still in love with you.' Beppi sounded jealous.

'He has a wife now. I see her all the time. She has a little baby boy.'

'You don't speak to her?'

'No ... although she seems nice ... and lonely maybe.'

'But she is Gianfranco's wife.'

'So I don't speak to her,' I agreed.

Sometimes I half-smiled at her, though, when we passed each other pushing our prams, and she half-smiled in return.

Just when things were feeling so much better, I noticed the signs again. My waist was growing thicker, my belly rounding and the smell of garlic frying in the kitchen of Little Italy made me feel nauseous. My baby was less than a year old and already I was pregnant again. I couldn't believe it.

This time even Beppi's joy was tentative. He wanted the new baby but he didn't want his wife to turn into a slow, sad stranger.

'This time it will be different,' I promised him. And it was.

For the second baby I felt too much. From the moment I held her in my arms, my mind wasn't big enough for all the worries that wanted to crowd into it. I walked around the house with baby clothes tucked beneath my blouse so my own body warmth would take away any last vestige of dampness. I woke ten times in the night to hover over the cot and check the baby was still breathing. I became obsessed with how much she was eating, how much she was sleeping, how often I had to change her nappy. It didn't help that the older child, sensing maybe that she had been so easily displaced, became fractious. Sometimes the sound of her crying could be heard in the restaurant.

Both Beppi and I were exhausted and unhappy. One morning I heard him muttering as he gave the baby her bottle and I realized he was calling her 'Addolorata'. Perhaps he hadn't meant it to be her name, but somehow it stuck. When she was christened in St Peter's even the priest looked surprised that our first little girl was named 'Pity' and now we'd chosen to call our second daughter 'Sorrow'.

I'm not sure we would have survived without Margaret. Beppi must have told her how bad things were and she took to coming over whenever she had spare time and taking one of the babies off my hands. I was reluctant at first because I'd got to the stage where I didn't trust anyone but myself to care for them properly.

'For God's sake, Catherine, I was a nanny, remember? Even the Contessa trusted me with her children.'

I grew to be grateful, especially when she took the babies for long walks. I'd hear the sound of their screaming growing fainter as Margaret pushed them away in their pram and louder again as they returned.

Sometimes, if he was around, Ernesto would walk with her to keep her company and she took to wearing a coy look on her face whenever his name was mentioned.

'I thought you weren't interested in Italian boys?' I said as it finally dawned on me what was going on. 'You told me you'd never have one.'

She giggled a bit and blushed. 'Well, Ernesto is different. He's so gentle and he hasn't got a terrible temper.'

'Still, I don't believe it. You and Ernesto!'

We both laughed then and for a moment it was like we were both back in our little room at Signora Lucy's.

Later Margaret lay on the bed beside me and got that look on her face that meant she wanted to give me advice.

'What?' I asked.

'This will pass, you know, over time.'

'How do you mean?'

'Lots of women are depressed after they've had a baby. Or they get a little bit obsessive about things.' Margaret wasn't a nanny any longer but she still thought she was an expert. 'Things will get better eventually, don't worry.'

'I'm not worrying,' I said, even though I did little else.

She must have had a word with my mother and they cooked up a plan together. Three or four times a week one of them would come and look after the babies and I was meant to go out somewhere. I'm not sure what they expected me to do – look round the shops perhaps or go to galleries. None of that appealed. Instead I went downstairs and helped out in Little Italy where at least I could be close to Beppi.

It was a relief to be out of that apartment, which had felt tiny when there were only two of us but was unbearable now there were four.

'We have to find something bigger,' I told Beppi one day as I was setting up and he was prepping for lunch. 'Something with a garden so the children have got somewhere to play when they get bigger.'

'We need a proper house,' Beppi agreed. 'But not too far away because I don't want to be sitting on that bus for hours each week like I did when I worked at the Greek restaurant.'

Margaret and I took to walking round Clerkenwell looking for properties for sale. I knew exactly what I wanted. Something tucked away in a quiet street with a patch of garden.

When we found the house behind St James's church-yard I knew it was the one for me. Perhaps I liked it because it wasn't so different from the place I'd grown up in on Balls Pond Road. It was tall and narrow with black-painted railings at the front. But instead of a busy road, it looked out over green grass and leafy trees. And all around it were little Italian cafés that reminded me of Anastasio's bar.

'Will it be too expensive, though?' Margaret asked.

'I don't know. Beppi and I never talk about money. He looks after all that.'

Beppi took a couple of hours off work and went to see the house. When he came back he was beaming. 'It is perfect, Caterina. I love it.'

'Not too expensive?'

He frowned. 'We'll have to get a loan. It's a risk. But as Ernesto says, if people don't take risks then nothing happens.'

'Will it mean you have to work harder than ever? Because if it does, I'd rather stay here.'

'Don't worry, Caterina.' He smiled. 'Things will work out. It will be fine.'

* * *

Beppi's Pasta

I should start by saying that even the Italian housewives these days buy the fresh pasta from supermarkets and are quite happy with the quality of products available. But if you have an hour to spare and don't mind the extra work, here is how I do it:

750 g strong white plain flour
4 large eggs
2 fl oz water

Place the flour on the kitchen table, make a well in the centre, add the eggs and some water, then mix the contents to obtain a thick paste. (Start mixing from inside the well if you don't want to lose the liquid.)

Knead for twenty minutes minimum. Sprinkle some flour if the mix is too wet, or more water if it is too dry. The end product must not be sticking to your hands or have any air bubbles inside. You can test this by cutting the mix in half with a knife; any bubbles will then show. Continue to work the mix until the bubbles disappear.

Cut up the quantity in three or four portions and wrap all but one in clingfilm to keep moist while you stretch the pasta. So what if you don't have one of those fancy pasta-making machines? My mother, she used a rolling pin all her life. I myself have used an old wine bottle to roll out the pasta dough. Really I have. It's not so hard. All you need are strong arms.

However, when using the machine, cut up one portion into several pieces, say six, and sprinkle with flour. Roll all the pieces on the first setting, than again on the medium setting and finally set the machine on the one before the last setting – meaning that if there were five settings you would finish with the fourth otherwise it would be too thin. (I am making this idiot-proof, you see.) Cut up strips of pasta to a manageable length and lay them on a cloth to dry or until you are ready to cook them.

Caterina's note: Not everyone wants pasta drying all over the house you know, Beppi. Had you ever thought of that?

19

The dress was hanging on the mannequin in the corner of the sewing room and it was everything Pieta had hoped it would be: a beautiful, elegant, shimmering thing. Now she knew for sure her sister was going to look like a princess.

But any happiness she felt to see the gown completed was tempered by other, more complicated feelings. Her mother's story had left Pieta more confused than ever. As she pottered round, covering the dress to protect it from dust and clearing up scraps of fabric and fallen beads, she tried to marry up the Beppi and Caterina of the story with the two people they'd become as they edged into old age.

Closing the door on the sewing room, Pieta thought about calling Addolorata. She knew she ought to share some of their family's history with her but couldn't quite make herself pick up the phone. After all, her sister had been given their mother's love when she had not. It seemed fitting now that she should keep her story.

Pieta kept casting her mind back to their childhood, trying to remember some inequality. But all she could recall were the many days when her mother closed her bedroom door and lay down for hours pleading a headache, and how she often seemed sad for no reason. There wasn't even the haziest recollection of ever feeling unloved.

It was nearly lunchtime and Pieta felt restless. The past few days had been lived between her mother's sewing room and her father's hospital bed. Now it was time to get out, to fill her lungs with London's petrol fumes and walk past cafés bristling with people. She needed to climb back into her own life again.

Her feet took her down towards Hatton Garden, the place her mother had been when she first realized Gianfranco had followed them to London. Was it really jealousy that brought him here, obsessive love for her mother, or something else? Pieta wondered. As she thought about the way her father's childhood friend had turned into his lifelong enemy, she turned the corner and found herself walking towards DeMatteo's Italian Grocer.

She stood outside the shop for a while, looking through the window at the shelves of dried Italian pasta, the mottled salami hanging from hooks and the cabinets filled with cheeses. Her father had been so excited about the store before he knew who it belonged to.

Michele was behind the counter. He glanced up and smiled a greeting.

As soon as he'd got rid of his customer, he came out to see her. 'Are you all right?' he asked.

'My father had a heart attack,' she told him.

'I know, I heard. But he's going to be OK, isn't he?'

'Yes, I think so. The doctors seem happy and his angioplasty went well.'

'How has your mother been coping? And your sister?'

'Mamma is fine, considering. She's catching up on her sleep at last. But Addolorata seems to have gone completely mad. I've hardly seen her for days and days. I think she's still blaming herself.'

Looking concerned, Michele took her arm. 'Come inside. I'll make you some coffee,' he said.

'No … I shouldn't.' For some reason the nicer he was to her the more she felt like crying. 'You know how things are with my father. If he hears I've been here he'll be furious and now is not the time to upset him. I shouldn't have come at all.'

Reaching into the shop, Michele flipped over the closed sign on the glass doorway of DeMatteo's. Then he shut the door firmly and locked up. 'Come on,' he said, turning back to her, 'you need a drink.'

'Won't your father mind you closing up like that in the middle of the day?'

'Probably,' he admitted and, taking her arm again, led her away.

They walked to a pub on the Farringdon Road that Pieta never went into but which, it quickly became clear, was Michele's local. The manager greeted him by name and poured him a glass of beer without waiting for his order.

'My friend needs something restorative,' Michele told him, and Pieta was given a pungent cocktail made with Stone's Green Ginger Wine.

They sat in a corner, well away from the other drinkers, and talked for a while about her father and the shock of his sudden illness.

'He always seemed so fit,' Pieta said, gulping down the warming drink faster than she'd meant to. 'He never sat still for a minute.'

Michele smiled. 'It must be an Italian thing. My father is exactly the same.'

'They were friends when they were little, you know.' Pieta wondered if Michele knew anything at all about their fathers' pasts. 'In some awful mountain town in southern Italy.'

'I know. I've been there.'

'Really?'

He drained his glass of beer. 'When I was a kid we used to go back for a month every summer. That was when my grandparents were alive. Don't you remember how my father used to shut the shop for the whole of August?'

'No, not really.'

He grimaced and gestured towards the bar for more drinks. 'I hated Ravenno because there was absolutely nothing to do there, just lots of visiting relatives, sitting down and behaving myself. The only good days were when my father took us to the beach, and that meant driving for miles over the mountains. But you've never been there?'

Pieta shook her head. 'My father has hardly been back. He was always so busy with the restaurant. I think he went once when his mother died and another time he went to Rome, but he never took us with him.'

'Maybe he'll decide he wants to go now. Having been ill might make him want to see Italy again.'

'I don't think so. There's no one there for him now, just a few cousins he barely ever speaks to.'

'What about his sister?'

'Isabella? She's dead, too.'

He looked shocked. 'When did that happen?'

'Oh, years ago.'

'That can't be right.' Michele sounded confused.

'Why do you say that?'

He paused for a moment as though considering what to say. 'Because she and my father used to write to each other,' he explained at last. 'I remember there was a big stink when my mother found the letters.'

Pieta felt light-headed. She was already halfway through her second drink and now she swallowed another big mouthful. 'So ... you're saying she's alive?'

'Yes, as far as I know she still is. But what made you think she was dead?' Michele asked. 'Is that what your father told you?'

'I think so ... I don't know.' Suddenly Pieta wasn't certain if someone had actually said the words, or if she and Addolorata had assumed she must be dead because her father hardly mentioned her.

'Her letters were always sent from Rome not Ravenno,' Michele added.

'But I don't understand why your father was writing to her.'

He looked awkward. 'Maybe they had some sort of fling,' he said, and she wondered if he knew more than he was letting on. 'I know my mother tried to put a stop to the letters, although whether she succeeded is another matter. My father has never liked being told what to do.'

Pieta was so astonished she accepted a third drink and finished it just as quickly as she had the previous two. Her face was flushed and she knew she ought to go home, but tearing herself away from Michele and their little corner of the bar wasn't easy. She sat there for another half-hour talking about Italy and their fathers, until Michele told her she looked exhausted and offered to walk her home.

There was a brief moment as he said goodbye outside her parents' house when she thought Michele was going to lean in and kiss her goodbye. Instead he touched her on the shoulder and told her to take care of herself and that he hoped he'd see her soon.

'Addolorata can't be right,' she thought woozily as she closed the front door behind her. 'He's not sweet on me at all.'

20

A headache and a dry throat woke Pieta a few hours later. She made coffee and toast, as though it were first thing in the morning rather than late afternoon, and sat on the doorstep in her dressing gown, trying to pull herself together. Michele occupied her thoughts as she sipped her coffee. There was a gentleness about him, a softness. It was so difficult to believe he was the son of the man who had tried to destroy her father.

Her coffee finished, Pieta stared out at the rows of vegetables and tried to decide how to fill her time now the dress had been completed. Weeds were snaking through the garden, and motes of dust and dirt had invaded the house, but she felt exhausted by the idea of tackling either.

And anyway, there was a bigger problem to worry about. Addolorata, stubborn in her shame and guilt, seemed to be avoiding her. Her sister had phoned a few times and been to visit their father, but had stayed away from both the house and Pieta as much as she could. It was difficult to know what to do. Should she go and check she was all right, or leave her to find her own way home?

Pieta went upstairs and dressed in comfortable blue jeans and a smock top. Grabbing a merino wrap in case she got cold, she headed out and started walking slowly towards Little Italy. But once she got to the main road she changed her mind. A black cab was cruising past with its orange 'For Hire' sign illuminated and it would have seemed a missed opportunity not to hail it. Sitting back and instructing the driver to take her to the hospital, she felt relieved. It was easier to put off the problem of her sister until another day.

When she arrived at the hospital Pieta was glad she'd chosen to come. Her father was pacing around impatiently while her mother sat in an armchair looking like she was the one who needed medical attention. The toll of the late nights spent sewing and her constant simmering anxiety about Beppi was showing.

'Mamma, look at you,' Pieta exclaimed. 'You need to go home and rest. I'll stay here with Papa. You take a break.'

'I'm fine—'

'No, you're not,' her father interrupted. 'Go home, Caterina. I'll be back there with you soon. See how I am a healthy man again. These doctors have fixed me with their little tubes and their drugs. Meanwhile you look terrible, *cara*. Go home and rest.'

But once she had gone, he lay down on his bed, shutting his eyes for a moment, and Pieta saw the change in him. Some of his strength and confidence had seeped away. He had aged by five years not a few days.

'Ah, my poor wife,' he murmured. 'How is she managing without me?'

'She's been fine, Papa. Stop worrying.'

'But what does she eat, Pieta? And is she sleeping?

256

She is not strong, your mother, she cannot manage by herself.'

'She coped alone when she lived in Rome,' Pieta reminded him.

Normally her father shrugged off references to the past but now he didn't seem to be so unwilling to follow his memories. Perhaps it was the boredom of being cooped up in hospital that had made him more talkative, or the lingering shock of having his body fail him.

'In Rome your mother lived in a terrible place full of prostitutes and run by a madwoman,' he recalled. 'I can't believe she stayed there.'

'What happened to her, Papa?'

'What do you mean?'

'Why did she change from being that person to the woman she is today?'

He closed his eyes again and for a moment she thought he was going to drift off to sleep again. And then he began to tell his side of the story.

*　*　*

I knew there was something really wrong with her when she made her father paint the apartment all those crazy colours. *Mannagia chi te muort* – bright red, purple, orange. You'd have died if you'd seen it. When Margaret and Ernesto moved in, the first thing they did was scrape it all off.

I thought things would be better when we moved into our house but if anything she got worse. Her world seemed to shrink into those four walls. For a while I managed to persuade her to waitress in the restaurant.

Just a couple of nights a week. Margaret or her mother would babysit. I thought it was helping but she only lasted about six months and then she retreated into the house again.

I blame myself. Once I had opened Little Italy I had to work long hours to make it a big success. The difference between a profit and a loss was very small in those early days. And then, once the money started coming in, I was determined to build a stronger business so my beautiful daughters would always have plenty of everything and never know what it was like to be hungry or cold like when I was a child in Ravenno. But I was so busy that I neglected Caterina, so she ended up spending too much time on her own.

Margaret always said lots of women get depressed after they gave birth. She promised Caterina would come out of it eventually and be herself again. But it never happened, not entirely. Gianfranco must share some of the blame for that. He was always there on the fringes of our lives, and although she never said so, I think he was following my Caterina for a while. He was a man I trusted too much. I'd been blind to his real character but she saw it from the start.

That's one of the things I loved about Caterina. She was so wise. But she was also sensitive. Always she worried about things before they happened, and I would have to comfort her and tell her everything would be all right. Sometimes it made me angry and I would shout at her. There were big arguments that would wake the babies and in the end everyone was screaming.

After a while it seemed easier for me to stay at Little

Italy. When I wasn't in my kitchen I'd sit outside and play cards with Ernesto. I avoided home and found any excuse to be in other places. After the restaurant was closed I'd go to Soho with Aldo the chef. He was a single man and he liked to drink at a little flamenco bar in a dark alley off Oxford Street. We were always surrounded by pretty girls and we'd buy them champagne and let them flirt with us. Often Aldo would leave with one of them but I always went home alone.

But there was one woman who intrigued me, a flamenco dancer called Inès who danced like she wanted to murder a man. So passionate, so fiery. And after she had finished on the stage she would drink a glass of sangria with me. The music was loud and when she spoke she came so close that I could feel her hot breath on my cheek. She'd be sweating from the dance, her make-up running and her face shining, but she didn't care. She seemed so strong and free that eventually I fell a little bit in love with her.

How would Caterina ever find out? I reasoned. She was locked away in her world of worry and I was safe. Yes, there were nights I never arrived home. We'd leave the flamenco bar once the birds were singing and go back to Inès's tiny basement flat near Fitzroy Square. And from there I would go straight to Little Italy. Caterina never said anything. I didn't think she cared.

Inès started asking more from me. She turned up at the restaurant one day because she wanted to see where I worked. Then she started dropping by mid-afternoon when she knew I would be outside playing cards with Ernesto. He warned me that I should make her stay away. Although I hadn't said a word to him, he seemed to understand what was going on. But I liked her being there. She was glamorous with her red lipstick and her glossy hair pulled back tightly from her face. She could be stormy, too. As soon as she realized I would never leave Caterina, she began to create scenes.

When my sister Isabella wrote to say my mother was very sick again and I should go home to Ravenno, I was sad to leave my restaurant and my girls. But it was a relief to escape Inès.

Italy was strange. While my life had been changing so much, everything in Ravenno seemed to have stayed the same. Even the old man who ran the market stall looked like he hadn't bothered to move from his stool. Being back there made me grateful for the new life I had, and grateful also to my Caterina for leading me to it.

As soon as I saw my mother I knew it wouldn't be long. There was no need for any doctor to tell me how sick she was. I sat beside her bed and held her hand for hours at a time. I like to think she found some comfort in knowing her only son was there.

It is a terrible thing to lose a mother, to know that you are on your own and no one will ever love the bones of you like she did. The day Mamma closed her eyes for the last time I felt cast adrift. Again I realized how grateful I was to have Caterina, the only person in the world who had ever loved me nearly as much as my mother did. And I felt guilty about the way I had been treating her.

After the funeral Isabella told me there was no reason for her to stay in Ravenno any longer and that she was going to shut up the house and move to Rome. Things were awkward between us because she'd done something that made me very angry and I'd found it hard to forgive her. For my mother's sake we had put all that aside in the last few days. Now Mamma was gone, we argued again.

I couldn't understand why she would move to Rome. She knew no one there, no friends or family. 'I think you should stay here and look after the house,' I told her. 'I'll send you enough money to get by.'

'I don't care what you think and I don't want your money,' Isabella said angrily. 'I'm going to Rome.'

She began throwing her few clothes into a suitcase and then she put on her good coat, slammed the door behind her and went to catch the next bus from the piazza. I was certain she wouldn't get far so I waited for two or three days. But I was wrong. She didn't change her mind and come home. I began to worry. Isabella had lived in Ravenno all her life and I couldn't imagine her faring well in the city.

Ravenno felt more depressing as each day went by and I was desperate to leave. I closed all the shutters, locked up the house and left the key beneath a rock in the garden just in case either of us ever did decide to go back there.

I caught the train to Termini and when I arrived all I could see were the dangers that would have been waiting for Isabella: the pickpockets ready to snatch what money she had; the gypsy children; and the men who preyed on young girls. I wished I knew where she had gone but Rome is a big place and I had no hope of finding her.

Instead I went to the Piazza Navona and wandered around the narrow streets remembering the time I'd spent there while I was courting Caterina. I even stopped at the café where she'd worked and was pleased to find the old owner, a Greek man called Anastasio, behind the counter. We drank a coffee together and I told him about my success with Little Italy. When he asked after Caterina it was difficult to know what to say. In truth he'd have barely recognized her if he saw her again.

'She's a mamma now. Two perfect little girls,' I boasted, pulling out the photos of my daughters I always carried in my wallet.

On the journey home there was plenty of time to reflect on what I'd lost and what I was in danger of losing. I promised myself I would break things off with Inès as soon as I got back.

But it wasn't easy. Caterina was more distant than ever and I was lonely and unhappy. It didn't take long before I slipped back into the comfort of being with Ines. While I was angry at myself for being so weak it was easier to see her than it was to make her stay away.

It must have been a year later that the postcard from Isabella arrived. On the front was a picture of the Spanish Steps and on the back she'd written that she was in trouble and needed me. I was angry but she was my sister and I couldn't refuse to help. So I went back to Rome and found her in a little two-room apartment not far from Termini. It was an ugly place, cramped and hot, and to my eyes Isabella looked coarsened by it. The trouble she'd found herself in was connected to a man, of course. I helped her move to a better place and arranged to send her money regularly. It was difficult for Isabella because she was proud, but she had no other choice.

This time, as I travelled home, I thought about the man I had become and realized I was not so different from the *scemo* who had caused all Isabella's problems. I was so ashamed of myself and for the second time I promised to end this craziness with Ines.

To begin with she found reasons to come to Little Italy. She would claim she was shopping in the market or meeting a friend for lunch. There was a scene or two when she realized I had given her up for good, and I was sorry because she wasn't a bad person, but Caterina was my wife and it was her love I wanted most.

But still it wasn't easy. At night Caterina slept with her back turned to me, she skirted round the edge of a room if I was in it and cut any conversation with me short. I hoped I hadn't left it too late and that all her love for me hadn't leaked away.

I hired another chef and cut down the hours I spent at Little Italy. Instead of working or playing cards with Ernesto, I stayed at home. Caterina seemed confused, almost shy of me, and I felt uncomfortable in the house, as though I was taking up too much of her space. So when spring came and the weather grew warmer I began spending more time out in the garden.

I worked the soil the way my mamma had shown me when I was a boy, planting herbs and vegetables in neat rows. When I saw the green shoots pushing up out of the soil it made me happy and so I planted more. Sometimes I'd see Caterina watching me through the kitchen window as she warmed her hands with a cup of tea. One afternoon I found her pinching out the laterals from a tomato plant. 'My father always used to get me to do this,' she said before melting away indoors.

As the summer went by she joined me in the garden more often. It seemed she enjoyed us working side by side. Together we fought the slugs that ate our lettuces, pulled off the caterpillars and tackled the weeds. Out in that garden, as the plants flourished around us, Caterina's love for me grew a little stronger, too.

She had changed. The girl she'd been was gone and the woman she'd become was frailer and more uncertain. Slowly I grew to accept that.

* * *

Pieta saw her father's eyelids droop. In a moment he would be asleep. She looked at his face, the way the wrinkles settled on each other where his skin was slackening and the greyness of the stubble on his cheeks. Her father had always been the fun one, playing rough and tumble with Addolorata, pushing her on a swing for hours, letting them get dirty, eat more ice-cream than was good for them and stay up late. At night, curled up in the bunk beds they'd slept in as children, they'd talked about how they preferred him to their mother.

All these years later Pieta felt disloyal. She hoped her mother's ear hadn't been pressed up against the bedroom door, that she hadn't suspected how her daughters felt. Her parents may have had failings like anyone else but their love for her was strong. Her face grew wet with tears as she remembered that they were getting older and would one day be gone, leaving her, in Beppi's words, cast adrift. She rested her head on her father's bedcovers, held his hand tightly and let herself cry.

It was late when she left the hospital but Pieta didn't feel tired. Disoriented by her second journey into the past she wandered down the brightly lit corridors towards the exit. She needed wine, she decided, as she sank into the back seat of a taxi. A bottle of crisp sauvignon blanc and someone to share it with.

She got the driver to take her to Little Italy, hoping Addolorata might be working the late shift. A part of her was still reluctant to face her sister's guilt and grief, but now she'd heard her father's side of the story she couldn't put off sharing it any longer.

Frederico was outside clearing one of the tables.

'Is she here?' Pieta asked.

'Of course she is. For days now she's been here day and night, and it isn't good for her or anyone else.' It wasn't like Frederico to speak so frankly, and Pieta could imagine how bad the atmosphere in Little Italy's cramped kitchen must be.

He brought her a glass of wine while she was waiting, and, as she drank it, she tried to decide what she should say. Her sister didn't have the patience for a long-winded story. She would only want the bare facts.

'I suppose you've come to talk to me about what happens when Papa gets out of hospital?' Addolorata looked hot, exhausted and sullen. 'You want to know whether I'm going to walk away from Little Italy?'

Pieta gulped down a mouthful of wine. 'Actually, that's not it at all. I came because there are some things I need to tell you.'

'What things?'

'Sit down and get Frederico to bring us more wine. This is going to take a while.'

When she had finished speaking Pieta realized she'd seen an entire range of emotions on her sister's face – shock, sadness, amazement, even horror.

'How could all of this have happened without us knowing?' Addolorata asked. By now there was a bottle of wine on their table and they'd drunk almost all of it.

'I know. I'm still not sure what to think. I feel we ought to do something but I've no idea what,' admitted Pieta.

Addolorata looked around at the familiar stuccoed walls of Little Italy. 'I think I know what I have to do.'

'Stay here?'

She nodded. 'How can I do anything else after what you've told me? I thought it was just a restaurant when really this place is his life. That's why it nearly killed him when I threatened to leave.'

'But he loves you ... he doesn't want you to be unhappy,' Pieta reminded her.

'Yes, I know.' Addolorata sounded defeated. 'So I suppose I'll just have to find a way to be happy here.'

21

Pieta was too wound up to go to bed. Her mind humming with its many new worries, she found herself in the garden pulling weeds by the yellow light cast through the kitchen window, picking ripe tomatoes and poking her finger into the soil of the raised herb garden to make sure it hadn't dried out.

She tugged out a last weed and went back into the house. All she wanted was to go to sleep so she could stop thinking.

But everything conspired to keep Pieta awake. Just as her thoughts were scrambling and she could feel herself beginning to tip into sleep, a dog barked or a car hooted its horn and she was fully conscious again, rolling over and trying not to open her eyes.

Shortly before dawn she gave up and occupied herself for a while, folding sweaters and rehanging dresses in the room that had become her wardrobe. As soon as she heard the hum of London waking up and going to work she pulled on some jeans and a loose scoop-necked top, tied a bright silk scarf around her throat and walked up the hill towards Islington and her favourite French pâtisserie.

She bought a box of almond croissants and sticky

little lemon cakes covered in icing, then hailed a black cab to take her back home again.

As the taxi pulled up outside the house, she noticed a woman standing beside the railings, staring up at it. Pieta was trying to balance the cake box and find some cash to pay for her fare when she realized the woman still hadn't moved.

'Hello? Are you looking for someone?' Pieta held the box against her chest.

'Are you one of the sisters with the sad names?' she asked.

'I'm Pieta.' She thought the woman gave her an appraising look when she heard her name. 'And you are?'

'I'm Gaetana DeMatteo, Michele's mother. I'm here to see Catherine if I can.'

It was Pieta's turn to be appraising. Michele's mother was slender and elegant. She was wearing slim-fitting jeans and high-heeled sandals, and her hair looked as if it had been expensively highlighted and carefully blow-dried into a flattering layered bob. Pieta felt drab in comparison.

'Does my mother know you're coming?'

'No, and to be honest I'm not sure she'll want to see me. But after what's happened, I think it's time I talked to her.'

'You'd better come in, then.' Pieta held out the box. 'I have cake. Lots of it.'

Her mother recognized Gaetana the moment she saw her. At first she looked surprised to find her standing on her doorstep, then she moved aside and asked her to come in.

'I'm sorry about your husband. I hope he's going to be all right,' Gaetana began as she settled at the kitchen table. Pieta busied herself making coffee and arranging the croissants and cakes on a plate.

'He's much better, thank you.' Her mother sounded formal. 'He'll be home from hospital very soon.'

'That's good.' Gaetana accepted a croissant and a cup of coffee but didn't touch either.

'Why have you come?' Pieta was surprised how calm and certain her mother sounded. 'If it's to tell me that Gianfranco wants to talk to Beppi, that the heart attack has made him realize it's time to make amends, then I'm sorry but it's too late.'

'No, that's not what I'm asking you,' said Gaetana. 'I know you and Beppi won't ever forgive him, but maybe you could begin to forget? It would be nice if we didn't have to stay away from Little Italy when we know it serves the best *zuppa di soffritto*. It would be good if you could come into DeMatteo's to buy our *sfogliatelle*, which are so much more delicious than these French croissants. All I'm asking is that we allow the hatred to be forgotten and are civilized to each other if we happen to meet somewhere in the neighbourhood.'

'We have no problem with you, Gaetana,' her mother said. 'But neither Beppi nor I can forget what your husband tried to do to us.'

Gaetana chewed a fingernail thoughtfully. 'He's hurt me, too, you know. For all those years he was having an affair with Beppi's sister Isabella. He'd go back to Italy, saying he was on business when really he was with her. For a while he even paid for her apartment near Termini. But you knew that?'

'Yes,' replied her mother quietly.

'You didn't know about Isabella's baby, though?'

Pieta saw the look of shock spread across her mother's face. 'There's a baby?'

'Yes, she had a little boy to my husband. She called him Beppi.'

Pieta's tiredness had disappeared. Every bit of her was buzzing, as though she'd drunk a week's worth of strong espresso. 'I have a cousin?' she asked.

Gaetana turned to her. 'You do. He's a few years younger than you, I believe. Your father knew, of course. He went to Rome to help Isabella move out of the apartment after she got pregnant, and he gave her money so she wouldn't have to accept anything more from Gianfranco. But she couldn't break away from him completely. Sometimes I wonder if she's still writing to him.'

For a moment there was silence and then her mother said, 'But Gianfranco only cared about hurting Beppi, didn't he? He never really loved Isabella?'

Gaetana didn't answer the question. Instead she sighed and said, 'My husband is in love with what could be and what might have been, never with what is.'

Although Pieta didn't really understand what she meant, her mother nodded as if she did.

No longer pretending to be on the fringes of the conversation, Pieta took a seat at the table. 'So you forgave him for having the affair with Isabella?' she asked Gaetana.

'No, but I tried to forget. Life can be short and very unpredictable, as your father has just shown us. I love my husband, despite his faults, so I want to spend my life with him.' Gaetana looked directly at her mother. 'Haven't you ever chosen to forget something out of love for your husband?'

Again there was a long silence. Pieta waited to hear what her mother would say but she also chose not to answer the question. 'So what do you want me to do?' she asked instead.

'Whatever you think best.' Gaetana stood up. 'It's up to you now, Catherine. I've said what I came to say.'

Addolorata seemed to have regained some of her old buoyancy. She'd come out of the kitchen to greet a table of old regulars, and was smiling as she accepted compliments for her food and suggested other things they might want to try: buffalo mozzarella flown in fresh from Campania; white peaches soaked in red wine.

The newspaper lying unread in front of her, Pieta waited at an empty table. She needed to tell her sister the final part of the story and see if she had any answers to the questions that were crowding into her mind. Had Michele perhaps suggested his mother come to them? Did he see their father's illness as a turning point, a chance to change the way things were?

And what of their father? How likely was it he would agree to forget a single thing Gianfranco had done? Even though it was true that he himself had made mistakes, she was certain he would be unyielding. In a way the feud had sustained him for all these years.

'What a mess it is,' she complained to Addolorata.

'I just can't see that there's any way to fix it. Are there any other families that are as crazy as ours?'

An odd little smile spread slowly across her sister's face. 'Well, I've worked out what I'm going to do.'

'Elope?'

'No, I'm going to invite Michele DeMatteo to my wedding. And I want my aunt Isabella there and my cousin Beppi, too.'

Pieta was horrified. 'You can't do that.'

'No? Why not?'

'Papa will have a meltdown. Do you want to give him another heart attack?'

Addolorata nodded at Frederico, who had delivered an espresso to their table. 'OK, so here's the thing,' she began once he had moved on. 'Papa has had his way over where we get married and hold the reception. He's chosen the wine and told me repeatedly what he thinks we should have on the menu. Meanwhile you've made me the gown you dreamed of seeing me in. I'm hugely grateful, don't get me wrong, just as I'm grateful that you've been running round organizing everything. I don't have time right now and even if I did, I doubt I'd care about all that stuff as much as you do. I don't even care that Mamma wants me to have Margaret and Ernesto's granddaughters as flower girls. That's fine by me. But the one thing I'd like to have some control over is the guest list. Give me that at least.'

Pieta saw Eden come into the restaurant. He smiled when he spotted them and raised his hand in a wave.

'I have to go.' Addolorata drained her coffee cup. 'Eden and I are going to some stupid class they're holding at St Peter's for couples who are about to get married. Papa said we had to, remember? It turns out he was right and it's obligatory so we couldn't get out of it.'

Pieta stared at her. She feared her sister really was foolhardy enough to add those extra three names to her guest list. 'Just tell me you won't try to invite Michele, please. Do you want to ruin your own wedding?'

'Stop worrying,' Addolorata said, and her tone was gentle now. 'Everything will be all right.'

The day her father came home was like a party. They'd bought a case of his favourite Barolo and arranged vegetables picked fresh from his garden on a big platter that they'd put in the centre of the kitchen table.

'I'll cook dinner,' Pieta offered.

'Are you sure?' her sister asked. 'I can bring something from the restaurant. It's no trouble.'

'No, no, I'd like to cook.'

Addolorata looked surprised but only said, 'OK then.'

When she thought her parents might be nearly home Pieta put on her father's favourite CD of Neapolitan love songs. The house smelled of the sauce she had bubbling on the stove and the room was filled with music. She hoped her papa would forget about his heart attack and be happy he was back in his own kitchen.

But the very first thing he did when he walked in was sniff the air and frown. Lifting the lid off the pan, he checked the contents. 'What's this?' He looked at it dubiously.

'It's a sauce for the pasta, Papa.'

He poked at it with a wooden spoon. 'The meat in here, it looks all shredded.'

'Yes, it is.'

'I never shredded the beef in my life. What made you think it was the thing to do?'

'I just thought it would be … nice.' Pieta tried not to sound offended.

'Nice … uh,' he said dismissively, and then he allowed his wife to settle him in a chair and bring him a glass of wine.

He didn't sit still for long. Soon he was striding about in his garden searching for signs of attack from the caterpillars that ate his cabbages and the insects that plagued his tomatoes. Every now and then he paced through the kitchen, looking at what Pieta was doing but saying nothing.

When she put the pasta pot on to boil, he could contain himself no longer. 'Salt the water once it is boiling,' he shouted at her urgently. 'Not before.'

Pieta tried to stay calm. This was just a taste of what her sister had to put up with in Little Italy each day. Besides, it was Papa's first night home and she didn't want it to end in a big fight.

When he sat down to eat, her father's expression was sour. He forked up a few strands of spaghetti and captured a little sauce. 'It would have been better with the pappardelle,' he complained as he swallowed his first mouthful.

Pieta pretended she hadn't heard him.

'This is really good.' Addolorata was eating with gusto. 'What did you do?'

'I might give you the recipe.' Pieta was watching her

father, who was chewing thoughtfully. 'Papa, do you like it?'

'Yes.' He sounded almost grumpy. 'It is very nice, very tasty.'

He wiped his plate clean with a crust of bread and later, when she went into the kitchen for a glass of water, she found him tasting the leftovers from a wooden spoon. 'Yes, yes, very nice,' he muttered to her. 'But better with the pappardelle.'

Pieta's Shredded Beef Ragù

Honestly, I've no idea when it comes to cooking. All I know is that I hate mince. Frankly, I don't think you should ever eat anything you could easily push down a plughole.

I wanted to make something delicious for Papa – a *ragù* but without the mince. So this I what I did:

I got a couple of big sirloin steaks and bashed them with a pestle so they were thin and tender. Then I fried them on both sides to seal them, because I've read that's what you're meant to do, and I put them in a saucepan with half a bottle of red wine and left them to poach.

I chopped an onion, some celery and a little garlic and fried them in olive oil, then added a jar of tomato passata, some tomato concentrate, a little salt and ground black pepper. I would have put some red chilli pepper in, too, but Mamma doesn't like it. Anyway, once that was bubbling I poured in the wine and steaks and let them simmer for a bit.

I had a couple of glasses of wine myself, then I pulled out the steaks, trimmed off the fat and shredded them with a knife and fork. I put the shredded beef back in with the tomatoes and let it all simmer away until the sauce had thickened and the beef was tender. Right at the end I put in a little fresh basil from the garden. And then I served it with some spaghetti. Although perhaps Papa is right and it would have been better with the pappardelle.

Addolorata's note: You know what, that's not bad. Maybe you didn't miss out on the cooking gene after all. I might put something like it on the menu at the restaurant.

Beppi's note: Not while I have anything to do with it … but it was very nice, Pieta, very tasty.

22

Everyone seemed to have disappeared. Pieta's parents had been gone all morning, she had no idea where, and when she phoned Little Italy to see if Addolorata had time for a late lunch, they told her she'd taken a few days' leave.

'Are you sure?' she asked Frederico. 'She keeps telling me how busy she is. How come she suddenly has time to take a holiday?'

'I don't know.' Frederico never allowed himself to be pulled into their family arguments. 'She only said there was an urgent matter she needed to take care of and she had to take time off. Maybe it has something to do with the wedding.'

Feeling disgruntled, Pieta put down the phone. She couldn't imagine why Addolorata would need time off work for the wedding since Pieta had already organized almost every detail of it herself. She had hired romantic white muslin sheers to drape the walls and ceiling of Little Italy and white linen tablecloths to use instead of the usual red-and-white checked ones. Down the centre of each long row of tables would be a river of sea salt, glistening like crystals, with little tea lights dotted through it, and she had hired pots of hot pink tropical orchids to provide a dramatic contrast.

The cake was a monster, four tiers high, covered in white icing and to be decorated with more pink orchids. She had found a band to play while they were eating so they could follow the Italian tradition of getting up to dance between the endless courses of food. And now she knew there were going to be flower girls, she had bought cute little fairy dresses for them. What was there left for Addolorata to worry about?

Then Pieta realized there was only one thing she could be doing. Buzzing with anxiety, she ran up to her sister's room. It was in the usual state of disarray – piles of clean clothes mingling with dirty ones, a rumpled bed and a dressing table covered with half-used bottles of foundation and squashed-looking lipsticks with lost tops. Pieta checked on top of the wardrobe. The suitcase that was always kept there had gone.

Moving a plate covered in toast crumbs and jam smears, she sat down heavily on the bed. 'Bloody Addolorata,' she said out loud. She knew if she searched through the drawers of the bedside table, her sister's passport and credit cards would be missing, too. It was obvious to Pieta that she had gone to Rome to look for their aunt. She'd said she'd do it and now she had. 'Oh, bloody hell.'

Pieta tried to take some comfort from the fact that Addolorata had only known about their aunt's existence for a matter of days. What were the chances of tracking her down in a city as big as Rome? The trouble was she knew how resourceful and determined her sister could be. Addolorata never stopped to worry about what the problems might be before she tried to do something. Instead she waded in and got on with it.

Even if she did find her, surely Isabella wouldn't come to London for the wedding? She wouldn't be that crazy. Pieta tried to convince herself, but somehow it wasn't working.

She needed a sympathetic person to talk to, someone who would understand the complexities of her family and tell her what to do. In Rome her mother had confided in the Greek bar-owner, Anastasio. He had been wise and kind. She needed a friend like him.

Pieta went back to her own room, a haven of order with no unwashed plates or clothes lying crumpled on the floor. She'd be able to think straight there.

She lay on her bed for a while and stared at the ceiling. Once her mind was made up, she sat at her dressing table and brushed her black hair until it was glossy, then started to apply her make-up methodically. Primer first so the foundation would sit properly. Then neutral shades of bone and brown for her eyelids, a dramatic sweep of black mascara and finally a slick of gloss on her lips.

Satisfied, Pieta turned her attention to what she should wear. She chose narrow jeans and a little top that showed off her slim figure more than she normally liked to, wedge-heeled sandals that gave her height, a green scarf tied round her throat and a spritz of fragrance.

She didn't want to waste time walking so she hailed a cab on Clerkenwell Green and told the driver where to drop her. When they pulled up outside DeMatteo's she saw to her relief that Michele was alone behind the counter.

He smiled when he spotted her. 'Hey, how are you? I hear your father's home.'

'I'm OK … sort of. Actually, I wondered if you'd have time for a drink.'

'Yeah, sure, if you'd like to.' He seemed surprised but pleased. 'My mother's out the back. I'll just get her to come in and mind the store for half an hour.'

Michele's mother raised her eyebrows when she saw Pieta. 'You look very nice today,' she said. 'Going somewhere special?'

'Just to the pub for a quick drink.'

Gaetana looked intrigued. 'Has your mamma said anything to your papa about my visit?'

'Honestly, I don't know.'

'Ah well,' said Gaetana coolly, slipping behind the counter. 'I've done what I can.'

Pieta hoped Michele didn't think she was brazen turning up out of the blue and asking him out for a drink, but she hadn't been able to think of anyone else she could talk to. Her friends wouldn't understand; they'd tell her she was overreacting. But Michele knew her family, had grown up with their fathers' feud and understood what could happen to the fiery Italian temperament once it was submerged in England's icy coolness.

He took her back to the same pub but this time she ordered a cold beer. 'That cocktail was delicious but it gave me a terrible headache,' she confessed.

'Yes, one is good but three isn't necessarily better.' He smiled. 'Still, I was impressed.'

They sat outside so she could smoke and picked up where they'd left off, chatting easily and laughing a lot. So when she started to tell him about Addolorata and her certainty that she was in Rome, she was surprised to see how uncomfortable Michele looked.

'Actually, Pieta, I sort of knew,' he admitted. 'Addolorata came to see me because she thought I might have an address for them.'

'But why would you have an address?'

His eyes met hers and he gave a half-shrug. 'Well, because your cousin Beppi is my half-brother, of course.'

Pieta felt slighted. He had known of little Beppi's existence while she had not. 'You didn't mention him the other day,' she said accusingly.

'I wasn't sure how much to say. I'm sorry. I should have told you.'

'But how did you know?' Pieta asked. 'Did your parents tell you about him?'

'No, but I'd listened to them argue about the situation for years and, given the way they shout at each other, I could hardly help overhearing. So one day, when they were both out, I went through my father's stuff, found some of Isabella's letters shoved behind the drawers of his desk and copied down her address. I don't have any other brothers or sisters,' he reminded her. 'My half-brother is the only one and I wanted to find him.'

'So did you meet him?' Pieta was fascinated now.

'I went to Rome. Just like my father had for all those years, I pretended I was going on business. But as soon as I got there I caught a taxi to the address on the letter.'

'And you found them?'

'I did. It was a bit of a shock for your aunt at first,

but once she realized why I'd come she was very wel-coming. I liked her. She was a lot of fun.'

'You didn't resent her for hurting your mother?'

'Well, yes, a bit,' Michele admitted. 'But my father was as much to blame for their affair as she was. And I liked my half-brother. I wanted to have a relationship with him, which meant I had to accept Isabella.'

'Oh God, and you gave the address to my sister.' Pieta put her head in her hands. 'Shit.'

'She said you wouldn't take the news very well.'

Pieta tried to explain why having her aunt and cousin at the wedding was likely to turn the whole thing into a disaster. But Michele began to argue with her, insisting it would be the best thing for everyone in the long run.

'Trust me, I know my father. He's going to go completely mental,' she insisted.

'Look, Pieta, I can understand why you don't want me there. Don't worry, I told Addolorata I wouldn't come. But it's your sister's wedding not yours. So don't you think you're being a bit unreasonable trying to dictate who she can and can't invite?' His words were hard but his voice gentle, and for some reason Pieta felt like crying.

'I'm only thinking of my father. I don't want to see him upset, especially since he's been so ill.'

'Are you sure it's just your father you're worried about?'

She stubbed out her cigarette and reached for an-other. 'I've put so much work into this wedding, I can't bear to see it ruined,' she admitted.

'Perhaps it won't be ruined,' Michele suggested.

'It might bring your family together again. Surely it's only been your father's pride that's kept him away from Isabella for all these years? And isn't family what weddings are all about – not ribbons, bows and fussy dresses?'

'But Isabella had a baby with your father, a man he hates,' Pieta argued. 'Papa would have seen that as part of Gianfranco's plot to destroy him.'

'My father ...' Michele paused. 'He's not such a bad man, you know. He had an affair but so do lots of husbands.'

'Yes, but there's more to it than that.'

'Tell me?'

'I would but ... it's not my story to tell.'

'Whatever it is, it happened a long time ago,' he reasoned.

'Not to my father. To him it all still feels like yesterday.' Pieta finished her drink and stood to go. She had been wrong to think this could be a good idea. 'Anyway, thanks for the drink, Michele. I'll see you around.'

She walked home feeling more disconsolate than ever. All she wanted to do was to shut the front door behind her and hide away inside the four familiar walls of their house.

Nikolas Rose had phoned three times to see when she was coming back to work and Pieta knew she couldn't it put off any longer. Her father's illness had bought her another week's leave but, like it or not, it was time to slip back into her familiar routine.

She sat on the doorstep, smoking a morning cigarette

and drinking her coffee. It felt a bit like returning to prison. She wasn't in the mood to deal with Nikolas or his fast-changing moods, and the thought of all the problems waiting for her was daunting. That flamboyant peony dress, for instance, which she had designed for Michele's fiancée. She wondered what had happened to it.

Sitting in a little pool of morning sunlight, enjoying the peace and quiet, Pieta wished she didn't have to go to work and that she could spend the day here instead, helping her father tend his vegetables.

Reluctantly she dressed in smart clothes and crammed a big handbag with office essentials: her diary, a notepad, her favourite pencils. Every item felt a little strange to her, even though it had only been three weeks since she'd last handled them.

As she walked towards Holborn she brooded on what Michele had said to her outside the pub. She didn't like the picture he had painted. Surely she wasn't that person? Living vicariously, always putting her father's feelings first, obsessively planning her sister's wedding. It made her sound as though she didn't have a life of her own.

Outside Nikolas Rose's salon she paused for a moment. She hoped he was in one of his charming moods otherwise the day was going to be a long one.

There was a mess waiting for her just as she'd expected. Her desk was covered in paper, her in-tray crammed full. Pieta sat down and began to work through it all carefully. Until it was sorted and everything in its proper place, she knew she wouldn't be able to concentrate.

The girls from the Make Room were pleased to see her. They came in and gave her snippets of gossip, one careful eye on the door in case Nikolas should arrive and find them whispering together.

'He's been in a terrible mood,' said Yvette, the salon's top seamstress. 'Yelling at us for no reason. The other day he threw his phone at the wall and then came in and demanded we find him another one.'

Pieta couldn't help smiling. 'What's been wrong with him, do you think?'

'Well, that client has been causing problems. The bride you did the rather gorgeous design for, the one with the ruffles and peonies. It's a shame because the girls were looking forward to having a go at that.'

Pieta was pleased Yvette had liked the design. She had a good eye and was usually not afraid to say when she thought something was wrong.

'So Nikolas has redone it?' she asked.

'Yes, he's made it restrained, tasteful and rather dull. I'm not surprised the poor girl doesn't like it. She told him she wanted your dress instead. That's when the phone hit the wall.'

'Well, it isn't really a Nikolas Rose gown,' Pieta conceded. 'It's not his look at all.'

'Maybe it's time he changed his look. He's been doing the same thing for years now. We're all thoroughly sick of it. Your design was different, something fun for a change.'

Yvette went back to her sewing and Pieta to clearing her in tray. Her mood had been lifted by the conversation. Suddenly she was beginning to feel creative again.

Order had been restored to her corner of the Design Room by the time Nikolas tripped in through the door. He was wearing a pale linen suit and a panama hat and, when he saw her, his pixie face lifted into a smile.

'Pieta, you're back, how marvellous. Why don't you make us some coffee and then I'll fill you in on everything?' He kissed her cheek, his lips barely making contact. 'I'm so glad to see you, darling. You're never allowed to take time off again, do you hear? I can't do without you.'

He continued to chatter away as she made his coffee exactly how he liked it – two strong shots and a tiny splash of low-fat milk. And then he took her through the designs they were working on, as well as the appointment book and the calendar. Things were busy and Pieta could imagine how stressed he'd been trying to handle it all without her. No wonder he'd been in such a bad mood.

He left the new version of Helene Sealy's peony gown until last. 'Oh yes, I sorted out your little hiccup with this dress,' he said casually. 'I just toned things down a bit, kept it classic. Better, you see?'

'What does the bride think of it?' Pieta couldn't help asking.

Nikolas scowled.

'Does she like it?' she prompted.

'She will like it, darling … by the time you've finished with her. She's coming in at lunchtime to try on the first calico.'

Pieta looked at the new design. There was nothing wrong with it. Nikolas had drawn up a nice strapless gown with a fuller skirt than the one she had planned.

The blowsy peonies had been toned down into tiny fabric daisies, and the ruffles and flounces had gone. It was nice but boring. She wondered how on earth she was going to talk the bride into it.

'Oh, and I'm not going to be here to see her,' Nikolas told her airily. 'But you'll be fine.'

There was no point in arguing with him. It never got her very far. But all morning she dreaded her meeting with Michele's unhappy fiancée. She had always made it a rule not to pressure a client into a gown they didn't feel comfortable with, never mind plainly didn't like. Other designers might be happy with the hard sell approach but for Pieta it was about creating trust and trying to get into the psyche of a client so she could design something that was truly 'them'.

When she was shown into the Champagne Room, Helene looked as pleased to see her as Nikolas had been. 'Oh good, you're back,' she said, as Pieta sat her down on the big white sofa. 'I've been having a bit of a fight with your boss. Did he tell you?'

'Fighting with him is a bad idea,' Pieta said wryly. In her lap was the presentation kit they made up for every bride: a silver folder tied with white taffeta ribbon and containing fabric swatches and copies of the drawings printed on silver paper. 'Why don't you take another look through these and then you can try on your calico.'

'There's no point, is there? I know I'm not going to like it.'

Pieta pretended she hadn't heard. 'The calico is going to give you a good idea of the shape of the dress and we'll be able to check for fit,' she said, adding as always, 'But it will look rather plain and won't fall in quite the same way as it will once the gown is made up in the final fabric.'

She offered Helene the presentation kit and, looking exasperated, the girl took it. 'I don't want this dress,' she said as she flicked through the drawings. 'I want the one you designed for me.'

'But Nikolas Rose thinks …' Pieta stopped. She couldn't be bothered with this any longer. 'Look, it was nice but it's not going to happen. This is my fault because I shouldn't have shown you the design. No dress that looks like that is ever going to come out of this salon.'

'Well, fine, it doesn't have to.' Helene sounded determined. 'You could do it for me in your own time. I bet you often do that for people to make some extra money?'

'No, I don't—'

'There's loads of time,' Helene interrupted. 'Me and my fiancé haven't set a new date for the wedding yet, so you could just work on it at your own pace.'

'I'd get fired if Nikolas found out,' she told Helene.

'How would he find out? I'm certainly not planning to invite him to my wedding.'

'I just can't do it. I'm sorry.'

'Will you at least think about it, please?' the girl pleaded. 'As I said, there's no rush. My fiancé and I have a lot going on in our lives right now and need a little time. But this is really important to me, so please don't decide here and now.'

'OK, I'll think about it.' Pieta didn't have the

strength to argue any more. 'But I promise you I'm very unlikely to change my mind.'

Helene smiled. 'You never know, though, do you? I'll keep my fingers crossed.'

When Nikolas came back from lunch he was still in an affable mood. 'So she tried the calico on? All OK?' he asked.

'Actually, no.' Pieta knew he wouldn't be happy. 'She's decided to put things on hold for a while.'

'Really?' He looked surprised. 'How long do we have till the wedding?'

'Well, that's the thing – they cancelled the original date and don't seem to have set a new one. I'm wondering if it's actually going to happen.'

Nikolas shook his head with a sort of theatrical weariness. 'Why didn't the girl tell us that? I suppose she thought we'd try to charge her a fortune for the work we've done so far, so she's creating a big fuss about not liking the design to try and get out of it. Poor little thing has been jilted.'

'Perhaps that's it,' Pieta agreed. She realized that in all her conversations with Michele he had only ever mentioned his fiancée to her that one time, ages ago, when she'd offered him her congratulations. It all seemed extremely odd.

That afternoon, as she tried to concentrate on her work, she found her mind returning to Helene's request. In some ways the peony gown demanded to be made. She wanted to take the fantasy off the page and turn it into a real dress, to help Helene find the right shoes and earrings, to advise her on her flowers. Although she wasn't quite so certain she wanted the girl to wear them all as she walked down the aisle towards Michele.

That night when she got home from work she felt exhausted. But still, as the cooking smells wafted up from the kitchen, she took out her sketch pad and started doodling. What flowed from her pencil was a dress with an asymmetric shoulder strap of fabric peonies edged in palest pink and a hemline caught up in a ruffle at the front to show a little leg. She remembered every detail of Helene's gown, even the fabric she had thought it would look best in.

Enthused she looked back over the sketches she'd made for the collection she planned to have one day. It had been a while since she'd picked them up and now they looked a little too restrained and tasteful. A bit too Nikolas Rose.

She pulled out more paper and let herself dream. The gowns she sketched were romantic and bold. Not every bride would have the confidence to wear one, but any woman who loved fashion as much as she did couldn't fail to be intrigued. Pieta began to feel excited. Perhaps this was her signature look. She'd certainly seen nothing quite like it in any of the bridal magazines.

When she heard her father shouting up to her that dinner was ready she was reluctant to put down her pencil. But there had been no time for lunch and she was hungry. Besides, whatever he'd been cooking smelled divine.

It was a lasagne, the first he'd made since coming home from hospital. Although the dried pasta was from his store in the pantry and the sauce something he had frozen weeks ago, still Pieta took this as a sign his strength was returning.

For the past week or so her father had walked around on an old man's legs. Feeling weak had made him sour. No one had escaped his mood and the household had been subdued. Now, though, as he pulled his lasagne out of the oven, he seemed buoyant. He gazed at it with satisfaction. 'What a shame your sister isn't here to see it, Pieta,' he boomed. 'Look at this.'

'It's beautiful,' she agreed.

'It will taste as good as it looks.'

As he filled the waiting plates with food, she asked casually, 'Papa, did Addolorata tell you where she was going?'

'No, I think she's somewhere with Eden, taking a break. Maybe the stress of planning a wedding is getting to her, eh?'

Pieta managed not to roll her eyes. 'Yes, maybe,' she muttered instead.

Her father put a simple dressing of oil and lemon on the salad and left the meatballs soaking in sauce in the oven. 'Two courses tonight,' he declared. 'I have made some delicious little *polpette* because I have to build up my strength after all that terrible hospital food. Those poor sick people having to eat that muck day after day. Remember them as you feast on your lasagne, Pieta.'

It did taste good. The thin layers of pasta almost melted in the mouth and the *besciamella* sauce gave it a wicked creaminess.

'Perfect,' her mother declared, managing to finish more than usual.

'It's a heavy dish but people always love it,' her

father agreed happily as he doled out a little more onto Pieta's plate. She tried to refuse but he wouldn't listen. 'Shut up and eat it,' he told her, and she didn't dare argue.

It was while they were tackling the second course that her mother decided to speak up. 'Gaetana DeMatteo called in the other day,' she said as if it were an ordinary occurrence.

Pieta looked at her mother sharply. It wasn't like her to raise a subject that might upset her father.

'She came here? To this house?' He sounded confused.

'That's right.' Her mother kept on eating.

'Why? What did she want?'

'She told us about Isabella and her child.'

'Uh,' he grunted. 'My sister was a silly girl and now she is a silly woman.' He pushed a meatball around his plate, his good mood gone.

'But that wasn't why she came,' her mother continued. 'She had a request to make.'

'Uh,' he grunted again, pretending not to be interested.

'She thinks it's time to forget the past.'

Her father tossed down his fork and pushed away the plate, leaving his last meatball uneaten.

'Don't be like that, Beppi. Just listen to me for a moment.' Her mother still sounded calm. 'All she's saying is that we should be able to buy a piece of pecorino cheese at DeMatteo's and they ought to feel like they can eat at Little Italy. And if we bang into each other at St Peter's or on the street then it shouldn't be so awkward.'

'Why?'

'Because it's more civilized.'

'Why do we have to be civilized?'

'Oh, Beppi, I know he hurt you more than anyone but—'

'*Stai zitta!* I don't want to talk about it.'

'Don't tell me to shut up, Beppi. I don't want to be shouted at. The fact is it's time this feud ended. No one is saying we have to be friends with Gianfranco. That will never happen. But we can be civilized. We can do that at least.'

Pieta looked at her parents. They seemed different to her now that she'd heard about their earlier lives, more vulnerable, less certain.

'I think Mamma is right,' she dared to say. 'He is a horrible man but why should we take it out on his wife and his son? They seem fine.'

Her father didn't even bother to grunt.

'Listen to Pieta, she is making sense,' her mother urged.

He scraped his chair back from the table. 'Shop at DeMatteo's then, *figlia*. It's your money, you earn it. Give it to him if you want to. But I'll tell you one thing. You have ruined my dinner!'

Pieta watched him as he stormed out of the kitchen. 'That didn't go well,' she said to her mother.

'I didn't expect it to. But give him time. He has spent years hating Gianfranco.'

'He loves hating him, doesn't he?'

'That's not true. I may have told you what happened but you weren't there. You don't know how it felt. He hates him for good reasons.'

Pieta cleared the plates and took care of the washing-up. As she scrubbed the baked crust of pasta and sauce from the oven dish she let her mind return to her usual worries. If her father refused even to talk about Isabella, how was he going to feel when she turned up at St Peter's dressed for a wedding?

That night, as she curled up in bed and tried to find sleep, she heard an unfamiliar sound echoing up from the floor below – her parents arguing. Their voices were raised, and although she couldn't work out what they were saying, she realized her mother was doing a lot of the shouting.

'They never argue,' she muttered, closing her eyes and pulling the duvet up over her ears. 'What the hell is going on with this family?'

23

Addolorata was home, her suitcase stuffed with buffalo mozzarella and salami, her clothes pushed in around the food.

'Eden and I went to Rome for a pre-wedding break,' she lied convincingly to them all. 'When we went on that course at St Peter's they told us it would be a good idea to spend some quality time together in the run-up to the wedding.'

Pieta didn't challenge her until later when they were alone together up in the sewing room, checking the fit of the gown after five days of Italian eating. That was when she began to say the things she'd been practising in her mind since she'd realized what Addolorata was up to.

'I can't believe you'd be so stupid,' she hissed as she helped Addolorata step into the gown. 'Can't you see how much it will upset him when he realizes you've been lying?'

'But Isabella is so lovely.' Her sister was in a buoyant mood. 'She's a brilliant cook and she made me this Roman dish with baby artichokes that would be great to have on the menu as a special—'

'Addolorata,' she interrupted. 'Can we just talk about the wedding for one minute? Did you invite her?'

'Yep.'

'And is she coming?'

'Yep.'

Pieta fastened her sister into the dress with gentle fingers but her tone was furious. 'Well, you'd better tell Papa, then. Give him some warning. He's not going to be happy.'

'It's my wedding and it's my problem.' Addolorata sounded bullish. 'So stop trying to tell me what to do. I have a plan, OK?'

'What plan?'

Addolorata didn't reply. She was gazing at herself in the mirror, turning her body to check her reflection from different angles. 'I'd forgotten how beautiful it is, Pieta. You're really talented, you know. Why you're still working for that idiot Nikolas Rose escapes me.'

'I know, I know.' Pieta sat down at the sewing table. 'I've been wondering the same thing all week because he's driving me insane. I'm starting to wish I could just walk out on him.'

'Well, why don't you leave and set up on your own? Now seems as good a time as any. There are probably a couple of clients you could steal to get you started, aren't there?'

Pieta told her about the peony gown and the drawings she'd been making for a small collection of samples.

'What are you waiting for? Get on with it,' Addolorata urged. 'Go into work tomorrow and tell him you're leaving.'

'Yes but what if—'

'Stop worrying about what might go wrong. Have

some faith in yourself. You made this perfect gown for me with no input from Nikolas Rose. Papa has always said he'll give you the money to get you started. You can find a studio, take out some ads in the bridal mags and make the peony gown as your first commission. Start thinking of it as exciting instead of scary.'

Pieta knew she was right. There was no sense in waiting any longer. As she helped her sister climb out of the gown, her mind ran over the possibilities.

'Resign tomorrow,' said Addolorata as she headed off to bed. 'Promise me you will.'

'Wait,' Pieta called after her. 'Your plan about the wedding...'

But Addolorata just threw a conspiratorial smile over her shoulder and shook her head. 'Tomorrow,' she reminded her.

'I'm going to resign from Nikolas Rose today.' Pieta thought if she told enough people then she had to make it happen.

Her mother looked up from her cornflakes. 'Really? Are you going to start your own business at last? Your father will be so excited. Beppi, Beppi, come inside. Pieta has some big news for you.'

Her father had soil on his hands and was dressed in nothing but an old pair of shorts. 'What news? What's happened?'

'I'm going to resign from my job today. Set up on my own.'

Forgetting his hands were dirty, Beppi grabbed Pieta's shoulders and kissed her on both cheeks. 'Finally! I'm so pleased,' he told her, trying to brush away the soil he'd left on her white shirt but only making it worse. 'It will be hard work, *figlia*, but I know you won't regret it.' He began chattering happily about all the ways he'd be able to help her.

On the way to work, Pieta risked stopping at DeMatteo's for a coffee and some breakfast. 'I'm going to resign from my job today,' she told Gaetana, accepting a wrapped pastry from her. 'I'm starting my own bridal design business.'

'Congratulations. If I come across any brides I'll send them to you.'

Pieta wanted to ask about Michele's fiancée but another customer came in and Gaetana moved off to serve him.

It had been easy telling other people but breaking the news to Nikolas Rose was another matter. Pieta spent most of the morning making sure her admin was up to scratch so someone else would be able to take over from her easily. She tidied her desk, put a few personal items in her oversized handbag and copied Helene Sealy's contact details and measurements into her diary. Once he knew she would be competing with him for business, Nikolas would want her to leave straight away.

She felt half-sick with nerves but she'd told almost everyone now so she had to do it. 'Nikolas, have you got a minute?' she asked.

He glanced at his watch. 'Yes, but only a minute. I have a lunch appointment.'

Pieta tried to remember to breathe. 'I've decided to resign,' she began nervously.

'Oh, Pieta, Pieta, not now,' Nikolas said, slipping

on a crimson Nehru jacket. 'If you want to screw more money out of me, then can we talk about it later when I get back from lunch?'

'No, actually I mean it. This isn't about a pay rise. I'm resigning and I'm going to set up on my own.'

'No, you're not.' He sounded certain. 'Leave what you've got here to go and work on your own in some pokey, overpriced studio and most likely go broke? I don't think so. You need Nikolas Rose and you know it.'

Pieta could feel herself weakening. 'I've got some ideas I want to work on and I can't do them here,' she tried to explain. 'It's not that I'm unhappy working for you, I just think it's time to move on.'

Nikolas gestured towards the door. 'If you want to leave, then off you go. But I don't think you do. I'm going for lunch and I'm confident you'll still be here when I get back. We'll talk about these ideas of yours then. Maybe you could do some sort of ready-to-wear diffusion line or something. I'll take a look at them at least.' He made it sound as if he were doing her a favour. As he walked out, his assistant at his heels, he called, 'I'll see you later.'

Pieta felt deflated. She sat at her desk for a moment, wishing there was something on it she could tidy. Some magazines to arrange in a neat pile, spines facing the same way, or even a few paper clips to put away. But she'd taken care of everything.

'So are you going to go, then?' Yvette had emerged from the Make Room.

'You overheard?'

She nodded. 'We all did. The door was open.'

'I don't know. I was so sure when I came in this morning but maybe he's right.'

'Why is he right?' Yvette came and sat down beside her. 'Tell me.'

'Well, it'll be hard. I'll have to take care of every dress from start to finish. There'll be no Make Room girls to do all the sewing and beading for me.'

'But beading is your favourite bit, isn't it?'

'Yes … but I won't have the support or the quality of clients. It's a risk.' These were all the things that had held her back for so long. 'And I don't want to leave you in the lurch in the middle of the summer season.'

'Pieta, we'll miss you, but he won't,' Yvette said briskly. 'There'll be another girl at this desk in no time. He'll train her up to produce the Nikolas Rose signature look and he'll use her the way he's used you.'

'But he was talking about a diffusion line using my new designs.'

Yvette shrugged. 'If he likes them I suppose he might, but he'll take all the credit for them.' She picked up Pieta's handbag and passed it to her. 'Don't you dare still be sitting here when he gets back. Come and say goodbye to us all and then go.'

There were a few tears as she hugged the Make Room girls goodbye and then Pieta walked slowly back through the Design Room, taking a last look at the place where she'd spent so many long hours. The grandeur of the Champagne Room reminded her of what she'd be losing. Nikolas was right to say that she'd never be able to afford anything like this. But as she shut the heavy doors behind her and walked down the stairs she felt the first stirrings of excitement. She was on her own.

The first place she went was Little Italy, hoping Addolorata might have time to share a celebratory glass of champagne. She found a bottle already on ice waiting for her.

'Did you do it?' asked her sister, joining her at one of the outdoor tables.

Pieta raised her glass. 'I needed a little help but I got there in the end. So here's to Pieta Martinelli, Bridal Designer.'

Addolorata let out a whoop and the lunch crowd turned to stare at them. 'That's fantastic! Well done.'

As they sipped their champagne, Pieta started making lists of all the things she had to do. 'A workshop is the first thing because I don't want to be based in Mamma's sewing room for more than a few weeks. I need somewhere stylish for the brides to come for their fittings. If I was sensible I'd have organized all this before I resigned.'

'You've spent your life being sensible,' her sister told her. 'It's great that you're taking a risk for once. And I bet that ...'

The rest of what she said was drowned out by the sound of drilling. Pieta realized that the shop next door to Little Italy, which until recently had been a travel agency, was boarded up. Inside someone was carrying out building work and there was a pile of paint cans stacked in the doorway.

'What's happening in there?' Pieta asked.

'Must be a new business,' Addolorata replied. 'The

travel agent's lease was up and he moved to Islington a couple of weeks ago.'

'I wonder what it'll be? I bet the rent on something with a nice shopfront like that is enormous.' She was starting to worry again. 'You know, I really ought to do a business plan and work out how much I can afford to pay …'

Addolorata topped up her glass. 'It's all going to be good. This is exciting, remember.'

They were just contemplating ordering a second bottle when Michele appeared. 'I heard your news, Pieta. Congratulations,' he called over the little hedge that separated the tables from the street market.

'Come and join us. We're celebrating,' Addolorata called back.

Michele glanced at Pieta, and she nodded. 'Yes, come on in. You're the excuse we need to get more champagne.'

Frederico raised an eyebrow when he saw Michele with them but he brought out a third glass and another bottle without saying anything.

'All these years and I've never sat at one of these tables,' Michele said.

'Well, that's a double reason to celebrate.' Addolorata raised her glass. 'Here's to changes. Good ones. To the end of a bad old era and a new beginning for us all.'

It was pleasant sitting there together. They sipped champagne and picked at some little dishes of food Frederico brought them: little balls of rice filled with melting mozzarella; deep-fried croquettes of potato; olives laced with garlic. Pieta didn't eat much. She was too busy listing all the things she needed to get her business off the ground.

'I'm sure you'll have your first client in no time,' Michele comforted her.

'Actually, I sort of already do,' she confessed. 'Your fiancée asked me to design her gown.'

The smile dropped from his face. 'She did what?'

'Yes, she came to me at Nikolas Rose a few weeks ago. And now she's going to be my first freelance commission.'

Michele's mouth had fallen into a grim line and his eyes refused to meet hers.

'She seems very nice,' she offered.

'Yes, she's nice,' Michele agreed in a tone that didn't invite further comment.

'Do you plan to get married at St Peter's?' Addolorata wasn't discouraged. 'Have you booked a date?'

'I haven't had time to think about it yet.' He was sounding more uncomfortable by the second. 'I didn't know Helene was going ahead with the dress. I haven't … we didn't …' He drained his glass. 'I really should go. Mamma is on her own at the shop. Thanks for the drink. I'll see you later.'

Intrigued, Pieta and Addolorata watched him escape.

'I'd love to know what's going on there. Did you see his face when you told him about the dress?' said Addolorata.

'I know, I know. But his fiancée insists she wants it made.'

'He must have changed his mind and not have

the guts to tell her. He's hoping she'll work it out for herself.'

Pieta didn't like the idea of Michele being such a coward. 'Surely not? There must be more to it than that.'

'I can't think what else it could be. So will you go ahead with the dress?'

Pieta finished her champagne. 'Well, I don't have any other clients. And if she ends up not wanting it then I can always use it as a sample. That dress feels like the beginning of something. I have to make it.'

As she walked home, Pieta passed the entrance to St Peter's. The Italian church was jammed into a row of tall buildings. From the outside it didn't look like much, but she knew that behind the small door were rows of marble columns, soaring domes, overwrought paintings and statues of the saints. It was like a little piece of baroque Italy hidden away in the centre of London.

On a whim, Pieta went in and sat quietly in one of the pews. She had long ago stopped accompanying her parents to mass but still she felt she belonged here. It was the stillness of St Peter's she loved and the history. Italian immigrants had been coming to the church for more than 150 years. Most were poor, scratching a living as street vendors or artisans, but this place had brought them peace and hope. Pieta closed her eyes and tried to empty her mind of all its worries. She thought about the thousands of lives that had passed through this place – those who had struggled and failed, and those who had succeeded. She was just a little part of it all, one more person trying to find a better life in this overcrowded city. And if she tried and failed no one would really notice but her. Bowing her head, she came as close to praying as she had for years.

When she arrived home there was another suitcase in the hall, but not Addolorata's this time. It was an old one, with a broken handle bound up with yellow tape. She found her mother in the kitchen, ironing her way through a pile of clean clothes and looking harried.

'What's going on?' Pieta asked.

'Your papa got cheap fares but we have to leave tomorrow and I don't know how I'm going to decide what to take and get us packed in time ...' She sounded half hysterical.

Confused, Pieta interrupted. 'What do you mean?'

'Italy,' her mother said. 'Beppi and I are going to Italy tomorrow. I haven't been back for thirty years. Imagine that.'

24

The old suitcase had been filled with neatly pressed clothes and the household was in uproar. Her father was darting around like an agitated bluebottle, her mother panicking in case she'd forgotten something important. Pieta couldn't get any sense out of either of them.

'But why Italy? Why now?' she kept asking.

'It was Beppi's idea. He wants to swim in the sea and eat *baccala*,' her mother said as she puffed up and down the stairs fetching things she thought she might need.

Her father's story was different. 'Your mamma wants to see Rome again. She put a coin in the Fontana di Trevi so she has to go back some day.'

Their suitcase was so full she could barely pick it up, so Pieta emptied out some of the things she was sure they wouldn't need and repacked everything carefully.

'Have you got all your pills in your hand luggage, Papa? Does your doctor say it's OK for you to travel?'

'*Si, si, cara.*' Already he was lapsing into Italian. 'I will be fine. And if I'm not then there are doctors and hospitals in Italy, too, you know.'

All the same, when she put them into a taxi, Pieta worried that they seemed too childlike to travel on their own. She waved until they turned the corner and were gone.

Without them the house felt bereft. The tick of the kitchen clock sounded louder than usual, her mother's newspaper waited folded and unread on the table, and in the garden the tomato plants dropped their ripe fruit on the ground unnoticed. Pieta made herself a coffee and went up to the sewing room. With no one there to interrupt her, she could spend as long as she liked working out a plan for her business

But she was too distracted to focus on what needed to be done. Instead she kept finding herself doodling a detail from the neckline of the peony gown or an idea for the cut of the hem. Giving up, she went and found her diary so she could look up Helene Sealy's number. Until she'd started on her dress she wouldn't be able to turn her mind to anything else.

Helene was thrilled when she heard why she was calling. 'You've left Nikolas Rose? That's fantastic news. So do I need to come and see you?'

'Not yet,' Pieta replied. 'I copied down your measurements so I can make up a body block from that. I'll call you once I've done the calico toile and you can come in for a first fitting then.'

'Thank you so much. I can't tell you how happy you've made me.'

'Are you sure, though?' Pieta couldn't help asking. 'Are you completely certain you want to go ahead with a dress given that you don't have a date for the wedding yet?'

'Yes, I'm sure.' There wasn't the slightest note of doubt in her voice.

Pieta spent the afternoon measuring out Helene's body block and wondering whether the wedding would actually happen. There was a part of her that hoped it wouldn't, even if it meant the peony dress never got worn. Michele kept sneaking into her consciousness. He had always been on the edge of her life, at the same schools and the same church, but because of the feud between their fathers she'd tried hard not to notice him. Ever since his mother had appeared on their doorstep, however, she'd found herself thinking about him, remembering their conversations in the pub and how easy it had been to chat to him. His curls were growing back now and his skin was a deeper olive from weekends of sunshine. She wondered what he did when he wasn't in the *salumeria*, where he went and who his friends were. And she wished she knew what was going on between him and his fiancée. As she carefully traced Helene's shape onto the cardboard and cut it into a pattern, Pieta tried not to imagine her new client wearing the peony dress as she stood beside him at the altar.

Pieta had never swung between elation and despair as often as she did in the next week. The time she spent working on the gown was sheer pleasure; it always left her feeling dreamy and sated. But the rest of her day was filled up with looking for a studio and planning for her business, and that wasn't going well at all.

'Everything is so expensive,' she told Addolorata late one afternoon as they shared a bottle of wine outside Little Italy. 'Even the really horrible places cost a fortune. I kind of knew they would but I was hoping I'd get lucky.'

Addolorata gave her an odd look. 'Don't rush into anything,' she said. 'Something will just turn up, you'll see.'

Both were starving so they ordered plates of risotto filled with earthy mushrooms and creamy with melted butter and Parmesan.

'I wonder how Mamma and Papa are getting on in Italy,' said Pieta as she savoured a rich, delicious forkful.

'Papa rang here the other day to make sure everything was all right.' Addolorata laughed. 'It's probably killing him being away from the place. But he said they were about to go south to Ravenno to see what sort of state the old family house is in.'

'How strange that he never sold it.'

'I suppose it's never been worth much. And maybe he felt that he couldn't sell up because it was his last link with Italy and his family.'

'I'd like to see it, wouldn't you?' Pieta had travelled to Florence and Venice but never further south. 'Even though Mamma made Ravenno sound awful, I'd still like to go there.'

The sound of drilling and hammering from the shop next door grew so loud it made conversation almost impossible for the rest of their meal. Pieta wondered if it was affecting Little Italy's business.

'How are you managing to put up with this all day?' she asked Addolorata when it finally stopped.

'Oh, hopefully they'll be finished soon,' she murmured, rubbing her finger round her empty plate and licking the last bits of risotto from it.

Pieta was still staring at the boarded-up shop in

disapproval when Eden appeared in the doorway wearing overalls that were covered in dust and streaks of white paint. He looked sheepish when he saw her.

'All right?' he said. 'Having a nice late lunch or early dinner ... which one is it?'

Pieta was confused. 'What are you doing in there? I thought you were working on a mansion block in Maida Vale.'

'Finished that the other week. This is just a favour I'm doing for a mate.'

'So what's the shop going to be then?'

'Er, well ...'

Addolorata jumped in. 'A clothes shop apparently. Eden is stripping the floors, painting the walls white and putting in a changing room, aren't you?'

'That's right.' He sounded relieved. 'It's not a big job. Be finished in a day or so.'

'Good thing, too,' said Pieta. 'That noise is hideous.'

He laughed and nodded, setting his dusty dreadlocks swinging. 'You don't get building work without noise. I don't even hear it now, you know. Anyway I just came out to see if there might be some coffee and a bowl of *tiramisu* going for a hungry worker.'

Addolorata stood up. 'There is, but you're not eating it out here looking like that. You'll lower the tone.'

Full of risotto, Pieta decided to walk home via the market. She wanted to buy some flowers to brighten up the sewing room. She might have stopped in at DeMatteo's to buy some freshly roasted coffee beans, but Gianfranco was behind the counter and glowered at her through the window. Clearly no one had told him it was time for them to be civilized with one another.

Pieta had tidied up as much as she could, propped a full-length mirror against the wall and put a large vase of white blooms in the corner but still her mother's sewing room was far from an ideal place to meet clients. Nikolas Rose had always impressed upon her the importance of presentation. Everything about bridal couture had to be special, he said, from the room where she received clients to the bag in which she packaged the finished gown. Pieta knew finding a proper studio ought to be her first priority but for some reason she couldn't think of anything but the peony dress.

Its calico toile was hanging on a rail and she hoped Helene wouldn't be disappointed when she saw it. No matter how carefully she explained that this stage was about stitching up some cheap fabric to make sure the fit and shape were right and that the calico was the mere shell of the dress that would come, brides always seemed a bit disappointed by how drab it was. Nervously Pieta laid out the drawings of her design with some fabric swatches on the table. She hoped this was going to go well.

The moment she heard the doorbell ring, she ran downstairs.

'Hi, come in,' she said to Helene. 'I'm sorry I don't have a proper studio. I'm working from my mother's sewing room, which is a bit different from Nikolas Rose's salon as you'll see. But come up anyway.'

'Actually I hated that Champagne Room,' Helene confessed as she followed her upstairs. 'It was really stuffy and old-fashioned. I never felt like I belonged there.'

As she helped her into her calico and made alterations to the shape and fit, Pieta automatically ran through the things she talked about with every bride. Had Helene thought about flowers? Would she wear her hair up or down? Did she need help choosing shoes or jewellery?

It was only when the girl was back in her own clothes and about to leave, that Pieta's curiosity got the better of her.

'Did you realize that I know your fiancé?' she asked.

'Oh, do you?' Helene smiled. 'He's lovely, isn't he? Michele is the first really good guy I've been out with. That's why I had to marry him. But how do you know each other?'

'His shop is round the corner from the restaurant my sister runs, Little Italy.'

'I know it. Haven't been there, though. For some reason Michele never wants to eat there. Probably sick of Italian food. He always likes a curry.' Helene smiled and Pieta was reminded what a pretty girl she was. 'Did you tell him you were designing my dress?' she asked.

'Actually I did. Should I not have?'

'Oh no, that's fine.' For the first time Pieta thought she heard a tiny wobble of doubt in Helene's voice.

'Great, well, I'll cost out the dress and let you know how much you owe me for the deposit.' Pieta tried to sound breezy. 'Oh, and I'm going to do another calico so I'll need to get you back in for a second fitting.'

When Helene left, she kissed Pieta on the cheek. 'Thank you. I've been having a really crappy time and this is the first thing that's gone right for me in ages.'

Shutting the door behind her, Pieta felt guilty for having hoped the wedding might not happen. Helene was a perfectly nice girl. How could she wish her so much unhappiness?

Pieta was busy making a second calico so she could be sure the changes she'd made to the peony gown would look and fit right. When the telephone rang, she nearly didn't bother to answer it.

'Family conference.' It was Addolorata, sounding shrill. 'At Little Italy in half an hour. Be here.'

'Hey, how can we have a family conference? Mamma and Papa are still in Italy.'

'Not any more. I think you'll find they're sitting outside the restaurant and fizzing at the bung for some reason. You'd better get here as fast as you can. Something's up.'

Pieta was faintly irritated. All she wanted to do was to work on this dress but there seemed to be endless interruptions – appointments with her bank manager, possible studios to view, and now her parents demanding she drop everything and rush over to Little Italy. She was pleased they were home but would have been grateful for a few more hours of peace to complete the calico. Feeling disgruntled, she changed into clean clothes and made herself presentable.

She found her parents sitting at one of Little Italy's outdoor tables, barely able to contain their excitement.

'*Ciao, bella*,' her father greeted her. His skin was tanned and his lips blistered from too much sun.

'Oh, Pieta.' Her mother clung to her and kissed her cheek. 'We've missed you. Is everything all right at the house?'

Beppi took control. He sat them down and asked Frederico to bring an antipasto platter and a bottle of chilled rosé wine.

'Your mother and I, we have some news,' he began. 'We made some big decisions while we were in Italy.'

Pieta noticed her mother was twisting a napkin nervously in her hands. 'What sort of decisions?' she asked.

'We've decided to buy a place in Italy. Something not far from a beach, perhaps as far south as Basilicata, so that I can have some sunshine and good food every summer.'

'Fantastic! A holiday house,' said Addolorata. 'That's great news.'

'Yes, but there's more, isn't there, Beppi?' her mother said. 'You'd better tell them the rest of it.'

'We've decided also to sell the house in Clerkenwell. We'll find something smaller for when we're in London. A little apartment somewhere.'

'Sell the house?' Pieta couldn't believe it. 'Are you sure, Papa?'

'Yes, it's time for a change,' he said.

'But what about Mamma?'

'Your mother agrees that we've been in the house too long. We want to have one last adventure before it's too late. So we'll spend time in Italy and you can come and visit us there. And we'll come back to London whenever we miss you.'

Addolorata nodded. 'I think it sounds great.'

Pieta tried to nod approvingly, too, but her mind was whirling with worries. Now she'd have to find a place to live as well as somewhere to work.

'The timing is right,' her father continued. 'Addolorata, once you are married you will move to Eden's house, of course. You spend half your time there anyhow. And Pieta, you are changing your life, too.'

'Yes …' Pieta wasn't sure what else to say.

'Your mamma and I thought you could live in the apartment above Little Italy while you get your business off the ground. It's not very big but it will be convenient. And at least you'll be able to eat properly.'

'Good idea.' Addolorata was sounding positive. 'We're just storing junk in it at the moment so we'll get it cleaned out and make it nice again.'

'Yes, sure … thanks.' Pieta was dazed.

'There's one more thing. The most important one for you, Pieta. Come with me.' He stood up and led her out onto the street.

'Where are we going?'

'You'll see.' He sounded excited again. 'Come on, come on, follow me.'

Grabbing her by the hand, he pulled her towards the shop next door to Little Italy. There was still some scaffolding up outside and a large tarpaulin had been gaffer-taped to it to hide the shopfront from view.

Eden appeared and helped her father tug down the tarpaulin. Pieta stared for a moment and then she felt tears spring into her eyes. Above the door of the shop was a small stylish sign. It read: 'Pieta Martinelli, Bridal Designer'.

'It's your shop. Go inside and take a look,' her father urged.

Through the doorway was a spacious room with white-painted walls and polished wooden floors. On one side was an ivory-coloured curtain that led to a large changing room with a mirrored wall. And through an archway was another room, decorated in similar style, with a drawing board and a work table.

'Do you like it?' Her father sounded anxious. 'We've left the finishing touches to you because we didn't want to get it wrong.'

'Like it?' Pieta wrapped her arms round him and kissed him. 'Of course I do. I love it. But I don't understand. Have you rented the place for me? It must have cost a fortune.'

'Rented?' He made a disapproving clicking noise with his tongue. 'One of the things my father-in-law taught me is that you never rent when you can buy. All the profits I made from Little Italy went into buying the buildings it occupied. I bought this one, too, because I thought one day we might want to expand the restaurant. And you see, it has all worked out. Addolorata gets Little Italy and you get this shop and some money to turn it into a business once we've sold the house.'

Pieta was overwhelmed. 'You don't have to do this—'

'Of course I do,' he interrupted. 'All those years I was working for you and Addolorata, for your futures. It makes me very happy that I can give them to you at last. Now you stay here, look around, make your plans. I'm going back to make sure my Caterina is all right. It is a big change. We must all look after her.'

Pieta stood for a while in the middle of the shop. She could see so much possibility. There was space for her to display a small collection of wedding jewellery, underwear and shoes, maybe even some bonbonnières. She would buy a sofa where the brides could sit during consultations and a couple of mannequins to dress in samples of her gowns and put in the window. Even the location was good. The fashion crowd she was aiming at would think it edgy and cool.

'It's so perfect,' she told everyone when she returned to the table. 'And I already have a name for it. I'm going to call it "The Italian Wedding".'

Her father considered the name for a second or two. 'The Italian Wedding? It's a good name,' he declared. 'I like it.'

They all ate dinner together outside Little Italy, with her father insisting on ordering.

'You don't want the *sartu*, Pieta. It is too heavy. Good for Eden maybe after all his hard work, but not for you. And Caterina, you are tired? Maybe just a little minestrone so you have room for pudding.'

Pieta kept stealing glances at her new shop. She was impatient to be in there and running her business, to be Pieta Martinelli, Bridal Designer at long last.

25

Addolorata had suddenly realized her wedding was only a fortnight away and was showing signs of panic.

'What did you say we're doing about flowers? And the photography? Oh God, I should have been involved with this, shouldn't I?'

'It's all organized. While you were busy running round Italy looking for long-lost relatives, I was sorting it out for you.' Pieta couldn't keep the tartness from her voice.

'I'm a terrible bride, aren't I?' Addolorata giggled. 'Lucky I've got you or the whole thing would have been a disaster.'

They were lying on Pieta's bed, side by side, like they used to on good days when they were kids. Having a sister had sometimes seemed a curse to Pieta. As teenagers there had been months when they refused to speak to each other, when clothes had been borrowed and spoilt and voices had been raised. Even now there were times when there was tension between them, when Addolorata accused her of saying one thing and meaning another, or when Pieta got tired of her sister's casual approach to everything in life except food.

'Your wedding still might be a disaster,' she pointed out. 'You haven't told me what your big plan is. How you're going to introduce Isabella and her son into the occasion without upsetting Papa.'

'Ah yes, that.' Addolorata pulled a rug over her and snuggled into it. 'Well, they're not going to come to the church ceremony, just the reception. Papa will be feeling emotional and have a couple of glasses of bubbly in him by the time he sees her. I think it'll be OK.'

'What if it isn't?'

'Oh, stop worrying. Come and help me decide what I'm going to do with my hair and make-up. You're good at that stuff.'

Pieta spent the next hour piling her sister's hair on her head and painting her face. Whatever else might happen on her wedding day, Addolorata was going to look beautiful.

'Our lives are going to change,' Pieta said wistfully, looking at their reflections in the mirror of her dressing table. 'Our family is being broken up.'

'Change isn't always a bad thing,' pointed out Addolorata. 'Although I never thought Mamma would leave this house. I'd love to know what happened in Italy to make them come home with all these plans.'

'I'll find out,' promised Pieta. 'Now come downstairs. Let's try on that wedding dress one last time.'

Pieta was curious about Italy, too, but she bided her time until her father was out playing cards with Ernesto. She found her mother up in the junk room, sitting beside an open box and poring over old photographs.

'I'm trying to make a start clearing out some of our stuff but I'm not getting very far,' she admitted. 'I keep finding things I'd forgotten I had. Did I ever show you this picture of you as a baby with my mother at the house in Balls Pond Road?'

'I don't think so.' Pieta sat down beside her and glanced at the picture. 'Ugly little thing, wasn't I?'

'No, you weren't, you were beautiful. Both of you were. Even though I wasn't much of a mother back then.'

'But you had postnatal depression, Mamma.' Pieta's voice was gentle. 'How come you never saw a doctor and got treatment for it?'

'In those days you just didn't. I don't think we even had a name for how I was feeling. My generation always thought you should soldier on and not bother the doctor.'

'Things might have been different if you had.'

'But they didn't turn out too badly in the end, did they?' Her eyes were glazing with tears. 'I have two beautiful and successful daughters, a good husband and exciting plans for the future.'

'Can you leave all this, though?' Pieta looked round the attic room. 'Do you really want to sell our house?'

'No, of course not. Leaving this house will be the hardest thing I've done in my life. But it doesn't make financial sense to keep it, I can see that.'

'Why, though?' Pieta persisted. 'What made you and Papa come up with this idea of living in Italy? Why leave here when you're perfectly happy?'

Her mother put the photograph back in the box and said thoughtfully, 'Partly because of your father's heart attack, I suppose, and the realization that so much of our lives lie behind us. And partly because of Italy.'

'You were only away for ten days and suddenly you decide to buy a house there. What happened exactly?'

'Come downstairs. We'll make a cup of tea and I'll tell you,' her mother promised.

* * *

Do you know that even the coffee smells different in Italy? It was the first thing we noticed when we got off the plane. Beppi had to have two cups of sweet espresso straight away. He had been scared of going back, I think. It had been so long and he knew how much things would have changed.

Rome wasn't so different, though. The streets around Termini still felt dirty and dangerous, the cafés spilled onto the pavements and the ancient buildings looked the same. It was busier and noisier than it had been in our day. The queue to see the Sistine Chapel snaked for what seemed like miles and we had to fight our way through a bank of tourists to spend time beside the Trevi Fountain. That put Beppi into one of his bad moods.

Both of us wanted to go back to the Piazza Navona. It was the place we first met and where we'd spent most of our time that summer. But it felt strange to be walking through it, like we were young just five minutes ago.

'It's more than thirty years since I first saw you sitting at that pavement café and then you came up and spoke to me,' Beppi reminisced as we walked past the rows of easels where artists were painting tourists' portraits or views of ancient Rome.

'It was you who spoke to me first,' I pointed out.

'No, no, you are remembering it wrong,' he insisted.

'You girls were keen to talk to us. We were young, cool and hanging out by the fountain. How could you resist, eh?'

There was still a bar where Anastasio's used to be. It had been refitted with modern chairs and tables instead of the old booths, and there was a new Gaggia coffee machine. I'd half hoped I'd find Anastasio there, an old man sitting with his newspaper and a beer at the corner table. But there was no sign of him and the haughty-looking young girl behind the counter shrugged when I mentioned his name.

'Anastasio?' A skinny man of about our age was sitting at the bar, dunking biscotti into a tall glass of caffe latte. 'He retired, went back to Greece years ago. He'd made his money and said he wanted to enjoy it before it was too late.'

'He was a kind person. I'm glad he did well,' I said in my rusty Italian.

The man sort of squinted at me and cocked his head on one side like a puppy. 'Do I know you? Have we met before?'

'I used to work here thirty years ago.'

The girl behind the bar looked disinterested in my memories but the thin man grinned. 'I remember a very pretty blonde English girl from back then. All the boys were after her. But that wasn't you, was it?'

'No, that was my friend Audrey.'

We sat down with our coffees and for a moment the past seemed more real to us than the present. There had been times when I'd been sad and lonely in Rome, but mostly what I remembered was the feeling of possibility. We felt as if anything could happen.

Beppi seemed to read my mind. 'We're still only in our sixties, you know,' he said. 'Life isn't over yet.'

'I know but I feel so old. And how did those years go by so fast without us noticing?'

'For a long time nothing changed. We stayed in the same house, worked in the same business. I think that has made it feel as though life has gone by faster.' Beppi looked at the scene on the street outside: the chaos of vans trying to edge down the narrow alley clotted with café tables and swarms of people; the woman standing on the pavement shouting a conversation with someone three floors up; the kids flying past on their scooters. 'I certainly never meant to stay away from Italy for so long. I'm a foreigner here, Caterina,' he said sadly.

That night we ate in the hotel restaurant where Beppi had once worked. It was still grand but scaled down from what he remembered.

'Tonight we don't worry about what anything costs,' he said as we walked in. Even though there was no one there he recognized, I think it gave him huge satisfaction to go back. He'd left in disgrace thanks to Gianfranco and now he was returning a successful man.

Naturally the food didn't meet with his approval.

'This saltimbocca needs more sage and the meat isn't tender enough. I don't believe it's even veal,' he said, pushing it round his plate cheerfully.

We ate in different restaurants every night, Beppi ordering more than we could ever manage: soups rich with chestnuts and chickpeas; oxtail stewed in rosemary and red wine; squid stuffed with little prawns. As he ate, he made notes to pass on to Addolorata.

'Beppi, stop it,' I said at last. 'If she needs inspiration she can come here herself. You have to back off now. Leave her to run Little Italy by herself.'

He looked hurt. 'I'm only trying to help.'

'I know but she doesn't need your help any more.'

We were eating in a tiny family-run place in Trastevere, with eight tables at the most. Beppi looked around at it speculatively. 'Perhaps we should open a little trattoria like this. Have a blackboard menu. I cook, you waitress, just like the old days.'

I laughed. 'No, Beppi, no.'

'I have to do something.' He sounded almost desperate. 'I can't sit at home all the time. If you retire you die, as I've said a hundred times before.'

'You have your garden, your cards with Ernesto and you could be on the committee that organizes the procession of Our Lady of Mount Carmel for St Peter's. There are lots of things you can do to fill your time.'

He looked sullen. 'But I don't want to fill my time.'

The next day he told me he was growing tired of Rome. 'We'll catch a train down south and find somewhere to stay near the coast,' he decided. 'And then we can make a day trip to Ravenno and see my mother's house, if it's still standing.'

My memories of Ravenno weren't happy ones and I was reluctant to go back there, but Beppi's mind was made up. He went and chatted to the concierge who, as luck would have it, had a cousin who knew someone with a seaside house in Marina di Maratea that he sometimes rented out. A couple of telephone calls were all it took to fix it.

From the moment we saw the little white house we

both fell in love. It was right by the Gulf of Policastro with just a bed of rock in front of it and a garden sloping up behind. The house was shaded by carob trees and inside it was very simple: a ceramic tiled floor, a wood burner in the kitchen, and whitewashed walls with brightly painted plates dancing across them.

The first thing Beppi did was rip off his clothes and climb the stone steps down to the sea. He dunked his head beneath the waves, immersing every bit of himself in the salty water.

'It is beautiful, Caterina. Come for a swim,' he shouted when he resurfaced.

I shook my head. I was happy up on the rocks in the shade of an overhanging carob tree that was dropping its long black pods all around me.

That afternoon we shopped for food together: sweet little cherry tomatoes, fresh basil, a bottle of Aglianico wine, a bulb of garlic. Beppi cooked a simple pasta dish and we carried the kitchen table and chairs out onto the rock and ate beside the sea.

'What a beautiful life,' said Beppi as he drank his wine and breathed in the salty air. 'Here I could be happy doing nothing.'

We put off going to Ravenno and over the next few days fell into an easy rhythm. A coffee and a pastry every morning at the café in the town, then shopping together for no more than a basket of food and home again so Beppi could swim in the sea and bake himself on the rocks. As the day cooled we'd take a walk, exploring little bays and leafy lanes, staring into the vegetable gardens of the peasant farmers and comparing them to our own.

'I would be happy to spend summers here,' Beppi kept saying.

To my surprise I agreed with him. If he could be happy here then so could I.

'We should come back for a few weeks next year,' I suggested. 'Maybe Pieta and Addolorata could come out and join us.'

'They would love it,' he agreed. 'How could they not?'

I'd have preferred to stay by the sea but sadly Ravenno could be avoided no longer. The road was just as I remembered it, twisting and turning round mountains and through tunnels, with Beppi behind the wheel of the rental car, swearing beneath his breath.

'*Cose da pazzi*, they all drive like lunatics,' he kept complaining.

'You used to drive a bit like that yourself,' I told him, trying not to look down into the ravine we were skirting.

Ravenno hadn't changed. Its green-shuttered stone houses clung like barnacles to the side of the mountain and, as we drove nearer, it seemed as unfriendly and forgotten as it always had.

'It's a godforsaken place,' I complained. 'How did you ever survive growing up here?'

'As a child it wasn't so bad. Every day there was an adventure to be found.'

'For you and Gianfranco?' I asked.

He nodded but said nothing.

We parked in the piazza and walked down to his mother's house. To our surprise there were vegetables planted in the freshly dug garden. Someone had

327

painted the front door blue and rolled rocks onto the roof to stop the terracotta tiles being lifted off by the winter winds.

'Someone is living here,' said Beppi, confused.

The window was open and he peered inside. '*Buon giorno*,' he called out. 'Is anybody there?'

We heard the sound of a baby crying and a mother's voice trying to soothe it.

'Hello, hello,' Beppi called out and rapped on the door.

The girl that opened it was young and very beautiful. She had jet-black hair that fell into ringlets round her face and eyes the colour of almonds.

'*Signore*?' the girl said questioningly. 'Can I help you? Are you a foreigner?'

'No, I am from Ravenno.' Beppi sounded indignant.

'Oh.' She sounded apologetic. 'I didn't recognize your accent. You don't sound like you come from round here.'

'This is my house.' Beppi had one foot in the door now. 'What are you doing here?'

The girl seemed unperturbed. She opened the door a little wider so he could see the humble room behind it. 'There must be some mistake, *signore*. This house belongs to my landlady Isabella Martinelli. She lives in Rome.'

Beppi looked taken aback. 'She has been letting the place?'

'Yes. The rent is low because, as you can see, the house is not much. When we moved in a year ago we had to tidy it up a lot. Fortunately my husband is a good worker.'

'Isabella has been letting this house?' Beppi was stunned.

The girl looked concerned. 'Are you all right, *signore*? I think you and your wife should come in and sit down while I get you both a glass of water.'

All the colour had drained from Beppi's face.

'That's very kind of you,' I said quickly. Taking his elbow, I led him inside.

She had made homely little touches to the place. Pretty curtains hanging at the window, a display of family photographs like Beppi's mother had once had, some wild flowers arranged in a large glass of water on the kitchen table.

'Isabella Martinelli is my husband's sister,' I explained to the girl. 'We haven't seen her or been back to Ravenno for many years. We expected the place to be empty.'

'You aren't going to make us leave? I have a young baby …'

'No, no, don't worry,' I reassured her. 'No one's going to make you move out. Isabella has the right to let the place to you if she wants to, doesn't she, Beppi?'

He nodded slowly. 'I expect she needs the money.' He paused for a moment and then asked the girl hesitantly. 'Have you seen her?'

'No, we arranged it all over the telephone. She doesn't come down here.'

I finished my water and touched Beppi's arm gently. 'We should go now. There's nothing to see here. Let's go back to the coast.'

'All right,' he agreed.

He made me walk once around the town with him

but didn't share any of his memories of the place. I expect they all included Gianfranco and he preferred not to speak of him.

It was a relief to get into the car and point it back towards Marina di Maratea. 'I don't ever want to go back there,' I told him.

'We don't have to.' He was driving faster than he had on the way there. 'If Isabella wants the house she can have it.'

We were back beside the sea in time for the sunset. Since we hadn't had time to shop for food we walked slowly to the little pizza restaurant up the road.

'Everywhere is polluted by Gianfranco,' Beppi complained. 'London, Ravenno, Rome. Everywhere I go I'm forced to remember him.'

'Not here, though,' I said as we took our seats and accepted menus from the waiter. 'Gianfranco never came to Maratea.'

'You are right.' Beppi frowned at the menu. 'This place is untouched by him.'

For the next day or so he was very quiet. He dozed in the sun, toasting his body brown, swam in the sea and cooked in the little kitchen.

One evening we were sitting outside on the rocks listening to the waves and watching the sun sink into the sea. Suddenly Beppi said, 'I have made my decision.'

'What decision?'

'We are going to buy this house and spend our summers here. Addolorata will be free to do whatever she likes at Little Italy without me interfering. And every time I turn a corner I won't have to worry that

I'm going to bump into Gianfranco. Here I can forget about him and the stupid feud and just enjoy my life … and my wife.' He smiled at me and I glimpsed the strong white teeth that could still crack a walnut.

I had been ready to argue but paused for a moment and thought about it. There was a possibility that Beppi was right. I couldn't deny that we had been happy these last few days together by the sea.

'It's fine for a week or so, but won't you get bored living here for an entire summer?' I asked.

'Perhaps,' he agreed. 'But we can keep a place in London so we can go back whenever we want.'

'How do you even know this place is for sale?' I was sure there would be an obstacle if I looked hard enough.

'Yesterday I was talking to the man in the wine shop while you were next door looking at the souvenirs. He seemed to think the owner would take an offer. It's worth a try.'

Neither of us mentioned our own house, the place that had been my refuge for so many years. I suspected Beppi's plan meant selling it but I wasn't ready to think about that yet.

Once the sun had set we went indoors. The day had been warm but now there was a chill in the air and it felt like the beginnings of autumn. Beppi lit the wood burner and we sat beside it, watching the flames flicker through the glass. That's when I decided that if this could be our future maybe I wouldn't mind leaving the past behind.

26

Life was chaotic. The house was up for sale and they were busy sorting through the belongings the family had accumulated over the past thirty years. Most days the dust drifted thickly through the air as they disturbed piles of books and cupboards filled with things they'd never really needed.

Everyone seemed on edge. Addolorata had the wedding jitters and was driving everyone insane with questions about all the little details she hadn't cared to mention until now. Pieta was trying to sort out her little apartment as well as her shop, and struggling to find time to finish the peony dress. And Beppi seemed to be spending hours on the phone, making arrangements for his new life in Italy.

'There's a lot to organize, a lot to be done,' he kept muttering.

With all the noise and fuss, Pieta had found it impossible to work in the sewing room so she'd decamped to her new shop. Even though things there weren't arranged quite to her satisfaction, at least it was peaceful and she had more space to cut the fabric and begin to sew the peony gown.

She was immersed in her work one morning when there was a knock on the door and she looked up to see

Michele waving a takeaway coffee and a box of pastries at her through the window.

'I've brought you some breakfast,' he said when she unlocked the door.

'You absolutely can't come in,' she told him. 'I'm just finishing your fiancée's dress and you're the last person who should see it.'

'It doesn't matter about that now.' He looked regretful. 'Let me in and I'll explain why.'

He sat down on the elegant white sofa that had just arrived and delivered a formal little speech. 'Helene was too upset to talk to you herself so I said I'd come,' he began. 'We've cancelled our plans to get married so she won't need the dress. Of course, I'll pay whatever is owing on it. And I'm sorry to have wasted your time.'

Pieta realized she was happy to hear the wedding was off and instantly felt guilty. 'It doesn't matter about the money,' she said, trying to keep her voice steady. 'I can keep the dress as a sample. I'll put it on one of the mannequins in the window.'

'That's kind of you.'

'But Michele, what I don't understand is why you've strung her along all this time.' Pieta rushed into the question without thinking. 'You knew weeks ago that you didn't want to go ahead with the wedding, didn't you? Were you just too afraid to tell her?'

'No, not afraid.' Michele shifted uncomfortably on the sofa. 'But I had my reasons.'

Having turned the conversation in this direction, Pieta couldn't help but pursue it. 'I know it's none of my business but I have to ask … what were your reasons?'

He shifted his feet uncomfortably. 'Helene has been having a bad time,' he began. 'Her mother has been seriously ill and then she lost her job and had to temp, which she hated. She kept saying our wedding was the only thing keeping her going. I thought telling her I'd changed my mind would destroy her.'

'And now?'

'Her mother is out of hospital, she's landed a good job and she seems a little stronger. It wasn't fair to put it off any longer. Helene is a lovely girl. She hasn't done anything wrong and I didn't want to hurt her any more than was necessary.'

Pieta wanted to ask him what had made him change his mind but she thought she'd probably pushed it too far already.

'Well, look, I appreciate you coming to let me know and please tell Helene not to worry about wasting my time because she hasn't,' she said briskly. 'Actually, it's thanks to her that I'm here instead of slaving away at Nikolas Rose.'

'The shop looks great,' he said, relieved to change the subject. 'Show me around.'

She spent half an hour chatting to him and then took him upstairs to the still dingy apartment and made him look at paint charts and fabric swatches as she described her plans for it.

'Sorry, I'm going on a bit, aren't I?' she laughed. 'But I'm excited by all this and a bit obsessive.'

'It's nice to see you so passionate about your life. And it'll be good having you here, living and working in the neighbourhood. I expect we'll see a lot more of each other.'

Pieta felt a little jolt of happiness. 'I expect so.'

They said goodbye out on the street amid the bustle of the market. Just as she was about to go, Michele reached out and touched her arm. 'I care about Helene, you know,' he said quietly. 'But I realized I was only with her because the person I'm really in love with seemed out of reach. That's why I couldn't marry her in the end.'

He turned away and headed back to stand behind the counter at his father's shop, leaving Pieta to return to work on the now unwanted peony dress and wonder if there was any sort of a message for her in Michele's last words.

The night before the wedding they had agreed to have a family dinner, just the four of them gathered round the kitchen table the way it had been for so many years.

'What will you cook?' Pieta asked her father. 'It had better not be anything too heavy, as that dress already fits Addolorata like a glove.'

'Heavy? My food isn't heavy.' Her father looked grumpy as he surveyed the contents of the larder. 'So much pasta in here. You must take some when you move to the apartment otherwise it will be wasted.'

Once he'd pulled out almost every pan, he began to chop garlic and parsley to make a *soffritto*. Watching it sizzle in warm olive oil Pieta remembered childhood summers, playing with Addolorata outside in the garden as the smell of their father's cooking drifted out of the kitchen window and made their mouths water. Soon their life in this house would be just a memory. Her father would rattle pans in another smaller kitchen and she would eat her meals alone in the apartment above Little Italy.

The thought made her feel so wretched that she couldn't watch her father cook any longer. Instead she went upstairs to sort her clothes into piles. Some would go to charity shops, others to vintage clothes stores. Even this was poignant. Every dress or shoe had a memory attached to it, however small, and Pieta felt as if she were giving her life away. But the apartment was tiny and there wasn't space for everything.

'Change can be good, remember?' Addolorata was standing in the doorway, smiling at her.

'So you say,' Pieta replied. 'It's not feeling so good right now, though. Only sad.'

'I know. For years I've been complaining about Mamma and Papa, and now I know they're not going to be around so much I'm going to miss them. Crazy, isn't it?' She pulled a floral print dress off the charity shop pile. 'Do you think this would fit me? I've always liked it.'

Pieta abandoned her sorting and zipped her sister into the dress, helping her find shoes and a handbag that would go with it.

'This is heaven,' Addolorata admitted. 'For years I've lusted after your wardrobe. And it fits me … just … almost.'

'As long as you don't put on any weight you'll get away with it.'

Addolorata started rifling through the piles of clothes in case there was anything else she fancied. 'You know it's going to be good having you living and working in the neighbourhood,' she said as she tugged out a blue top. 'We'll see a lot of each other.'

'That's funny. Michele said more or less the same thing.' Pieta had told her sister that his wedding was off but not about the rest of their conversation.

'Well, you know what I think …'

'Yes, yes.'

Addolorata turned to her. 'Now things are changing and Papa will be in Italy for so much of the year, maybe we can stop tiptoeing around his stupid feud. And you can see Michele if you want to.'

'Oh, I don't know.' Pieta kept her tone casual. 'Michele said he is in love with someone who's out of his reach so—'

Rolling her eyes, her sister interrupted, '*You're* the girl who is out of his reach, Pieta. It's so incredibly, blindingly obvious.'

'Well, we'll see.' Pieta didn't want to think about it. She tossed over one of her old gypsy-style skirts. 'This would look good on you. Try it on.'

The kitchen table was so covered with dishes of food that Pieta couldn't help sighing when she saw it. She knew who would be left with the washing-up at the end of her father's feast.

'We have baked red onions stuffed with pecorino cheese and *braciole* with a beautiful *ragù*,' announced Beppi. 'To start there is a little spaghetti served with the sauce I braised the meat in. Perfect, very simple. Oh and some *caponata*, because I found some good aubergines and also some artichoke hearts with a sauce made of almonds. I had the artichokes in the freezer.

We had to use them up. But Addolorata, your sister says you mustn't eat too much the night before your wedding so just have a small taste of everything.'

Seated at the head of the table, her mother seemed dazed.

'Are you all right, Mamma?' Pieta asked.

She smiled wanly. 'It's all happening so fast, isn't it?' She looked at the plate of spaghetti Beppi put down before her as if she wasn't quite sure what to do with it. 'I don't think I'd expected things to change so quickly.'

Once the pasta had been served, her father took his seat. He wouldn't stay there for long. Between mouthfuls of food he liked to jump up and down, checking on whatever was still warming in the oven, handing out more serviettes or piling plates in the sink. Pieta didn't think she'd ever seen him eat a whole meal without leaping up from his chair every few minutes.

'I have some news,' he declared once the pasta course was finished. 'The house in Marina di Maratea is ours. It cost a little more than I wanted to pay but that's OK. It's perfect, as you will see, and so it's worth it.'

'What about our house? Is it sold yet?' asked Pieta.

'We have an offer on it. I don't think it will be long before it sells.'

Pieta imagined another family sitting round a table in this kitchen, planting flowers where her father's vegetables had once been, making the place their own. 'That's good,' she said faintly.

'I didn't think it would happen so quickly,' her mother repeated.

For a while there was an awkward silence. No one

knew what to say. The only sound was the clinking of serving spoons against dishes as they piled more food onto their plates.

'Tomorrow my little girl is getting married,' Beppi said at last. 'Selling houses, moving to Italy – none of that is important right now. The only thing I want to think about is Addolorata and Eden's wedding.'

Pieta raised her glass to meet his. 'Here's to Addolorata and Eden,' she said.

'May they always be as happy as Caterina and I are right now,' her father added, clinking his glass against hers.

Addolorata took a sip of wine and then said, 'Papa, about tomorrow. Promise me that, whatever happens, you won't lose your temper.'

'But what will happen?' he asked.

'Just promise me.'

'Of course, of course. This day is about you and Eden, not me. Why would I want to lose my temper?'

Just as Pieta had predicted, there was too much food. After dinner she packed the leftovers away in the fridge and tackled the dishes.

'I'll only have one lonely little plate to wash up when I'm in the apartment,' she said, handing a dish to Addolorata to dry. 'I'll live on egg on toast.'

'For a couple of days maybe, and then you'll be in the restaurant looking for something more delicious. Or you can phone down and we'll send meals up to you.'

Pieta watched her sister put the dish back in the cupboard it had lived in for as long as she could re-member. 'It'll be OK, won't it?'

Addolorata took a dripping plate and rubbed the tea towel over it. 'I hope so, but who knows? Anything could happen. That's what makes life interesting.'

The morning of Addolorata's wedding was almost unbearably poignant. Sitting out on the back doorstep, drinking coffee and sharing a morning cigarette with her sister for the last time, Pieta already felt nostalgia for the life that was slipping away.

'What made you so certain that Eden was the one you wanted to marry?' she asked Addolorata.

'I don't really know. He just felt more like family than a boyfriend right from the very beginning. Even when we argue or he comes home drunk and snores all night I can't imagine life without him.'

'I don't think I've ever felt like that about anyone.'

'Really? No one?'

'Maybe with Michele a little bit,' Pieta conceded, 'which is kind of mad because he's not even my boyfriend. But somehow he already feels like family.'

'I tried to get him to come to the wedding,' Addolorata admitted. 'But he said no because he didn't want to cause any trouble with Papa.'

'How can he be so nice and yet his father so awful?'

'People aren't necessarily like their parents. We're not, are we?'

Pieta smiled. Addolorata couldn't see how like their father she was, just as, until a few weeks ago, she hadn't realized how much she took after their mother.

'Well, let's hope you're like them when it comes to having a long marriage,' was all she said.

'Yes, they seem happier than ever now, don't they?

There's been something very sweet about them since Papa had his heart attack. Have you noticed how they keep holding hands?' Addolorata looked thoughtful for a moment. 'If Eden and I can have that in thirty years' time then perhaps I wouldn't mind taking after them.'

It was a bright day but there was no warmth in the sun. Even the season was changing. The cigarette finished, the sisters moved from their seat on the step and closed the back door behind them.

'Let's go and start your hair and make-up,' said Pieta. 'And get you ready to be a bride.'

27

To Pieta the ceremony seemed to be over too quickly. One minute she was sitting in St Peter's waiting for the bride to arrive and wishing the priests hadn't replaced the old votive candles with the electric version you lit by putting a coin in a slot. The next, Eden and Addolorata were standing on the church steps as everyone showered them with confetti and took photographs.

The moment he saw his daughter in her dazzling gown Beppi had become emotional. 'So beautiful, so perfect,' he had muttered in Pieta's ear throughout the wedding service, and she had noticed how, from time to time, he gave her mother's hand a squeeze. At the altar, his dreadlocks pulled back neatly into a ponytail, Eden had done the same with Addolorata.

Now, taking one last look at the happy scene on the church steps, Pieta turned away reluctantly and headed to Little Italy. She wanted to make sure every last thing was ready for the wedding party. The dining room had been transformed and her vision of gauzy white drapes, flickering candles, crystals of sea salt and dramatic pink orchids was as elegant as she'd hoped it might be. To her eyes it all looked perfect.

The next time Pieta had a chance to look about her,

the elegant tables were overflowing with half-filled glasses of wine, plates of food and baskets of bread. The roar of Italian voices was deafening. Everyone was talking at once, gesticulating to make their points, filling their glasses, and then drinking and eating some more. Pieta had counted five courses so far – some just little tastes, a few prawns on a plate, a tiny mound of risotto – but she knew there was much more to come. Up on the dance floor wide-hipped women jiggled to the music, as balding old men tried to twirl them round. Her mother's friend Margaret was up there with her husband Ernesto, laughing at something he'd said. Addolorata was whispering in the ear of the head waiter Frederico, unable to stop working even today. Eden and a bunch of his friends were outside smoking cigars. But so far there was no sign of Isabella and her son. And then Pieta saw her, a stranger hovering in the doorway. Her nose was a little too broad and her teeth were crooked, but she had a vivacity about her that gave her face so much life you quickly stopped noticing she was no beauty.

Pieta's mother must have looked up and spotted Isabella, too, because her mouth dropped open slightly and she reached over and touched Beppi's shoulder. Deep in conversation with someone, he ignored her for a moment so she tapped him again. This time he turned and, following her gaze, saw his sister in the doorway. For a moment nobody moved. Like cats at night-time they froze and stared at each other. And then Isabella took two steps forward and a tall young man followed her inside. Very slowly, Beppi got to his feet but he made no move towards them.

Pieta couldn't bear it any longer. Jumping up, she pushed her way behind people's chairs to get to the doorway.

'Hello, you must be Isabella.' She kissed the woman on both cheeks. 'I'm Pieta, your niece. Welcome to Little Italy.'

'Thank you,' Isabella said in hesitant English. 'I'm still not sure we should have come, but my son Beppi wanted to and I thought he deserved to meet his family.'

She stepped sideways and the dark young man came forward. He looked amazingly like photos Pieta had seen of her father as a younger man. She greeted him and then turned to scan the room for her sister.

Addolorata was already heading towards them, smiling. 'I'm so glad you came. I was worried you'd changed your minds.' She held out her arms to embrace them.

As a group, they all turned towards Beppi, to check his reaction. He was still staring at them, unmoving.

'Come and say hello to him,' Pieta encouraged. 'He wants you to. It's only his pride holding him back.'

When Isabella spoke to her father it was in a dialect that, to Pieta's ear, was harsher and more guttural than Italian, and impossible to understand. For a moment his face stayed stony and unresponsive but, when she gestured towards her son and Beppi looked at him properly for the first time, it softened.

'You look like you could be my own son, not Gianfranco's,' he said in wonder. 'You have my face as well as my name.'

'I'm so very happy to meet you at last.' The boy's

Italian was pure but shyness made his voice soft, and Pieta had to strain to hear him. 'All my life my mother has told me stories of your childhood in Ravenno.'

Frederico, as observant as ever, brought over some extra chairs and they all crammed together around the table. Soon Isabella and young Beppi had glasses of wine and plates of food in front of them like all the other wedding guests. Pieta felt almost faint with relief. The most difficult moment had passed. Now she could relax.

An hour later, feeling hot and over-full, she made her way outside. She thought she might take a break from the party and walk to the end of the street to help her digestion. But as she left Little Italy she saw Michele. He must have just finished work and was standing there, staring into the restaurant filled with so many of his friends and neighbours. He smiled when he saw her.

'Is my brother inside?' he asked.

She nodded. 'They arrived about ten minutes ago.'

'And how was it? How did your father take it?'

'He was very shocked but glad, too, I think. At least, I think he will be eventually. This is a very emotional day for him.'

'I should go.' Michele looked regretful. 'Say *auguri* to your sister from me.'

'No, stay.' The words were out before Pieta had time to think properly.

He shook his head. 'Things are going well in there. I don't want to be the one to cause trouble.'

'Just come and sit outside with me and I'll get Frederico to bring something out for you. A glass of wine and a little food. And I'll tell your brother you're here. Wouldn't you like to say hello?'

'Yes, of course I would. But only if you're certain …'

Pieta smiled. 'Yes, I'm sure. I really am.'

With some reluctance he followed her in through the flower-covered bridal archway and sat down with her at one of the outdoor tables.

She went inside to find Frederico and then returned to her parents' table. Her father was sitting beside young Beppi, his face filled with sadness and regret. 'I don't know you,' she heard him say. 'I don't know you at all.'

She whispered quickly in the boy's ear and then went back outside to sit with Michele in the cool air, listening to the noise of the party. As they shared a bottle of wine Pieta wondered how these new people were going to change her family, which had already, in the past few weeks, altered so much.

It was a scene Pieta had never imagined she would see. Inside Little Italy the waiters were clearing up while a few last people finished their wine or had a final dance. Outside, gathered around one of the tables, were her father, her cousin Beppi and Michele. There was a bottle of brandy open and all three men were smoking fat cigars. Her father, more than a little drunk on champagne and high on emotion, was showing them through his memories.

He had been shocked at first when he'd found Pieta talking to Michele outside. 'What does he think he's doing here?' he'd hissed at her.

But young Beppi had stopped him, holding up a

hand and saying quickly, 'He is my brother, *zio*. My family. He came to see me.'

Her father seemed to lose the will to be angry. He'd called for Frederico to bring the brandy and cigars and sat down with them.

'When I was your age,' he began, nodding at young Beppi, 'I looked up to Gianfranco. I had worshipped him for years. Looking back now I can see he was never worthy of it. Even when we were boys his true character was there to be seen by anyone who was looking properly. I didn't see it, of course. I followed him, copied him, did things that now I sometimes remember and feel ashamed of.

'To begin with it was just the usual mischief, like knocking on people's doors and running away, or hiding and squirting passers-by with water. I'm sure all boys did things like that. But as we grew older Gianfranco always wanted to go one step further. We stole things from people who didn't have much. Little trinkets, nothing we really wanted, just stealing for the thrill of it. We killed things – small animals, birds – and pretended we were hunting when now I realize it was something else.'

Pieta had never heard any of this before. 'It was about power,' she guessed.

'That's right.' Her father drew on his cigar. 'Power over me and everything else.'

Michele had been listening carefully, his expression unchanging. 'You've thought about this a lot over the years, haven't you?' he said softly.

Beppi looked surprised, almost as though he had for-gotten he was talking to two of Gianfranco's sons. 'I've had a lot of time to think,' he said in a voice that was just as soft. 'It's not that I blame your father entirely. I could have said no. Gone my own way. But in Ravenno there was not much to do and Gianfranco always created some excitement. I was too naive to realize that one day he would turn against me, too. Later on he did a lot of things – tried to steal my Caterina, got me fired from my job. I've been angry for a long time but now I see it was in him from the very beginning. He was never the friend I wanted him to be.'

Michele couldn't help but try to defend his father. 'He's made mistakes, we all do. But he's not a bad man. He has been a good father to me. He loves me.'

Beppi shrugged. 'It's easy to love your children,' he said dismissively. 'It doesn't necessarily mean you're a good person.'

The two men stared at each other and for a moment Pieta thought the wedding was going to end in a fight after all.

'But can't you do what Michele's mother suggested, Papa?' she interjected. 'End this feud? Just be civil to one another.'

'Yes, *cara*, I could be civil. Smile when I walk past him, nod a greeting. But it wouldn't be sincere. And so what would be the point of doing it?'

Pieta looked at Michele helplessly. It seemed the situation would never be resolved.

'Fine, you hate my father.' Michele sounded sad rather than angry. 'So be it. But does that mean you also have to hate me? I don't understand why you have to take this out on me and my brother.'

Pieta's father poured a little more brandy into all

their glasses. 'Perhaps I've made mistakes,' he conceded. 'I wanted to protect my family from Gianfranco, that's all. It seemed best to stay away from anything to do with him.'

'Even after all these years?' Michele said.

'What does time have to do with it? You three may not realize it but in thirty years' time you'll still be the same people, just older and more tired. Time goes by so quickly and it doesn't change you in any of the ways you think it will.'

'And now?' Michele asked. 'You're sharing brandy with us. Is that just because we're at the end of an emotional day and you're a little drunk? Tomorrow will you refuse to acknowledge us again?'

Pieta stared at her father, willing his response.

'Drunk? Yes, maybe a little.' Beppi sipped at his brandy thoughtfully. 'But for me this is a time of endings and new beginnings. Don't keep asking me to be civil to your father. It won't happen. Not ever. I hate him as much now as I did all those years ago. But you boys ... I was wrong to take my feelings out on you.' He stared at the nephew that looked so like him. 'I've wasted so much time ...'

'It's not too late, Papa,' Pieta said, resting a hand on his arm. 'There is still time for you to get to know cousin Beppi ... and Michele, too.'

They sat outside for a long time, wrapping up in coats when it grew cold. Everyone was reluctant to be the first to leave. But when Pieta saw the sky lightening she realized it was time to break up the group.

She said goodbye to Michele beside the bridal archway of wilting flowers.

'Will you be at work later? I'll bring you some lunch,' he promised.

'Either there or up in the apartment. I've got a lot to sort out.'

'I'll see you later then.' Michele kissed her quickly on the cheek.

'Yes, later.'

Although she was tired, Pieta wasn't quite ready to go home. There was a sense of sadness about the house and she was still feeling celebratory. So instead she unlocked the door of her new shop and slipped inside.

The place felt as though it had been waiting for her. The mannequin dressed in the peony gown, the pristine new white sofa and the shelves she had begun to stock with accessories were all as she had left them. She sat down on the sofa and sighed out a breath. In a way it was a relief that Addolorata's wedding was over. It had caused her so much stress. But when they'd turned out the lights in Little Italy, she'd also felt sad because it marked the end of an era.

Pieta stared at the peony gown. She knew it was the right time for all of them to stop clinging to the past. Addolorata was living with Eden now, her parents were becoming gypsies and she was in charge of her own life at last.

Standing up, she began to ease the peony dress off the mannequin. She couldn't help herself. The finished gown had never been worn and she wanted to see how it fell, to bring it to life for the first time.

She climbed into it and, although it was awkward, managed to fasten up the back by herself. Then she turned to face the mirror. It was extraordinary to see herself in a bridal gown. She had created so many and yet never worn one. And although the fit wasn't exactly right, Pieta was pleased with what she saw.

The peony gown was sexy but not overtly so. It was fun without being fussy, detailed but not over-embellished. She turned slowly to see her reflection from the back and, as she did, spared a thought for Michele's fiancée Helene. This was her dream gown. How sad it was that she would never get to wear it.

Pieta walked the length of the shop to check how the dress would move with her and then twirled a few steps back to the mirror. Sad for Helene perhaps, but not for her. Michele had found his way through the chinks in her life and, although she was scared of tempting fate, she could already imagine them spending more time together. Later today he would bring her lunch. Perhaps tomorrow they would go out to dinner. The next day, who knew?

There was always the chance it would all come to nothing but, for the first time in her life, Pieta dared to dream. As she stood in front of the mirror in her little shop, staring at the reflection of herself transformed into a bride, she allowed herself to believe that one day it might happen to her for real.

* * *

I'm sitting on the rocks in front of our little white house, watching Beppi swimming in the sea. Every day he strikes out a little further and I'm terrified he'll reach the point where the water is so deep it's more black than blue. I'm not sure what I'd do if he did get into trouble. I certainly couldn't jump in and save him. But it makes me feel better sitting here, watching his grey head bobbing above the waves.

'Don't swim out too far,' I call as always, but he ignores me. His arms are cutting through the waves and he's feeling younger and stronger than he does on land.

Beppi never could sit still for long. He cycles up to the village every day to buy food even though it's a steep climb. His face is tanned and his eyes look clearer. He says he's had no chest pains but I can't help worrying. We're so far away from a hospital here that I can't imagine what would happen if something went wrong.

But let me describe our house. All this salty sea air had left it looking faded so the first thing Beppi did was have it repainted a brilliant white. He paid a man from the village to do it but hung over him the entire time to make sure he was getting it right. Then he varnished all the woodwork and filled window boxes with pretty flowers. It's my job to water them every evening or they'd soon shrivel and die in the summer heat.

Now he has started making a vegetable garden in the small space at the back of the house. He's out there with his shirt off first thing every morning, piling on mulch and compost, and shining with sweat as the sun comes up. When he gets really hot he jumps into the sea and pushes himself to see how far out he can go. That's when I come out and sit on the rocks. I bring a book with me and pretend to be reading it but in actual fact I never take my eyes off him.

Once he's had his swim, we'll drive up to the village

together. There's a little café where we like to drink coffee and share a pastry. The owner has already started greeting us as if we're regulars, and we catch up with all the local gossip. It may only be a little place but a lot goes on here.

Sometimes I do get lonely. I miss my house and wish I could be safe inside its walls again. But mostly I feel like a different person here, younger and stronger, like Beppi when he's out swimming in the sea.

In a few weeks they'll all be here: Addolorata with her husband and their little baby girl, Pieta with her fiancé Michele. It's taken a while for Beppi to welcome both men into his family, Michele especially because of all those things that happened in the past. But it's all right now. Mostly it's all right.

Beppi is in the deep water. He has turned and is waving at me. He knows I don't want him to head out any further and I'm sure he's teasing me. He turns back as if to keep swimming but I don't bother calling out to him. He won't hear me and, even if he could, he wouldn't listen.

But then he changes his mind and begins to swim back towards me, surely and strongly like a young man, the water running off his body. And I sit up here on the rocks, my book in my hands, watching and waiting for him.

How Beppi Cooks His Lasagne

So now you know how to make the *ragù* and your own pasta. But to make a beautiful lasagne you have to bring everything together in the end, just like telling a story.

So you've already made the pasta and now you half-fill a big pan with water and bring it to the boil. Add a spoonful of oil to stop the strips of pasta sticking to one another and a generous pinch of salt. If cooking the pasta while it is still fresh, it only needs to boil one minute, a little longer if it has been allowed to dry.

I would only boil small quantities each time. Then put it in a colander, cool under a cold water tap and let it drain.

Now get a big baking dish and smear some of the *ragù* sauce in it and then place layers of pasta, covering each layer with a generous amount of sauce. Complete the job by topping the last layer with *besciamella* sauce. I suppose I'm going to have to tell you how to make that as well?

2 oz of butter
2 tbsp of plain flour
1 pint of milk
ground nutmeg
salt and pepper

Place the butter in a small saucepan, heat it gently till

it melts, add the flour and stir for a couple of minutes until the mixture is crumbly, add the milk slowly and keep stirring until all the solids have liquefied. Add the salt, pepper and nutmeg, bring to a gentle boil and cook till it has thickened.

When satisfied, pour the *besciamella* on top of the lasagne, place the dish in a hot oven at about 180°C and cook for thirty to forty-five minutes depending on the size of the dish.

This should be enough to feed a crowd. All this work, all those hours, and they will fall on it and eat it in minutes. But what can I do? Everybody loves my beautiful lasagne.

Addolorata's note: And you say my food is too complicated, Papa.

Acknowledgements

This book is dedicated to my mother and father who planted the seed for the story. In her youth my mother actually did hitchhike to Italy with her girlfriends. She met my father on the streets of Rome, fell in love with him and took him home to Liverpool. There, after a close encounter with Scouse (the local dish, a kind of stew) he begged his three sisters to send him recipes. He used to haunt the aisles of the supermarket on a Saturday afternoon until they marked down the 'exotic' vegetables like red peppers and aubergines, then bring them home and cook up a storm. All of Beppi's recipes in this book are things he's been cooking for us for years.

My parent's story is the *soffritto* for this book, the all-important base that gives it its flavour. But Beppi and Caterina are not my father and mother. They and all the other characters in this book are inventions. I dreamt them up and set them on their course and from time to time they surprised me.

As well as my parents I'd like to thank – as always – my editor Yvette Goulden and also my agent Caroline Sheldon for stepping into the breach. Also thanks to bridal designer Theresa Lim for sharing her time and knowledge and to my husband Carne for always being happy to accompany me on research trips so long as they involve being in Italy, eating and drinking.

Finally I owe a huge debt of gratitude to my first agent, the late Maggie Noach and to the late Angela D'Audney, two extraordinary women who never knew each other but who, in different ways, helped me get this far.

More recipes from Beppi

So now I am going to let you into a secret. The lasagne it is just the first course. When we serve it to the English people they love it. Always they ask for seconds. Then we serve them the main course, the meat, vegetables ... they see it and grow pale. Trust me it is funny.

So now I will show you some dishes to serve after the lasagne. My *polpette* (you call them meatballs) and a delicious dish with the peppers. Both serve four to six people depending how hungry you are.

Beppi's polpette recipe

About half a kilo good steak mince
2 eggs
rye bread or stale bread (one big slice)
chopped flat parsley
grated parmesan
salt and pepper

First of all start up a Neapolitan sauce or ragu like I showed you before. While the sauce is cooking, soak the bread in water and then squeeze dry. Mix it with the mince and all the other ingredients using a fork or better still your hand. Then put some oil in a frying pan and warm it on a low heat.

Shape the meatballs, roll them in some flour, then fry lightly turning them over once. Finally remove them from frying pan and let them cook for ten to fifteen minutes in the sauce on a very low setting.

They will be good served with pasta or separately with the peppers and a green salad.

A delicious dish with peppers

6 peppers (capsicums) red, yellow, green, all the
   colours
anchovies
capers
black olives
a little dry bread

Cut up the peppers, remove all traces of seeds and slice them in thin strips. Then add them to the hot oil, add salt and pepper and stir fry on a low heat for fifteen to twenty minutes. When nearly cooked add some anchovies, capers and olives and let them cook for only a few minutes. Finally add some dry small pieces of bread and mix so it absorbs the liquid and oil.

Beppi's note: And see how you use up the stale bread? No waste. Perfect!

Why I wrote this story
(and why you should write one too!)

Having written two novels while working full time as a magazine journalist I was feeling a bit worn out and came up with what seemed like a genius plan. I would get my English mother to write down the story of how she met my Italian father back in 1959. It's the romantic and daring tale of how she hitched from Liverpool to Rome with two friends and ended up coming home with a husband. I had visions of my mother producing 30,000 words or so that I would flesh out into a fabulous novel. Cheating a bit, yes, but genius all the same.

Unfortunately it didn't quite work out like that. My mother's reminiscences filled only a couple of pages. It was a long time ago, she insisted, and that was all she could remember. But by then I was in love with the idea of writing a novel about discovering who your parents really are – not just the people who nurtured and raised you but had crazy adventures, wild passions and deep disappointments.

So I wracked my brains and tried to remember the stories I'd been told when I was growing up. Of course, back then I was a dreamy sort of child who only half listened to anything that was said to me. And I didn't much like being half-Italian. It singled me out from the other kids, I had a different name, ate different food. When my father tried to talk to me in Italian I stuck my fingers in my ears and cried. And when his friends came round to our little bungalow in Merseyside to play cards and argue in loud voices I steered well clear.

In the summer we'd drive to Italy in whatever rattly old car my father had at the time. Those holidays involved an awful lot of sitting round in dusty yards or hot kitchens listening to adults yabber in Italian. The tedium was punctuated by the horror of being made to kiss hairy-faced old ladies or submitting to having your cheek pinched (the cuter you were the harder they pinched!).

The town my father comes from is well off the tourist trail and back when I was a child they hadn't seen many extremely tall, ginger-headed, pale people on their streets. So when my brother and I ventured out we were like Pied Pipers, picking up a following of astonished Italian kids who stared at us and shouted insults.

Although I was officially half-Italian, I never felt like one of them. I didn't speak the language fluently enough to hold a proper conversation with my grandfather, aunts or cousins. Mainly what I did during those long summer holidays was sit around and observe people. I saw the way they lived life bigger than we English people tend to. They shouted more, talked with their hands, let their passions get the better of them. Food was all-important. They'd drive for miles to get the best spit-roasted chicken or the freshest mozzarella. When the whole family went to the beach we didn't take plastic-wrapped, squashed cheese sandwiches like at home, but vast trays of baked pasta and slow-cooked beef. Everyone hired little cabins and you'd sit there, passing tastes of food from family to family, eating for half the afternoon. I remember seeing a video my uncle had made and in every shot I was chewing something.

It was very clear to me that I had much more freedom than my female cousins. They left school young, helped out at home and then were expected to marry and have children. If they wanted to go shopping they were chaperoned by a brother or parent. Their lives revolved round the kitchen and the family.

This was the 70s but southern Italy was still a place governed by tradition. Peasants rode in carts pulled by pure white oxen. Brides came with dowries. Many things were still done the same way they had been a hundred years earlier ... or at least so it seemed to me.

When I started writing fiction these were the memories that came back to me and laced themselves through my first two novels, *Delicious* and *Summer at the Villa Rosa* (also known as *The Gypsy Tearoom*). But for my third book I needed fresh ideas and new memories. And all I had were those couple of pages of my mother's reminiscences that she'd typed up for me.

As another writer once said to me, if you don't live then you have nothing to write about. And as luck would have it real life intruded on my writing. To pay the bills I took a part-time job – this time editing a bridal magazine. This was ironic as weddings have never really been my thing. I come from a family of serial elopers and didn't have the whole production with the bouffy dress and elaborate ceremony. But as I styled fashion shoots and researched articles I became fascinated by the world of weddings from the designing of glorious frocks to the ribbons on the wedding favours that match a detail in the invitation ...

Writing a novel is a bit like cooking something special. Ideas have to marinate for a while and then you layer flavours until the balance is right. From my sudden interest in weddings Pieta Martinelli, bridal designer, was born. Like me she was half Italian and also, just like me, she didn't know enough about her parents. (After that our paths diverge. I don't have a wardrobe full of fabulous clothes and a figure to show them off, nor could I design a dress if my life depended on it.)

In the end my parents' history provided the *soffritto* for the book, the all-important base that gives it its flavour. But the story stretched way beyond that.

And I was left with a sense that everyone should write down their life story, fill it with pictures, recipes, memories, feelings, make it a rich and varied thing. Fancy prose isn't important, neither is expensive binding. It can be little more than a scrapbook. And maybe some day there'll be a Pieta Martinelli in your life who'll come along and read it to get a sense, not just of who you are, but where they came from.

So what are you waiting for ...?

Maratea

The trouble with Italy is it's really, really full. Not just with Italians but with tourists who travel from all around the world to swarm over the ancient monuments of Rome and Florence, along the canals of Venice and around the hairpin bends of the Amalfi Coast. It's still worth fighting your way through the crowds to see iconic places like the Trevi Fountain or the Coliseum but for a sense of the real Italy you have to escape somewhere most tourists haven't discovered yet.

I'm going to let you in on my Italian secret. It's called the Costa di Maratea. Some people compare it to the more famous Amalfi Coast because it's a series of villages linked by a winding coastal road with breathtaking views of the turquoise sea and the steep, bare mountains of Basilicata. It's less dramatic than Amalfi, true, but it's also much cheaper and far less crowded even though it's only two hours drive south of Naples.

The historic part of Maratea lies halfway up the northern slope of Mount San Biagio. This is where I like to go every morning to sit at one of the outdoor tables at the café in the piazza, drink espresso, eat *sfogliatelle* (a particularly yummy crisp pastry filled with ricotta cheese and candied orange peel) and watch Italian life going on all around me. Here the shops close at lunchtime and don't open again till about 5 p.m. so mornings are busy. Everyone is out, shopping for fresh food, gossiping with friends or, like me, enjoying morning coffee. From my table I can see the man who owns the linen shop trying to hawk his wares, the butcher leaning in his doorway waiting for his next customer and a tiny old lady dressed in black enjoying the sunshine. Life is lived out on the streets here and the locals, quick to spot a new face, are greeting me with a friendly *buongiorno* after just a couple of days.

But even I can't sit around eating pastries all morning and anyway there are plenty of places to explore. Maratea was founded in the 13th century although most of its buildings date from a few hundred years after that. It's a cluster of churches, monasteries and crumbling old houses built around steep, narrow alleyways. Above the town itself is a white statue of Christ the Redeemer (like the one in Rio De Janeiro only smaller) that was built in the 1960s. You can drive up there and walk around its base enjoying the sweeping views down over the quaint Porto di Maratea and its small marina.

Or you can take a short drive south into the neighbouring region of Calabria. Here there is a bigger town called Praia a Mare that is home to the most amazing church I've ever visited. The Sanctuary of the Madonna Della Grotta is built inside an enormous cave. The altar and pews sit beneath the dripping stalactites and, while it is amazingly beautiful, it's so damp and chilly that I can't imagine worshipping here would be much fun.

Tradition is still very much respected in this part of Italy and every Sunday afternoon the locals, young and old, go to 'fare la passeggiata' along Praia's tree-lined boulevard. This involves dressing up in your best clothes and walking back and forth, stopping every now and then to greet friends. The same thing happens at the same time in towns all around south Italy. In the old days it was the perfect way for Mamma to show off her daughters to potential husbands.

In many ways this part of Italy offers a glimpse of life the way it has been lived for centuries. Local farmers graze their cattle on the hillsides and you can often hear the clanging of bells the cows wear around their necks. Old peasants cultivate fava beans and artichokes as well as a few rows of grapes for their own wine on their tiny holdings of land, and families still cook the local Lucano cuisine robustly flavoured with spicy sausage and hot chilli pepper.

I like to visit in May when Maratea celebrates the Festa Di San Biagio, honouring its patron saint with processions, feasting, music and fireworks. Or in late September when the summer crowds are gone but it's still warm enough to sit on the shingle beaches and swim in the Mediterranean Sea.

For me this is a special place. So much so that I stole it, gave it a thin disguise by changing its name to Triento, and used it in my last novel, *Summer at the Villa Rosa* (also known as *The Gypsy Tearoom*). And I've returned there again for the next story I'm working on.

There are probably more beautiful places to visit in Italy and certainly there are many that are more famous. But there's something about this secret little corner of the country that's so charming I hope I'll be travelling back there for many years to come. I just have to remember not to tell too many people about it ...